PENGUIN BOOKS

THE HOTEL EDEN

Ron Carlson's stories have appeared in *Harper's*, *Esquire*, *Gentleman's Quarterly*, *North American Review*, and elsewhere. He is the author of two previous collections, *The News of the World* and *Plan B for the Middle Class*, and the novels *Betrayed by F. Scott Fitzgerald* and *Truants*. He teaches creative writing at Arizona State and lives in Scottsdale. "I write about my personal experiences," Carlson says, "whether I've had them or not. I send myself on the journey. If it's not personal, I don't want to be involved."

Praise for *The Hotel Eden*

"A funny and poignant collection . . . Carlson produces clean and assured prose and animates familiar situations with imaginative twists, masterfully reported details and enough emotional honesty to fill a book twice this size." —*Publishers Weekly* (starred review)

"Carlson is a comic genius, but he is also a poet of humiliation, loss, and precarious existence." —*Amazon.com*

"Carlson is one of the most accomplished short-story writers in the nation." —*Portland Oregonian*

"Wicked and funny. . . Ron Carlson's characters include all of us as we are—glorious, desperate, generous, capable of nurturing as well as killing." —Mark Richard

"I read Ron Carlson's stories again and again. . . . [they are] authentic, honest, hilarious, and full of a kind of hard-won hopefulness." —Pam Houston

"The vigor of Mr. Carlson's imagination is exceeded only by the surprise and force of his emotion." —Padgett Powell

THE
HOTEL
EDEN

STORIES

RON CARLSON

PENGUIN BOOKS

PENGUIN BOOKS

Published by the Penguin Group
Penguin Putnam Inc., 375 Hudson Street,
New York, New York 10014, U.S.A.
Penguin Books Ltd, 27 Wrights Lane, London W8 5TZ, England
Penguin Books Australia Ltd, Ringwood, Victoria, Australia
Penguin Books Canada Ltd, 10 Alcorn Avenue,
Toronto, Ontario, Canada M4V 3B2
Penguin Books (N.Z.) Ltd, 182–190 Wairau Road,
Auckland 10, New Zealand
Penguin India, 210 Chiranjiv Tower, 43 Nehru Place,
New Delhi 11009, India

Penguin Books Ltd, Registered Offices:
Harmondsworth, Middlesex, England

First published in the United States of America by
W. W. Norton & Company, Inc. 1997
Published in Penguin Books 1998

1 3 5 7 9 10 8 6 4 2

Copyright © Ron Carlson, 1997
All rights reserved

PUBLISHER'S NOTE
These are works of fiction. Names, characters, places, and incidents
either are the product of the author's imagination or are used fictitiously,
and any resemblance to actual persons, living or dead, events,
or locales is entirely coincidental.

THE LIBRARY OF CONGRESS HAS CATALOGED THE HARDCOVER AS FOLLOWS:
Carlson, Ron
The Hotel Eden, stories / Ron Carlson.
p. cm.
Contents: The Hotel Eden—Keith—The prisoner of Bluestone—Zanduce at
second—The house goes up—What we wanted to do—note on the type—The
chromium hook—Nightcap—Dr. Slime—Down the green river—Oxygen.
ISBN 0-393-04068-2 (hc.)
ISBN 0 14 02.7389 1 (pbk.)
1. Title
PS3553.A733H68   1997
813'.54—dc20   96–42425

Printed in the United States of America
Composed in Granjon with display set in Nova Augustea Composition
Designed by JAM Design

Except in the United States of America, this book is sold subject to the condition
that it shall not, by way of trade or otherwise, be lent, re-sold, hired out, or otherwise
circulated without the publisher's prior consent in any form of binding or cover other
than that in which it is published and without a similar condition including
this condition being imposed on the subsequent purchaser.

for Walter DeMelle

CONTENTS

ACKNOWLEDGMENTS

SOME OF THE stories in this collection appeared, sometimes in slightly different form, in the following publications: *Double-Take*: "Nightcap"; *Esquire*: "The Hotel Eden"; *Harper's*: "Zanduce at Second," "A Note on the Type," "What We Wanted to Do," "The Chromium Hook"; *Gentlemen's Quarterly*: "The Prisoner of Bluestone"; *Salt Lake City Magazine*: "Nightcap"; *The Southern Review*: "Down the Green River"; *Tell*: "Keith"; *Western Humanities Review*: "Dr. Slime"; *Witness*: "What We Wanted to Do," "Oxygen."

Special thanks to the editors of these publications, particularly Will Blythe, Colin Harrison, Ben Metcalf, Tom Mallon, and Dave Smith.

"Keith" also appeared in the anthology *Success Stories of the Nineties;* and "A Note on the Type" was published as a letterpress book from Mile Wide Press (Penland, North Carolina) in an edition of one hundred copies, each with a cover of galvanized roof flashing and type hand-set by the determined Eileen Wallace, 1996. "A Note on the Type" also appeared in *The Writ-*

ACKNOWLEDGMENTS

ing Path 2, edited by Michael Pettit, University of Iowa Press, 1996.

I would also like to express my gratitude to Gail Hochman for constant and everlasting faith; Marianne Merola for her encouragement; to Ed Dee for the Jack Frost line; to Bill Mai for kindnesses in the Old World; to Christopher Merrill for his enthusiasms; to David Kranes for friendship and astute reading; to Michael Phillips for help in the snow; to Carol Houck Smith for tenacity and grace; to Ashley Barnes for her smart efforts on my behalf; and to Elaine and Nick and Colin for all these delicious years and those to come.

I

Let me make this kind of mistake with you,

let me tell you everything.

THE HOTEL EDEN

THAT YEAR THE place we would go after hours was the Hotel Eden. It had a cozy little bar in the parlor with three tiny tables and four stools at the counter. You had to walk sideways to get around, and it had a low ceiling and thick old carpets, but it had a roomy feeling and it became absolutely grand when Porter was there. Over the course of the spring he told us a hundred stories in the Eden and changed things for us.

The barman was a young Scot named Norris who seemed neither glad nor annoyed when we'd come in around midnight after closing down one of the pubs, the Black Swan or the Lamb and Flag or the forty others we saw that cold spring. Pub hours then were eleven o'clock last call, and drink up by eleven-fifteen. Porter would set his empty pint glass on the whatever bar and say to Allison and me, "The Eden then?" He'd bike over, regardless of where we were, out on the Isle of Dogs or up in Hampstead, and Allison would get us a cab.

Norris would have the little curtain pulled down above the

bar, a translucent yellow sheet that said, "Residents Only." He drew it down every night at eleven; hotels could serve late to their guests. Porter had done some favor for the manager of the Hotel Eden when he'd come to London years before, and he had privileges. They became in a sense our privileges too, though—as you shall see—I was only in the Eden alone on one occasion. The curtain just touched your forehead if you sat at the bar.

We often arrived ahead of Porter, and Norris would set us up with pints of lager, saying always, "Hello, miss," when he placed Allison's glass. The Eden didn't have bitter. I remember the room as always being empty when we'd arrive, and it was a bit of a mystery at first as to why Norris was still even open. But there were times when there was a guest or two, a man or a man and a woman, having a brandy at one of the tables. We were quiet too, talking about Allison's research at the museum—she had a year in London to work on her doctorate in Art History. But it was all airy, because we were really just waiting for Porter. It was as if we weren't substantial enough to hold down our stools, and then Porter would come in, packing his riding gloves into his helmet, running a hand through his thick black hair, saying, "Right enough, Norris, let's commence then, you gloomy Northlander," and gravity would be restored. His magnetism was tangible, and we'd wait for him to speak. When he had the pint of lager in his hand, he'd turn to Allison and say something that would start the rest of the night.

One night, he lifted his glass and said, "Found a body today." Then he drank.

Allison leaned in: "A dead man?"

"Dead as Keats and naked as Byron." We waited for him to go on. His was the voice of experience, the world, the things that year that I wanted so much.

"Where?" I asked.

"Under the terrace at the Pilot."

"The place on the river?" Allison asked. He'd taken us walking through the Isle of Dogs after we'd first met and we'd stopped at half a dozen pubs which backed onto the Thames.

"Right, lady. Spoiled my lunch, he did, floating under there like that."

Allison was lit by this news. We both were. And there it was: the night kicked in at any hour, no matter how late. When Porter arrived, things *commenced*. We both leaned closer. Porter, though he'd just sucked the top off his pint, called Norris for another, and the evening was launched.

We always stayed until Porter leaned back and said, "It's a night then." He didn't have an accent to us, being American, but he had the idiom and he had the way of putting his whole hand around a glass and of speaking over the top of a pint with the smallest line of froth of his upper lip, something manly really, something you'd never correct or try to touch off him, that was something to us I can only describe as being *real*. He'd been at Hilman College years before Allison and me, and he knew Professor Mills and all the old staff and he'd even been there the night of the Lake Dorm Fire, the most famous thing about Hilman really, next to Professor Mills, I suppose. I spent a hundred hours with him in the Eden that spring, like Allison, twelve inches across that little round table or huddled as we were at the bar, and I memorized Porter really, his face, the smooth tan of red veins running up under his eyes, as if he'd stood too close to some special fire, and his white teeth, which he showed you it seemed for a purpose. His nose had been broken years ago. We played did you know so-and-so until Allison, who was still a member of Lake Sorority, brought up the fire.

"Oh yes," he said. "I was there. What's the legend grown to now? A hundred ghosts?"

"Six," Allison laughed. "There's always been six."

"Always," he protested. "You make it sound ancient. Hey, I was there. February." Then he added with authority and precision: "Fifteen years ago."

"Someone had stopped the doors with something; the six girls couldn't get out."

Porter drew on his beer and looked at me. "Hockey sticks. It was a bundle of hockey sticks through the door handles."

"That's right."

"Oh." He looked from me to Allison. "It was awful. A cold night at Hilman, and you know, it could get cold, ten degrees, old snow on the ground hard as plastic, and the colossal inferno. From the quad you could see the trapped figures bumping into the glass doors. A group of us came up from town, the Villager had just closed, you ever drink there?"

"It's now a cappuccino place," Allison said. "The Blue Dish."

"Ah, the old Villager was a capital dive. That bar could tell some tales. It's where I met our Professor Mills. Anyway, they closed at one, and when I stepped out into the winter night, there was this ethereal light pulsing from the campus like a heartbeat, and you had to go. There was no choice. I knew right away it was Lake, fully engaged, as they say, a fire like no other, trying to tear a hole in the world." Allison and I were mesmerized, and he finished: "It singed the sycamores back to Dobbs Street, and that's where a group of us stood. It hurt to look. In the explosive light, I could see figures come to the glass, they looked like fish."

When he'd finish talking like that, telling this story or that—he'd found a downed ultralight plane in the Cotswolds once on a walking tour and had had to secure the pilot's compound leg fracture—Allison and I would be unable to move. It was a spell. It's that simple. You see, we were graduate students and we weren't used to this type of thing. I'd tell you what we were used to but it all seems to drop out of memory like the bottom of a wet cardboard box. We were used to nothing: to weeks at the library at Hilman in Wisconsin and then some vacation road trips with nothing but forced high jinx and a beach. There was always one of our friends, my roommate or Allison's roommate, who would either read Dylan Thomas aloud all the way to Florida and then refuse to leave the car or get absolutely drunk for a week and try to show everyone his or her genitals as part of a discussion of our place in the universe. We were Americans and we knew it. I was twenty-three and Allison was twenty-four. We hadn't done anything, we were scholars. I'd finished my master's degree in meteorology at Northern near Hilman and was doing what—nothing. Allison got her grant. Going to England was a big deal for us. She was going to do her research at the British Museum. I was going to cool out and do London. Then we met Porter.

Allison's mentor at Hilman, the famous Professor Julie Mills, had given us some telephone numbers, and after we found a flat in Hampstead and after Allison had established a routine with her work, we called the first guy. His name was Roger Ardreprice, the assistant curator of Keats's House, and he had us meet him over there as things were closing up one cold March night. He was a smug little guy who gave us his card right away and walked with both hands in his jacket pockets and finished all his sentences with "well um um." We walked over to the High Street and then down to the Pearl of India with him talking about Professor Mills, whom he called Julie. Evidently he'd met other of her students in former years, and he assumed his role as host of all of London with a kind of jaded enthusiasm; it was clear he'd seen our kind before. It was at the long dinner that we met two other people who had studied at Hilman with the famous Professor Julie Mills. One was a quiet well-dressed woman named Sarah Garrison who worked at the Tate, and the other was a thirtyish man in a green windbreaker who came late, said hello, and then ate in the back at a table by the kitchen door with two turbaned men who evidently were the chefs. This was Porter.

Of course, we didn't talk to him until afterward. Roger Ardreprice ran a long dinner which was half reverential shop-talk about Julie Mills and half sage advice about life in London, primarily about things to avoid. Roger had a practiced world-weary smile which he played all night, even condescending to Sarah Garrison, who seemed to me to be a real nice woman. It was a relief when we finally adjourned sometime after eleven and stepped from the close spicy room onto the cold sidewalk. Sarah took a cab and Roger headed down for his tube stop, and so Allison and I had the walk up the hill. I remember the night well, the penetrating cold wind, our steps past all the shops we would eventually memorize: the newsdealer, the kabob stand, the cheese shop, the Rosslyn Arms. We were a week in London and the glow was very much on everything, even a chilly night after a strange dinner. Then like a phantom, a figure came suddenly from behind us and banked against the curb, a man on a bicycle. He pulled the goggles off his head and said, "Enough curry with Captain Prig then?" He grinned the most beguiling grin, the corners of his mouth puckered. "Want a pint?"

"It's after hours," I said.

"This is the most interesting city in the world," he said. "Certainly we can find a pint." He stopped a cab and spoke to the driver and herded us inside, saying, "See you in nineteen minutes."

And so we were delivered to the Hotel Eden. That first night we waited in front on the four long white stone steps until we saw him turn onto the street, all business on his bicycle, nineteen minutes later. "Yes, indeed," he said, dismounting and taking a deep breath through his nose as if sensing something near. "The promise of lager. Which one of you studied with Julie Mills?"

Allison said, "I did. I do. I finish next year."

"Nice woman," he said as he pulled open the old glass door of the hotel. "I slept with her all my senior year." Then he turned to us as if apologizing. "But we were never in love. Let's have that straight."

I thought Allison was going to be sick after that news. Professor Mills was widely revered, a heroine, a goddess, certainly someone who would have a wing of the museum named after her someday. Then we went into the little room and met Norris and he drew three beautiful pints of lager, gold in glass, and set them before us.

"Why'd you eat with the cooks?" Allison asked Porter.

"That's the owner and his brother," Porter said. His face was ruddy in the half-light of the bar. "They're Sikhs. Do you know about the Sikhs?"

We shook our heads no.

"Don't mess with them. They're merciless. Literally. The man who sat at my right has killed three people."

I nodded at him, flattered that he thought I'd mess with anyone at all, let alone a bearded man in a turban.

"I'm doing a story on their code." Porter drank deeply from his glass. "Besides, your Mr. Roger Ardreprice, Esquire, has no surplus love for me." He smiled. "And you . . ." He turned his glorious smile to Allison, and reached out and took her shiny brown hair in his hand. "You're certainly a Lake. We'll have to get you a tortoiseshell clip for that Lake hair." Lake was the prime sorority at Hilman. "What brings you to London besides the footsteps of our Miss Mills?—who founded Lake, of course, a thousand years ago."

Allison talked a little about the Egyptian influence on the Victorians, but it was halfhearted, the way all academic talk is in a pub, and my little story about my degree in meteorology felt absolutely silly. I had nothing to say to this man, and I wanted something. I wanted to warn him about something with an exacting and savage code, but there was nothing. I wasn't going to say what I had said to my uncle at a graduation party, "I got good grades."

But Porter turned to me, and I can still feel it like a light, his attention, and he said, with a kind of respect, "The weather. Oh that's very fine. The weather," he turned to me and then back to Allison, "and art. That is absolutely formidable." He wasn't kidding. It was the first time in the seven months since I'd graduated that I felt I had studied something real, and the feeling was good. I felt our life in London assume a new dimension, and I called for another round.

That was the way we'd see him; he would turn up. We'd go four, five days with Allison working at the museum and me tramping London like a tourist, which I absolutely was, doing only a smattering of research, and then there'd be a one-pound note stapled to a page torn from the map book *London A to Z* in our mailbox with the name of a pub and an hour scribbled on it. The Flask, Highgate, 9 p.m., or Old Plover, on the river, 7. And we'd go. He would have seen the Prince at Trafalgar Square or stopped a fight in Hyde Park and there'd be a bandage across his nose to prove it. He was a character, and I realize now we'd never met one. I'd known some guys in the dorms who would do crazy things drunk on the weekend, but I'd never met anybody in my life who had done and seen so much. He was out in the world, and it all called to me.

He took us to the Irish pubs in Kilburn, all the lights on, everyone scared of a suitcase bomb, the men sitting against the wall in their black suits drinking Guinness. We went to three different pubs, all well lit and quiet, and Porter told us not to talk too loud or laugh too loud or do anything that might set off these powder kegs. "Although there's no real danger," he added, pointing at Allison's L. L. Bean boots. "They're not going to harm an American schoolgirl. And such a beautiful member of the Lake."

Maybe harm was part of the deal, the attraction, I know it probably was for me. I'd spend two days straight doing some of my feeble research, charting rainfall (London has exactly fifteen rain days per month, year-round), and then, with my shoulders cramping and my fingers stained with the wacky English marking pens we bought, I'd be at the Eden bent over a pint looking into Porter's fine face and it would all go away. He showed up early in March with his arm in a sling and a thrilling scrape across his left cheekbone. Someone had opened a car door on him as he'd biked home one night. The gravel tracks where he'd hit the road made a bright fan under his eye. His grin seemed magnified that night under our concern.

"Nothing," he said of it. "The worst is I can't ride for a week. It puts me in the tube with all the rest of you wankers." He laughed. "Say, Norris," he called. "Is there any beer in here?" I saw Allison's face, the worry there, and knew she was a goner. And I was a goner too. I'd never had a scratch on my body.

Porter was too much, and I knew that this is the way I did it, had crushes, and I'd fallen for two or three people before: Professor Cummins, my thesis chair, with his black bowl of hair and bright blue eyes, a cartoon face really, but he'd traveled the world and in his own words been rained on in ninety-nine countries; and Julie Mills, who worked so closely with Allison. I'd met her five or six times at receptions and such, and her intensity, the way she set her hand below my shoulder when speaking to me as if to steady me for the news to come, and the way there was a clear second between each of her words, these things printed themselves on me, and I tried them out with no success. I tried everything and had little success generating any conviction that I might find a personality for me.

And now Allison kidded me when we'd have tea somewhere or a plowman's platter in a pub: "You don't have to try Porter's frown when you ask for a pint," she'd say. "This isn't the Eden." And I'd taken certain idiomatic inflections from Porter's accent, and when they'd slip out, Allison would turn to me, alert to it. I would have stopped it if I could. I started being assertive and making predictions, the way Porter did. We'd gone to Southwark one night, and after a few at a dive called Old Tricks, we'd stood at the curb afterward, arm in arm in the chill, and he'd said, "Calm enough now," and he'd scanned the low apartment buildings on the square, "but this will all be in flames in two years. Put it in your calendar." And when I got that way with Allison, even making a categorical statement about being late for the tube or forgetting the umbrella, she'd say, "Put it in your calendar, mate." I always smiled at these times and tried to shrug them off. She was right, after all. But I also knew she'd fallen too. She didn't pick up the posture or the walk, but Allison was in love with this character too.

One night in March, he met us at the Eden with a plan. I was a meteorologist, wasn't I? It was key for a truly global understanding of the weather for me to visit the north Scottish coast and see the effects of the Gulf Stream firsthand. "Think of it, Mark," he said, his face lit by the glass of beer. "The Gulf Stream. All that water roiling against the coast of Mexico, warming in the equatorial sun, then spooling out around the corner of Florida and up across the Atlantic four thousand miles still warm as it pets the forehead of Scotland. It's absolutely tropical. Palm trees. We better get up there."

Well, I didn't have anything to do. I was on hold, taking a year off we called it sometimes, and I looked at Allison there in the Eden. She raised her eyebrows at me, throwing me the ball, and smiled. Her hair was back in the new brown clip Porter had given her. "Sounds too good to pass up," she said. "Mark's ready for an adventure."

"Capital," Porter said. "I'll arrange train tickets. We'll leave Wednesday."

Allison and I talked about it in our flat. It was chilly all the time, and we'd get in the bed sometimes in the early afternoon and talk and maybe have a snack, some cheese and bread with some Whitbred from a canister. She came home early from the museum the Tuesday before I was to leave with Porter. There was a troubled look on her face. She undressed and got in beside me. "Well," she said. "Ready for your adventure?" Her face was strange, serious and fragile, and she put her head into my shoulder and held me.

"Hey, don't worry," I said. The part of her sweet hair was against my mouth. "You've got the people at the museum if you need anything, and if something came up you could always call Roger Ardreprice." I patted the naked hollow of her back to let her know that I had been kidding with that last, but she didn't move. "Hey," I said, trying to sit up to look her in the eyes, comfort her, but she pushed me back, burrowed in.

PORTER AND I left London in the late afternoon and clacked through the industrial corridor of the city until just before the early dark the fields began to open and hedgerows grow farther apart. Porter had arrived late for the train and kicked his feet up on the opposite seat, saying, "Sorry, mate, but I've got the ticket right here." He withdrew a glass jar from his pack and examined it. "Not a leak. Tight and dry." He held the jar like a trophy and smiled at me his gorgeous smile. "Dry martinis, and we're going to get *very* tight." Then he unwrapped two white china coffee cups and handed me one. There was a little gold crown on each cup, the blue date in Roman numerals MCMLIII. He saw me examining the beautiful cup and said, "From the coronation. But there are no saucers and—in the finest tradition of the empire—no ice."

Well, I was thrilled. Here I was rambling north in a foreign country, every mile was farther north in Britain than I'd ever been, etc., and Porter was dropping a fat green olive in my cup and covering it with silver vodka. "This is real," I said aloud, and I felt satisfied at how it felt.

"To Norris," I said, making the first toast, "and the Eden, hoping they're happy tonight."

"Agreed," Porter said, drinking. "But happy's not the word, mate. Norris is pleased, but never happy. He's been a good friend to me, these English years."

"We love him," I said, speaking easily hearing the "we," Allison entering the sentence as a natural thing. It was true. We'd often remarked as we'd caught the tube back to Hampstead or as we'd headed toward the Eden that Norris was wonderful. In fact he was one of eight people we knew by name in that great world city.

"Allison seems a dear girl." Porter said. It was a strange thing, like a violation, the two of us talking about her.

"She's great," I said, simply holding place.

"Women." Porter raised his cup. "The great unknowable."

I thought about Allison, missing her in a different way. We were tender people, that is, *kids,* and our only separations had been play ones, vacations when she'd go home to her folks and I'd go home to my folks, and then we moved in together after graduating with no fanfare, tenderly, a boy and a girl who were smart and well-meaning. Our big adventure was going off to England together, which everyone we knew and our families thought was a wonderful idea, and who knows what anybody meant by that, and really, who knows what we meant at such a young age, what we were about. We were lovers, but that term would have embarrassed us, and there are no other words which come close to the way we were. We liked each other a lot, that's it. We both knew it. We were waiting for something to happen, something to do with age and the world that would tell us if we were qualified, if we were in love, the real love. And here I was on a train with a stranger, each mile sending me farther from her into a dark night in a foreign country. I thought about her in the quilts of our small bed in Hampstead. The first martini was working, and it had made me large: I was a man on a train far from home.

We got drunk. Porter grinned a lot and I actually made him giggle a few times with my witty remarks. The vodka evidently made me very clever. About nine o'clock we went up to the club car, a little snack bar, and bought some Scotch eggs. This was real life, I could feel it. I'd had a glimpse of it from time to time with Porter, but now here we were.

One long afternoon after we'd first met him, he took us on a walk through the Isle of Dogs. He'd had us meet him at the Bridge & Beacon near the foot of London Bridge and we'd spent the rest of the day tramping the industrial borough of the Isle. The pubs were hidden among all the fenced construction storage lots and warehouses. We'd walk a quarter mile down a street with steel sheeting on both sides and then down a little alley would be the entry to the Bowsprit or the Sea Lion or the Roman Arch, places that had been selling drinks for three hundred years while the roads outside, while everything outside, changed. They all had a dock and an entry off the Thames. For us it was enchanting, this lost world at once rough, crude, and romantic. Two steps down under a huge varnished beam into a long room of polished walnut and brass lamps, like the captain's quarters on a ship, we'd follow Porter and sit by the window where the river spread beneath us. He'd call the barman by name and order three pints. I mean, we loved this stuff. We were on the inside.

"Do you know the opening of *Heart of Darkness?*" he asked. We'd never read it. "Right here," he said, sweeping his hand at the window. "At anchor here on a sloop in the sea reach of the Thames." And then he'd pull the paperback from his pocket and read the first two pages. "Geez, that makes a man thirsty, eh, Mark?" He'd bump me and we'd drink up.

It was a long tour. We left the London Bridge sometime after five and didn't cross under the river in the tunnel at Greenwich until almost eleven. I remember scurrying through the long tiled corridor far beneath the river behind Porter as he dragged us along in a hurry because the pubs were going to close and we'd miss the last train back to Hampstead. We were all full of beer and Allison and I were dislocated, a feeling I got used to and came to like, as we came out into the bright cold air and saw the *Cutty Sark* moored there. This was life, it seemed to me, and I ran into the Red Cloak on Porter's footsteps. I was bursting and so pleased to be headed for the men's when he took my arm and pulled me to the bar. "Let's have a pint first, just to savor the night," he said. I wasn't standing upright, having walked with a bladder cramp for half a mile, and now the pain and pressure were blinding. I gripped the glass and met his smile. Allison came out of the ladies' and came over. "Are we being macho or just self-destructive?" she said.

"We're playing through the pain," Porter said. "We're seeing if the Buddhists are right with their wheel of desire and misery." I could barely hear him; there was a rushing in my ears, a cataract of steady noise. Disaster was imminent. Porter took a big slug of the bitter, and I mirrored his action. We swallowed and put down the glasses. "Excuse me," he said. "Think I'll hit the loo." And he strolled slowly into the men's. A blurred moment later I stood beside him at the huge urinals, dizzy and reclaimed. "We made it, mate," he said. "Now we've got to pound down a thousand beers and catch the train."

It had been a strange season in London for me. It was all new and as they say exciting, but I couldn't figure out what any of it meant. Now on the train to the north coast with Porter, I actually felt like somebody else who had never had my life, because as I saw it, my life—high school, college, Allison—hadn't taught me anything. For the first time I didn't give a shit about what happened next. The little play dance of cause and effect, be a good student, was all gone.

"You're not married," I said. It seemed late on a train and you could talk like that.

He looked at me. "It's not clear," he said. "In the eyes of men or the eyes of God?" I must have been looking serious, because he added, "No. I'm not married. Nearly happened once, but no, it was the timing, and now I've got plenty to do."

"Oh," I said.

"It was a girl at Hilman," he said. "I'd have done it too, but it got away from us. There's a time for it and you can wait too long." He pointed at me. "You and Allison talking about it?"

"No, not really. I mean, I don't know. I guess we are, kind of, being over here together. But we've never talked about it really." Now he was just smiling at me, the kid. That's what I wanted to say: hey, I'm a kid here; I'm too young. I'm too young for anything.

Porter drank. He was the first person I'd met who drank heavily and didn't make a mess. When the guys in the dorm drank the way he did every night we saw him, you wouldn't see them for three days. "Well, just remember there's a time and if it gets away, it's gone. Be alert." It sounded so true what he said. I'd never had a talk like this on a train and it all sounded true. It had weight. I wondered if the time had come and gone. I thought about Allison at thirty or forty, teaching art history at Holyoke or someplace. She'd be married to someone else, a man who appeared to be older than she, some guy with a thin gray beard.

"How do you know if the time is right or if the time is coming up? How do you know about this timing?" I held out my beau-

tiful white coffee cup, and Porter carefully filled it with the silver liquid. My future seemed vast, unchartable. "Whose fault
was it when you lost this girl?"

Porter rolled his head to look at me. He looked serious.
"Hers. Mine. She could have fixed it." He gave me a dire, ironic
look. "And then it was too late."

"What was her name?"

"It's no longer important."

"Was she a Lake?"

The window with the cabin lights dimmed was a dreamy
plate of our faint reflection torn up by all the white and yellow
lights of industrial lots and truck parks. "Yeah," he said. "They
all were. She wore her hair like Allison does and she looked that
way." He had grown wistful and turned quickly to me with a
grin. "Oh, hell, they all look that way when they're twenty-two."
After a while, Porter sat up and again topped my cup with
vodka.

In Edinburgh, we had to change trains. It was just before
dawn, and I felt torn up by all the drinking. Porter walked me
across to our connection, the train for Cape Wrath, and he went
off—for some reason—to the stationmaster's office. Checking
on something. He was going to make a few calls and then we'd
be off again, north to the coast. I'd wanted to call Allison, but
what would I say? I missed her? It was true, but it sounded like
kid stuff somehow. It bothered me that there was nothing appropriate to say, nothing fitting, and the days themselves felt like
they didn't fit, like I was waiting to grow into them. I sat sulking
on the train in Edinburgh station. I was sure—that is, I suspected—that there was something wrong with me. I hadn't seen
a fire or found a body or stopped a fight or *been* in one, really,
nor could I say what was going to happen, because I could not

read any of the signs. I wanted with all my teeth for something real to claim me. Anyway, that's as close as I can say it.

When Porter came back I could see him striding down the platform in the gray light like a man with a purpose. He didn't seem very drunk. He had a blue package under his arm. "Oh, matey, bad luck," he said, sitting opposite me in our new compartment. It was an older train, everything carpet and tassels and wood in remarkably good condition. It was like a time warp I was in, sitting there drunk while Porter told me he was going back to London. "Have to." He tapped the package. "They've overnighted all the data and I've got to compose the piece by tomorrow." He shook my hand heartily. "Wish me luck. And good luck to you. You'll love Cape Wrath. I once saw a submarine there off the coast. Good luck to you and your Gulf Stream." He smiled oddly with that last, a surreal look, I thought from my depth or height, distance anyway, and he was gone.

Well, I couldn't think. For a while I worked my face with my hands, carefully hoping that such a reasonable gesture might wake me, help me get a grip. But even after the train moved and then moved again, gaining momentum now, I was blank. Outside now the world was gray and green, the misting precipitation cutting the visibility to five hundred feet. This was part of a typical spring low pressure that would engulf all of Great Britain for a week. I didn't really know if I wanted to go on alone, but then I didn't know where I was going. I didn't know if I wanted to get off the train, because I didn't really know why I was on the train in the first place. I felt a little sick, a kind of shocky jangling that would resolve itself into nausea but not for about an hour, and so I put my feet on the opposite seat, closed my eyes, and waited.

Porter had been to our flat once. It was the day I had gone to the Royal Weather Offices in London, and when I came back, he and Allison were drinking our Whitbred at the tiny table. The place was a bed-sitter, too small for three people. I sat on the bed, but even so every time one of us moved the other two had to shift. Evidently Porter had come to invite us to some funky bar, the last mod pub off Piccadilly, he said. Allison's face was rosy in the close room. I told them about my day, the tour I'd taken, and Porter got me talking about El Niño, and I got a little carried away, I guess. I mean, I knew this stuff. But I remember them exchanging glances and smiling. I was smiling too, and I remember being happy waving my arms around as the great cycles of the English climate.

Now I felt every ripple of every steel track as it connected to the one before it, and I knew with increasing certainty that I was going to be sick. But there was something more than all the drink rising in me. Something was wrong. I was used to that feeling, that is, that things were not exactly as I expected, but this was something else. That blue package that Porter had carried back. I'd seen it all night, the corner of it, sticking out of the blown zipper of his leather valise. He'd had it all along. What was he talking about?

It was like that for forty minutes, my stomach roiling steadily, until we stopped at Pitlochry. When I stood up, I felt the whole chemistry seize, and I limped to the loo and after a band of sweat burst onto my forehead, I was sick, voluminously sick, and then I was better, that is, just stricken not poisoned. My head felt empty. I hurried to the platform and wrangled with the telephone until I was able to reach Roger Ardreprice. I had tried Allison at home and at the museum, and then I called Roger at work and a woman answered the phone: "Keats's House."

"Listen," I started after he'd come to the phone. Then I didn't know what to say. Why was I calling? "Listen," I said again. "I'm uneasy about something. . . ."

"Where are you calling from?" he asked.

"I'm in Scotland. I'm in someplace, Pitlochry. Porter and I were going north to the coast."

"Porter, oh, for god's sakes, you didn't get tangled up with Porter, did you? What's he got you doing? I should have said something."

The phone box was close, airless, and I pressed the red-paned door open with my foot. "He's been great, but . . ."

"Oh my, this is bad news. Porter, for your information, probably started the Lake fire. He was tried for it, you know. He is bloody bad news. You keep yourself and that young woman away from him. Especially the girl. What's her name?"

I set my forehead against one of the glass panes of the phone booth and breathed through my mouth deeply two or three times. "Allison," I said.

"Right," Roger Ardreprice said from London. "Don't let him at her."

I couldn't hear very well now, a kind of static had set up in my head, and I set the phone back on the cradle.

The return train was a lesson in sanity. I felt the whole time that I would go crazy the next minute, and this powerful about-to-explode feeling finally became a granite rock which I held on my lap with my traveling case. I thought if I could sit still, everything would be all right. As the afternoon failed, I sat perfectly still through the maddening countryside, across the bridges and rivers of Great Britain with my body feeling distant and infirm in the waxy shadow of my hangover. Big decisions, I learned that day, are made in the body, and my body recoiled at the thought of Porter.

From King's Cross I took a cab to the museum. I didn't care about the expense. It was odd then, being in a hurry for the first time that spring, impatient with the old city, which now seemed just a place in my way. Allison wasn't there. I called home. No answer. I checked in the Museum Pub, where we'd had lunch a dozen times; those lunches all seemed a long time ago. I grabbed another taxi and went home. Our narrow flat seemed like a bittersweet joke: what children lived here? The light rain had followed me south, as I knew it would, and in the mist I walked up to the High Street and had a doner kebab. It tasted good and I ate it as I drifted down to the tube stop. There was no hurry now. Rumbling through the Underground in the yellow light, I let my shoulders roll with the train. Everyone looked tired, hungover, ready for therapy.

I'd never been to the Hotel Eden alone, and in the new dark in the quiet rain, I stood a moment and took it in. It was frankly just a sad old four-story white building, the two columns on each side of the doors peeling as they had for years on end. Norris was inside alone, and I took a pint of lager from him and sat at one of the little tables. The beer nailed me back in place. I was worn out and spent, but I was through being sick. I had another pint as I watched Norris move in the back bar. It would be three hours before Allison and Porter came in from wherever they were, and then I would tell them all about my trip to Scotland. It would be my first story.

KEITH

THEY WERE LAB partners. It was that simple, how they met. She was *the* Barbara Anderson, president of half the school offices and queen of the rest. He was Keith Zetterstrom, a character, an oddball, a Z. His name was called last. The spring of their senior year at their equipment drawer she spoke to him for the first time in all their grades together: "Are you my lab partner?"

He spread the gear on the counter for the inventory and looked at her. "Yes, I am," he said. "I haven't lied to you this far, and I'm not going to start now."

After school Barbara Anderson met her boyfriend, Brian Woodworth, in the parking lot. They had twin red scooters because Brian had given her one at Christmas. "That guy," Barbara said, pointing to where Keith stood in the bus line, "is my lab partner."

"Who is he?" Brian said.

Keith was the window, wallpaper, woodwork. He'd been

there for years and they'd never seen him. This was complicated because for years he was short and then he grew tall. And then he grew a long black slash of hair and now he had a crewcut. He was hard to see, hard to fix in one's vision.

The experiments in chemistry that spring concerned states of matter, and Barbara and Keith worked well together, quietly and methodically testing the elements.

"You're Barbara Anderson," he said finally as they waited for a beaker to boil. "We were on the same kickball team in fourth grade and I stood behind you in the sixth-grade Christmas play. I was a Russian soldier."

Barbara Anderson did not know what to say to these things. She couldn't remember the sixth-grade play . . . and fourth grade? So she said, "What are you doing after graduation?"

"The sky's the limit," he said. "And you are going off to Brown University."

"How did you know that?"

"The list has been posted for weeks."

"Oh. Right. Well, I may go to Brown and I may stay here and go to the university with my boyfriend."

Their mixture boiled and Keith poured some off into a cooling tray. "So what do you do?" he asked her.

Barbara eyed him. She was used to classmates having curiosity about her, and she had developed a pleasant condescension, but Keith had her off guard.

"What do you mean?"

"On a date with Brian, your boyfriend. What do you do?"

"Lots of things. We play miniature golf."

"You go on your scooters and play miniature golf."

"Yes."

"Is there a windmill?"

"Yes, there's a windmill. Why do you ask? What are you getting at?"

"Who wins? The golf."

"Brian," Barbara said. "He does."

BARBARA SHOWED THE note to Trish, her best friend.

REASONS YOU SHOULD GO WITH ME
A.   You are my lab partner.
B.   Just to see. (You too, even Barbara Anderson, contain the same restless germ of curiosity that all humanity possesses, a trait that has led us out of the complacency of our dark caves into the bright world where we invented bowling— among other things.)
C.   It's not a "date."

"Great," Trish said. "We certainly believe this! But, girl, who wants to graduate without a night out with a bald whatever. And I don't think he's going to ravish you—against your will, that is. Go for it. We'll tell Brian that you're staying at my house."

KEITH DROVE A Chevy pickup, forest-green, and when Barbara climbed in, she asked, "Why don't you drive this to school?"

"There's a bus. I love the bus. Have you ever been on one?"

"Not a school bus."

"Oh, try it," he said. "Try it. It's so big and it doesn't drop you off right at your house."

"You're weird."

"Why? Oh, does the bus go right to your house? Come on, does it? But you've got to admit they're big, and that yellow paint job? Show me that somewhere else, I dare you. Fasten your seat belt, let's go."

The evening went like this: Keith turned onto Bloomfield, the broad business avenue that stretched from near the airport all the way back to the university, and he told her, "I want you to point out your least favorite building on this street."

"So we're not going bowling?"

"No, we're saving that. I thought we'd just get a little something to eat. So, keep your eyes open. Any places you can't stand?" By the time they reached the airport, Barbara had pointed out four she thought were ugly. When they turned around, Keith added: "Now, your final choice, please. And not someplace you just don't like. We're looking for genuine aversion."

Barbara selected a five-story metal building near downtown, with a simple marquee above the main doors that read INSURANCE.

"Excellent," Keith said as he swung the pickup to the curb. He began unloading his truck. "This is truly garish. The architect here is now serving time."

"This is where my father used to work."

Keith paused, his arms full of equipment. "When . . ."

"When he divorced my mom. His office was right up there." She pointed. "I hate driving by this place."

"Good," Keith said with renewed conviction. "Come over here and sit down. Have a Coke."

Barbara sat in a chaise longue that Keith had set on the flood-lit front lawn next to a folding table. He handed her a Coke. "We're eating here?"

"Yes, miss," he said, toting over the cooler and the little propane stove. "It's rustic but traditional: cheese omelets and hash brown potatoes. Sliced tomatoes for a salad with choice of dressing, and—for dessert—ice cream. On the way home, of course." Keith poured some oil into the frying pan. "There is nothing like a meal to alter the chemistry of a place."

On the way home, they did indeed stop for ice cream, and Barbara asked him: "Wasn't your hair long last year, like in your face and down like this?" She swept her hand past his eye.

"It was."

"Why is it so short now?"

Keith ran his hand back over his head. "Seasonal cut. Summer's a-coming in. I want to lead the way."

IT WAS AN odd week for Barbara. She actually did feel different about the insurance building as she drove her scooter by it on the way to school. When Trish found out about dinner, she said, "That was you! I saw your spread as we headed down to Barney's. You were like camped out, right?"

Wonder spread on Barbara's face as she thought it over. "Yeah, it was cool. He cooked."

"Right. But please, I've known a lot of guys who cook and they were some of the slickest. *High School Confidential* says: 'There are three million seductions and only one goal.'"

"You're a cynic."

"Cynicism is a useful survival skill."

IN CHEMISTRY, IT was sulfur. Liquid, solid, and gas. The hallways of the chemistry annex smelled like rotten eggs and jokes abounded. Barbara winced through the white wispy smoke as Keith stirred the melting sulfur nuggets.

"This is awful," Barbara said.

"This is wonderful," Keith said. "This is the exact smell that greets sinners at the gates of hell. They think it's awful; here we get to enjoy it for free."

Barbara looked at him. "My lab partner is a certifiable . . ."

"Your lab partner will meet you tonight at seven o'clock."

"Keith," she said, taking the stir stick from him and prodding the undissolved sulfur, "I'm dating Brian. Remember?"

"Good for you," he said. "Now tell me something I don't know. Listen: I'll pick you up at seven. This isn't a date. This isn't dinner. This is errands. I'm serious. Necessary errands—for your friends."

Barbara Anderson rolled her eyes.

"You'll be home by nine. Young Mr. Brian can scoot by then. I mean it." Keith leaned toward her, the streams of baking acrid sulfur rising past his face. "I'm not lying to you."

WHEN SHE GOT to the truck that night, Keith asked her, "What did you tell Brian?"

"I told him I had errands at my aunt's and to come by at ten for a little while."

"That's awfully late on a school night."

"Keith."

"I mean, why didn't you tell him you'd be with me for two hours?" He looked at her. "I have trouble lending credibility to a relationship that is almost one year old and one in which one of the members has given another an actual full-size, roadworthy motor vehicle, and yet it remains a relationship in which one of the members lies to the other when she plans to spend two hours with her lab partner, a person with whom she has inhaled the very vapors of hell."

"Stop the truck, Keith. I'm getting out."

"And miss bowling? And miss the search for bowling balls?"

Half an hour later they were in Veteran's Thrift, reading the bowling balls. They'd already bought five at Desert Industry Thrift Shops and the Salvation Army store. Keith's rule was it had to be less than two dollars. They already had PATTY for Trish, BETSY and KIM for two more of Barbara's friends, an initialled ball B.R. for Brian even though his last name was Woodworth ("Puzzle him," Keith said. "Make him guess"), and WALT for their chemistry teacher, Mr. Walter Miles. They found three more in the bins in Veteran's Thrift, one marked SKIP, one marked COSMO ("A must," Keith said), and a brilliant green ball, run deeply with hypnotic swirls, which had no name at all.

Barbara was touring the wide shelves of used appliances, toys, and kitchen utensils. "Where do they get all this stuff?"

"You've never been in a secondhand store before, have you?"

"No. Look at all this stuff. This is a quarter?" She held up a large plastic tray with the Beatles' pictures on it.

"That," Keith said, taking it from her and placing it in the cart with their bowling balls, "came from the home of a fan of the first magnitude. Oh, it's a sad story. It's enough to say that this is here tonight because of Yoko Ono." Keith's attention was taken by a large trophy, standing among the dozen other trophies on the top shelf. "Whoa," he said, pulling it down. It was huge, over three feet tall: six golden columns, ascending from a white marble base to a silver obelisk, framed by two embossed silver wreaths, and topped by a silver woman on a rearing motorcycle. The inscription on the base read: WIDOWMAKER HILL CLIMB — FIRST PLACE 1987. Keith held it out to show Barbara, like a man holding a huge bottle of aspirin in a television commercial. "But this is another story altogether." He placed it reverently in the basket.

"And that would be?"

"No time. You've got to get back and meet Brian, a person who doesn't know where you are." Keith led her to the checkout. He was quiet all the way to the truck. He placed the balls carefully in the cardboard boxes in the truck bed and then set the huge trophy between them on the seat.

"You don't know where this trophy came from."

Keith put a finger to his lips—*"Shhhh"*—and started the truck and headed to Barbara's house. After several blocks of silence, Barbara folded her arms. "It's a tragic, tragic story," he said in a low voice. "I mean, this girl was a golden girl, an angel, the light in everybody's life."

"Do I want to hear this tragic story?"

"She was a wonder. Straight A's, with an A plus in chemistry. The girl could do no wrong. And then," Keith looked at Barbara, "she got involved with motorcycles."

"Is this her on top of the trophy?"

"The very girl." Keith nodded grimly. "Oh, it started innocently enough with a little red motor scooter, a toy really, and she could be seen running errands for the Ladies' Society and other charities every Saturday and Sunday when she wasn't home studying." Keith turned to Barbara, moving the trophy forward so he could see her. "I should add here that her fine academic standing got her into Brown University, where she was going that fateful fall." Keith laid the trophy back. "When her thirst for speed grew and grew, breaking over her good common sense like a tidal wave, sending her into the arms of a twelve-hundred-cc Harley-Davidson, one of the most powerful two-wheeled vehicles in the history of mankind." They turned onto Barbara's street, and suddenly Barbara ducked, her head against Keith's knee.

"Drive by," she whispered. "Just keep going."

"What?" Keith said. "If I do that Brian won't see you." Keith could see Brian leaning against his scooter in the driveway. "Is that guy always early?"

Keith turned the next corner, and Barbara sat up and opened her door. "I'll go down the alley."

"Cool," Keith said. "So you sneak down the alley to meet your boyfriend? Pretty sexy."

She gave him a look.

"Okay, have fun. But there's one last thing, partner. I'll pick you up at four to deliver these bowling balls."

"Four?"

"Four a.m. Brian will be gone, won't he?"

"Keith."

"It's not a date. We've got to finish this program, right?"

Barbara looked over at Brian and quickly back at Keith as she opened the truck door. "Okay, but meet me at the corner. There," she pointed, "by the postbox."

SHE WAS THERE. The streets of the suburbs were dark and quiet, everything in its place, sleeping, but Barbara Anderson stood in the humming lamplight, humming her elbows. It was eerily quiet and she could hear Keith coming for two or three blocks before he turned onto her street. He had the heater on in the truck, and when she climbed in he handed her a blue cardigan, which she quickly buttoned up. "Four a.m.," she said, rubbing her hands over the air vent. "Now this is weird out here."

"Yeah," Keith said. "Four o'clock makes it a different planet. I recommend it. But bring a sweater." He looked at her. "You look real sleepy," he said. "You look good. This is the face you ought to bring to school."

Barbara looked at Keith and smiled. "No makeup, okay? It's

four a.m." His face looked tired, and in the pale dash lights, with his short, short hair he looked more like a child, a little boy. "What do we do?"

"We give each of these babies," Keith nodded back at the bowling balls in the truck bed, "a new home."

They delivered the balls, placing them carefully on the porches of their friends, including Trish and Brian, and then they spent half an hour finding Mr. Miles's house, which was across town, a tan split-level. Keith handed Barbara the ball marked WALT and made her walk it up to the front porch. When she returned to the truck, Keith said, "Years from now you'll be able to say, 'When I was seventeen I put a bowling ball on my chemistry's teacher's front porch.'"

"His name was Walt," Barbara added.

At five-thirty, as the first gray light rose, Barbara Anderson and Keith walked into Jewel's Café carrying the last two balls: the green beauty and COSMO. Jewel's was the oldest café in the city, an all-night diner full of mailmen. "So," Barbara said, as they slid into one of the huge maroon booths, "who gets these last two?" She was radiant now, fully awake, and energized by the new day.

The waitress appeared and they ordered Round-the-World omelettes, hash browns, juice, milk, coffee, and wheat muffins, and Barbara ate with gusto, looking up halfway through. "So, where next?" She saw his plate. "Hey, you're not eating."

Keith looked odd, his face milky, his eyes gray. "This food is full of the exact amino acids to have a certifiably chemical day," he said. "I'll get around to it."

But he never did. He pushed his plate to the side and turned the place mat over and began to write on it.

"Are you feeling all right?" Barbara said.

"I'm okay."

She tilted her head at him skeptically.

"Hey. I'm okay. I haven't lied to you this far. Why would I start now? You know I'm okay, don't you? Well? Don't you think I'm okay?"

She looked at him and said quietly: "You're okay."

He showed her the note he had written:

Dear Waitress: My girlfriend and I are from rival families—different sides of the tracks, races, creeds, colors, and zip codes, and if they found out we had been out bowling all night, they would banish us to prison schools on separate planets. Please, please find a good home for our only bowling balls. Our enormous sadness is only mitigated by the fact that we know you'll take care of them.

With sweet sorrow—COSMO

In the truck, Barbara said, "Mitigated?"

"Always leave them something to look up."

"You're sick, aren't you?" she said.

"You look good in that sweater," he said. When she started to remove it, he added, "Don't. I'll get it after class, in just," he looked at his watch, "two hours and twenty minutes."

BUT HE WASN'T there. He wasn't there all week. The class did experiments with oxidation and Mr. Miles spent two days explaining and diagramming rust. On Friday, Mr. Miles worked with Barbara on the experiments and she asked him what was wrong with Keith. "I'm not sure," her teacher told her. "But I think he's on medication."

Barbara had a tennis match on Tuesday afternoon at school, and Brian picked her up and drove her home. Usually he came in for an hour or so on these school days and they made out a little and raided the fridge, but for the first time she begged off, claiming homework, kissing him on the cheek and running into her house. But on Friday, during her away match at Viewmont, she felt odd again. She knew Brian was in the stands. When she walked off the court after the match it was nearly dark and Brian was waiting. She gave Trish her rackets and Barbara climbed on Brian's scooter without a word. "You weren't that bad," he said. "Viewmont always has a good team."

"Brian, let's just go home."

"You want to stop at Swenson's, get something to eat?"

"No."

So Brian started his scooter and drove them home. Barbara could tell by the way he was driving that he was mad, and it confused her: she felt strangely glad about it. She didn't want to invite him in, let him grope her on the couch. She held on as he took the corners too fast and slipped through the stop signs, but all the way home she didn't put her chin on his shoulder.

At her house, she got the scene she'd been expecting. "Just what is the matter with you?" Brian said. For some reason when he'd gone to kiss her, she'd averted her face. Her heart burned with pleasure and shame. She was going to make up a lie about tennis, but then just said, "Oh Brian. Just leave me alone for a while, will you? Just go home."

Inside, she couldn't settle down. She didn't shower or change clothes. She sat in the dark of her room for a while and then, using only the tiny spot of her desk lamp, she copied her chemistry notes for the week and called Trish.

It was midnight when Trish picked her up quietly by the mailbox on the corner. Trish was smoking one of her Marlboros and blowing smoke into the windshield. She said, *"High School Confidential,* Part Five: Young Barbara Anderson, still in her foxy tennis clothes, and her old friend Trish meet again at midnight, cruise the Strip, pick up two young men with tattoos, and are never seen alive again. Is that it? Count me in."

"Not quite. It goes like this: two sultry babes, one of whom has just been a royal bitch to her boyfriend for no reason, drive to 1147 Fairmont to drop off the week's chemistry notes."

"That would be Keith Zetterstrom's address, I'd guess." Trish said.

"He's my lab partner."

"Of course he is," Trish said.

"He missed all last week. Mr. Miles told me that Keith's on medication."

"Oh my god!" Trish clamped the steering wheel. "He's got cancer. That's that scary hairdo. He's sick."

"No he doesn't. I checked the college lists. He's going to Dickinson."

"Not for long, honey. I should have known this." Trish inhaled and blew smoke thoughtfully out of the side of her mouth. "Bald kids in high school without earrings have got cancer."

KEITH WAS IN class the following Monday for the chemistry exam: sulfur and rust. After class, Barbara Anderson took him by the arm and led him to her locker. "Thanks for the notes, partner," he said. "They were absolutely chemical. I aced the quiz."

"You were sick last week."

"Last week." He pondered. "Oh, you mean because I wasn't

here. What do you do, come every day? I just couldn't; it would take away the something special I feel for this place. I like to come from time to time and keep the dew on the rose, so to speak."

"I know what's the matter with you."

"Good for you, Barbara Anderson. And I know what's the matter with you too; sounds like a promising relationship."

Barbara pulled his folded sweater from the locker and handed it to him. As she did, Brian came up and said to them both: "Oh, I see." He started to walk away.

"Brian," Keith said. "Listen. You don't see. I'm not a threat to you. How could I be a threat to you? Think about it." Brian stood, his eyes narrowed. Keith went on: "Barbara's not stupid. What am I going to do, trick her? I'm her lab partner in chemistry. Relax." Keith went to Brian and took his hand, shook it. "I'm serious, Woodworth."

Brian stood for a moment longer until Barbara said, "I'll see you at lunch," and then he backed and disappeared down the hall. When he was gone, Barbara said, "*Are* you tricking me?"

"I don't know. Something's going on. I'm a little confused."

"You're confused. Who are you? Where have you been, Keith Zetterstrom? I've been going to school with you all these years and I've never even seen you and then we're delivering bowling balls together and now you're sick. Where were you last year? What are you doing? What are you going to do next year?"

"Last year I got a C in Spanish with Mrs. Whitehead. It was gruesome. This year is somewhat worse, with a few exceptions, and all in all, I'd say the sky is the limit." Keith took her wrist. "Quote me on that."

Barbara took a sharp breath through her nose and quietly began to cry.

"What?" Keith said. "If I do that Brian won't see you." Keith could see Brian leaning against his scooter in the driveway. "Is that guy always early?"

Keith turned the next corner, and Barbara sat up and opened her door. "I'll go down the alley."

"Cool," Keith said. "So you sneak down the alley to meet your boyfriend? Pretty sexy."

She gave him a look.

"Okay, have fun. But there's one last thing, partner. I'll pick you up at four to deliver these bowling balls."

"Four?"

"Four a.m. Brian will be gone, won't he?"

"Keith."

"It's not a date. We've got to finish this program, right?"

Barbara looked over at Brian and quickly back at Keith as she opened the truck door. "Okay, but meet me at the corner. There," she pointed, "by the postbox."

SHE WAS THERE. The streets of the suburbs were dark and quiet, everything in its place, sleeping, but Barbara Anderson stood in the humming lamplight, hugging her elbows. It was eerily quiet and she could hear Keith coming for two or three blocks before he turned onto her street. He had the heater on in the truck, and when she climbed in he handed her a blue cardigan, which she quickly buttoned up. "Four a.m.," she said, rubbing her hands over the air vent. "Now this is weird out here."

"Yeah," Keith said. "Four o'clock makes it a different planet. I recommend it. But bring a sweater." He looked at her. "You look real sleepy," he said. "You look good. This is the face you ought to bring to school."

Barbara looked at Keith and smiled. "No makeup, okay? It's

face, more serious, be strong. Good. Now walk just like this, little stab steps, real slow."

They started down the hallway, creeping along one side. "How far is it?" Barbara said. People passed them walking quietly in groups of two or three. It was the end of visiting hours. "A hundred yards to the elevators and down three floors, then out a hundred more. Keep your face down."

"Are people looking at us?"

"Well, yes. They've never seen a braver couple. And they've never seen such chemical pajamas. What are those little deals, lambs?"

They continued along the windows, through the lobby and down the elevator, in which they stood side by side, their four hands clasped together, while they were looking at their tennis shoes. The other people in the car gave them room out of respect. The main hall was worse, thick with people, everyone going five miles an hour faster than Barbara and Keith, who shuffled along whispering.

In the gift shop, finally, they parted the waters. The small room was crowded, but the people stepped aside and Keith and Barbara stood right at the counter. "A package of chewing gum, please," Keith said.

"Which kind?" said the candy striper.

"Sugarless. My sister and I want our teeth to last forever."

THEY RAN TO the truck, leaping and swinging their arms. Keith threw the bag containing their clothes into the truck bed and climbed into the cab. Barbara climbed in, laughing, and Keith said, "Come on, face the facts: you feel better! You're cured!" And she slid across the seat meaning to hug him but it changed for both of them and they kissed. She pulled him to her side and they kissed again, one of her arms around his neck and one of her hands on his face. They fell into a spin there in the truck, eyes closed, holding on to each other in their pajamas, her robe open, their heads against the backseat, kissing. Barbara shifted and Keith sat up; the look they exchanged held. Below them the city's lights flickered. Barbara cupped her hand carefully on the top of Keith's bald scalp. She pulled him forward and they kissed. When she looked in his eyes again she knew what was going to happen, and it was a powerful feeling that gave her strange new certainty as she went for his mouth again.

There were other moments that surfaced in the truck in the night above the ancient city. Something Keith did, his hand reminded her of Brian, and then that thought vanished as they were beyond Brian in a moment. Later, well beyond even her notions of what to do and what not to do, lathered and breathing as if in toil, she heard herself say, "Yes." She said that several times.

SHE LOOKED FOR Keith everywhere, catching glimpses of his head, his shoulder, in the hallways. In chemistry they didn't talk; there were final reports, no need to work together. Finally, three days before graduation, they stood side by side cleaning out their chemistry equipment locker, waiting for Mr. Miles to check them off. Keith's manner was what? Easy, too confident, too neutral. He seemed to take up too much space in the room. She hated the way he kept his face blank and open, as if fishing for the first remark. She held off, feeling the restraint as a physical pang. Mr. Miles inventoried their cupboard and asked for their keys. He had a large ring of thirty or forty of the thin brass keys. Keith handed his to Mr. Miles and then Barbara Anderson found her key in the side of her purse and handed it to the teacher. She hated relinquishing the key; it was the only thing she had that meant she would see Keith, and now with it gone something opened in her and it hurt in a way she'd never hurt before. Keith turned to her and seeing something in her face, shrugged and said, "The end of chemistry as we know it. Which isn't really very well."

"Who are you?" Barbara said, her voice a kind of surprise to her. "You're so glib. Such a little actor." Mr. Miles looked up from his check sheet and several students turned toward them. Barbara was speaking loudly; she couldn't help it. "What are you doing to me? If you ask me this is a pretty chickenshit good-bye." Everyone was looking at her. Then her face would not work at all, the tears coming from some hot place, and Barbara Anderson walked from the room.

Keith hadn't moved. Mr. Miles looked at Keith, alarmed. Keith whispered: "Don't worry, Mr. Miles. She was addressing her remarks to me."

THERE WAS ONE more scene. The night before graduation, while her classmates met in the bright, noisy gym for the year-book-signing party, Barbara drove out to the airport and met Keith where he said he'd be: at the last gate, H-17. There on an empty stretch of maroon carpet in front of three large banks of seats full of travelers, he was waiting. He handed her a pretty green canvas valise and an empty paper ticket sleeve.

"You can't even talk as yourself," she said. "You always need a setting. Now we're pretending I'm going somewhere?"

He looked serious tonight, weary. There were gray shadows under his eyes. "You wanted a goodbye scene," he said. "I tried not to do this."

"It's all a joke," she said. "You joke all the time."

"You know what my counselor said?" He smiled thinly as if glad to give her this point. "He said that this is a phase, that I'll stop joking soon." Their eyes met and the look held again. "Come here," he said. She stepped close to him. He put his hand on her elbow. "You want a farewell speech. Okay, here you go. You better call Brian and get your scooter back. Tell him I tricked you. Wake up, lady. Get real. I just wanted to see if I could give Barbara Anderson a whirl. And I did. It was selfish, okay? I just screwed you around a little. You said it yourself: it was a joke. That's my speech. How was it?"

"You didn't screw me around, Keith. You didn't give me a whirl." Barbara moved his hand and then put her arms around his neck so she could speak in his ear. She could see some of the people watching them. "You made love to me, Keith. It wasn't a joke. You made love to me and I met you tonight to say—good for you. Extreme times require extreme solutions." She was whispering as they stood alone on that carpet in their embrace. "I wondered how it was going to happen, but you were a surprise. Way to go. What did you think? That I wanted to go off to college an eighteen-year-old virgin? That pajama bit was great; I'll remember it." Now people were deplaning, entering the gate area and streaming around the young couple. Barbara felt Keith begin to tremble, and she closed her eyes. "It wasn't a joke. There's this: I made love to you too. You were there, remember? I'm glad for it." She pulled back slightly and found his lips. For a moment she was keenly aware of the public scene they were making, but that disappeared and they twisted tighter and were just there, kissing. She had dropped the valise and when the mock ticket slipped from her fingers behind his neck, a young woman in a business suit knelt and retrieved it and tapped Barbara on the hand. Barbara clutched the ticket and dropped her head to Keith's chest.

"I remember," he said. "My memory is aces."

"Tell me, Keith," she said. "What are these people thinking? Make something up."

"No need. They've got it right. That's why we came out here. They think we're saying goodbye."

SIMPLY PUT, THAT was the last time Barbara Anderson saw Keith Zetterstrom. That fall when she arrived in Providence for her freshman year at Brown, there was one package waiting for her, a large trophy topped by a girl on a motorcycle. She had seen it before. She kept it in her dorm window, where it was visible four stories from the ground, and she told her roommates that it meant a lot to her, that it represented a lot of fun and hard work but her goal had been to win the Widowmaker Hill Climb, and once she had done that, she sold her bikes and gave up her motorcycles forever.

THE PRISONER OF
BLUESTONE

THERE WAS A camera. Mr. Ruckelbar was helping load the crushed sedan onto DiPaulo's tow truck when an old Nikon camera fell from the gashed trunkwell and hit him on the shoulder. At first he thought it was a rock or a taillight assembly; things had fallen on him before as he and DiPaulo had wrestled the ruined vehicles onto the tiltbed of DiPaulo's big custom Ford, and of course DiPaulo wasn't there to be hit. He had a bad back and was in the cab working the hydraulics and calling, "Good? Are we good yet?"

"Whoa, that's enough!" he called. Now Ruckelbar would have to clamber up and set the chains. DiPaulo, he thought, the wrecker with the bad back.

It was a thick gray twilight in the last week of October, chilly now with the sun gone. This vehicle had been out back for too long. The end of summer was always bad. After the Labor Day weekend, he always took in a couple cars. He stored them out in a fenced lot behind his Sunoco station, getting twenty dollars a week until the insurance paperwork was completed, all of them the same really, totaled and sold to DiPaulo, who took them out to Junk World, his four acres of damaged vehicles near Torrington. Ruckelbar was glad to see this silver Saab go. It had been weird having the kid almost every afternoon since it had arrived, sitting out in the crushed thing full of leaves and beads of glass, just sitting there until dark sometimes, then walking back toward town along the two-lane without a proper jacket, some boy, the brother he said he was, some kid you didn't need sitting in a totaled Saab, some skinny kid maybe fourteen years old.

Ruckelbar cinched the final chain hitch and climbed down. "What'd you get?" It was DiPaulo. The small old man had limped back in the new dark and had picked the camera up. "This has got to be worth something."

"It's that kid's. It was his sister's car."

DiPaulo handed him back the camera. "That kid. That kid doesn't need to see this. I'd chuck it in the river before I let him see it. He's nutty enough." DiPaulo shook his head. "What's he going to do when he sees the car is finally gone?"

"Lord knows," Ruckelbar said. "Maybe he'll find someplace else to go."

"Well, that car's been here a long time, summer's over, and that camera," DiPaulo poked it with one of his short stained fingers, "is long gone to everybody. Let you leave the sleeping dogs asleep. Just put it in a drawer. You listen to your old pal. Your father would." DiPaulo took Ruckelbar's shoulder in his hand for a second. "See you. I'll be back Wednesday for that van. You take care." The little old man turned one more time and pointed at Ruckelbar. "And for god's sakes, don't tell that kid where this car is going."

DiPaulo had known Ruckelbar's father, "for a thousand years

before you came along," he'd say, and Ruckelbar could remember DiPaulo saying "Leave sleeping dogs asleep" throughout the years in friendly arguments every time there was some sort of cash windfall. The elder Ruckelbar would smile and say that DiPaulo should have been a tax attorney.

After DiPaulo left, Ruckelbar rolled the wooden desk chair back inside the office of the Sunoco station and locked up. The building was a local landmark really, such an old little stone edifice painted blue, sitting all alone out on Route 21, where the woods had grown up around it and made it appear a hut in a fairy tale, with two gas pumps. The Bluestone everyone called it, and it was used to mark the quarry turnoff; "four miles past the Bluestone." It certainly marked Ruckelbar's life, was his life. He had met Clare at a community bonfire at the Quarry Meadows when she was still a student at Woodbine Prep, and above there at the Upper Quarry, remote and private, one night a year later she had helped him undo both of them in his father's truck and urgently had begun a sex life that wouldn't last five years.

Ruckelbar was a sophomore at the University of Massachusetts when his father had a heart attack in the station that March and died sitting up against the wall in the single-bay garage. Ruckelbar was twenty and when he came home it would stick. Clare was back from Sarah Lawrence that summer, and it was all right for a while, even good, the way anything can be good when you're young. It was fun having a service station, and after closing they'd go to the pubs beyond the blue-collar town of Garse, roadhouses that are all gone now. It was thrilling for Clare to sit in his pickup, the station truck, the same truck in which she arched herself against him at Upper Quarry and the same truck he drives now, as he rocked the huge set of keys in the latch of Bluestone and then extracted them and turned to her for a night. But she didn't think he was serious about it. He was to be an engineer; his father had said as much, and then another year passed, his mother now ill, while he ran the place all winter, plowing the snow from around the station with a blade on the old truck that his father had welded himself. When spring came it was a done deal. The wild iris and the dogwoods burst from every seam in the earth and the world changed for Ruckelbar, his sense of autonomy and worth, and he knew he was here for life. Even by the time they married, Clare had had enough. When she saw that the little baby girl she had the next year gave her no leverage with him, she stopped coming out with box lunches and avoided driving by the place even when she had to drive to Garse going by way of Tipton, which added four miles to the trip. She let him know that she didn't want to hear about Bluestone in her house and that he was to leave his overalls at the station, his boots in the garage, and he was to shower in the basement.

He'd gone along with this somehow, gone along without an angry word, without many words at all, the separate bedroom in the nice house in Corbett, and now after nearly twenty years, it was their way. After the loss of Clare and then the loss of the memory of her in his truck and in his bed came the loss of his daughter, which he also just allowed. Clare had her at home and Clare was determined that Marjorie should understand the essential elements of disappointment, and the lessons started with his name. Now, at seventeen, Marjorie was a day student at Woodbine, the prep school in Corbett, and her name was Marjorie Bar, shortened Clare said for convenience and for her career, whatever it would be. And Ruckelbar had let that happen too. He could fix any feature of any automobile, truck, or element of farm equipment, but he could not fix this.

AT HOME AFTER a silent dinner with Clare, he broke the rule about talking about the station and told her that DiPaulo had picked up the car, the one the boy had been sitting in every day for weeks. She didn't like DiPaulo—he'd always been part of the way her life had betrayed her—and she let her eyes lift in disgust and then asked about the boy, "What did he do?" They were clearing the supper dishes. Marjorie ate dinner at school and arrived home after the evening study hall. It was queer that Clare should ask a question, and Ruckelbar, who hadn't intended his comment to begin a conversation, was surprised and not sure of how he should answer.

"He sat in the car. In the driver's seat."

This stopped Clare midstep and she held her dishes still. "All day?"

"He came after school and walked home after dark." It was the most Ruckelbar had spoken about the station in his kitchen for five or six years. Clare resumed sorting out the silverware and wiping up. Ruckelbar realized he wanted to ask Clare what to do about the camera. "Do you remember the accident?" he asked. "The girl?"

"If it's the same girl. The three young people from Garse. She was a tramp. They were killed on Labor Day or just before. They went off the quarry road."

Ruckelbar, who hadn't seen the papers, had known about the accident, of course. The police tow truck driver had told him about the three students, and the vehicle was crushed in so radical a fashion anyone could see it had fallen some distance onto the rock. Clare seemed to know more about it, something she'd read or heard, but Ruckelbar didn't know how to ask, and in a moment the chance was lost.

"Who's a tramp?" Marjorie entered the kitchen, putting her bookbag on a chair.

"Your father has some lowlife living in a car."

Ruckelbar looked at her.

"Any pie?" Marjorie asked her mother. Clare extracted a pumpkin pie from the fridge. Under the plastic wrap, it was uncut, one of Clare's fresh pumpkin pies. Ruckelbar looked at it, just a pie, and he stopped slipping. He'd already exited the room in his head, and he came back. "I'd like a piece of that pie, too, Clare. If I could please."

"You didn't get any?" Marjorie said. "You must really smell like gasoline tonight." She was actually trying to be light.

"He's not a lowlife, Clare," he said to her as she set a wedge of pie before him and dropped a fork onto the table. Even Marjorie, who had silently sided with her mother every time she'd had the chance, looked up in surprise at Clare. "It's the boy whose sister was killed last summer."

"Sheila Morton," Marjorie said.

"The tramp," Clare said.

Ruckelbar took a bite of pie. He was going to stay right here. This was the scene he'd drifted away from a thousand times. They were talking.

"She was not a tramp," he said. "This boy is a nice boy."

"He's disturbed," Clare said. "God, going out there to sit in the car?"

"Sheila was a slut," Marjorie said. "Everybody knew that."

The moment had gone very strange for all of them together like this in the kitchen. An ordinary night would have found Ruckelbar in the garage or his bedroom, Marjorie on the phone, and Clare at the television. They all felt the vague uncertainty of having the rules shift. No one would leave and no one knew how it would end; this was all new.

"She was, Dad," Marjorie said, setting Ruckelbar back in his chair with the word "Dad," which in its disuse had become monumental, naked and direct. They all heard it. Marjorie went on, "She put out, okay? One of those guys was from Woodbine. What do you think they were doing? They were headed for the Upper Quarry. It's where the sluts go. You don't try that road unless you're going to put out."

Ruckelbar had stopped eating the pie. He put down his fork and turned: Clare was gone.

A sunny Saturday in New England the last day in October: Ruckelbar lives for days like these, maybe this day in particular, the sun even at noon fallen away hard, but the lever of heat still there, though more than half the leaves are down and they skirl across Route 21 and pool against the banks of old grass. Ruckelbar sits in his old wooden office chair, which he pulls out front on days just like this, the whole scene a throwback to any fall afternoon thirty years ago, that being Clare's word, "throwback," but for now he's free in what feels like the very last late sunlight of the year. It's Halloween, he remembers; tonight they turn their clocks back. It doesn't matter. For now, he's simply going to sit in the place which has become the place he belongs, a place where he is closest to being happy, no, pleased he never moved, pleased to have this place paid for and not be running the Citgo in town chasing in circles regardless of the money, pleased to have the only station in the twelve miles of Route 21 between Garse and Corbett, nothing to look at across the street but trees rolling away toward Little Bear Mountain. Ruckelbar won't make fifty dollars the whole day and he simply leans back in the sunshine, pleased to have his tools put away and the bay swept and the office neat, just pleased to have the afternoon. As he sits and lifts his face to the old sun, he feels it and he's surprised that there is something else now, something new swimming underneath the ease he always feels at Bluestone, something about last night, and he tries to dismiss it but it will not be dismissed. It took years to achieve this separate peace and now something is coming undone.

Last night Ruckelbar had gone to Clare's room. After Marjorie had finished her pie and left the kitchen, her dishes on the table still, he'd sat as their talk played again in his head, burning there like a mistake. He hadn't known the Morton girl and in defending her he'd let his wife be injured. But he felt good about it somehow, that he had protested, and his mind had opened in the realization that something in him had been killed when they'd changed Marjorie's name, and he'd hated himself for not protesting then, but he knew too that he'd always just gone along. He lifted the two plates from the table and then put them down where they were. He went to Marjorie where she talked on the phone in the den and he stood before her until she put her palm over the speaker and said, annoyed, "What?" He said, "Get off the phone and go put your dishes away. Now." He said it in such a way that she spoke quickly into the telephone and hung up. Before she could rise, he added, "I think you should watch your language around your mother; I'm sure you didn't please her tonight in speaking so freely. She's worked hard to raise you correctly and you disappointed her."

"You started it," Marjorie said.

"Stop," he said. "You apologize to her tomorrow. It will mean a lot to her. You're everything she's got." Ruckelbar wanted to touch his daughter, put his hand on her cheek, but he didn't move, and in a moment Marjorie left the room. He had not done it too many times to reach out now, and besides, his hands, he always knew, were never really clean.

Ruckelbar went upstairs and knocked at his wife's door and then, surprising himself, went into the dark room. She was in bed and he sat beside her, but could do no more. He knew she was awake and he willed himself to put his arm around her, but he could not, pulling his fists up instead to his face and smelling in his knuckles all the scents of Bluestone.

In the early afternoon, a Chevy Two convertible pulls in to the gas pumps. At first Ruckelbar thinks it is two nuns, but when the two women get out laughing in their full black dresses, he sees they are gotten up as witches. One puts her tall black hat on and pulls a broom from the backseat ready to mug for any passing cars. Ruckelbar steps over. The bareheaded witch is switching on the pump. "Let me get that for you," he offers. "You'll smell like gasoline at your party."

"Great," the girl says. They are both about his daughter's age. "What are you going to be?" she asks him.

"This is it," Ruckelbar says, indicating his gray overall.

"Okay," the other witch says, "so what are you, the Prisoner of Bluestone?" They laugh and Ruckelbar has to laugh there in the sunshine. Girls. His daughter would not believe that he laughed with these girls; there'd be no way to explain it to her. The valve clicks off and he replaces the nozzle. As he does, the broom witch takes it from him and holds it as if to gas the broom.

"This, get this," she says. "Let's get out your camera, Paul." She's read his name in the patch. The other witch has grabbed her broom now and poses with her friend. Hearing his name and their laughter elates him and without hesitation, as if he'd planned it, he ducks into the station and retrieves the Nikon camera. He takes their picture there, two tall witches in the sunshine, and as he does, a passing car honks a salute. One of the witches steps out now seeing the bright blue station as if for the first time and says, "What is this, a movie set? I love it that you actually sell gas." She throws her broom and hat back into the car. The other girl, the driver, reaches deep into her costume, here and there, to find her money. She has some difficulty. Her hat falls off and Ruckelbar holds it for her, finally exchanging it for the nine dollars she pays him.

"Happy Halloween," she says, getting into the car. "I like your outfit. I hope they come to let you out someday."

The other girl has been at the car's radio and a song that Ruckelbar seems to remember rises around them. As the girls begin to pull away, she calls, "You can use that picture in your advertising!" And she throws him a flamboyant kiss.

All day long the traffic is desultory, five cars an hour pass Bluestone, the sound they make on Route 21 is a sound Ruckelbar knows by heart. He knows the trucks from the cars and he knows the high whine of the school buses. He knows if someone is speeding and he can tell if a car's intention is to slow and turn in. Just before sunset he hears that sound and a little white Ford Escort coasts into the gravel yard of the station, parking to one side. There is something odd about it and Ruckelbar thinks it is more costumes, two people, one wrapped like the Mummy, but then he sees it is a rental, and when the man and the woman get out and the man has the head bandage, he knows it is the owners of the Dodge van come to get whatever they'd left inside. People come the week after an accident and get their stuff. He stands and waves at the young people and then goes to unlock the chainlink gate, trying not to look at the man's head, which is swollen crazily over the unbandaged eye.

The woman strides directly for the van as Ruckelbar says, "Take your time, I don't close until six. No rush."

The woman calls from where she's slid open the side door of the van, "Bring the basket, Jerry. It's in the back."

So now it's Ruckelbar bending into the little Ford and extracting a huge plastic laundry basket because the man Jerry says he's not supposed to bend over until the swelling subsides in a week. "I have to sleep sitting up." Jerry's about thirty, his skull absolutely out of whack, a wrong-way oval, the skin on his exposed forehead about to split, shiny and yellow. Ruckelbar can smell the varnish of liquor on his breath. When he pulls the basket from the small backseat to hand it to Jerry, the young man has already wandered out back.

Ruckelbar takes the basket around to the open side of the van and offers it there, but the woman is on her knees on the middle seat bent into the far back, trying to untangle the straps of a collapsed child seat. Her cotton shift is drawn up so that her bare thighs are visible to him. Her underpants are a shiny satin blue and the configuration of her white thighs and the way they meet in the blue fabric seem a disembodied mystery to Ruckelbar. Ruckelbar looks away and steps back onto the moist yellow grid of grass where the Saab sat for eight weeks. He can hear the woman now, a soft sucking, and he knows she is weeping. He sets the basket there in the twilight and he walks back to the office. He is lit and shaken; he feels as he did when the witch said his name. On his way he hears Jerry break the mirror assembly from the van door and he turns to watch the young man throw it into the woods and then spin to the ground and grab his head.

Out front the sun is gone, the day is gone, it feels nothing but late. The daylight seems used, thin, good for nothing. He carries his chair back into the office and there in the new gloom is the boy, arms folded, leaning against the counter.

"You scared me," Ruckelbar says. "Hello." He sets the chair behind his steel desk and switches on the office fluorescents. He's lost for a moment and simply adds, "How are you?"

"Where's my sister's car?" the boy asks. He looks different close like this in the flat light; he's taller and younger, his pale face run with freckles. He's wearing a red plaid shirt unbuttoned over a faded black T-shirt.

"The insurance company came and got it. It was theirs." The boy takes this in and makes a face that says he understands. "Remember, I told you about this a couple of weeks ago?" The boy nods at him and then turns to the big window and looks out. His eyes are roaming and Ruckelbar sees the desperation.

The camera sits on the old steel desk, and in a second Ruckelbar decides what to do; if the boy recognizes it, he'll give it to him. Otherwise, he'll let this sleeping dog be. It feels like a good decision, but Ruckelbar is floating in a new world, he can tell. They can hear the loud voices outside, the man and the woman in the back, and Ruckelbar switches on the exterior lights.

"Where would the insurance take that car?"

"I don't know," Ruckelbar says.

"Would they fix it?"

"Probably part it out," Ruckelbar says. "They don't fix them anymore, many of them."

"It had been a good car for Sheila," the boy says. "Better than any of her friends had."

"I hear good things about the Saab," Ruckelbar says. "You want a Coke, something, candy bar?"

"I don't know why I'm out here now," the boy says. Their reflections have come up in the big windows. Ruckelbar drops quarters in the round-shouldered soda machine, another throwback, and opens the door for the boy to choose. "Root beer," the boy says, extracting the bottle.

"You live in Garse?" Ruckelbar asks him.

"Yeah," the boy says. His eyes are still wide, darting, and Ruckelbar can see the rim of moisture. The world outside is now set still on the pivot point of light, the glow of the station lights running into the air out over the road through the trees all the way to the even wash of silver along the horizon of Little Bear Mountain, and above the mountain like two huge ghosts floats the mirror image of the two of them. The leaves lie still. Standing by the door Ruckelbar can feel the air falling from the dark heavens, a faint chill falling from infinity. Tomorrow night it will be dark an hour earlier.

Now Ruckelbar hears the woman's voice from outside, around the building, a cry of some sort, and then the rental Escort does a short circle in the gravel in front of the Sunoco pumps and rips dust into the new dusk as it mounts Route 21 headed for Corbett. Ruckelbar and the boy have stepped outside. They watch the car disappear, turning on its lights after a few seconds on the pavement.

"There's a bonfire at the quarry tonight," Ruckelbar says. "Garse does it. You going?"

"We'd have gone with Sheila. She liked that stuff; she liked Halloween." The boy follows him back inside.

"You want a ride home?" Ruckelbar says, knowing instantly that it is the wrong thing to say, the offer of sympathy battering the boy over the brink, and now the boy stands crying stiffly, chin down, his arms crossed tighter than anything in the world.

Ruckelbar's heart heaves; he knows about this, about living in his silent house where a kind word would have broken him.

They stand that way, as if after an explosion, not knowing what to do; all the surprises in the room have been used up. Everything that happens now will be work. Ruckelbar is particularly out of ideas; he's not used to having anyone in the office for longer than it takes to make change. His father sometimes sat in here and chewed the fat with his cronies, DiPaulo and others, but Ruckelbar has never done it. He doesn't have any cronies. Now he doesn't know what to do. Ruckelbar points at the boy. "You go ahead, get the truck, bring it around front." He hands the boy his keys. The boy looks at him, so he goes on. "It's all right. You do it. You know my truck." With it dark now, Ruckelbar can see himself in the front window, a man in overalls. He's scared. It feels like something else could happen. He reaches for the phone and calls Clare, which he doesn't do three times a year. "Clare," he says, "I'm bringing somebody home who needs a warm meal. We're coming. It's not something we can talk over. We'll be about fifteen minutes, okay, honey? Did you hear me? Can you put on some of your tea?" He has never said anything like this to Clare in his life. The only people who are ever in their house are Clare's sister every other year and a few of Marjorie's friends who stand in the entry a minute or two.

"Paul," she says, and his name again jolts Ruckelbar. She goes on, "Marjorie spoke to me."

"I'm glad for that, Clare."

"She's a good girl, Paul."

"Yes, she is."

There is a pause and then Clare adds the last. "She misses her father. She said that today." Ruckelbar draws a quick breath and sees his truck like a ghost ship drift up front in the window. He lifts a hand to the boy in the truck. What he sees is a figure caught in the old yellow glass, a man in there. Ruckelbar thought everything was settled so long ago.

He turns off the light before he can see what the image will do, and he grabs his keys and the camera. Outside, the boy has slid to the passenger side. When Ruckelbar climbs in the boy says, in a new voice, easy and relaxed, "Nice truck. It's in good shape."

"It's a '62," Ruckelbar says. "My dad's truck. If you park them inside and change the oil every twenty-five hundred miles, they keep." He puts the camera on the seat. "This was in your sister's car."

The boy picks it up. "Cool," he says, hefting it. "This is a weird place," the boy says. "Who painted it blue?"

Ruckelbar is now in gear on the hardtop of Route 21. He looks back at Bluestone once, a little building in the dark. "My father did," he says.

ZANDUCE AT SECOND

By his thirty-third birthday, a gray May day which found him having a warm cup of spice tea on the terrace of the Bay-side Inn in Annapolis, Maryland, with Carol Ann Menager, a nineteen-year-old woman he had hired out of the Bethesda Hilton Turntable Lounge at eleven o'clock that morning, Eddie Zanduce had killed eleven people and had that reputation, was famous for killing people, really the most famous killer of the day, his photograph in the sports section every week or so and somewhere in the article the phrase "eleven people" or "eleven fatalities"—in fact, the word *eleven* now had that association first, the number of the dead—and in all the major league baseball parks his full name could be heard every game day in some comment, the gist of which would be "Popcorn and beer for ten-fifty, that's bad, but just be glad Eddie Zanduce isn't here, for he'd kill you for sure," and the vendors would slide the beer across the counter and say, "Watch out for Eddie," which had come to supplant "Here you go," or "Have a nice day," in conversations even away from the parks. Everywhere he was that famous. Even this young woman, who has been working out of the Hilton for the past eight months not reading the papers and only watching as much TV. as one might watch in rented rooms in the early afternoon or late evening, not really news hours, even she knows his name, though she can't remember why she knows it and she finally asks him, her brow a furrow, "Eddie Zanduce? Are you on television? An actor?" And he smiles, raising the room-service teacup, but it's not a real smile. It is the placeholder expression he's been using for four years now since he first hit a baseball into the stands and it struck and killed a college sophomore, a young man, the papers were quick to point out, who was a straight-A student majoring in chemistry, and it is the kind of smile that makes him look nothing but old, a person who has seen it all and is now waiting for it all to be over. And in his old man's way he is patient through the next part, a talk he has had with many people all around the country, letting them know that he is simply Eddie Zanduce, the third baseman for the Orioles who has killed several people with foul balls. It has been a pernicious series of accidents really, though he won't say that.

She already knows she's not there for sex, after an hour she can tell by the manner, the face, and he has a beautiful actor's face which has been stunned with a kind of ruin by his bad luck and the weight of bearing responsibility for what he has done as an athlete. He's in the second thousand afternoons of this new life and the loneliness seems to have a physical gravity; he's hired her because it would have been impossible not to. He's hired her to survive the afternoon.

The day has been a walk through the tony shopping district in Annapolis, where he has bought her a red cotton sweater with tortiseshell buttons. It is a perfect sweater for May, and it looks wonderful as she holds it before her; she has short brunette hair, shiny as a schoolgirl's, which he realizes she may be. Then a walk along the pier, just a walk, no talking. She doesn't because he doesn't, and early on such outings, she always follows the man's lead. Later, the fresh salad lunch from room service and the tea. She explores the suite, poking her head into the bright bathroom, the nicest bathroom in any hotel she's been in during her brief career. There's a hair dryer, a robe, a fridge, and a phone. The shower is also a steamroom and the tub is a vast marble dish. There is a little city of lotions and shampoos. She smiles and he says, Please, feel free. Then he lies on the bed while she showers and dresses; he likes to watch her dress, but that too is different because he lies there imagining a family scene, the young wife busy with her grooming, not immodest in her nakedness, her undergarments on the bed like something sweet and familiar. The tea was her idea when he told her she could have anything at all; and she saw he was one of the odd ones, there were so many odd ones anymore willing to pay for something she's never fully understood, and she's taken the not understanding as just being part of it, her job, men and women, life. She's known lots of people who didn't understand what they were doing; her parents, for example. Her decision to go to work this way was based on her vision of simply fucking men for money, but the months have been more wearing than she could have foreseen with all the chatter and the posturing, some men who only want to mope or weep all through their massage, others who want to walk ahead of her into two or three nightspots and then yell at her later in some bedroom at the Embassy Suites, too many who want her to tell them about some other bastard who has abused her or broken her heart. But here this Eddie Zanduce just drinks his tea with his old man's smile as he watches the stormy summer weather as if it were a home movie. They've been through it all already and he has said simply without pretension. No, that's all right. We won't be doing that, but you can shower later. I'll have you in town by five-thirty.

THE ELEVEN PEOPLE Eddie Zanduce has killed have been properly eulogized, the irony in the demise of each celebrated in the tabloid press, the potentials of their lives properly inflated, and their fame—brief though it may have been—certainly far beyond any which might have accompanied their natural passing, and so they needn't be listed here and made flesh again. They each float in the head of Eddie Zanduce in his every movement, though he has never said so, or acknowledged his burden in any public way, and it has become a kind of poor form now even in the press corps, a group not known for any form, good or bad, to bring it up. After the seventh person, a girl of nine who had gone with her four cousins to see the Orioles play New York over a year ago, and was removed from all earthly joy and worry by Eddie Zanduce's powerhouse line drive pulled foul into the seats behind third, the sportswriters dropped the whole story, letting it fall on page one of the second section: news. And even now after games, the five or six reporters who bother to come into the clubhouse—the Orioles are having a lackluster start, and have all but relinquished even a shot at the pennant—give Eddie Zanduce's locker a wide berth. Through it all, he has said one thing only, and that eleven times: "I'm sorry; this is terrible." When asked after the third fatality, a retired school principal who was unable to see and avoid the sharp shot of one of Eddie

Zanduce's foul balls, if the unfortunate accidents might make him consider leaving the game, he said, "No."

And he became so stoic in the eyes of the press and they painted him that way that there was a general wonder at how he could stand it having the eleven innocent people dead by his hand and they said things like "It would be hard on me" and "I couldn't take it." And so they marveled darkly at his ability to appear in his uniform, take the field at all, dive right when the hit required it and glove the ball, scrambling to his knees in time to make the throw either to first or to second if there was a chance for a double play. They noted that his batting slump worsened, and now he's gone weeks in the new season without a hit, but he plays because he's steady in the field and he can fill the stands. His face was the object of great scrutiny for expression, a scowl or a grin, because much could have been made of such a look. And when he was at the plate, standing in the box awaiting the pitch, his bat held rigid and ready off his right shoulder as if for business, this business and nothing else, the cameras went in on his face, his eyes, which were simply inscrutable to the nation of baseball fans.

And now, at thirty-three he lies on the queen-size bed of the Bayside Inn, his fingers twined behind his head, as he watches Carol Ann Menager come dripping into the room, her hair partially in a towel, her nineteen-year-old body a rose-and-pale pattern of the female form, five years away from any visible wear and tear from the vocation she has chosen. She warms him appearing this way, naked and ready to chat as she reaches for her lavender bra and puts it of all her clothing on first, simply as convenience, and the sight of her there bare and comfortable makes him feel the thing he has been missing: befriended.

"But you feel bad about it, right?" Carol Ann says. "It must hurt you to know what has happened."

"I do," he says, "I do. I feel as badly about it all as I should."

And now Carol Ann stops briefly, one leg in her lavender panties, and now she quickly pulls them up and says, "I don't know what you mean."

"I only mean what I said and nothing more," Eddie Zanduce says.

"What was the worst?"

He still reclines and answers: "They are all equally bad."

"The little girl?"

Eddie Zanduce draws a deep breath there on the bed and then speaks: "The little girl, whose name was Victoria Tuttle, and the tourist from Austria, whose name was Heinrich Vence, and the Toronto Blue Jay, a man in a costume named William Dirsk, who was standing on the home dugout when my line drive broke his sternum. And the eight others all equally unlikely and horrible, all equally bad. In fact, eleven isn't really worse than one for me, because I maxed out on one. It doesn't double with two. My capacity for such feelings, I found out, is limited. And I am full."

Carol Ann Menager sits on the bed and buttons her new sweater. There is no hurry in her actions. She is thinking. "And if you killed someone tonight?"

Here Eddie Zanduce turns to her, his head rolling in the cradle of his hands, and smiles the smile he's been using all day, though it hasn't worn thin. "I wouldn't like that," he says. "Although it has been shown to me that I am fully capable of such a thing."

"Is it bad luck to talk about?"

"I don't believe in luck, bad or good." He warms his smile

one more time for her and says, "I'm glad you came today. I wouldn't have ordered the tea." He swings his legs to sit up. "And the sweater, well, it looks very nice. We'll drive back when you're ready."

ON THE DRIVE NORTH Carol Ann Menager says one thing that stays with Eddie Zanduce after he drops her at her little blue Geo in the Hilton parking lot and after he has dressed and played three innings of baseball before a crowd of twenty-four thousand, the stadium a third full under low clouds this early in the season with the Orioles going ho-hum and school not out yet, and she says it like so much she has said in the six hours he has known her—right out of the blue as they cruise north from Annapolis on Route 2 in his thick silver Mercedes, a car he thinks nothing of and can afford not to think of, under the low sullen skies that bless and begrudge the very springtime hedgerows the car speeds past. It had all come to her as she'd assembled herself an hour before; and it is so different from what she's imagined, in fact, she'd paused while drying herself with the lush towel in the Bayside Inn, her foot on the edge of the tub, and she'd looked at the ceiling where a heavy raft of clouds crossed the domed skylight, and one hand on the towel against herself, she'd seen Eddie Zanduce so differently than she had thought. For one thing he wasn't married and playing the dark game that some men did, putting themselves closer and closer to the edge of their lives until something went over, and he wasn't simply off, the men who tried to own her for the three hundred dollars and then didn't touch her, and he wasn't cruel in the other more overt ways, nor was he turned so tight that to enjoy a cup of tea over the marina with a hooker was anything sexual, nor was she young enough to be his daughter, just none of it, but she could see that he had made his pact with the random killings he initiated at the plate in baseball parks and the agreement left him nothing but the long series of empty afternoons.

"You want to know why I became a hooker?" she asks.

"Not really," he says. He drives the way other men drive when there are things on their minds, but his mind, she knows, has but one thing in it—eleven times. "You have your reasons. I respect them. I think you should be careful and do what you choose."

"You didn't even see me," she says. "You don't even know who's in the car with you."

He doesn't answer. He says. "I'll have you back by five-thirty."

"A lot of men want to know why I would do such a thing. They call me young and beautiful and talented and ready for the world and many other things that any person in any walk of life would take as a compliment. And I make it my challenge, the only one after survive, to answer them all differently. Are you listening?"

Eddie Zanduce drives.

"Some of them I tell that I hate the work but enjoy the money; they like that because—to a man—it's true of them. Some I tell I love the work and would do it for free; and they like that because they're all boys. Everybody else gets a complicated story with a mother and a father and a boyfriend or two, sometimes an ex-husband, sometimes a child who is sometimes a girl and sometimes a boy, and we end up nodding over our coffees or our brandies or whatever we're talking over, and we smile at the wisdom of time, because there is nothing else to do but for them to agree with me or simply hear and nod and then smile, I do tell good stories, and that smile is the same smile you've been giving yourself all day. If you had your life figured out any better than I do, it would have been a different day back at your sailboat motel. Sorry to go on, because it doesn't matter, but I'll tell you the truth; what can it hurt, right? You're a killer. I'm just a whore. I'm a whore because I don't care, and because I don't care it's a perfect job. I don't see anybody else doing any better. Show me somebody who's got a grip, just one person. Survive. That's my motto. And then tell stories. What should I do, trot out to the community college and prepare for my future as a medical doctor? I don't think so."

Eddie Zanduce looks at the young woman. Her eyes are deeper, darker, near tears. "You are beautiful," he says. "I'm sorry if the day wasn't to your liking."

She has been treated one hundred ways, but not this way, not with this delicate diffidence, and she is surprised that it stings. She's been hurt and neglected and ignored and made to feel invisible, but this is different, somehow this is personal. "The day was fine. I just wish you'd seen me."

For some reason, Eddie Zanduce responds to this: "I don't see people. It's not what I do. I can't afford it." Having said it, he immediately regrets how true it sounds to him. Why is he talking to her? "I'm tired," he adds, and he is tired—of it all. He regrets his decision to have company, purchase it, because it has turned out to be what he wanted so long, and something about this girl has crossed into his view. She is smart and pretty and— he hates this—he does feel bad she's a hooker.

And then she says the haunting thing, the advice that he will carry into the game later that night. "Why don't you try to do it?" He looks at her as she finishes. "You've killed these people on accident. What if you tried? Could you kill somebody on purpose?"

At five twenty-five after driving the last forty minutes in a silence like the silence in the center of the rolling earth, Eddie Zanduce pulls into the Hilton lot and Carol Ann Menager says, "Right up there." When he stops the car, she steps out and says to him, "I'll be at the game. Thanks for the tea."

AND NOW at two and one, a count he loves, Eddie Zanduce steps out of the box, self-conscious in a way he hasn't been for years and years and can't figure out until he ticks upon it: she's here somewhere, taking the night off to catch a baseball game or else with a trick who even now would be charmed by her unaffected love for a night in the park, the two of them laughing like teenagers over popcorn, and now she'd be pointing down at Eddie, saying, "There, that's the guy." Eddie Zanduce listens to the low murmur of twenty-four thousand people who have chosen to attend tonight's game knowing he would be here, here at bat, which was a place from which he could harm them irreparably, for he has done it eleven times before. The announcers have handled it the same after the fourth death, a young lawyer taken by a hooked line shot, the ball shattering his occipital bone the final beat in a scene he'd watched every moment of from the tock! of the bat—when the ball was so small, a dot which grew through its unreliable one-second arc into a huge white spheroid of five ounces entering his face, and what the announcers began to say then was some version of "Please be alert, ladies and gentlemen, coming to the ballpark implies responsibility. That ball is likely to go absolutely anywhere." But everybody knows this. Every single soul, even the twenty Japanese businessmen not five days out of Osaka know about Eddie Zanduce, and their boxes behind first base titter and moan, even the four babies in arms not one of them five months old spread throughout the house know about the killer at the plate, as do the people sitting behind the babies disgusted at the parents for risking such a thing, and the drunks, a dozen people swimming that abyss as Eddie taps his cleats, they know, even one in his stuporous sleep, his head collapsed on his chest as if offering it up, knows that Eddie could kill any one of them tonight. The number eleven hovers everywhere as does the number twelve waiting to be written. It is already printed on   best-selling T-shirt, and there are others, "I'll be 12th," and "Take Me 12th!" and "NEXT," and many others, all on T-shirts which Eddie Zanduce could read in any crowd in any city in which the Orioles took the field. When he played baseball, when he was listed on the starting roster—where he'd been for seven years—the crowd was doubled. People came as they'd come out tonight on a chilly cloudy night in Baltimore, a night that should have seen ten thousand maybe, more likely eight, they flocked to the ballpark, crammed themselves into sold-out games or sat out—as tonight—in questionable weather as if they were asking to be twelfth, as if their lives were fully worthy of being interrupted, as if—like right now with Eddie stepping back into the batter's box—they were asking, Take me next, hit me, I have come here to be killed.

Eddie Zanduce remembers Carol Ann Menager in the car. He hoists his bat and says, "I'm going to kill one of you now."

"What's that, Eddie?"

Caulkins, the Minnesota catcher, has heard his threat, but it means nothing to Eddie, and he says that: "Nothing. Just something I'm going to do." He says this stepping back into the batter's box and lifts his bat up to the ready. Things are in place. And as if enacting the foretold, he slices the first pitch, savagely shaving it short into the first-base seats, the kind of ugly truncated liner that has only damage as its intent, and adrenaline pricks the twenty-four thousand hearts sitting in that dangerous circle, but after a beat that allows the gasp to subside, a catch-breath really that is merely overture for a scream, two young men in blue Maryland sweatshirts leap above the crowd there above first base and one waves his old brown mitt in which it is clear there is a baseball. They hug and hop up and down for a moment as the crowd witnesses it all sitting silent as the members of a scared congregation and then a roar begins which is like laughter in church and it rides on the night air, filling the stadium.

"I'll be damned," Caulkins declares, standing mask off behind Eddie Zanduce. "He caught that ball, Eddie."

Those words are etched in Eddie Zanduce's mind as he steps again up to the plate. He caught the ball. He looks across at the young men but they have sat down, dissolved, leaving a girl standing behind them in a red sweater who smiles at him widely and rises once on her toes and waves a little wave that says, "I knew it. I just knew it." She is alone standing there waving. Eddie thinks that: she's come alone.

The next pitch comes in fat and high and as Eddie Zanduce swings and connects he pictures this ball streaming down the line uninterrupted, too fast to be caught, a flash off the cranium of a man draining his beer at the very second a plate of bone carves into his brain and the lights go out. The real ball though snaps on a sharp hop over the third baseman, staying in fair territory for a double. Eddie Zanduce stands on second. There is a great cheering; he may be a killer but he is on the home team and he's driven in the first run of the ballgame. His first hit in this month of May. And Eddie Zanduce has a feeling he hasn't had for four years since it all began, since the weather in his life changed for good, and what he feels is anger. He can taste the dry anger in his mouth and it tastes good. He smiles and he knows the cameras are on him but he can't help himself he is so pleased to be angry, and the view he has now of the crowd behind the plate, three tiers of them, lifts him to a new feeling that he locks on in a second: he hates them. He hates them all so much that the rich feeling floods through his brain like nectar and his smile wants to close his eyes. He is transported by hatred, exulted, drenched. He leads off second, so on edge and pissed off he feels he's going to fly with this intoxicating hatred, and he smiles that different smile, the challenge and the glee, and he feels his heart beating in his neck and arms, hot here in the center of the world. It's a feeling you'd like to explain to someone after the game. He plans to. He's got two more at bats tonight, the gall rises in his throat like life itself, and he is going to kill somebody—or let them know he was trying.

THE HOUSE GOES UP

As you can see, I've got a nice body. But you can't get a house
to go up with just a body. Other women think it's a body. I can't
tell you how many times I've heard about it. They think it's just
some sex thing. And sex is part of it, but if it was just having a
good body, I couldn't even get them to sell the station wagon. So
I've got this nice body and I take care of it in ways most women
don't, but getting the house to go up is simpler than you'll ever
know. It's got everything to do with men, how easy men are,
how absolutely wide-eyed and pleased with themselves they are;
how ripe to fall in love.

Men are simple. If you even knew what blank tablets they are,
even the ones married ten, twelve years. In fact these guys are
sometimes the simplest, the worst. You'd think they had not
been out of the house at night for years or seen a woman in a
public place, such as the Castaway, which is where they see me.

There they are, boys in men's clothing. Some guy has lived in the same house with a woman for years, and what he knows about women can best be described as zero. I'm not saying I don't take advantage of this. I work with the materials at hand, I admit it. What am I supposed to do, make it hard on myself? Just because it's easy doesn't mean it's not worth doing. I'm going to be—in many ways—their first woman.

So I wear this lace. The lace in their household is long gone, believe me, and I wear this camisole, something none of them have ever seen, even the lawyers. They weren't really looking until they met me. And they like this: a skirt, zipper in the back. How exotic! And a blouse like this: silk, French cuffs. I mean, they don't understand these things. It is so easy. By the time they've lit your cigarette, by the time they've moved one barstool down from their friend who is also appraising you carefully, you can sense the house ready to move. I wear simple, understated jewelry, these are tiny zirconium, kind of classy, and I don't wear a necklace with this blouse. Gaudy jewelry is not necessary. Neither is cleavage. Not at all. And, I've got cleavage. I could show them a cleavage, but if I did that, if I hypnotized them with grand curves that started them scratching their palms, the house would never even quiver. They'd take charge and do the stupid things men do to get something they want. Cleavage is no good; men understand cleavage. It won't work at all.

The same with tight jeans. Why would you do that? To show them something they can have? Men understand tight jeans. As the woman said, cleavage is cleavage, coming or going. It's as simple as the man himself. What you need is mystery. My rule is three layers. I wear three layers: everywhere.

This is not about sex, do you see? This is about real estate. This is about getting someone's attention. This is about making him think that it's all his idea, which actually will happen as easily as rain falls, and eventually he'll be in love . . . and the rest will follow.

When I was married, we lived not far from here really, on a funky little street that dead-ended into a golf course, and my husband, who I understood less then than I do now, laid a flagstone patio and lined it with a short and pretty flagstone wall. It was a place to have cocktails in the afternoons and we did that for a few years. It was good, or so I thought at the time, and now I see that it was neither bad nor good. It was something we did out of doors. It was different from drinking at the Castaway.

In the Castaway I do very little. I sit at the bar for an hour and then I sit alone at a little table near the bar for the rest of the night. I drink Wallbangers or Sunrises or Sombreros, drinks the men are not going to drink, drinks they don't understand. Sometimes I smoke and sometimes I don't smoke. I keep my cigarettes in this. It's not really silver, but they've never even seen a cigarette case before. I say very little and smile shyly. They like it if I seem hurt somehow as if the last man in my life was a beast, a cretin, a rude rotten son of a bitch, and though I never use those words all I have to do is nod quietly and eventually the men will. They are all heroes ready to show me—if I will allow it—that men can be decent, caring individuals. "That son of a bitch," they'll say. "Didn't he understand anything?" And then they'll order me another drink once I tell them what I'm drinking, and we'll grin about how different that is from their Miller Lite or Seagram's and Seven, and it's a moment I love and try to extend any way I can, this man at my table, his hand in the air like a man, making an order for a woman he is in the process of saving. And though he won't make a move that night or offer his number or his card—if he has one—or ask for mine or really stay at the table when his friend at the bar signals that it is time to go, when I look up at him for the last time, keeping my head down, our eyes will meet and I will see it: the house is going up.

Of course he'll know where to find me the next Thursday night, same table. This time he'll come alone and we'll have a heart-to-heart; rather, he'll have a heart-to-heart and it will be all so high school, him leaning over the table, his eyes moist, meaning every word: the big things he'd always wanted to do, I mean not just drivers, even if he's a judge or a chemist, the things he's been kept from, the tragedy of time, of compromise, of—really—marriage. I'll listen without moving. It's terrifically poignant, let me tell you. Once in a while a song will come on the jukebox, "Stand by Your Man," or "Fools' Parade," and I'll sigh and let him know that the music has affected me, and I'll see the look in his eyes triple. Eventually he'll fall silent having said more to me in two hours than he's said in years and then he'll ask if I want to dance. I'll shake my head. The line: I'm not a girl who really dances. You should see him swell to hear this. Then, depending on my mood—if I'm up for hurrying things—I'll ask if it's okay if we get out of here. "I mean, could we just sit in your car for a while?"

Once you've sat in his car, it's a done deal. He'll want to do something. What I let him do is kiss me once and then I shake that off and hold his hand in both of mine. No one has done that for him in years. You hold a man's hand in both of your hands for ten minutes and he'll love you forever. That is what love is. I sit there and hint, faintly, at how hard things are for me, but how optimistic I am about tomorrow, and then I'll kiss him quickly on the cheek and get out of his car and into mine and drive home.

The rest is rote. I'll send him a note—to his office—during

the week thanking him for taking the time to talk to me, to share his feelings, saying that his being open meant so much to me. His wife isn't writing him notes anymore and he'll call and want to see me right away. And it's funny, but when you do see him, it won't be sex. I either bring him here or we go to a motel, and either way, there'll be a lot of pacing. The sudden charge of being alone in private will drive him mad. He'll want to dive for me, but he respects me too much, and besides, he's my savior, my hero. See how simple it all is, how simple men are? Oh, we'll end up in a clinch, again some agony right out of high school, where he'll get a couple of layers past the slip or camisole in absolute wonderland at such things, all that lace, and him so steamed up, he'll never get to skin. It's so goofy, him standing up quickly and tucking in his shirt, and me on the bed propped up on one arm, and now I'll show him a little cleavage, and I'll look as serious as I ever have looked serious and I'll try to smile, but what I'll say is: "I want to see you again. I need you. No, never mind, go on, go home. I'll be all right." By this time he will have come over to the bed and I'll level with him. "I'm a girl who doesn't do this," I'll say. "But I want you again. All of you. I feel so funny, but: *I need it.*"

And so it goes. You'll give him some little presents and he'll buy you a couple of expensive things that make you wonder, a thousand-dollar watch and a real nice Walkman, and you'll teach him new sex tricks for a month or two until his wife finds out. It always takes the wife longer than I planned. Where is that girl? But oddly enough, it won't matter to my guy, because, you see, he loves me. He's not up for five bad scenes and ten months of therapy. This marriage is over. Kids and all. So much for Fido, the tennis club, every single thing that has kept him from being all he could be.

This is a tricky period for me. I'll tell him that we'd better not see each other for a while; it's only good sense. He'll take a room somewhere and call me five times a day. I feel guilty, I'll say. I'm confused. Meanwhile, I'll cruise his neighborhood waiting for the moment which got me into this whole deal. I mean, I'm happy all the while, I'm happy right now, I'm naturally a happy person, but I'm not really happy happy until I see the FOR SALE sign stabbed into the front lawn.

The house goes up. They have to deal with the realty, some tired schoolteacher, dry as old bread and dumb as a stick, and they have to think: seven percent. This stranger who can't speak grammatical English—a person who must have bored her classes to death for years without end in social studies—is going to get seven percent of our house.

And then they have to divide the possessions, think about all the stuff they've brought into the house for years and years— it goes miles beyond the stereo and houseplants; there are roomsful.

Later, six, ten weeks, after I've let him know that there is no way I can continue with him, that to be a "homewrecker" is more than I can bear and that I'm sure he's better off without me—I am, after all, just a damaged soul floating through the universe. After he's history, I'll drive by his house again. Sometimes I'll go by the garage sale; there she is, the wife, with four aisles of their lives spread in the sun. She won't know me. Maybe I'll buy something, a little wall mirror or a little hibachi for the terrace. If there's a box of tapes, I'll buy a cassette or two for my new Walkman.

I don't gloat. I do what I do. But I get a rush in these weeks, the aftermath. I love to drive by and just read the FOR SALE sign again. On the dry days of fall, it swings sometimes in the wind and I slow to hear the creaking. A healthy tuft of grass grows around the post like a hairy halo. The house is now empty, and the whole yard takes on a dusty, wild look, vacant. It could use a little water, but, of course, the mower, a red Toro with a grass catcher, that's long gone. That will never cut this grass again.

And between men sometimes I simply drive, float the neighborhoods at twilight before I go to the bar, and I admire the smooth blue lawns shimmering under the wheezing evening sprinklers and I watch the yellow squares of windows light against the night, maybe a porch lamp will illuminate a flagstone terrace. I love that. Flagstone. There is nothing that speaks of marriage more than well-laid flagstone and a short stone wall. I drive slowly past these formidable homes and I see the FOR SALE signs on every block. There is nothing, not even flagstone, that can prevent a house from going up.

I I

"Well, sir, what do you suggest:

we stand here and shed tears

and call each other names?

Or shall we go to Istanbul?"

Sydney Greenstreet as Caspar Gutman
in *The Maltese Falcon*

WHAT WE WANTED TO DO

WHAT WE WANTED to do was spill boiling oil onto the heads of our enemies as they attempted to bang down the gates of our village, but, as everyone now knows, we had some problems, primarily technical problems, that prevented us from doing what we wanted to do the way we had hoped to do it. What we're asking for today is another chance.

There has been so much media attention to this boiling oil issue that it is time to clear the air. There is a great deal of pressure to dismantle the system we have in place and bring the oil down off the roof. Even though there isn't much left. This would be a mistake. Yes, there were problems last month during the Visigoth raid, but as I will note, these are easily remedied.

From its inception I have been intimately involved in the boiling oil project—research, development, physical deployment. I also happened to be team leader on the roof last month when we had occasion to try the system during the Visigoth attack, about which so much has been written.

(It was not an "entirely successful" sortie, as I will show. The Visigoths, about two dozen, did penetrate the city and rape and plunder for several hours, but *there was no pillaging*. And make no questions about it—they now know we have oil on the roof and several of them are going to think twice before battering down our door again. I'm not saying it may not happen, but when it does, they know we'll be ready.)

First, the very concept of oil on the roof upset so many of our villagers. Granted, it is exotic, but all great ideas seem strange at first. When our researchers realized we could position a cauldron two hundred feet directly above our main portals, they began to see the possibilities of the greatest strategic defense system in the history of mankind.

The cauldron was expensive. We all knew a good defense was going to be costly. The cauldron was manufactured locally after procuring copper and brass from our mines, and it took—as is common knowledge—two years to complete. It is a beautiful thing capable of holding one hundred and ten gallons of oil. What we could not foresee was the expense and delay of building an armature. Well, of course, it's not enough to have a big pot, pretty as it may be; how are you going to pour its hot contents on your enemies? The construction of an adequate superstructure for the apparatus required dear time: another year during which the Huns and the Exogoths were raiding our village almost weekly. Let me ask you to remember that era—was that any fun?

I want to emphasize that we were committed to this program—and we remain committed. But at every turn we've met problems that our researchers could not—regardless of their intelligence and intuition—have foreseen. For instance: how were we to get a nineteen-hundred-pound brass cauldron onto the roof? When had such a question been asked before? And at each of these impossible challenges, our boiling oil teams have come up with solutions. The cauldron was raised to the roof by means of a custom-designed net and hoist including a rope four inches in diameter which was woven on the spot under less than ideal conditions as the Retrogoths and the Niligoths plundered our village almost incessantly during the cauldron's four-month ascent. To our great and everlasting credit, we did not drop the pot. The superstructure for the pouring device was dropped once, but it was easily repaired on-site, two hundred feet above the village steps.

That was quite a moment, and I remember it well. Standing on the roof by that gleaming symbol of our impending safety, a bright brass (and a few lesser metals) beacon to the world that we were not going to take it anymore. The wind carried up to us the cries of villagers being carried away by either the Maxigoths or the Minigoths, it was hard to tell. But there we stood, and as I felt the wind in my hair and watched the sporadic procession of home furnishings being carried out of our violated gates, I knew we were perched on the edge of a new epoch.

Well, there was some excitement; we began at once. We started a fire under the cauldron and knew we would all soon be safe. At that point I made a mistake, which I now readily admit. In the utter ebullience of the moment I called down—I did not "scream maniacally" as was reported—I called down that *it would not be long,* and I probably shouldn't have, because it may have led some of our citizenry to lower their guard. It was a mistake. I admit it. There were, as we found out almost immediately, still some bugs to be worked out of the program. For instance, there had never been a fire on top of the entry tower before, and yes, as everyone is aware, we had to spend more time than we really wanted containing the blaze, fueled as it was by the fresh high winds and the tower's wooden shingles. But I hasten to add that the damage was moderate, as moderate as a four-hour fire could be, and the billowing black smoke surely gave further intruders lurking in the hills pause as they considered finding any spoils in our ashes!

But throughout this relentless series of setbacks, pitfalls, and rooftop fires, there has been a hard core of us absolutely dedicated to doing what we wanted to do, and that was to splash scalding oil onto intruders as they pried or battered yet again at our old damaged gates. To us a little fire on the rooftop was of no consequence, a fribble, a tiny obstacle to be stepped over with an easy stride. Were we tired? Were we dirty? Were some of us burned and cranky? No matter! We were committed. And so the next day, the first quiet day we'd had in this village in months, that same sooty cadre stood in the warm ashes high above the entry steps and tried again. We knew—as we know right now—that our enemies are manifold and voracious and generally rude and persistent, and we wanted to be ready.

But tell me this: where does one find out how soon before an enemy attack to put the oil on to boil? Does anyone know? Let me assure you it is not in any book! We were writing the book!

We were vigilant. We squinted at the horizon all day long. And when we first saw the dust in the foothills we refired our cauldron, using wood which had been elevated through the night in woven baskets. Even speaking about it here today, I can feel the excitement stirring in my heart. The orange flames licked the sides of the brass container hungrily as if in concert with our own desperate desire for security and revenge. In the distance I could see the phalanx of Visigoths marching toward us like a warship through a sea of dust, and in my soul I pitied them and the end toward which they so steadfastly hastened. They seemed the very incarnation of mistake, their dreams of a day abusing our friends and families and of petty arsony and lewd public behavior about to be extinguished in one gorgeous wash of searing oil! I was beside myself.

It is important to know now that everyone on the roof that day exhibited orderly and methodical behavior. There was professional conduct of the first magnitude. There was no wild screaming or cursing or even the kind of sarcastic chuckling which you might expect in those about to enjoy a well-deserved and long-delayed victory. The problems of the day were not attributable to inappropriate deportment. My staff was good. It was when the Visigoths had approached close enough that we could see their cruel eyes and we could read the savage and misspelled tattoos that I realized our error. At that time I put my hand on the smooth side of our beautiful cauldron and found it only vaguely warm. Lukewarm. Tepid.

We had not known then what we now know. *We need to put the oil on sooner.*

It was my decision and my decision alone to do what we did, and that was to pour the warm oil on our enemies as they milled about the front gates, hammering at it with their truncheons.

Now this is where my report diverges from so many of the popular accounts. We have heard it said that the warm oil served as a stimulant to the attack that followed, the attack I alluded to earlier in which the criminal activity seemed even more animated than usual in the minds of some of our townspeople. Let me say first: I was an eyewitness. I gave the order to pour the oil and I witnessed its descent. I am happy and proud to report that the oil hit its target with an accuracy and completeness I could have only dreamed of. We got them all. There was oil everywhere. We soaked them, we coated them, we covered them in a lustrous layer of oil. Unfortunately, as everyone knows, it was only warm. Their immediate reaction was also what I had hoped for: surprise and panic. This, however, lasted about one second. Then several of them looked up into my face and began waving their fists in what I could only take as a tribute. And then, yes, they did become quite agitated anew, recommencing their assault on the weary planks of our patchwork gates. Some have said that they were on the verge of abandoning their attack before the oil was cast upon them, which I assure you is not true.

As to the attack that followed, it was no different in magnitude or intensity from any of the dozens we suffer every year. It may have seemed more odd or extreme since the perpetrators were greasy and thereby more offensive, and they did take every stick of furniture left in the village, including the pews from the church, every chair in the great hall, and four milking stools, the last four, from the dairy.

But I for one am simply tired of hearing about the slippery stain on the village steps. Yes, there is a bit of a mess, and yes, some of it seems to be permanent. My team removed what they could with salt and talc all this week. All I'll say now is watch your step as you come and go; in my mind it's a small inconvenience to pay for a perfect weapon system.

So, we've had our trial run. We gathered a lot of data. And you all know we'll be ready next time. We are going to get to do what we wanted to do. We will vex and repel our enemies with boiling oil. In the meantime, who needs furniture? We have a project! We need the determination not to lose the dream, and we need a lot of firewood. They will come again. You know it and I know it, and let's simply commit ourselves to making sure that the oil, when it falls, is very hot.

THE CHROMIUM HOOK

JACK CRAMBLE

EVERYBODY KNOWS THIS, that we pulled in the driveway and I found the hook when I went around to Jill's door. It was caught in the door handle, hanging there like I don't know what. I didn't know what it was at first, but when Jill got out she knew, and she started screaming, for which I don't blame her. Her father came out and made like where had we been and did we know it was almost one o'clock. He's a good guy, but under real pressure, I guess, since his wife had her troubles. Anyway, he looks at the hook, and then he looks Jill over real good, suspicious-like, like we'd been up to something, which we definitely had not. We had been, as everybody knows, up at Conversation Point with our debate files, and the time got away from us. I was helping her with her arguments, asking questions, like that, things like "What are the drawbacks of an international nuclear-test-ban treaty?" And she would fish around in her file

box and try to find the answer. Her one shot at college is the debate team, and their big meet with Northwoods was a week
from that Saturday. It was Mr. Royaltuber who called the police,
and the word got out.

JILL ROYALTUBER

IT WAS THE scaredest I've ever been, and when I think of how
close that homicidal maniac came to getting us and doing whatever he was going to do with that big vicious hook, my blood
runs cold. Jack was really brave. He wanted to get out of the car
after we heard the first noises, the scrapings, and see what it was,
but I wouldn't let him. Sometimes boys just don't have any
sense. We'd already heard about the escaped homicidal maniac
on the radio. They'd interrupted *Wild Johnny Hateras's Top
Twenty Country Countdown* with the news bulletin that some
one-armed madman had escaped the loony bin on Demon Hill
and was sort of armed and dangerous. And of course Discussion
Point is right there by the iron fence of the nuthouse. We had
gone up to Discussion Point to work through some problems I'd
been having since my mom left, and Jack was talking to me
about being strong and saying he'd be there for me and not to
get too depressed and to look on the sunny side of things, that
Mom was better off in the hospital—she certainly seemed happier. So Jack was being that thing, supportive, which I love. A
boyfriend who is captain of football is one thing, and a boyfriend
who is captain of football and supportive is another. But I kept
him from getting out of the car after we heard the noises. The
wind had come up a little and it was dark as dark, and I said,
"Let's just get out of here." Jack wasn't afraid. He wanted to
stay. But I told him it was late, and then we heard the scratching

closer, against the car, and it felt like it was right on my bare spine. "Pull out!" I yelled, and he gunned the engine of his Ford—it's a wonderful car, which he did all the work on—and we headed for home.

DR. STEWART NARKENPIE, DIRECTOR, THE SPINARD PSYCHIATRIC INSTITUTE

IT IS NOT a loony bin. It is not a nuthouse or a funny farm. It's not even an insane asylum. It is, as I've been telling everyone in this community for the twenty-two years I've lived here, the Spinard Psychiatric Institute, a center for the treatment of psychological disorders. It is a medical hospital, the building and grounds of which occupy just under two hundred acres on the top of Decatur Hill, and it employs thirty-eight citizens from the lovely town of Griggs, including Mr. Howard Lugdrum, who was injured seriously in last week's incident. I have spoken to the Rotary Club once a year for forever, as well as to the Lions and the Elks and the Junior Achievement and the graduating class of the high school and the Vocational Outreach in the Griggs Middle School, explaining what we do and how we do it and that the Spinard Psychiatric Institute is not a loony bin or any other kind of bin, and I am not getting through. It is not a bin! Even though a large portion of our community has had family and friends enter the Institute as patients only to be returned to the community after treatment in better shape than before, and even though most everybody has visited the grounds—if not for personal reasons, then certainly at our annual Community Picnic on the South Lawn—there still persists this incurable sense that once you pass under the Spinard stone arch you are entering the twilight zone. Yes, we do have a big iron fence, because some of our patients get confused and could possibly wander away, and yes, the buildings, some of them, have bars over the windows for the safety of our patients, and some of our patients wear restraints when out-of-doors, but they are dangerous to no one but themselves. I cannot say how weary I am of setting the record straight. It is not a nuthouse, and I am not a mad scientist. We don't have any mad scientists, mad professors, or mad doctors. No one's mad. We don't use that term. We do have some disturbed patients, but we're treating them, and there is a chance—with rest counseling, and medication—that they will get better. We do not perform operations except as they become medically necessary. We had an appendectomy last fall. We do not operate on the brain. We do not—as the high school paper suggests regularly—do brain transplants, dissections, or enlargements. Most recently I had to speak with Wild Johnny Hateras at KGRG, the radio station in Griggs, about the prank news bulletin on Halloween, which is just the kind of thing that keeps any understanding between the Institute and the town in tatters and is responsible, I think, for the harm resulting from last Saturday's incident, about which we've heard so much.

MR. HOWARD LUGDRUM

IT HURT. DON'T you think that hurt? Everybody talks about the kids: oh, they were scared, they were frightened and nervous, oh, they were terrified. Well, think about it—had two trespassers yanked off *their* prosthesis? In the course of doing their job, were either of *them* pulled from their feet and dragged till an arm came off, and left there tumbling in the dirt? As it turns out, I was lucky I was wearing my simple hook and the straps broke; if I'd been wearing my regular armature, those two little criminals would have dragged me to death, and we'd have murder here instead of reckless endangerment.

ROD BUDDAROCK

IF ANYBODY, ONE person, says anything, one thing, about my buddy Jack Cramble being up there at Passion Point to do anything, one thing, besides help little Jill Royaltuber with family problems, such as they are, I'll find that person and use his lying butt to wipe up Main Street. I'm not joking here. I know Jack from being co-captain of football, and I know what I'm saying. Of course, he could have come to the team party out at the Landing, but here was a girl who had some troubles and he was there to help. There's been a lot of talk about what they were really doing. Jack made that crack about debate, which was too bad, because he couldn't get within two miles of the debate team—I'm a better debater than Jack and Jill put together—but he only said that to protect Jill's reputation, such as it is. She's a nice girl, but a little confused. It was only last year that her mom went bonkers, and Jill herself went a little nuts about that time, but she is no slut. If anybody, one person, says anything about Jill Royaltuber being a wide-mouthed, round-heeled slut, I'll find that person and trouble will certainly rain down upon his or her head like hot shit from Mars.

MR. HOWARD LUGDRUM

I'D SEEN THE car before. It's a two-door Ford, blue-and-white. There are five or six cars I see there by our north fence in the pine grove. They bring their girlfriends up from town in the good weather, and we find the empty beer bottles and condoms. The kids call it Passion Point. We had a timed light system there until a few years ago, but the Environmental Protection Agency asked us to dismantle it because of the Weaver's bat, a protected species that hunts there at night. The deal about the parking is that the grove is our property and we stand liable for any harm. Two kids climb in the backseat of some old clunker with a faulty exhaust and the Institute would be sued until the thirteenth of never. I mean, these are kids at night in old cars. What we've done is put the grove on the watchman's tour, and one of us takes the big flashlight and shines it on a few bare butts every night of the week. Until last week, it's been kind of funny—I mean, you see some white rear end hop up, and then the cars start up and wheel out like scurrying rats. Once interrupted, they don't come back. Until the next night. Like I said, these are kids.

I'm in charge of the buildings and grounds at the Institute, and I like my work there; it's been a good place to me.

SHERIFF CURTIS MANSARACK

THE MOST FREQUENTLY asked question is "When you bust a beer bust, do you keep the beer?" For Pete's sake. Every weekend I roust one or two of these high school beer parties, most often on the hill or down at Ander's Landing. Sometimes, though, there'll be a complaint and I'll be called to a private residence. A lot of these kids know me by now, and they know that about eleven-thirty old Sheriff Mansarack will slip up in his cruiser and flash the lights long enough for every drunk sophomore to run into the bushes so that I can cite the two or three seniors too drunk to flee.

I was in the middle of such a raid last Saturday night, Halloween, a night when I know for a sure fact that there is going to be trouble, and I got the call from Oleena Weenz, our dispatcher. There had been, in her words, a "vicious assault by a pervert," and she directed me to the address on Eider Street where I found Mr. Rick Royaltuber and the two young people and heard the story. I knew the boy, Jack Cramble, and had seen him play football earlier that night when Griggs beat Bark City, and I was kind of surprised that he wasn't down with the rest of the team drinking beer at the Landing. I also knew Mr. Royaltuber, as I had taken the call when his wife went off the deep end a year ago. When a guy helps you subdue his wife and pries her fingers off a rusty pair of kitchen scissors while you hold her kicking and screaming on your lap on the front porch in front of all the neighborhood, you remember him. That was a bad deal, embarrassing for me to get caught off guard. I mean, she looked normal. I hadn't seen the scissors. And it was bad for old Royaltuber too, with her shrieking out about him porking what's-her-name, the wife of old Dr. Dizzy up at the loony bin, and rattling those scissors at us. Hey, sometimes kitchen tools are the worst. And she was strong.

Anyway, I spoke to Mr. Royaltuber and I saw the hook there on the car door. It was a regular artificial arm, straps and all, one of them torn, and it scared me too. I mean, when that thing came off, it had to hurt. I took the report, but it wasn't all in line, and to tell the truth neither was the front of the Royaltuber girl's shirt. She was misbuttoned the way you are after putting away your playthings in a hurry.

The Cramble boy kept at me to get back up there right away before the pervert got somebody else, saying things like Wasn't I the sheriff? Wasn't I supposed to do something? Well, I could

see *he* wanted to do something, something that had been interrupted up at Passion Point, so I just told them all it was going to
be all right, which it was, and I headed back to the Landing,
where I was able to run off about ten kids and confiscate a case
and a half of Castle Moat, which is not my favorite, but it'll do.

MR. HOWARD LUGDRUM

I NEVER MARRIED. Years ago, after my accident, I changed my
plans about a career in tennis and went up to college near Brip-
pert and got into their vocational-ed program in hotel management.

I was pretty numbed out after Cassie's family moved who
knows where. This is a long time ago now. Her girlfriend Maggie Rayne hung around with me for a while, and then I think she
saw the limits of a man with one hand and moved on. Her father
was a professor at the medical school, and I was clearly out-
classed. So, anyway, I never married. I didn't realize the torch
was still lit—or really how alive I could feel—until I saw Cassie
again a year ago, when she was carried up here kicking and
screaming, spitting and cursing, her eyes red and her hair wild,
the most beautiful thing I've seen in, let's see, seventeen years.

MRS. MARGARET RAYNE NARKENPIE

I HAD NOT planned on a mountaintop in Bushville. I had not
actually thought I would—after seven years of graduate study
and three years at the Highborn Academy—find myself banished to the left-hand districts of Forsaken Acres, dressing for
dinner at the macaroni-and-cheese outlet, opting for the
creamed tuna on special nights. I had lived in a wasteland as a

girl, and I thought I was through with it. Let's just say, for the sake of argument, that marrying the highest-ranking doctor in my father's finest class, a tall, good-looking psychiatrist of sterling promise who could have written his ticket anywhere in the civilized world, I was expecting to live in a place where there was more than one Quicky Freeze and a Video Hut. I had dared to think London, New York, even Albuquerque. I had not imagined Griggs. My husband—who has his Institute and his staff and his many duties and all his important vision for psychiatric health care—can't even see Griggs. So, the way I live here and whom I associate with in this outpost of desolation is, it would seem to me, my business.

Mr. Royaltuber handles all the television and monitor maintenance and repair for the Spinard Institute. He has also helped us with the satellite dish and the cable connections we use at home. He's a nice man, and I have lunch with him from time to time. We've become, under the circumstances and in this barren place, friends. I met his wife only once, when I was at his home. It was less than pleasant.

MR. WILD JOHNNY HATERAS, RADIO PERSONALITY, KGRG

IF ANYBODY PRETENDS to be hurt or surprised by our little prank, they're bad actors. Everybody in this burg knows what we do on Halloween with the "important news bulletin" and the hook. We've been doing it since I started spinning platters here twelve years ago. Nick goes out and slips a dozen of the phony hooks on car doors, and then I interrupt the program with my announcement about the maniac. I think of it as our little annual contribution to birth control, all those kids jumping up when I cut into "Unchained Melody" with my homicide-and-hook news brief. When we started, we used those plastic hooks from the costume shop in Orpenhook, but, sad to say, gang, it's impossible to scare anybody anymore with a plastic hook. Don't tell *me* the world's a better place. So now we get them in Bark City, little steel hooks that at least look authentic for a few minutes. But this will probably be the last year we send Nick out with anything at all, because of the trouble up by the nuthouse, and because he's afraid of getting shot. Can you believe that? You go out on Halloween to have a little fun anymore and you run a good chance of getting plugged? Hey, Griggs, wake up, all is not well. If you can't harass the teenagers without running the risk of getting killed, this town is in trouble.

MRS. CASSIE ROYALTUBER

IT'S FUNNY WHAT people think. You try to put a pair of kitchen scissors in the doctor's wife one afternoon and they think (a) you're crazy, or (b) you're desperately in love with your sweet husband, or (c) you caught her in bed with your husband, with whom she's been sleeping for two years, and therefore you're just slow to catch on, since everybody, absolutely everybody else in this village, which is not exactly full of geniuses, has known about the affair since the first week, or (d) that you're all three: crazy, in love, and slow to catch on.

Well, it is simply exhilarating to be liberated from (a) the slings and (b) the arrows of public opinion and to take it for what it is, which is (a) irrelevant and (b) as absolutely wrong as it can be.

Who in their right mind—which is where I find myself—would consider that the television repairman's wife might have another reason? Who would grant the past its due, the vast sweeping privilege of history and justice? Who would guess that (a) I knew Mrs. Narkenpie before she and her doctor moved to Griggs, in fact before she was Mrs. Narkenpie, when she was simply Margaret Rayne, and that (b) she was the prime reason I had been forcibly removed from my one true love so many years ago, and that (c) I had chosen those scissors not for the convenience of their being right there in the drawer but because they were appropriate—I wanted to cut her the way she cut my Howard.

And the things I screamed I screamed on purpose. How are you going to get into the loony bin unless they think you're loony?

ROD BUDDAROCK

WHAT HE DOES is take the beer. This seems to be his only deal as a cop, to drive around on weekends and take beer from kids. And he keeps the beer. Some kids just go ahead and buy his brand, which is the Rocary Red Ale—fifteen dollars a case at any Ale and Mail. Isn't there any crime to stop? How do you get a job like that—free car and free beer? Hey, I'll sign up. As is, I'm glad I'm a senior and out of here next spring. He comes into our Halloween party last Saturday, the same night that there's a maniac with a hook roaming all over Griggs, attacking kids, slashing at everything in sight, and he busts us, scaring everybody shitless and causing Ardeen Roster to break her nose running away in the bushes, and he writes *me* a ticket for it. Then, while some monster with one arm has practically taken over the whole town, he takes our beer, and there's still about three and a half cases of Red Pelican—which you have to drive to Orpenhook to even find—so I'm forced to live the rest of my life picturing this civic wart pounding down our Pelicans every afternoon on his deck while he dreams up his next law enforcement strategy. Life is hard on the young, man, count on it.

MR. HOWARD LUGDRUM

I'M GOING TO NEED to get my hook back. There's a lot of work up here that requires two hands. We've got leaves to rake, tons, and a lot of other seasonal preventive maintenance—storm windows, snowplow prep work—and I can't load and deliver firewood effectively without my prosthesis. I'd appreciate its return as soon as possible.

MR. RICK ROYALTUBER

CASSIE WAS NEVER even cranky all these years. I mean, of all people, she's the last I'd expect to crack up. It was tough to send her off. It hurt me to put her up on the hill, but there it was, we couldn't deny she'd lost control of her senses when she tried to harm Mrs. Narkenpie. How do you think I feel knowing she's up there, locked up in a nuthouse night and day, wearing a straitjacket or what-have-you. But the doctor said it was for the best, and I believe him. These things, so many of them, are beyond ordinary folks.

SHERIFF CURTIS MANSARACK

INCIDENTAL TO MY call on the Royaltubers Halloween night, I had the Cramble boy pop open his trunk, and I found the following:

nylon rope, 100 yards
hammer
hatchet
power screwdriver
small grappling hook
duct tape, two rolls
canvas, 12x12
flashlights, two
pepper spray, two canisters
bolt cutters
Doritos, large bag, taco-flavored

JILL ROYALTUBER

I NEVER SAW his face. I never saw anything really. All I heard was some vibrations, I guess—maybe footsteps in the leaves, and then a kind of metallic clicking like scritch, scritch, and I was begging Jack to pull out, to just pull out of there. We hadn't been doing anything. Jack had hurt his hand in the game against Bark City, and I had been massaging that. We were trying to relax.

MRS. CASSIE ROYALTUBER

I LOVED HOWARD from Moment Number One, when we met seventeen years ago, on the night of the construction of our high school's homecoming float, which was a big ram. We were the Cragview Rams. He and I were part of the tissue brigade, two dozen kids handing Kleenex each to each in a line that ended at the chicken-wire sculpture, which slowly filled with the red, white, and blue paper. He was standing next to me and our hands touched once a second as the tissue flowed through us, my left hand, his right hand, which he would lose that spring, touch, touch, touch. He was the first tender boy I ever knew, and I was happy when he invited me to the homecoming dance. There is no need to explain every delicate step of that fall, Moment Number Two and Moment Number Three, except to say that when we gave our hearts, we gave our hearts completely, and everything else followed. It was the year I died and went to heaven for a while.

Moment Number Four I discovered that I was pregnant, and even that seemed magical, until my father found out thanks to my jealous classmate, wicked Maggie Rayne, who also told him that Howard and I always met after school in the Knopdish junkyard. And it was there, Moment Number Five, that my father found us in the rear seat of an old VW van, which had been like a haven for us, and he yanked me out onto the ground and slammed that rusty door forever, or so I thought, on my one good thing—Howard Lugdrum.

Howard, I heard, lost his arm in the "accident," and my father moved us far away, here to Griggs. The Moments now go unnumbered. Before the summer was over, young, handsome Ricky Royaltuber was coming round, and I didn't care, I did my part. I wasn't even there, and I guess I've been away a long time.

I didn't care when Maggie Rayne moved to town with her fancy doctor, and I didn't care that she went after and got Ricky. It freed me in a way. I can hardly remember who came and went in our house—Jill's friends, neighbors, boys.

But when I heard that the stars had relented and uncrossed and again lined up my way, that Howard had come to Griggs, working at this very loony bin in which I now live, I woke up, and in a major way. Afternoons, he comes in with a cup of tea, and we sit and he lets me hold it while we talk. These days are sweet days again, full of sweet moments. Even now I can see him through these bars, cleaning the windows of the van with the big circles of his left hand.

JACK CRAMBLE

I DON'T CARE who knows it now: I was going to spring her. Last year, when I was a nobody from nowhere, she was the only person in town who would listen. I was the new kid in town then, not captain of the football team, and she was always there for me. I told her everything. It was easier and better than talking to my own folks, and she was different, a woman, more woman than anybody I'll ever meet again. I loved her and I loved the way she talked, putting my problems in perspective a, b, c, or 1, 2, 3. To keep seeing her I started dating that dipweed Jill, who has been nothing but a pain in the neck with all her "sharing," "caring," and "daring." Such a girl. Such a needy little girl. Just thinking about her makes my skin crawl. Let's go up to the Point, she'd say, so she could crawl all over me. I'll tell you flat, she knows nothing about being a real woman like her mother. We went up there on Halloween after the game so I could scope out the fence and the approach to Cassie's room. The plan was for midnight. Of course, Jill jumped me when we parked, and lucky for me the watchman came along or I'd have had to go all the way. As it was, her pants were already to her ankles, and he got a hell of a view of her bare ass in the window.

But it hasn't deterred me. Cassie and I are meant to be together, that's clear, regardless of the age difference. I'm going back up there in a night or two and busting her out. Football season's over, and it's time to be me. My heart knows what to do, and it says, Scale the wall, break her out!

MR. HOWARD LUGDRUM

SHE WAS HERE almost a year before she told me. Though I knew instantly we'd pick up where we left off, my heart steady through the years to the one woman I loved, Cassie waited to be sure it was still me, I guess, that a man with one arm could be trusted. So last week we were at tea in her room after her counseling session, and she looked at me funny and told me something amazing: I have a daughter! A daughter! Having Cassie back in my life after so long seemed almost too much for me to bear, and now . . . a child. Well, not a child but a young woman. And, Cassie told me, I could see her if I went by the north pine grove sometime after nine that night, Halloween. I'd see a blue-and-white Ford and my daughter would be in it! It was all I could do to get the afternoon hours out of the way; it was a waiting like no waiting I have ever known. My daughter! As it happened, I don't know if I saw her or not, just somebody's butt in the moonlight.

SHERIFF CURTIS MANSARACK

FALL IN GRIGGS is a good thing: the leaves change color and there's football and the smell of the first wood fires. Halloween's my last big chance to score a beer bust, and I almost never miss. I didn't miss this year. Every year there's a hook, sometimes more than one, and it takes a week or two for things to quiet down. I don't mind the hooks; the waxed windows are worse. I'd trade the waxed windows for two more hooks. Soon it will snow and life gets real easy: there's no cop better than old Jack Frost.

PERSON BEHIND LAST TREE IN THE TWILIGHT

At night, as I drift through these woods, I tap my hook from time to time against my leg and the feel of the hard iron spurs me on past fence and fern, past drooping branches and the cobbed underbrush. What I need is an older-model American car parked alone in the dark, one with a grip handle I can snare. The lift handles are no good, and everything anymore has the aerodynamic lift handles. I want a '60 Fairlane or a '58 Chevrolet, a car with bench seats big enough for two young people to get comfortable and tangle up their clothing and their brainwaves so that they forget the dark, the woods, the person with a hook, every Halloween, approaching through the leaves.

A NOTE
ON THE TYPE

NO ALPHABET COMES along full-grown. A period of development is required for the individual letters to bloom and then another period for them to adjust to their place in the entire set, and sometimes this period can be a few weeks or it can be a lifetime. No quality font maker ever sat down and wrote out A to Z just like that. It doesn't happen. Getting Ray Bold right required five months, these last five months, an intense creative period for me which has included my ten-week escape from the state facilities at Windchime, Nevada, and my return here one week ago. Though I have always continued sharpening my letters while incarcerated, most of the real development of Ray Bold occurred while I was on the outside, actively eluding the authorities. There's a kind of energy in the out-of-doors, moving primarily along the sides of things, always hungry, sleeping thinly in hard places, that awakens in me the primal desire toward print.

And though Ray Bold is my best typeface and the culmination

of my work in the field, I should explain it is also my last—for the reasons this note on the type will illuminate. I started this whole thing in the first place because I had been given some time at the Fort Nippers Juvenile Facility in Colorado—two months for reckless endangerment, which is what they call Grand Theft Auto when you first start in at it, and I was rooming with Little Ricky Grudnaut, who had only just commenced his life as an arsonist by burning down all four barns in the nearby town of Ulna in a single night the previous February. Juvenile facilities, as you can imagine, are prime locations for meeting famous criminals early in their careers, and Little Ricky went on, as everyone now knows, to burn down eleven Chicken Gigundo Franchise outlets before he was apprehended on fire himself in Napkin, Oklahoma, and asked to be extinguished.

But impulsive and poultry-phobic as he may have become later, Little Ricky Grudnaut gave me some valuable advice so many years ago. I'd moped around our cell for a week—it was really a kind of dorm room—staring at this and that, and he looked up from the tattoo he was etching in his forearm with an old car key. It was Satan's head, he told me, and it was pretty red, but it only looked like some big face with real bad hair—and he said, "Look, Ray, get something to do or you'll lose it. Make something up." He threw me then my first instrument, a green golf pencil he'd had hidden in his shoe.

It was there in Fort Nippers, fresh from the brutality of my own household, that I began the doodling that would evolve into these many alphabets which I've used to measure each of my unauthorized sorties from state-sponsored facilities. Little Ricky Grudnaut saw my first *R* that day and was encouraging. "It ain't the devil," he said, "but it's a start."

I HAVE DECIDED to accept the offer of reduced charges for full disclosure of how and where I sustained my escape. In Windchime I had been sharing a cell with Bobby Lee Swinghammer, the boxer and public enemy, who had battered so many officials during his divorce proceedings last year in Carson City. Bobby Lee was not happy to have a lowly car thief in his cell and he had even less patience with my alphabets. I tried to explain to him that I wasn't simply a car thief, that I was now, in the words of the court, "an habitual criminal" (though my only crime had been to steal cars which I had been doing for years and years), and I tried to show him what I was working on with Ray Bold. Bobby Lee Swinghammer's comment was that it looked "piss plain," and it irked him so badly that he then showed me in the next few weeks some of his own lettercraft. These were primarily the initials *B* and *L* and *S* that he had worked on while on the telephone with his attorney. And they are perfect examples of what is wrong with any font that comes to life in prison.

The design is a result of too much time. I've seen them in every facility in which I have resided, these letters too cute to read, I mean flat-out baroque. Serifs on the *T*'s that weigh ten pounds; Bobby Lee had beaked serifs on his *S*'s that were big as shoes. His *B* was three-dimensional, ten feet deep, a *B* you could move into, four rooms and a bath on the first floor alone. I mean he had all afternoon while his lawyer said "We'll see" a dozen different ways, why not do some gingerbread, some decoration? I kept my remarks to a minimum. But I've seen a lot of this, graffiti so ornate you couldn't find the letters in the words. And what all of that is about is one thing and it's *having time*. I respect it and I understand it—a lot of my colleagues have got plenty of time, and now I've got some again too, but it's a style that is just not for me.

I became a car thief because it seemed a quick and efficient way to get away from my father's fists, and I became a font maker because I was caught. After my very first arrest—I'd taken a red Firebird from in front of a 7-Eleven—in fact in my first alphabet, made with a golf pencil, I tried my hand at serification. I was thirteen and I didn't know any better. These were pretty letters. I mean, they had a kind of beauty. I filigreed the C's and G's and the Q until they looked like they were choking on lace. But what? They stood there these letters so tricked up you wouldn't take them out of the house, too much makeup, and you knew they weren't any good. For me, that is. You put a shadow line along the stem of an R and then beak the tail it's too heavy to move.

The initials that Bobby Lee Swinghammer had been carving into the back of his hand with a Motel 6 ballpoint pen looked like monuments. You could visit them, but they were going absolutely nowhere.

And that's what I wanted in this last one, Ray Bold, a font that says "movement." I mean, I was taking it with me and I was going to use it, essentially, on the run. Bobby Lee was right, it is plain but it can travel light.

I want to make it clear right here, though Bobby Lee and I had our differences and he did on occasion pummel me about the head and upper trunk (not as hard as he could have, god knows), he is not the reason I escaped from Windchime. I have escaped, as the documents point out, eleven times from various facilities throughout this part of the west, and it was never because of any individual cellmate, though Bobby Lee was one of the most animated I've encountered. I like him as a person and

I'm pleased that his appeal is being heard and that soon he will
be resuming his life as an athlete.

I walked out of Windchime because I had the chance. I found
that lab coat folded over the handrail on our stairs. Then,
dressed as a medical technician, with my hair parted right down
the middle, I walked out of there one afternoon, carrying a clipboard I'd made myself in shop, and which is I'll admit right here
the single most powerful accessory to any costume. You carry a
clipboard, they won't mess with you.

Anyway, that windy spring day I had no idea of the direction
this new alphabet would take. I knew I would begin writing;
everybody knew that. I always do it. I've been doing it for more
than twenty years. When my father backhanded me for the last
time I fled the place but not before making my *Ray* on his sedan
with the edge of a nickel. It wasn't great, and I don't care to
write with money as a rule, but it was me, my instinct for lettercraft at the very start.

I also knew I'd be spending plenty of time in the wilderness,
the high desert there around Windchime and the forests as they
reach into Idaho and the world beyond. I know now that, yes,
landscape did have a clear effect on the development of Ray
Bold, the broad clean vistas of Nevada, the residual chill those
first few April nights, and the sharp chunk of flint I selected to
inscribe my name on a stock tank near Popknock. That first *Ray*
showed many clues about the alphabet to come: the *R* (and the *R*
is very dear to me, of course) made in a single stroke (the stem
bolder than the tail); the small case *a*, unclosed; and the capital *Y*,
which resembles an *X*. These earmarks of early Ray Bold would
be repeated again and again in my travels—the single stroke, the
open letter, the imprecise armature. To me they all say one
thing: energy.

I made that *Ray* just about nightfall the second night, and I was fairly sure the shepherd might have seen me cross open ground from a rocky bluff to the tank, and so, writing there in the near dark on the heavily oxidized old steel tank while I knelt on the sharp stones and breathed hard from the run (I'd had little exercise at Windchime), I was scared and happy at once, which as anyone knows are the perfect conditions under which to write your name. *Ray.* It was a beginning.

"Why do it?" they say. "You want to be famous?" It is a question so wrongheaded that it kind of hurts. Because what I do, I do for myself. Most of the time you're out there in some dumpster behind the Royal Food in Triplet or you're sitting in a culvert in Marvin or in a boxcar on a siding in Old Delphi (all places I've been) and what you make, you better make for yourself. There aren't a whole lot of people going to come along and appreciate the understated loop on your *g* or the precision of any of your descenders. I mean, that's the way I figured it. When I fell into that dumpster in Triplet I was scratched and bleeding from hurrying with a barbed-wire fence, and I sat there on the old produce looking at the metal side of that bin, and then after I'd pried a tenpenny nail from a wooden melon crate I made my *Ray,* the best I knew how, knowing only I would see it. And in poor light. I made it for myself. It existed for a moment and then I heard the dogs and I was on the run again.

There was once a week later when I took that gray LeBaron in Marvin and it ran out of gas almost immediately, midtown, right opposite the Blue Ribbon Hardware, and I could see the town cop cruising up behind, and I took off on foot. And I can run when there's a reason, but as I run I always think, as I was thinking that day: where would I make my *Ray.* The two are linked with me: to run is to write. That day after about half a mile, I crawled into a canal duct, a square cement tube with about four inches of water running through the bottom. And with a round rock as big as a grapefruit sitting in that cold irrigation water, I did it there: *Ray*. It wasn't for the critics and it wasn't for the press. They wouldn't be along this way. It was for me. And it was as pure a *Ray* as I've ever done. I couldn't find that place today with a compass.

At times like that when you're in the heat of creation, making your mark, you don't think about hanging a hairline serif on the Y. It seems pretty plainly what it is: an indulgence. Form should fit function, the man said, and I'm with him.

After Marvin, that night in the water, I got sick and slept two or three days in hayfields near there. As everyone knows I moved from there to that Tuffshed I lived in near Shutout for a week getting my strength back. The reports had me eating dog food, and I'll just say to that I ate some *dog food,* dry food, I think it was Yumpup, but there were also lots of nuts and berries in the vicinity and I enjoyed them as well.

Everyone also knows about the three families I met and traveled with briefly. The German couple's story just appeared in *Der Spielplotz* and so most of Germany and Austria are familiar with me and my typeface. I hope that their tale doesn't prevent other Europeans from visiting Yellowstone and talking with Americans at the photo-vistas. I'm still amused that they thought I was a university professor (because I talked a little about my work), but on a three-state, five-month run from the law you're bound to be misunderstood. The two American families seemed to have no difficulty believing they'd fallen into the hands of an escaped felon, and though I did interrupt their vacations, I thought we all had a fine time, and I returned all of their equipment except the one blue windbreaker in good condition.

THOUGH I HAVE decided to tell my story, I don't see how it is going to help them catch the next guy. Because those last five weeks were not typical in the least. Fortunately, by the time I arrived in Sanction, Idaho, Ray Bold was mostly complete, for I lost interest in it for a while.

Walking through that town one evening, I took a blue Country Squire station wagon, the largest car I ever stole, from the gravel lot of the Farmers' Exchange. About a quarter mile later I discovered Mrs. Kathleen McKay in the back of the vehicle among her gear. When you find a woman in the car you're stealing, there is a good chance the law will view that as kidnapping, so when Mrs. McKay called out, "Now who is driving me home?" I answered, truthfully, "Just me, Ray." And at the four-way, when she said left, I turned left.

Now it is an odd thing to meet a widow in that way, and the month that followed, five weeks really, were odd too, and I'm just getting the handle on it now. Mrs. McKay's main interests were in painting pictures with oil paints and in fixing up the farm. Her place was 105 acres five miles out of Sanction and the house was very fine, being block and two stories with a steep metal snow roof. Her husband had farmed the little place, she said, but not very well. He had been a Mormon from a fine string of them, but he was a drinker and they'd had no children, and so the church, she said, had not been too sorry to let them go.

She told me all this while making my bed in the little outbuilding by the barn, and when she finished, she said, "Now I'm glad you're here, Ray. And I hope tomorrow you could help me repair the culvert."

I had thought it would be painting the barn, which was a grand building, faded but not peeling, or mowing the acres and acres of weeds, which I could see were full of rabbits. But no, it was replacing the culvert in the road to the house. It was generally collapsed along its length and rusted through in two big places. It was a hard crossing for any vehicle. Looking at it, I didn't really know where to start. I'd hid in plenty of culverts, mostly larger than this one, which was a thirty-inch corrugated-steel tube, but I'd never replaced one. The first thing, I started her old tractor, an International, and chained up to the ruined culvert and ripped it out of the ground like I don't know what. I mean, it was a satisfying start, and I'll just tell you right out, I was involved.

I trenched the throughway with a shovel, good work that took two days, and then I laid her shiny new culvert in there pretty as a piece of jewelry. I set it solid and then buried the thing and packed the road again so that there wasn't a hump, there wasn't a bump, there wasn't a ripple as you crossed. I spent an extra day dredging the ditch, but that was gilding the lily, and I was just showing off.

And you know what: she paid me with a pie. I'm not joking. I parked the tractor and hung up the shovel and on the way back to my room, she met me in the dooryard like some picture out of the *Farmer's Almanac,* which there were plenty of lying around, and she handed me an apple pie in a glass dish. It was warm and swollen up so the seams on the crosshatch piecrust were steaming.

Well, I don't know, but this was a little different period for old Ray. I already had this good feather bed in the old tack room and the smell of leather and the summer evenings and now I had had six days of good work where I had been the boss and I had a glass pie dish in my hands in the open air of Idaho. What I'm saying here is that I was affected. All of this had affected me.

To tell the truth, kindness was a new thing. My father was a crude man who never hesitated to push a child to the ground. As a cop in the town of Brown River he was not amused to have a son who was a thief. And my mother had more than she could handle with five kids and preferred to travel with the Red Cross from flood to fire across the plains. And so, all these years, I've been a loner and happy at it I thought, until Mrs. McKay showed me her apple pie. Such a surprise, that tenderness. I had heard of such things before, but I honestly didn't think I was the type.

I ate the pie and that affected me, two warm pieces, and then I ate a piece cool in the morning for breakfast along with Mrs. McKay's coffee sitting over her checked tablecloth in the main house as another day came up to get the world and I was affected further. I'm not making excuses, these are facts. When I stood up to go out and commence the mowing, Mrs. McKay said it could wait a couple of days. How'd she say it? Like this: "Ray, I believe that could wait a day or two."

And that was that. It was three days when I came out of that house again; it didn't really make any difference to those weeds. I moved into the main house. I can barely talk about it except to say these were decent days to me. I rode a tractor through the sunny fields of Idaho, mowing, slowing from time to time to let the rabbits run ahead of the blades. And in the evenings there was washing up and hot meals and Mrs. McKay. The whole time, I mean every minute of every day of all five weeks, I never made a *Ray*. And this is a place with all that barnwood and a metal silo. I didn't scratch a letter big or small, and there were plenty of good places. Do you hear me? I'd lost the desire.

But, in the meantime I was a farmer, I guess, or a hired hand, something. I did take an interest in Mrs. McKay's paintings, which were portraits, I suppose, portraits of farmers in shirt-sleeves and overalls, that kind of thing. They were good paintings in my opinion, I mean, you could tell what they were, and she had some twenty of the things on her sunporch, where she painted. She didn't paint any of the farmers' wives or animals or like that, but I could see her orange tractor in the back of three or four of the pictures. I like that, the real touches. A tractor way out behind some guy in a painting, say only three inches tall, adds a lot to it for me, especially when it is a tractor I know pretty well.

Mrs. McKay showed some of these portraits at the fair each year and had ribbons in her book. At night on that screen porch listening to the crickets and hearing the moths bump against the screens, I'd be sitting side by side with her looking at the scrapbook. I'd be tired and she would smell nice. I see now that I was in a kind of spell, as I said, I was affected. Times I sensed I was far gone, but could do nothing about it.

One night, for example, she turned to me in the bed and asked, "What is it you were in jail for, Ray? Were you a car thief?"

I wasn't even surprised by this and I answered with the truth, which is the way I've always answered questions. "Yes," I said. "I took a lot of cars. And I was caught for it."

"Why did you?"

"I took the first one to run away. I was young, a boy, and I liked having it, and as soon as I could I took another. And it became a habit for me. I've taken a lot of cars I didn't especially want or need. It's been my life in a way, right until the other week when I took your car, though I would have been just as pleased to walk or hitchhike." I had already told her that first day that I had been headed for Yellowstone National Park, though I didn't tell her I was planning on making Rays all over the damn place.

After a while that night in the bed she just said, "I see." And she said it sweetly, sleepily, and I took it for what it was.

WELL, THIS DREAM doesn't last long. Five weeks is just a minute, really, and things began to shift in the final days. For one thing I came to understand that I was the person Mrs. McKay was painting now by the fact of the cut fields in the background. The face wasn't right, but maybe that's okay, because my face isn't right. In real life it's a little thin, off-center. She'd corrected that, which is her privilege as an artist, and further she'd put a dreamy look on the guy's face, which I suppose is a real nod toward accuracy.

"Are these your other men?" I asked her one night after supper. We'd spoken frankly from the outset and there was no need to change now, even though I had uncomfortable feelings about her artwork; it affected me now by making me sad. And I knew what was going on though I could not help myself. I could not go out in the yard and steal her car again and pick up my plans where I'd dropped them. I'll say it because I know it was true, I was beyond affected, I was in love with Mrs. McKay. I could tell because I was just full of hard wonder, a feeling I understood was jealousy. I mean there were almost two dozen paintings out there on the porch.

But my question hit a wrong note. Mrs. McKay looked at me

while she figured out what I was asking and then her face kind of folded and she went up to bed. I didn't think as it was happening to say I was sorry, though I was sorry in a second, sorrier really for that remark than for any of the two hundred forty or so vehicles I had taken, the inconvenience and damage that had often accompanied their disappearance. What followed was my worst night, I'd say. I'm a car thief and I am not used to hurting people's feelings. If I hurt their feelings, I'm not usually there to be part of it. And I cared for Mrs. McKay in a way that was strange to me too. I sat there until sunrise when I printed a little apology on a piece of paper, squaring the letters in a way that felt quite odd, but they were legible, which is what I was after: "I'm sorry for being a fool. Please forgive me. Love, Ray." I made the Ray in cursive, something I've done only three or four times in my whole life. Then I went out to paint the barn.

It was midmorning when I turned from where I stood high on that ladder painting the barn and saw the sheriff's two vehicles where they were parked below me. I hadn't heard them because cars didn't make any whump-whump crossing that new culvert. When I saw those two Fords, I thought it would come back to me like a lost dog—the need to run and run, and make a *Ray* around the first hard corner. But it didn't. I looked down and saw the sheriff. There were two kids in the other car, county deputies, and I descended the ladder and didn't spill a drop of that paint. The sheriff greeted me by name and I greeted him back. The men allowed me to seal the gallon of barn red and to put my tools away. One of the kids helped me with the ladder. None of them drew their sidearms and I appreciated that.

It was as they were cuffing me that Mrs. McKay came out. She came right up and took my arm and the men stepped back for a moment. I will always remember her face there, so serious and pure. She said, "They were friends, Ray. Other men who have helped me keep this place together. I never gave any other man an apple pie, not even Mr. McKay." I loved her for saying that. She didn't have to. You have a woman make that kind of statement in broad daylight in front of the county officials and it's a bracing experience; it certainly braced me. I smiled there as happy as I'd been in this life. As the deputy helped me into the car I realized that for the first time *ever* I was leaving home. I'd never really had one before.

"Save that paint," I said to Mrs. McKay. "I'll be back and finish this job." I saw her face and it has sustained me.

THEY HAD FOUND me because I'd mowed. Think about it, you drive County Road 216 twice a week for a few years and then one day a hundred acres of milkweed, goldenrod, and what-have-you are trimmed like a city park. You'd make a phone call, which is what the sheriff had done. That's what change is, a clue.

So, HERE I AM in Windchime once again. I work at this second series of Ray Bold an hour or two a day. I can feel it evolving, that is, the font is a little more vertical than it was when I was on the outside and I'm thickening the stems. And I'm thinking it would look good with a spur serif—there's time. It doesn't have all the energy of Ray Bold I, but it's an alphabet with staying power, and it has a different purpose: it has to keep me busy for fifteen months, when I'll be going home to paint a barn and mow the fields. My days as a font maker are numbered.

My new cellmate, Victor Lee Peterson, the semifamous archer and survivalist who extorted all that money from Harrah's in

Reno recently and then put arrows in the radiators of so many state vehicles during his botched escape on horseback, has no time for my work. He leafs through the notebooks and shakes his head. He's spent three weeks now etching a target, five concentric circles on the wall, and I'll say this, he's got a steady hand and he's got a good understanding of symmetry. But, a target? He says the same thing about my letters. "The ABC's?" he said when he first saw my work. I smile at him. I kind of like him. He's an anarchist, but I think I can get through. As I said today: "Victor. You've got to treat it right. It's just the alphabet but sometimes it's all we've got."

I I I

If you haven't gambled for love in the moonlight,

then you haven't gambled at all.

—"The Moonlight Gambler,"
lyrics by Bob Hilliard, music by Phil Springer

NIGHTCAP

I WAS FILING deeds, or rather, I had been filing deeds all day, and now I was taking a break to rest my head on the corner of my walnut desk and moan, when there was a knock at my door. My heart kicked in. People don't come to my office. From time to time folders are slipped under my door, but my clients don't come here. They call me and I copy something and send it to them. I'm an attorney.

Still and all, I hadn't been much of anything since Lily, the woman I loved, had—justifiably—asked me to move out three months ago. Simply, these were days of filing. I didn't moan that often, but I sat still for hours—hours I couldn't bill to anyone. I wanted Lily back, and the short of it is that I'm not going to get her back in this story. She's not even *in* this story. There's another woman in this story, and I wish I could say there's another man. But there isn't. It's me.

And now the heavy golden doorknob turned, and the woman

entered. She wore a red print cowboy shirt and tight Levi's and under one arm she held a tiny maroon purse.

"Wrong room," I said. I had about four wrong rooms a week.

"Jack," she said, stepping forward. It was either not the wrong room or really the wrong room. "I'm Lynn LaMoine. Phyllis told me that if I came over there was a good chance I could talk you into going to the ball game tonight."

Well. She had me sitting down, half embarrassed about having my moaning interrupted, overheard, and her sister, Phyllis, Madame Cause-Effect, the most feared wrongful death attorney in the state, somehow knew that I was in limbo. I steered the middle road; it would be the last time. "I like baseball," I said. "But don't you have a husband?"

She nodded for a while, her mouth set. "Yeah," she said. "I was married, but . . . maybe you remember Clark Dewar?"

"Sure," I said. "He's at Stover-Reynolds."

She kept nodding. "A lawyer." Then she said the thing that sealed this small chapter of my cheap fate. "Look, I just thought it might be fun to sit outside in the night and watch the game. I'm not good at being lonely. And I don't like the lessons."

It was a page from my book, and I jumped right in. "We could go to the game," I told her. "The Gulls aren't very good, but I've got an old classmate who's coach, and the park organist is worth the price of admission."

At this she smiled so that just the tips of her front teeth showed and stood on one leg so that her shape in those Levi's cut a hard curve against the door behind her. I heard myself saying, "And the beer is cold and it's not going to rain." I explained that I didn't have a car and gave her my address. As a rule I try not to view women as their parts, but—as I said—my moaning had been interrupted and the whole era had me in a hammerlock, and as Lynn turned, her backside involuntarily brought to mind a raw word from some corner of my youth: tail.

THAT NIGHT as I eased into her car I realized that this was the first time I had been in a car alone with a woman for four weeks. For a moment, nine or ten seconds, it actually felt like a date. Ten tops. Though I hadn't accomplished anything with my life so far, I was showered and shined and the water in my hair was evaporating in a promising way, and we were going to the ball game.

I looked over at Lynn in her black silky skirt and plum sweater. She looked like a lot of women today: good. I couldn't tell if this was the outfit of a woman in deep physical need or not. The outfit didn't look overtly sexual, or maybe it did but so did everything else. And then I realized that in the muggy backwash late in this sour month, I felt the faint but unmistakable physical stir of desire. I've got to admit, it was a relief. I took it as a sign of well-being, possibly good health. It was a feeling that well-directed could get me somewhere.

As we arrived, turning onto Thirteenth South under the jutting cement bleachers of Derks Field, I smiled at myself for being so simple. I glanced again at Lynn's wardrobe. You can't tell a thing anymore by the way people dress; it only helps in court. No one dresses like a prostitute these days, not even the prostitutes. And besides, in my eight-year-old Sears khakis and blanched blue Oxford-cloth shirt from an era so far bygone only the Everly Brothers would have remembered it, I looked like the person in trouble, the person in deep, inarticulate need.

IN THE AMBIGUITY in which American ballparks exist, and they are a ragtag bunch, Derks Field is it. It is simply the loveliest garden of a small ballpark in the western United States. The stadium itself is primarily crumbling concrete poured the year I was born and named after John C. Derks, the sports editor at the *Tribune* who helped found the Pacific Coast League, Triple A Baseball, years ago. Though it could seat just over ten thousand, the average crowd these days was a scattered four hundred or so. This little Eden is situated, like most ballparks, in a kind of tough low-rent district spotted with small warehouses and storage yards for rusting heavy equipment.

As a boy I had come here and seen Dick Stuart play first base for the Bees; it was said he could hit the ball to Sugarhouse, which was about six miles into deep center. And my college team had played several games here my senior year while the campus field was being moved from behind the Medical School to Fort Douglas, and I mean Derks was a field that made you just want to take a few slides in the rich clay, dive for a liner in the lush grass.

Lynn and I parked in the back of the nearby All-Oil gas station and walked through a moderately threatening bevy of ten-year-old street kids milling outside the ticket office. When the game started, they would fan out across the street and wait to fight over foul balls, worth a buck apiece at the gate.

I love the moment of emerging into a baseball stadium, seeing all the new distance across the expanse of green grass made magical by the field lights bright in the incipient twilight. The bright cartoon colors on the ads of the home-run fence make a little carnival of their own, and above the "401 Feet" sign in straight-away center, the purple mountains of the Wasatch Front strike the sky, holding their stashes of snow like pink secrets in the last daylight.

I felt right at home. There was Midgely, the only guy who

stayed with baseball from our college squad, standing on the dugout steps just like a coach is supposed to look; there were all the teenage baseball wives sitting in the box behind the dugout, their blond hair buoyant in the fresh air, their babies struggling in the lap blankets; there was the empty box that our firm bought for the season and which no one *ever* used; there beyond first in the general admission were Benito Antenna's fans, a grouping of eight or nine of the largest women in the state come to cheer their true love; and there riding the summer air like the aroma of peanuts and popcorn and cut grass were the strains of Steiner Brightenbeeker's organ cutting a quirky and satanic version of "How Much Is That Doggie in the Window?" I could see the Phantom of the Ballpark himself pounding out the melody in his little green cell, way up at the top of the bleachers next to the press box.

"What?" Lynn said, returning from a solo venture underneath the bleachers. She handed me a beer and a bag of peanuts. She had insisted on buying the tickets, too. Evidently I was being hosted at the home park tonight.

"Nothing. That guy's an old friend of mine." I pointed up at Steiner. Lynn was being real nice, I guess, but I felt a little screwy. Seeing Steiner and being in a ballpark made me think for a minute the world might want me back. He had played at our parties.

And it is my custom with people I don't know to pay my own way, at least, but as she had handed me the plastic cup, I had accepted it without protest. My financial picture precluded many old customs, even those grounded on common sense. I would keep track and pay her back sometime. Besides, early in the game, so to speak, I didn't have the sense not to become indebted to this woman.

"Don't you want a beer?" I asked her. She demurred, and retrieved a flask of what turned out to be brandy from her purse along with a silver thimble. I don't have the official word on this, but I don't think you drink brandy at the ballpark. Certain beverages are married to their sports, and I still doubt whether baseball, even the raw, imprecise nature of Triple A, had anything to do with brandy. Brandy, I thought, taking another look at my date as we stood for Steiner's version of "The Star Spangled Banner," which he sprinkled with "Yellow Submarine," brandy is the drink for quoits.

I don't know; I was being a jerk. It wasn't a first. Blame it this time on the eternal unrest that witnessing baseball creates in my breast. There you are ten yards from the field where these guys are *playing*. So close to the fun. I loved baseball. The thing I regretted most was that I hadn't pressed on and played a little minor-league ball. Midgely himself and Snyder, the coach, talked to me that last May, but I was already lost. Nixon was in the White House and baseball just didn't seem relevant activity.

That isn't my greatest regret. I regretted ten other things with equal vigor—well, twelve say. Twelve tops. One in particular. Things that I wanted not to have happened. I wanted Lily back. I wanted to locate the little gumption in my heart that would allow me to step up and go on with my life. I wanted to be fine and strong and quit the law and reach deep and write a big book that some woman on a train would crush to her breast halfway through and sigh. But I could see myself on the table at the autopsy, the doctor turning to the class and looking up from my chest cavity a little puzzled and saying, "I'm glad you're all here for this medical first. He didn't have any. There's no gumption here at all."

I took a big sip of the beer and tried to relax. Brandy's okay in a ballpark, a peccadillo; it was me that was wrong. Lynn rooting around in her big leather purse for her silver flask and smiling so sweetly under the big lights, her face that mysterious thing, varnished with red and amber and the little blue above the eyes, Lynn was just being nice. I thought that: she's just being nice. Then I had the real thought: it's a tough thing to take, this niceness, good luck.

The most prominent feature of any game at Derks is the approximate quality of the pitching. By the third inning we had seen just over a thousand pitches. These kids could throw hard, but it was the catcher who was doing all the work. The wind-up, the pitch, the catcher's violent leap and stab to prevent the ball from imbedding itself in the wire backstop. Just watching him spearing all those wild pitches hurt my knees: up down up down.

I started in, as I always do, explaining the game to Lynn, the fine points. What the different stances indicated about the batters; why the outfielders shifted; how the third baseman is supposed to move to cover the return throw after a move to first. Being a frustrated player, like every other man in America, I wanted to show my skill.

After a few more beers, I settled down. The air cooled, the mountains dimmed, the bright infield rose in the light. I leaned back and just tried to unravel. I listened to Steiner's music, now the theme song from *Exodus*, and I could faintly hear his fans singing, "This land is mine, God gave this land to me . . ." Steiner made me smile. He played what he wanted, when he wanted. In nine innings you could hear lots of Chopin and Liszt, Beethoven, Bartok, and Lennon. He'd play show tunes and commercial jingles. He played lots of rock and roll, and I once heard his version of *An American in Paris* that lasted an inning and a half. He refused to look out and witness the sport that transpired below him. He had met complaints that he didn't get into the spirit of the thing by playing the heady five-note preamble to "Charge!" one night seventy times in a row, until not only was no one calling "Charge!" at the punch line, but the riff had acquired a tangible repulsion in the ears of the management (next door in the press box), and they were quick to have it banished forever. As long as the air was full of organ music, they were happy.

When Steiner did condescend and play "Take Me Out to the Ball Game," he did it in a medley with "In-A-Gadda-Da-Vida" by Iron Butterfly and "Sympathy for the Devil" by the Rolling Stones. The result, obviously, was an incantation for demon worship which his fans loved. And his fans, a group of ten or twelve young kids, done punk, sat below the organ loft with their backs to the game, bobbing their orange heads to Steiner's urgent melodies. This also mollified the management's attitude toward Steiner: the dozen general admission tickets he sold to his groupies alone.

As the game progressed through a series of walks, steals, overthrows, and passed balls, Lynn sipped her brandy and chattered about being out, how fresh it was, how her husband had only taken her to stockholders' meetings, how she didn't really know what to say (that got me a little; shades of actual dating), how being divorced was so different from what she supposed, not really any fun, and how grateful she was that I had agreed to come.

I held it all off. "Come on, this is great. This is baseball."

"Phyllis said you liked baseball."

I didn't lie: "Phyllis is a shrewd cookie."

"She's a good lawyer, but her husband is a shit too." Lynn

tossed back her drink. "You know, Jack, I honestly didn't know anything about marriage when I married my husband. I mean anything." Lynn sipped her brandy. "Clark came back from his mission and he seemed so ready, we just did it. What a deal. He told me later, this is much later, in counseling that he'd spent a lot of time on his mission planning, you know, our sex life. I mean, planning it out. It was awful." She lifted her tiny cup again, tossing back the rest of the drink.

"But," she began again, extending the word to two syllables, "divorce is worse. I don't like being alone. At all. But it's more than that." She looked into my face. "It's just . . . different. Hard." I saw her put her teeth in her lip on the last word, and she closed her eyes. When they opened again, she printed up a smile and showed me the flask. "Are you sure you wouldn't like any?"

"No," I said, kicking back my chair and standing. "I'll get another beer. Be right back."

Under the grandstand, I stood in the beer line and tried to pretend she hadn't shown me her cards. A friend of mine who has had more than his share of difficulty with women not his wife, especially young women not his wife, real young women, called each episode a "scrape." That's a good call. I'd had scrapes too. My second year in law school I took Lisa Krinkel (now Lisa Krink, media person) on a day trip to the mountains. We had a picnic on the Provo River, and I used my skills as a fire-tender and picnic host, along with the accessories of sunshine and red wine, to lull us both into a nifty last-couple-on-earth reverie as we boarded my old car in the brief twilight and headed for home. As always, I hadn't really done anything, except some woody wooing, ten kisses and fingers run along her arm; after all—though I might pretend differently for a day—I was going with Lily by then. Lisa and I pretended differently all the way home. I remember thinking: What are you doing, Jack? But Lisa Krinkel against me in the front seat kept running her fingernails across my chest in a chilling wave down to my belt buckle, untucking my shirt in the dark and using those fingernails lightly on my stomach, her mouth on my neck, warm, wet, warm, wet, until my eyes began to rattle. Finally, I pulled into the wide gravel turnout by the Mountain Meadow Café and told her either to stop it or deliver.

I wish I could remember exactly how I'd said that. It was probably something like: "Listen, we'd better not keep that up because it could lead to something really terrible which we both would regret forever and ever." But as a man, you can say that in such an anguished way, twisting in the seat obviously in the agonizing throes of acute arousal, a thing—you want her to know—so fully consuming and omnivorous that no woman (even the one who created this monstrous lust) could understand. You writhe, breathing melodramatic plumes of air. You roll your eyes and adjust your trousers like an animal that would be better off in every way put out of its misery. And, as I had hoped, Lisa Krinkel did put me out of my misery with a sudden startling thrust of her hand and then another minute of those electric fingernails and some heavy suction on my neck.

Then the strangest thing happened. When she was finished with my handkerchief, she asked me if we could pray. Well, that took me by surprise. I was just clasping my belt, but I clasped my hands humble as a schoolboy while she prayed aloud primarily to be delivered from evil, which was something I too hoped to be delivered from, but I sensed the prayer wasn't wholly for me as she sprinkled it liberally with her boyfriend's name: Tod. She went on there in the front seat for twenty minutes. I mean if prayers work, then this one was adequate. That little "Tod" every minute or so kept me alert right to the *amen*. We mounted the roadway and drove on in the dark. It had all changed. Now it seemed real late and it seemed a lot like driving my sister home from her date with Tod. Later I started seeing her on television, where she was a reporter for Channel 3, and it was real strange. Her hair was different, of course, blond, a professional requirement, and her name was different, *Krink,* for some reason, and I could barely remember if I had once had a scrape with this woman (including a couple of four-day nail scratches), if she was a part of my history at all. I mean, watching the news some nights it seemed impossible that I had ever prayed with Lisa Krink.

One of the primary cowardly acts of the late twentieth century is standing beneath the bleachers finishing a new beer before buying another and joining your date. I stood there in the archway, smacking my shoes in a little puddle of water on the cement floor, and tossed back the last of my beer. How lost can you be? The water was from an evaporative cooler mounted up in the locker-room window. It had been dripping steadily onto the floor for a decade. Amazing. I could fix that float seal in ten minutes. I'd done it at our house when Lily and I first moved in. And yet, I stood out of sight wondering how I was going to fix anything else. I bought another beer and went out to join Lynn. Just because you're born into the open world doesn't mean you're not going to have to hide sometimes.

Lynn looked at me with frank relief. I could read it. She thought I had left. I probably should have, but you can't leave a woman alone on this side of town, regardless of how bad the baseball gets.

The quality of Double A baseball is always strained. I could try to explain all the reasons, but there are too many to mention. It is not just a factor of skill or experience, because some of the most dextrous nineteen-year-olds in the universe took the field at the top of every inning along with two or three seasoned vets, guys about to be thirty who had seen action a year or two in the majors. No, it wasn't ability. The problem came most aptly under the title "attitude," and that attitude is best defined as "not giving a shit." It's exacerbated by the fact that not one game in a dozen got a headline and three paragraphs in the *Register* and none of the games were televised. And who—given the times— is going to leave his feet to stop a hot grounder down the line if his efforts are not going to be on TV?

Night fell softly over the lighted ballpark, unlike the dozens of flies that pelted into the outfield. The game bore on and on, both squads using every pitcher in the inventory, and Midgely and the other coach getting as much exercise as anyone by lifting their right and then their left arms to indicate which hurler should file forward next. The pitchers themselves marched quietly from the bull pen to the mound and then twenty pitches later to the dugout and then (we supposed) to the showers. By the time the game ended, after eleven (final score 21 to 16), there were at least four relievers who had showered, shaved, and dressed and were already home in bed.

In an economy measure, the ballpark lights were switched off the minute the last out, a force at second, was completed, and as the afterimage of the field burned out on our eyeballs, we could hear the players swearing as they bumbled around trying to pick their ways into the dugout. Lynn and I fell together and she took my arm so I could lead us stumbling out of the darkened stadium. It was kind of nice right there, a woman on my arm for a purpose, the whole world dark, and through it all the organ music, Steiner Brightenbeeker's mournful version of "Ghost Riders in the Sky." Outside, under the streetlights, the three dozen other souls who had stuck it out all nine innings dispersed, and Lynn and I crossed the street to her car. I looked back at the park. Above the parapet I could see Steiner's cigarette glowing up there in space. I pointed him out to Lynn and started to tell her that I had learned a lot from him, but it didn't come out right. He had always been adamant about his art. He was the one who told me to do something on purpose for art; to go without for it. To skip a date and write a story. That if I did, by two a.m. I'd have fifteen pages and be flying. I couldn't exactly explain it to her, so I just mentioned that he had done the music for the one play I'd ever written a thousand years ago and let it go at that.

At the car we could still hear the song. Steiner would play another hour for his fierce little coterie. The Phantom of the Ballpark.

Lynn and I went to her apartment in Sugarhouse for a nightcap. Now that's a word. Like *cocktail,* which I rarely use, it implies certain protocol. It sounds at first like you are supposed to drink it and get tired, take a few sips and yawn politely and then go to your room. A nightcap. I asked for a beer.

Her apartment was furnished somewhat like the interior of a refrigerator in white plastic and stainless steel, but the sofa was a relatively comfortable amorphous thing that seemed to say, "I'm not really furniture. I'm just waiting here for the future."

The only thing I knew for sure about a nightcap was that there was a moment when the woman said, "Do you mind if I slip into something more comfortable?" I was flipping quickly through the possible replies to such a question when Lynn came back with a pilsner glass full of Beck's for me and a small snifter of brandy for herself. She did not ask if she could slip into something more comfortable; instead she just sat by me in the couch or sofa, that thing, and put her knee up on the seat and her right hand on my shoulder. For a moment then, it was nifty as a picture. I thought: Hey, no problem, a nightcap. This is easy.

"How's your nightcap?" I asked Lynn. We hadn't really talked much in the car or parking it in the basement or riding the elevator to her floor or waiting for her to find her keys and I didn't know how we were doing anymore. Isn't that funny? You see a friend playing the organ in the dark, and you fall asleep at the wheel. I sipped the beer and I had no idea of what to say or do next.

"I love baseball," she breathed at me. She smelled nice, something of brandy and a new little scent, something with a European city in the name of it, and her hand on my shoulder felt good, and I realized, as anyone realizes when he hears a woman tell him a lie when she knows it is a lie and that he is going to know it is a lie and that the rules have been changed or removed and that frankly, he should now do anything he wants to, it's going to be all right. He's not going to get slapped or told, "You fool, what are you doing!" It's a realization that sets the adrenaline on you, your heart, your knees, and I sat there unable to move for a moment as the blood beat my corpuscles open.

When I did move, it was to reach for her, slowly, because that's the best moment, the reach, and I pulled her over toward me to kiss her, but she came with the gesture a little too fully and rolled over on top of me, setting her brandy skillfully on the floor as her mouth closed on mine.

It had been a while for this cowboy, but even so, she didn't quite feel right in my arms. Her body was not the body that I was used to, that I associated with such pleasures, and her movements too had an alien rhythm which I didn't at first fully appreciate. I was still being dizzied by these special effects when she started in earnest. It wasn't a moment until we were in a genuine thumping sofa rodeo, she on top of me, riding for the prize. My head had been crooked into the corner, stuffed into a spine-threatening pressure seal, and Lynn was bent (right word here) on tamping me further into the furniture. She did pause in her frenzy at one point, arch up, and pull her skirt free, bunching it at her waist. It was so frankly a practical matter, and her rosy face shone with such businesslike determination, that it gave me a new feeling: fear. Supine on that couch device, I suddenly felt like I was at the dentist. How do these things turn on us? How does something we seem to want, something we lean toward, instantly grow fangs and offer to bite our heads off?

I remember Midgely at the plate during a college game, going after what he thought was the fattest fastball he'd ever seen. It was a slow screwball, and when it broke midway through his swing and took him in the throat, he looked betrayed. He was out for a week. He couldn't talk above a whisper until after graduation. And right now I was midswing with Lynn, and I could tell something ugly was going to happen.

Meanwhile, with one halfhearted hand on her ass and the other massaging the sidewall of her breast, I was also thinking: You don't want to be rude. You don't want to stand, if you could, and heave her off and run for the door. With her panties tangled to her knees like that she'd likely take a tumble and put the corner of something into her brain. There you are visiting her in the hospital, coma day 183, the room stuffed with bushels of the flowers you've brought over the last six months, and you're saying to her sister Phyllis, the most ardent wrongful-death attorney in the history of the world, "Nightcap. We'd had a nightcap."

No, you can't leave. It's a night-cap, and you've got to do your part. You may know you're in trouble, but you've got to stay.

A moment later, Lynn peaked. Her writhing quadrupled suddenly and she went into an extended knee-squeeze seizure, a move I think I had first witnessed on *Big Time Wrestling,* and then she softened with a sigh, and said to me in her new voice, breathy and smiling, a whisper really, "What do you want?"

It's a great question, right? Even when it is misintended as it was here. It was meant here as the perfect overture to sexual compliance, but my answers marched right on by that and lined up. What do I want? *I want my life back. I want to see a chiropractor. I want baseball to be what it used to be.*

But I said, "How about another beer? I should be going soon, but I could use another beer."

When she left the room, shaking her skirt down and then stepping insouciantly out of her underpants, I had a chance to gather my assertiveness. I would tell her I was sorry, but not to call me again. I would tell her I wasn't ready for this mentally or physically. I would tell her simply, Don't be mad, but we're not right for each other *in any way.*

When Lynn reappeared with my beer, I sucked it down quietly and kissing her, took my ambivalent leave. The most assertive thing I said was that I would walk home, that I needed the air. Oh, it was sad out there in the air, walking along the dark streets. Why is it so hard to do things on purpose? I felt I had some principles, why wouldn't they apply? Why couldn't I use one like the right instrument and fix something? Don't answer.

I walked the two miles back to the corner where I used to live, the lost Ghost Mansion. It was as dark as a dark house in a horror film. Was the woman I loved asleep in there? I turned and started down the hill toward my apartment. Oh, I was separated all right, and none of the pieces were big enough to be good for anything. I said Lily's name and made one quiet resolution: no more nightcaps. At all.

DR. SLIME

THIS IS ABOUT the night Betsy told me she was leaving, the night that marked the end of a pretty screwy time all around. Everyone I knew was trying to be an artist, or really was an artist on some scale, and this was in Utah, so you can imagine the scale. Betsy had been almost making a living for several years as a singer, local work for advertising agencies and TV and radio, and my brother Mitchell, who loved her and with whom she lived, was an actor and model for television ads and local theater and whatever movie work came to town. I mean these were people who had consciously said, "I'm going to be an artist no matter what," and that seemed kind of crazy and therefore lovable because it is more interesting than anything nine to five, and I found myself taking care of them from time to time over a three-year period, sponsoring meals and paying their rent two or three times a year, and hanging out with them generally, because I am a regular person, which put me in awe of their refusal to cope with daily duties, and I'll just say it here, rather than let it sneak in later and have you think I'm a vile snake: I came to develop, after the first few months of catching midnight suppers after Mitch's shows and lunches downtown with Betsy after her auditions or after she'd recorded some commercial or other, a condition that anyone in my regular shoes would have developed, I mean not a strange or evil condition, but a profound condition nevertheless, and the condition that I bore night and day was that I was deeply and irrevocably in love with Betsy, my brother's lover, though as you will see it netted me nothing more than a sour and broken heart, broken as regular hearts can be broken, which I probably deserved, no, certainly deserved, and a condition regardless of its magnitude that allowed me to do the noble, the right thing, as you will also see, since I think I acted with grace or at least minor dexterity under such pressure.

I am not an artist. I am a baker for a major supermarket chain and it is work I enjoy more than I should perhaps, but I am dependent on my effort yielding tangible results, and at the end of my shift I go home tired and smelling good. On the day I'm talking about here I came home to my apartment about six a.m. having baked three flights of AUNT DOROTHY's turnovers all night—apple, peach, and raisin—I am AUNT DOROTHY—and found an envelope under the door containing fifteen twenties, the three hundred dollars that Mitch owed me. The note read "THERE IS MORE WHERE THIS CAME FROM. M." Every time he paid me back, this same note was enclosed. It meant that he had found work. His last gig for a smoked-meat ad paid him eight hundred dollars a day for four days, the only work he had in seven months. Mitch was feast or famine.

I put the money in the utility drawer in the kitchen; I would be lending it to him again. I didn't know what it was this time, but Betsy had called a couple of times this week worried, asking about him, what he was doing. He had a big bruise on his neck, and a slug of capsules, unidentifiable multicolored capsules, had begun appearing in the apartment.

"He's an actor," I told her. This is what I used to tell our parents when they would worry. It was a line, I had learned, that was the good news and the bad news at once.

"Yeah, well, I want to know what part beats him up and has him carting drugs."

I wanted to say: So do I, that no-good, erratic beast. Why don't you just drop him and fall into this baker's bed, where you'll be coated in frosting and treated like a goddess. I'll put you on a cake; I'll strew your path with powdered sugar and tender feathers of my piecrusts, for which I am known throughout the Intermountain West.

I said: "Don't worry, Betsy, I'll help you find out."

IT WAS THAT night that she came over to my place on her scooter about seven o'clock and told me she knew something and asked me would I help her, which meant Just Shut Up and Get on the Back. She wore an arresting costume, a red silk shirt printed with little guitars and a pair of bright blue trousers that bloomed at the knees and then fixed tight at the ankle cuff. I scanned her and said, "What decade are we preparing for?"

"Forties," she said, locking up. "Or nineties. You ready? Have you eaten?" I had only been on that red scooter two or three times and found it a terrible and exquisite form of transportation, and the one legitimate opportunity this baker had for putting his hands on the woman who quickened his yeasty heart, in other words, Betsy, my brother's lover, his paramour, his girlfriend, his, his, his.

We took the machine south on State Street. It was exhilarating to be in the rushing air, but the lane changes and a few of the stops made me feel even more tentative than I already did. I held Betsy's waist gingerly, so that at the light on Ninth, he turned and said, "Doug, this is a scooter, hold on for god's sakes. We're friends. Don't start acting like a god damned man." And she clamped my hands onto her sides firmly, my fingers on the top of her hipbones.

That was good, because it made me feel comfortable resting my chin on her shoulder too, as half a joke, and I could feel her smiling as we passed under the streetlights. But the joke was on me, nuzzling a woman of the future, who was I kidding? She smelled fresh, only a little like bread, and though I didn't know it, this was the very apex of my romantic career.

We passed through the rough darkness on Thirty-third South and could see the huge trucks working under lights removing the toxic waste dump where Vitro Processors had been, and then on the rough neon edge of West Valley City, Betsy pulled into Apollo Burger Number Two, a good Greek place. When we stopped I felt the air come up around my face in a little heat. I quickly sidestepped into the bathroom to adjust myself in my underwear; at some point in the close float out here, holding Betsy, my body had begun acting like *a god damned man.*

We ate pastrami burgers and drank cold milk sitting at a sticky picnic table in front of the establishment. It wasn't eight o'clock yet and Betsy assured me we had plenty of time. She knew where we were going because she had asked the driver of the van who had pulled up at their apartment two hours ago. He had come in looking for Mitchell and had told her: Granger High School, eight o'clock. She knew something else, but wasn't telling me.

"He's got to stop taking these stupid nickel-and-dime jobs," she said, as she made a tight ball of her burger wrapper.

"All work has its own dignity," I said—it was one of Mitch's lines.

"Bullshit, it's exploitation. I'm through with it."

"You're not going to sing anymore?"

She stood and threw the paper into a barrel. "I didn't say that."

On the scooter again, I didn't nuzzle. The dinner and the little lesson had taken the spirit out of it for me. I just squinted into the wind and held on. Thirty-fifth South widened into a thick avenue of shopping plazas separated by angry little knots of fast-food joints. Betsy maneuvered us a mile or two and then turned left through a tire outlet parking lot and around a large brick building that I thought was a JC Penney but turned out to be Granger High. We cruised through the parking lot, which was full, and she leaned the scooter against the building. The little marquee above the entrance read: *Welcome Freshmen,* and then below: *Friday, Mack's Mat Matches, 8:00 p.m.*

We stood in a little line of casually dressed Americans at the door and paid four-fifty each for a red ticket which let us into the crowded gymnasium. A vague whomp-whomp we'd been hearing in the hall turned out to be two beefy characters in a raised wrestling ring in the center of the gym slamming each other to the mat.

"Wrestling," I said to Betsy as she led me through the crowd, searching for seats.

"Looks like it."

I followed her, stepping on people's feet all the way across the humid room. There were many family clusters encircled by children standing on the folding chairs and then couples of slumming yuppies, the guy in bright penny loafers and a pastel Lacoste shirt, and sprinkled everywhere small gangs of teenagers in T-shirts waving placards which displayed misspelled death threats toward some of the athletes.

Betsy and I ended up sitting well in the corner of the gym right in the middle of a boiling fan club for the Proud Brothers. Two chubby girls next to me wore Proud Brothers Fan Club T-shirts in canary yellow (the official color) and on the front of each was a drawing of a wrestler's face. The whole club (twelve or so fifteen-year-olds, boys and girls) was hot. They were red in the face and still screaming. Over in the ring, one man would hoist the other aloft and half our neighbors would squeal with vengeful delight, the other half would gasp in horror, and then, after twirling his victim a moment, the wrestler would hurl his opponent to the mat and ka-bang! the whole room would bounce, and the Proud Brothers Fan Club would explode. The noise wanted to tear your hair out. Finally, I noticed that one of the participants had entangled the other's head in the ropes thoroughly and was prancing around the ring in a victory dance. The man in the ropes hung there, his tongue visible thirty rows back, certainly dead. The referee threw up the winner's hands, the bell gonged about twenty times, and the Proud Brothers Fan Club screamed one last time, and the whole gym lapsed into a wonderfully reassuring version of simple crowd noise.

The two girls beside me had fallen into a sisterly embrace, one consoling the other. One girl, her face awash in sweat and tears, peered over her friends' shoulders at me. "Were those the Proud Brothers?" I asked her.

She squeezed her eyes shut in misery and nodded. Her friend turned around to me fully in an odd shoulder-back posture and pulled her T-shirt down tight in what I thought was a gesture meant to display her nubby little breasts, but then she pointed beneath the distorted portrait on the shirtfront to the name below: TOM. Her friend, the bereaved, stood and showed me her breasts too, which were much larger and still heaving from the residual sobs so much that it was difficult to recognize the face on her shirt as human, but I finally read the name underneath: TIM.

"And it was Tim who was just killed?" I asked. She collapsed into her friend's arms again.

Betsy nudged me sharply. "What'd you say to her?" She tapped my arm with her knuckle. "You're going to get arrested. These are children."

By now they had carried the body of one brother away and the other brother had finished his prancing, and the announcer, a little guy in a tux, crawled into the ring with a bullhorn.

"Ladies and gentlemen . . ." he began and before he had finished rolling *gen-tull-mn* out of his mouth, Betsy turned to me and I to her, the same word on our lips: "Mitch!"

We both sat up straight and watched this guy very carefully. It was Mitchell all right, but they had him in a pompadour toupee, a thin mustache, and chrome-frame glasses. What gave him away was his voice and arrow posture and the way he held his chin up like William Tell. He had a good minor strut going around the ring, blasting his phrases in awkward, dramatic little crescendoes at the audience. *"Wee are pleeezd! Tooo pree-zent! A No! Holds! Barred! Un-Ree-Strik-Ted! Marr-eeed Cupples! Tag-Team-Match! Fee-chur-ring Two Dy-nam-ic Du-os! Bobbie and Robbie Hansen! Ver-sus. Mario and Isabella Delsandro!"*

Evidently these were two new dynamic duos, because the crowd was quiet for a moment as people twisted in their seats or stood up to evaluate the contestants. And both couples looked good. Bobbie and Robbie Hansen, I never did find out which was which, were a beefy though not unattractive blond couple who wore matching blue satin wrestling suits. The Delsandros were very handsome people indeed. Mario nodded his beautiful full hairdo at the fans for a moment before dropping his robe and revealing red tights. But it was Isabella who decided the evening. She also had curly black hair and a shiny red suit, but when she waved at the audience, they quieted further. There were some gasps. The girls next to me actually covered their mouths with their hands; I hadn't seen that in real life ever. This was the deal: there was a tuft of hair under each of her arms. It was alien enough for this crowd. Mormon women shave under their arms; it's doctrine. The booing started a second later and when the bell sounded, the fans had made their choice.

When Mitchell ducked out of the ring, Betsy said, "Announcer. That's not bad."

"They've got him up like Sammy Davis, Jr."

"But," she added, "where does an announcer get a black eye?"

I was having trouble taking my eyes from the voluptuous Mrs. Delsandro, who now as the *unclean woman* was getting her ears booed off.

"You're right," I said. "We better stay around, find out what he's up to."

I won't detail the match (or the one after it featuring the snake and the steel cage), but in a sophisticated turn of fate, the Delsandros won. I bounced in my chair the whole forty minutes watching Robbie and Bobbie have at the luckless Mario and Isabella. They were pummeled, tossed, and generously bent.

Then, late in the match, Robbie or Bobbie (Mr. Hansen) was tor-
turing Mrs. Delsandro, twisting her arm, gouging her eyes, rendering her weaker and weaker. Mr. Delsandro paced and wept
in his corner, pulling his hair out, praying to god, and generally
making manifest my very feelings for the woman in the ring.
Finally Mr. Hansen climbed on the turnstile and leapt on the
woozy woman, smashing her to the mat. He was going for the
pin. He lay across Mrs. Delsandro this way and that, maneuver-
ing cruelly, but every time the referee would slap the mat twice,
she'd squirm away. Robbie Hansen or Bobbie Hansen, whatever
his name was, was relentless. Mr. Mario Delsandro prayed in his
corner of the ring. Evidently his prayers were answered, because
about the tenth time the referee slapped the mat twice, Isabella
Delsandro bucked and threw Mr. Hansen clear and in a second
she was on him. It was such a relief, half the fans cheered.

What she did next sealed the Hansens' fate. She whomped
him a good one with a knee drop and then ducked and hoisted
him aloft, belly to heaven, in a refreshing spinal stretch. Well, it
took the crowd, who thought they were rooting for the home
team, less than a second to spot Mr. Hansen as a sick individual.
His blue satin shorts bulged precisely with the outline of his
skewered erection, and Mrs. Delsandro toured him once around
the ring for all to see and then dropped him casually on his head.
By now they were urging her, in loud and certain terms, to kill
Mr. Hansen. Wrestling is one thing. Transgressing the limits of
a family show is entirely another. I heard cries which included
the phrases *decapitate, assassinate,* and *put him to sleep.*

She responded by giving him the Norwegian Fish Slap, the
Ecuadoran Neck Burn, and the Tap Dance of Death, and then,
before tagging her wonderful husband, she stood over the pros-

trate and slithering Mr. Hansen, her legs apart, her hands on her hips, and she raised her chin triumphantly and laughed. Oh god, it was passion, it was opera, it was giving me the sweats.

When Mario Delsandro leaped into the ring, he swept up his beautiful dark wife and kissed her fully on the mouth. The crowd sang! Mr. Hansen thought he would use the opportunity to crawl away home, but no! Still in the middle of the most significant kiss I've ever witnessed in person, Mr. Delsandro stepped squarely in the middle of Mr. Hansen's back and pressed him flat.

There was never any hope for Mr. Hansen anyway. Among the spectators of his rude tumescence was his wife, Robbie or Bobbie, Mrs. Hansen, and she stood at her corner, her arms crossed as if for the final time, and sneered at him with all her might. Mario Delsandro took his time punishing Mr. Hansen: the German Ear Press, the Thunder Heel Spike, the Prisoner of War, the Ugandan Skull Popper, and the complicated and difficult-to-execute Underbelly Body Mortgage. A few times, early in this parade of torture, Mr. Hansen actually crawled away and reached his corner, where Mr. Delsandro would find him a second later, pleading with his wife to tag him, please tag him, save his life. She refused. At one point while he was begging her for help, she actually turned her back and called to the audience, "Is there a lawyer in the house?" No one responded. The attorneys present realized that to get in between two wrestlers would probably be a mistake.

After taking his revenge plus penalty and interest, Mr. Delsandro tagged the missus, and she danced in and pinned the comatose Mr. Hansen with one finger. The Delsandros kissed and were swept away by the adoring crowd. Mrs. Hansen stalked off. There was a good chance she was already a widow, but the crowd was on its feet and I couldn't see what ever happened to her husband, Mr. Hansen, Robbie or Bobbie.

stalked off. There was a good chance she was already a widow, but the crowd was on its feet and I couldn't see what ever happened to her husband, Mr. Hansen, Robbie or Bobbie.

stalked off. There was a good chance she was already a widow, but the crowd was on its feet and I couldn't see what ever happened to her husband, Mr. Hansen, Robbie or Bobbie.

Mitchell announced the next match, using the same snake oil school of entertaining, which was about right, because, as I said, it involved a snake and a steel cage and five dark men in turbans.

When that carnage was cleared, we found out what we wanted to know. Another announcer, a round man dressed in a black suit carrying what looked like a Bible in his hand, climbed into the ring and introduced the final match of the evening, a grudge match, a match between good and evil if there ever was one, a match important to the very futures of our children, et cetera, et cetera, and here to defend us is David Bright, our brightest star!

Ka-lank! The lights went out. Betsy grabbed my arm. "David Bright?" she said. "Mitch is David Bright?"

"Come to save us all."

An odd noise picked across the top of the room and then exploded into a version of "Onward Christian Soldiers" so loud most people ducked. A razor-edge spotlight flashed on, circling the room once, and then focusing on a crowded corner. In it appeared a phalanx of brown-shirted security guards, all women, marching onward through the teeming crowd. When the entourage reached the ring, we heard the announcer say, "Ladies and gentlemen: David Bright! Our Brightest Star!" And the lights went on and a blond athlete stepped into the ring. He raised his arms once and then took several ministeps to the center of the ring, where he lowered his head in what was supposed to be prayer and bathed in the tumult.

"That's not Mitch." I squinted. "Is it?"

"No," Betsy said. "Look at that guy. There's a lot of praying at these wrestling matches. Is it legal?"

When the crowd slowed a bit and David Bright had gone to his corner and begun a series of simple stretches, the announcer started to speak again. He said, "And his opponent . . ." and couldn't get another word out for all the booing.

I sat down and pulled Betsy to her chair. We looked at each other in that maelstrom of noise. It was a throaty, threatening roar that was certainly made in the jungles when men first began to socialize.

"I think we're about to see Mitch." I told her.

"It sounds as if we're about to see him killed."

"We'll be able to tell by his theme song."

The announcer had continued garbling in the catcalls, and then the lights went out and the spot shot down, circling, and then the sound system blared static and by the first three notes of the song that followed I knew we were in trouble. It was "White Rabbit" by the Jefferson Airplane. The spot fixed on the other corner of the room, and here came a Hell's Angel in a sleeveless black leather jacket, swatting his motorcycle cap at the fans, *get your hands off*. Well, it was a big guy, a large hairy Hell's Angel, a perfect Hell's Angel in my opinion, because it was not my brother Mitchell, and Betsy knew that too, because we exchanged grateful and relieved looks. However, when the Angel reached the ring, he didn't climb up, but bent down and this dirty, skinny person in a red satin robe who had been behind him stepped on the Hell's Angel's back and entered the bright lights of the ring. This guy was Mitchell.

This guy put his face right into all the booing as if it were the sweetest wind on earth. This guy moved slowly, confidently, like Hotspur, which I saw Mitchell play at the Cellar Theater, and he reached into the roomy pockets of his red satin robe and threw handfuls of something at the crowds.

"What's that?" I asked the Proud Brothers fan beside me. The cheerful chubby girl had been my source of information all night.

"Drugs," she said. "He always tries to give drugs to the kids."

I could see pills being thrown back into the ring.

Mitchell was laughing.

The announcer closed down his diatribe, which no one could hear, and then yelled, pointing at Mitchell: *"Dr. Slime!"* The booing now tripled, which gave Mitchell such joy he reached down and scooped up a handful of capsules and ate them, grinning.

The bell sounded and Mitchell was still in his robe. David Bright had come forward to wrestle, but Mitchell waved a hand at him, *just a minute,* and poured something on the back of his hand and then snorted it, blowing the residue at the fans. He laughed again, a demented laugh, just like Mephistopheles, which I saw him play at the University Playhouse, coiled his robe, forgot something, unrolled it, removed a syringe, laughed, threw the syringe at the fans, rerolled his robe, and threw it in David Bright's face. David was so surprised by the unfair play that my brother, Dr. Slime, was able to deliver the illegal Elbow Drill to his kidneys. Then while David staggered around on his knees in a daze, removing the robe from his head, Dr. Slime strutted around the ring eating drugs off the mat and waggling his tongue and eyes at those at ringside. From time to time, he'd stop chewing and kick David Bright about the face. The crowd was pissed off. They had rushed the ring and now stood ten deep in the apron. Mitchell could have walked out onto their faces.

He was milking it. I'd seen him do this one other time, in *Macbeth*, running the soliloquies to twice their ordinary length because he sensed an audience with a high tolerance for anguish. Now he knelt and took something from his sock and then snorted it. He leaped in frenzied drug-induced craziness, lest anyone forget he was a maniac, a drug fiend. He whacked the woozy David Bright rapid-fire karatelike blows. He was a whirling dervish.

Then while David Bright still tried to shake off his drubbing and climb to his feet, something happened to Dr. Slime. Something chemical. He kicked David Bright, knocking him down, and raised his arms, his fingers clenched together in (what my female neighbor told me was) his signature attack, the Crashing Bong, and prepared to bring it down on David Bright, ending a promising career. Then Dr. Slime stopped. There he was, mid-ring, his arms up as if holding a fifty-pound hammer, and he froze. Then, of course, he began vibrating, shaking himself out of the pose, his head trembling sickeningly like a tambourine, his hands fluttering full-speed. He began to jerk, drool, and grunt.

His demise couldn't have come at a worse time. David Bright, our brightest star, suddenly came to and stood up. He looked mad. The rest of the match took ten seconds. David Bright, who must have outweighed Mitchell by sixty pounds, picked him up like a rag doll, sorting through his limbs like a burglar, finally grabbing his heels and beginning to spin him around and around like the slingshot that other David used.

Betsy was on my arm with both her hands and when David

Bright let go of Mitchell and Mitchell left the ring and sailed off into the dark, she screamed and jumped on my back to see where he landed. We couldn't see a thing.

The crowd was delighted and David Bright took three or four polite bows, curtsies really, and humbly descended from the light. Betsy was screaming her head off: "You beasts! You fucking animals! I'll kill you all!" Things like that. Things that I would have loved to hear her cry for me.

I was crazy to go find Mitchell or his body or who was responsible for this heinous mayhem and file felony charges, suit, something, but Betsy was broken down, screaming into my shirt by now, and I held her and said *There there*, which is stupid, but I was so glad to have anything to say that I said it over and over.

The auditorium emptied and finally we ended up sitting, worn out, in our seats in the empty corner of the room. My good friend the Proud Brothers fan disappeared and then returned with two yellow T-shirts and gave them to me. "Here," she said. "Glad to meet you. You two are welcome to the club if you can make it next Friday."

I looked down at Betsy, her face wrecked, and I felt my own blood awash with the little chemicals of fear and anger. And love.

"You got the right spirit," the girl said and turned to leave.

We couldn't find Mitchell. We went back through both of the entrances the wrestlers had used, finally running into the school janitor, who simply said, "They don't stay around not one second. They get right in the motor home." He left us alone in the dark corridor.

"Why would he do this?" she said. "Why would he get hooked up with these sleazoid sadists?" She was as beautiful as worried girls get late at night in an empty school.

"I don't know."

"Well, find out!" She said this as an angry order, and then caught herself and smiled. "We've got talk to him; get him out of this."

"Save him," I said.

"What are you saying?" She tilted her head, focusing on me.

"Nothing." Then I decided to go on. "It's just . . . Betsy, I saw him strutting around that ring, playing that crowd."

"And?"

"And: he loved it."

Betsy folded her arms. "He loved having his neck broken."

I wanted to say, Listen, Betsy, it's art. It's all worth it. I had some new information on this subject, having witnessed the Delsandros wrestle, having witnessed their soaring struggle, and having had my heart in their hands, I was a new convert, but what could I say, some guy who is Aunt Dorothy every night in a bakery? I said, "Let's not fight."

She shook her head at me a minute, a phrase in body language that seemed to mean *you pathetic man*. And then we prowled the vacant corridors of Granger High School for a while, from time to time calling, "Mitchell!"

We went into the second-floor girls' room, because we could see the light under the door, and inside she turned to me and said, "Oh hell." It was a four-stall affair, primarily public-school gray with plenty of places to put your sanitary napkins. I could see the back of Betsy's beautiful head in the mirror. There was an old guy standing next to her and when I spoke I realized he was a screwed-up baker out of town for a night with his brother's girlfriend. He looked in serious need of a blood transfusion, exercise, good news.

"Dr. Slime?" I said to the stalls.

"What a night," Betsy said. "It doesn't matter. He's gone." She leaned against the counter and folded her arms. "He told me I should tell you my news."

"Good, okay," I said, leaning against the counter too and folding my arms. We stood like that, like two girlfriends in the girls' room.

"I'm going to L.A. Next week. I have some interviews with agents and two auditions."

"Auditions?" I said. I am a baker. It is not my job to catch on quickly. I looked at her face. She was as beautiful as any movie actress; with her mouth set as it was now and the soft wash of freckles across her nose and her pale hair up in braids, she looked twenty. She was smart and she could sing. "You're going to L.A. You're not coming back here."

"No, I guess I'm not," she said.

"Does Mitchell know?"

"Mitchell knows.

"How hurt is he?"

"That would be a stupid question, wouldn't it, Doug? Don't you think?"

I took my stupid question and the great load of other stupid questions forming in my ordinary skull out of the girls' room and through the dark hallways of Granger High and out into the great sad night. The parking lot was empty and I stood by the red scooter as if it were a shrine to the woman I loved, I ached for, in other words Betsy, who now walked toward me across the pavement, and who now, I realized, wasn't exactly my brother's lover anymore, a notion that gave me an odd shiver. I was as confused as bakers get to be.

"How certain are these things you've got out there?"

"How certain? How certain is my staying here, singing jingles for the next ten years? Come on, Doug: I want to be a singer." She mounted the scooter and waited.

"You are a singer, Betsy. The best. I love your singing. And so, this is your move, right?"

She nodded.

"And it's worth Mitchell?"

She started the machine and the blue exhaust began to roil up into the night. It wasn't a real question and she was right not to answer. Through the raining flux of emotions, worry about Mitchell, love for Betsy, the answer had descended on me like a ton of meringue. I knew the answer. *It was worth it*. It's funny about how the world changes and how art can turn the wheel. I had seen the Delsandros and I had seen my brother, a talented person, an artist, fly through the air to where I knew not, but I knew it was worth it. To be thrown that way in front of two thousand people, well, I'd never done it and I never would, but I know that Mitchell even as he squirmed through the terrific arc of his flight thought it was worth it. That's what art is, perhaps, the look I had seen on his face.

Is this clear? I was annoyed to my baker's bones at these two people and I wanted them to be mine forever. But they were both flying and I was proud of that too. I then climbed on behind my lost love, a woman who sings like an angel and drives a scooter like the devil, that is, Betsy, and I kissed her cheek. Just a little kiss. I wasn't trying anything. "Let us go then," I said, "and see if we can find our close friend Dr. Slime."

DOWN THE
GREEN RIVER

WE WERE FINE. We were holding on to a fine day on the fine
Green River in the mountains of Utah five hours from Salt Lake
with the sun out and Toby already fishing, when his mother,
Glenna, said, "We're sinking." She had been a pain in the ass
since dawn. I wanted nothing more than to argue, prove her
wrong, but I couldn't because there was real water in the bottom
of the raft. You're supposed to leave your troubles behind when
you float a river, but given our histories, that was a fat chance.

We were that strange thing: old friends. I'd known Glenna
since college; she had been Lily's roommate and there was a time
when we were close as close. She had been an ally in my quest
for Lily. We'd had a thousand coffees at their kitchen table and
she'd counseled and coached me, been a friend. Then after college she had married my pal Warren, which had been her mistake, and I had not married Lily, which had recently
(twenty-two days ago) become mine. Warren had not been good
to Glenna. His specialty was young women and he used his posi-

tion as editor of the *Register* to sharpen it. She had grown embit-
tered to say the least, and I wanted now simply to cut that deal—
old friends or not—call her a sour unlikable bitch and get on
with the day my way; if I had known that she was going to be
the photographer for the news story I was writing, I'd have
stayed in town.

She had her suitcase—something that has no business even
near a raft—balanced on the side tube, and she held her camera
case aloft in the other hand. It was dripping. The suitcase made
me mad. I was just mad. Glenna had been to Lily's wedding a
month (twenty-two days) ago. She had talked to Lily. Now I
could see the water over the tops of her shoes in the deep spaces
where she stood. It was not common to tear a raft on the gravel,
but it happened. I looked downriver for a landing site. The
banks were both steep cutaways, but there was a perfect sandbar
off to the right side, and I paddled us for it.

After the three of us dragged the raft clear of the water and
unloaded the gear, spreading it out to dry, I set Toby at the
downstream point with a small Mepps spinner and went back to
repair the raft. Glenna was sitting on her suitcase, checking her
camera. Her god damned suitcase. Warren had assigned me the
story and her the photographs. "Floating the Green"—it would
run in Thursday Sports.

I was trying not to think. I had taken the job to get out of
town and because I needed the money. Warren said the photographer would pick me up at four a.m., and there in the dark
when I saw Glenna's '70 Seville, the same car she'd had at
school, my heart clenched. We had all spent a lot of time in that
car. And I knew she'd seen Lily. Twenty-two days. If I had been
ready, been able to commit; if I had been thirty percent mature;
if I had not assumed being more "interesting" than Lily's other

dates would keep me first, then I might not have been standing on a sandbar with my teeth in my lip. Did I want to ask Glenna a few questions? Does Lily miss me? Has she said my name? Where should I send her tapes? Yes. Would I? Hey, I had a raft to fix, and as I said, I was trying not to think.

Now sitting on her suitcase on a sandbar, she stretched and reached in her bag for another Merit, which she lit and inhaled. "How'd he talk you into this one?" she said as smoke.

"He mentioned the beauty of nature." I waved up at the sunny gorge, the million facets of the exposed cliffs. "The clear air, the sweet light . . ."

"Bullshit, Jack."

"The money, which I need." I flopped the raft upside down. There were a dozen black patches of various sizes on the bottom, but I could find no new hole. Using my knife, I tested the edges of all the old patches, and, sure enough, one large one was loose. "What about you? You don't need another photo credit."

She pointed at Toby where he fished from the edge of the sand. "I'm here because you know how to do whatever it is we're going to do and you can show it to Toby in some semblance of man-to-boy goodwill and something will have been gained." She flipped the butt into the Green River. "About the rest, I could give a shit. If Warren wants me out of town so he can chase Lolita, so be it."

I bent to my work, scraping at the old patch. I peeled it off and revealed a two-inch L-shaped tear. I wiped the area down and prepared my own new patch with the repair kit while the sun dried the bottom of the raft. I didn't like that phrase *so be it*. There's gloom if not doom in that one.

And sure enough, a moment later Glenna spoke again. "Jack," she said. "Something's happening with the water." Her imprecision almost cheered me, then I looked and saw our sand-bar was shrinking. Toby had reeled in and was walking back, stepping with difficulty in the soft sand.

"Jack," he said. "The water's rising."

I stood still and watched it for a moment. The clear water crawled slowly and surely up the sand. The water was rising.

"My patch isn't dry. Load everything on the raft as it is." I set the cooler and my pack on the upside-down raft and Glenna put her suitcase and Toby placed the sleeping bags and the loose stuff in a heap on the raft. She paused long enough to snap a few photographs of our disaster.

The water inched up, covering our feet, lifting at the raft.

"We're going to get wet now, aren't we?" Glenna said.

"Yes," I said. "Just hold on to the raft and we'll float it down to the gravel spit." I pointed downstream two hundred yards.

"Why is the water rising?" Toby said, laying his pole onto our gear.

"Power for Los Angeles," I told him.

"Some guy's VCR timer just kicked in so he can record *Divorce Court* while he's out playing tennis," Glenna said. "This water is cold!"

Finally enough water crept under the raft to lift it free and we walked it down into the deeper water of the fresh, cold Green River. "Jack," Glenna said, blaming me for hydroelectric power everywhere, "this fucking water is cold!"

"Just hold on," I said to Toby as the water rose toward my chin. "This will be easy."

That is when I saw the next thing, something over my shoulder, and I turned as a small yellow raft drifted swiftly by. There were four women crowded into it. They appeared to be naked.

AN HOUR LATER, we started again. We had clambered out of
the river onto the gravel, unloaded the raft, and let the patch air-
dry for thirty minutes while Toby and I chose our next series of
flies and Glenna, stripped down to her tank top and Levi's, commenced drinking cans of lemon and cherry wine coolers. Then
we turned the raft over again, reloaded it, and tenderly made
into the river. I immediately pieced Toby's fly rod together, at-
tached the reel, and geared him up with a large Wooly Caddis,
the kind of mothy thing that bred thickly on this part of the
river. I clipped a bubble five feet from the fly so it would be
easier, this early in the day, to handle. Sitting on the side of raft,
I began to organize my tackle, and I had to consciously slow myself down. My blood was rich with the free feeling I always get
on a river. The sunshine angled down with its first heat of the
day on my forearms as I worked, and I realized that my life was
a little messy, but for now I was free. It was okay. I was now
afloat in a whole different way. It was a feeling a boy has. I
smiled with a little rue. Even in a life that is totally waxed, there
are still stupid pleasures. It was morning, and I smiled; come on,
who hasn't screwed up a life?

Toby had a sharp delivery on his cast, which we worked on
for a while as the raft drifted along the smooth sunny river. He
was still throwing the line, not punching it into place, but he
mastered a kind of effective half-and-half with which he was
able to set the fly in the swollen riffles about half the time. It was
now late in the morning, but there was enough shade on the
water that the fishing could still be good.

I started working the little nymph in the quiet shady pools
against the mountain as we'd pass. Once, twice, drift, and back. I
saw some sudden shadows and I was too quick on the one rise

I had. Glenna was sitting on her awful suitcase, back against the raft tube, her arms folded, drinking her coolers, quiet as Sunday school behind her oversize dark glasses. From time to time I had to set my rod down and avert the canyon wall or a small boulder or two in the river with the paddle and center us again.

Then later in the morning Glenna took a series of photographs of Toby as he knelt and fly-cast from his end of the raft. She was able, in fact, to film his first fish, a nice twenty-inch rainbow trout which answered the caddis in an odd rocky shallow, coming out of the water to his tail, and Toby, without a scream or a giggle, worked the fish into the current and fifty yards later into our now hot boat. He was a keeper, and Toby said, finally letting his enthusiasm show, "The first one I caught from a raft, ever." I killed the fish on my knee, showing Toby how to tap it smartly behind the cranium, and put him in my creel.

"It's awfully good luck to have the first fish be a keeper," I told him. "Now our nerves are down and we can be generous with the newcomers." Even Glenna seemed pleased watching us, as if her expectations for this sojourn were somehow being met.

I thought about the article I would write. I could have written it without coming, really. I knew the Green by the back. I would talk about the regulations (flies and lures only—no bait); I would talk about the boat launch and the fluctuating river level; I would say take along a patch kit. I would not mention anything that happened next.

The sun had straightened into noon, and the fishing had slowed considerably. I had taken two little trout from pools in the lee of two boulders, handling them with exaggerated care for Toby's information and then returning them to the water.

Then, around the next bend, there was a long slow avenue of river and I found out I had been right about the four rafters. They had been nude. About a half mile down, under a sunny gray shale escarpment, there was a party in session. Eleven or twelve rafts of all sizes had been beached, and fifty or sixty people loitered in the area in a formless nude cocktail party.

"Fish this side of the raft," I said to Toby, adjusting his pole opposite the nudists. Just as I settled him, with a promise of lunkers in that lane, Glenna spotted the other rafters and determined the nature of the activity. She was working down her third wine cooler, a beverage which evoked her less subtle qualities, and she cried out, "Check this out!"

A dozen or so of these noble campers sat bare-assed on a huge fallen log along the river, nursing their beers, taking the sun, watching the river the way people wait for a bus. I heard one call out, "Raft alert! Raft ho!" There was some laughter and a stir of curiosity about our little craft as it drew closer.

I wondered what it was about the wilds that made all these young lawyers feel impelled to take off their clothing. Is it true that as soon as most folks can't see the highway anymore, they immediately disrobe? We came abreast the naked natives in an eerie slow-motion silence. They stopped drawing beer from the keg, quit conversations, stood off the log. Many turned toward us or took half a step toward the river. Glenna was leaning dangerously out of the raft on that side, another wine-cooler casualness (she was just full of wine coolers), and Toby had swiveled fully around from his fishing duties, striking me in the ear with the tip of his rod. I lifted it from his hands.

One bold soul strode down to the edge of the river, waggling himself in the sunshine. He lifted his cup of beer at us and called, "Howdy! What ya doing?" Behind him, still standing against the log, was a slender, dark-haired girl who looked a lot like Lily. She was about as tall and had the posture. Her breasts were pure white, the two whitest things I'd ever seen at noon on a river, a white that hurt the eyes, and her pubic hair glinted red in the bright sunlight. Oh, I don't need to see these things. I need to fish and have my heart start again and be able to breathe without this weight in my chest. I could not physically stop looking at the girl.

"The same thing you are," Glenna answered the young man. "Fishing with worms!" She laughed a full raw laugh back in her throat, leaning so hard on the side of the raft that a quick stream of cold river water sloshed in. As Glenna continued staring the man down and chortling, I thought, This is where it comes from: the devil and the deep blue sea. I am caught, for a moment, between the devil and the deep blue sea. I looked down into the crystal green slip of the river; the stones shimmered and blinked, magnifying themselves in the bent waterlight.

Slowly, we slid past the naked throng. It seemed a blessing that Glenna had not thought to take any photographs. I shifted some of the gear out of the new bilgewater and cast one terrible glance back at the girl and her long bare legs. The arch of her ass along that large smooth log caught my heart like a fishhook. Toby had collapsed like a wet shirt and was sitting on the bottom of the raft, soaking. He bore all the signs of having been electrocuted. I doused his face in a couple handfuls of river water to put out the expression on his face, and sat him up again with his fishing pole and a new lure, a lime-green triple teaser which looked good enough for us to eat. I almost had him convinced that it was still possible to fish in this world when I heard Glenna groan and I felt the raft shift as she stood.

I cursed the pathetic confectioneer who had invented wine coolers and turned to see Glenna reach down and pull her tank top over her head, liberating Romulus and Remus, the mammoth breasts. Shuddered by the shirt, they rippled for a moment and then settled in the fresh air.

"No topless fishing," I said to her. "Don't do that." I handed her the shirt.

She threw it in the river. "I'm not going to fish," she said back to me. Toby had put his pole down again. This river trip had become more dangerous than he'd ever dreamed. I put one hand on his shoulder to restrain him from leaping into the sweet Green River. When I felt him relax, I turned back to Glenna and her titanic nudity. It was still a day. The sun touched off the river in a bright, happy way. We fell out of the long straight stretch into a soft, meandering red canyon. It was still a day.

"Look, Glenna," I said. She had opened another wine cooler. "Look. We're going to fish. This is a raft trip and we're going to fish. It would help everything if you would take your drink and turn around and face forward. Either way, you're going to get a wicked sunburn." I moved the three plastic-covered sleeping bags in such a way as to make her a backrest. She looked at me defiantly, and then she turned her back and settled in.

It was still a day. I took the bubble off Toby's line and showed him how to troll the triple teaser. "There are fish here," I told him. "Let's go to work." I tied an oversize Royal Coachman on my line and began casting my side of the river, humming—for some reason—the Vaughn Monroe version of the ominous ballad "Ghost Riders in the Sky." I knew the words, even the yippie-ai-ais.

WE PASSED LITTLE HOLE at three o'clock and I knew things would get better. Ninety-nine percent of the rafters climb out at Little Hole and we could see two dozen big GMC pickups and

campers waiting in the parking lot. We'd already passed a
flotilla of Scout rafts all tethered together in a large eddy taking
fly-casting lessons. It was a relief to see that they didn't have
enough gear to spend the night on the river.

It had been an odd scene, all those little men in their deco-
rated uniforms, nodding seriously into the face of their leader, a
guy about my age who was standing on a rock with his flyrod,
explaining the backcast. It was his face as it widened in surprise
that signaled the troop to turn and observe what would be for
many of them the largest breasts they would ever witness in person no matter how long they lived. Glenna had smiled easily at
all of them and waved sweetly at their leader. I said nothing, but
put my pole down and paddled hard downstream, just in case
Glenna had really got to the guy and brought out the incipient
vigilante all Scout leaders have. I didn't want to be entangled in
some midstream citizen's arrest.

Anyway, it was a relief to pass Little Hole and know that we
would see no more human beings until tomorrow noon when
we'd land at Brown's Park and the end of trail, so to speak.

By this time, Glenna was relaxed. She'd slowed her drinking
(and her speech and about everything else) and seemed to be in a
kind of happy low-grade coma, bare-breasted in the prow of our
ship like some laid-back figurehead. Toby had been doing well
with the triple teaser, taking three small trout, which we'd re-
leased. He handled the fish skillfully and made sure they returned to the river in good shape. I had had nothing on the
Coachman, but it was not the fly's fault. I had been casting in
time with "Ghost Riders in the Sky":

> Then cowboy change your ways today, (cast)
> Or with us you will ride, (cast)

and a fish would have been lucky to even catch a glimpse of its fur.

> A-trying to catch the Devil's herd (cast)
> Across these endless skies. (cast)

So there had been a little pressure, but now the long green shadows dragged themselves languorously across the clear water. It was late afternoon. We were past Little Hole. It was still a day. We dropped around two bends and were suddenly in the real wilderness, I could feel it, and I felt that little charge that the real places give me.

I had been here before, of course, many times with Lily. In the old days I thickened my favorite books in the bottom of rafts. Lily and I would leave the city Friday night, spend two days fishing scrupulously down the Green River, and drive back five hours from Brown's Park in the dark, arriving back in town in time for class with a giveaway suntan and the taste of adrenaline in my mouth. My books, *The Romantic Poets, The Victorian Poets, Eons of Literature,* were all swollen and twisted, their pages still wet as I sat in class, some of them singed where I had tried to dry them by the fire. Those trips with Lily were excruciatingly one-of-a-kind ventures—the world, planet and desire, fused and we had our way with it. I remember it all. I remember great poetry roasting cheerily by the fire in some lone canyon while Lily and I lay under the stars. Those beautiful books, I still have them.

MY LINE TRIPPED once hard and then I felt another sharp tug as my Royal Coachman snapped away in the mouth of what could only be a keeper. I set the hook and measured the tension. The trout ran. I gave him line evenly as the pressure rose, and he broke the surface, sixty yards behind us in the dark swelling river.

"Whoa!" Toby said.

"Watch your line, son," I told him. "It's the perfect time of night."

But even as I worked the trout stubbornly forward in the river, I was thinking about Lily. I'd never grown up and now fishing wasn't even the same.

THAT FISH WAS a keeper, a twenty-inch brown, and so were the two Toby took around the next bend as we passed under a monstrous spruce that leaned over the water. Four hills later we drifted into the narrows of Red Canyon. It was the deep middle of the everlasting summer twilight, and I cranked us over to the bank, booting the old wooden oars hard on the shallow rocky bottom. We came ashore halfway down the gorge so we could make camp. The rocky cliffs had gone coral in the purple sky and the river glowed green behind us as we unloaded the raft.

Glenna finally grabbed another T-shirt and struggled into it, something about being on land, I suppose, and said, "Oh, I gotta pee!" stepping stiffly up the sage-grown shore.

By the time she returned, the darkness had thickened, and Toby and I had a small driftwood fire going and were clearing an area for the tents. Glenna hugged herself against the fresh air coming along the river. She was a little pie-faced, but opened another wine cooler anyway. I fetched a flannel shirt from my kit and gave it to Toby, and then I settled down to the business of frying those fish. Since we were having cocktails, Glenna already reclining before the fire, I decided to take the extra time and make trout chowder.

Here's how: I retrieved my satchel of goodies, including a half pint of Old Kilroy, which is a good thing to sip if you're going to be cooking trout over an open fire while the night cools right down. In there too was a small tin of lard. You use about a table-spoon of lard for each trout, melting it in the frying pan and placing the trout in when the pan is warm, not hot. If the pan is too hot the fish will curl up and make it tricky cooking. If you don't have lard or butter, it's okay. Usually you don't. Without it you have to cook the trout slower, preventing it from sticking and burning in the pan by sprinkling in water and continuously prodding the fish around. Cut off the heads so the fish will fit into the pan. Then slice both onions you brought and let them start to cook around the fish. At the same time, fill your largest pot with water and put it on to boil. In Utah now you have to boil almost all your water. There is a good chance that someone has murdered his neighbor on instructions from god and thrown him in the creek just upstream from where you're mak-ing soup. Regardless, with a river that goes up and down eight inches twice a day, you have a lot of general cooties streaming right along. This is a good time to reach into the pack and peel open a couple cans of sardines in mustard sauce as appetizers, passing them around in the tin along with your Forest Master pocketknife, so the diners can spear a few and pass it on.

Okay, by the time your water boils, you will have fried the trout. When they've cooled, it will be easy to bone them, starting at the tail and lifting the skeleton from each. This will leave you with a platter of trout pieces. Add a package of leek soup mix (or vegetable soup mix) to the boiling water and then a package of tomato soup mix (or mushroom soup mix) and then the fried onion and some garlic powder. Then slip the trout morsels into the hot soup and cook the whole thing for another twenty min-utes while you drink whiskey and mind the fire. You want it to thicken up. Got any condensed milk? Add some powdered milk at least. Stir it occasionally. Pepper is good to add about now, too. When it reaches the consistency of gumbo, break out the bowls. Serve it with hunks of bread and maybe a slab of sharp cheddar cheese thrown across the top. It's a good dinner, easier to eat in the dark than a fried trout, and it stays hot longer and contains the foods that real raftsmen need. Bitter women who have been half naked all day drinking alcoholic beverages will eat trout chowder with gusto, not talking, just sopping it up, cheese, bread, and all. Be prepared to serve seconds.

AFTER HER SECOND bowl, her mouth still full of bread, Glenna said, "So, quite a day, eh, Jack?"

"Five good fish," I said, nodding at Toby. "Quite a day."

"No, I mean . . ."

"I know what you mean." I moved the pot of chowder off the hot ring of rocks around the fire and set it back on the sand, securing the lid. "We rescued a day from the jaws of the nudists."

The cooking had calmed me down, and I didn't want to get started with Glenna, especially since she was full of fructose and wine. Cooking, they say, uses a different part of your brain and I know which part, the good part, the part that's not wired all screwy with your twelve sorry versions of your personal history and the four jillion second guesses, backward glances, forehead-slapping embarrassments. The cooking part is clean as a cutting board and fitted accurately with close measurements and easy-to-follow instructions, which, you always know, are going to result in something edible and nourishing, over which you could make real conversation with someone, maybe someone you've known since college.

I ran the crust of my bread around the rim of my bowl and ate the last bite of chowder. It was good to be out of the raft, sitting on the ground by the fire, but I could feel there was going to be something before everybody hit the hay.

"Did you have fun, honey?" Glenna said to Toby. "Are you glad you came?"

"Yeah."

"Do you like old Jack here?"

"Aw, he's okay," I said and smiled at Toby.

"I've known Jack a long time."

"I know," Toby said.

"When did we meet, Jack?"

I broke some of the driftwood smaller in my hands and fed the fire back up. Toby had already filled the other kettle with water and I balanced it over the flames on three rocks.

"You want some coffee?" I said. I did not want to get started on the old world. We had met in the lobby of Wasatch Dorm my junior year. Glenna had come up to take my picture for the *Chronicle.* It was the Christmas of the White Album and Warren had decided I should run for class president. That afternoon she introduced me to her roommate, Lily Westerman.

"I don't think so," she said, showing me her bottle of Cabernet Lemon-Lime.

"Get your cup, Toby," I said. When I heard the boiling water cracking against the side of the kettle, I poured him a cup of hot chocolate. I fixed myself a cup of instant coffee and poured in a good lick of whiskey. Toby was standing to one side, a bright silhouette in the firelight.

"I think I'll go to bed," he said. "You guys are going to talk ancient history for a while. Dad was a big man on campus. This was during the war and he ran the paper, and Mom was the head photographer. You were all students, sort of, and Jack was going with Lily, who was Mom's roommate, and their house was like a club in the days when things mattered." He sipped his chocolate and toasted us. He knew how smart he was. "This was years ago."

"He's older than I am."

"Oh Jack," Glenna said, suddenly looking at me with eyes as cool and sober as the night. "Everybody's older than you are. That's always been your thing. It's kind of cute—about half." She must have seen me listening too hard, because she immediately waved her hand in front of her face and said, "Jack, ignore me. I'm drunk. That's what I do now: the drunk housewife."

"I don't believe her," I told Toby.

"I don't either," he said.

"Are you mad at your mother for embarrassing you today?" Glenna said. She was slumped against a rock opposite me. Her voice was now husky from too much sun, too much wine, too much lemon-lime.

"Mom," Toby said. "I'm tired. It was a pretty wild day. Good night." And he stepped down through the sage to his tent.

Halfway in the dark, he turned. "But Mom, you know what you said to that guy today, the naked guy?"

"Yeah?"

"It wasn't right. We weren't fishing with worms. The Green River is artificial flies and lures only."

"Okay, honey."

"But it was pretty funny, given the situation." He nodded once at us. "Good night." Toby disappeared in the dark.

"He's a good kid," I said.

She nodded the way people nod when their eyes are full and to speak would be to cry.

"It's okay," I said. "It was a good day." I looked at her

slumped on her suitcase, her hideous and beautiful suitcase, which seemed now simply something else trying to break my heart.

"Oh, Jack, I'm sorry. I'm so surprised by what I do, what anybody does. I guess I'm surprised any of it gets to me. If we'd just met, this would be a fun trip. If we were strangers. We're two people who know too much."

It was the worst kind of talk I'd ever heard around a campfire, and I wanted it to go away. "You're all right," I said. "You've got Toby." That, evidently, of course, was exactly the wrong thing to say and I sensed this from what I could hear in Glenna's breath. She was going to cry. The whole night seemed wrong.

I could hear a high wind in the junipers, but it was quiet in our camp. The campfire fluttered and sucked, settling down. I stared into the pink coals and watched them pulse white. I could see the bright edge of light on the cliff tip that meant in an hour the moon would break over the canyon. The other noise that came along sure as sure was the soft broken sucking of Glenna crying. She had her hand over her face in a gesture of real grief. I watched her for a moment, holding myself still. I was going to cry too, but I was going to try to wait for the moon. Finally, I went around the dying fire and sat by her.

"Hey, Glenna. Glenna," I whispered. "Did you bring any sunburn stuff?"

She shook her head no.

"Here," I said, handing her my tube of aloe. "Use this tonight. Okay? Use plenty. You surely scorched yourself." I could feel the heat from her sunburn as I sat by her.

"He's a good kid," she said.

"He's a great kid."

She shuddered and drew up in a series of short serious sobs. When that wave passed, I said, "What's the matter?" We were both speaking quietly.

She shook her head again, this time as if shaking something off. She said, "You're bright and young and you get married and you kind of always have money and then, bang-o, a thousand people later you're sunburned and eating fish in the big woods with an old friend and only the smallest part of it seems like the center of your life anymore. What's that about?"

I was beyond speaking now, lost in a widening orbit miles from our little fire. I knew she was going to go on. "There is a message, you know. From Lily. We saw her at the wedding." It had taken her all day but she had finally said Lily's name. "It's terrible, of course. We were eating cake and she came over to our table and said to tell Jack hello. So, *hello.*"

Now I had to hold her. Someone offers you that kind of last hello and whether you're camped by the river or not, you'll probably hug her, feeling her pulsing sunburn, and sit there thinking it all over for a little while. I had forever turned some corner in my life this month (twenty-two days), but I hadn't known it until Glenna said hello. Like it or not I was through being a boy.

So be it.

We sat there quietly and soon—over the steady low flash of the river—I could hear Toby, down in his tent, humming. It was something familiar, a sad ballad involving the devil's cattle and a long ride.

OXYGEN

In 1967, the year before the year that finally cracked the twentieth century once and for all, I had as my summer job delivering medical oxygen in Phoenix, Arizona. I was a sophomore at the University of Montana in Missoula, but my parents lived in Phoenix, and my father, as a welding engineer, used his contacts to get me a job at Ayr Oxygen Company. I started there doing what I called dumbbell maintenance, the kind of makework assigned to college kids. I cleared debris from the back lot, mainly crushed packing crates that had been discarded. That took a week, and on the last day, as I was raking, I put a nail through the bottom of my foot and had to go for a tetanus shot. Next, I whitewashed the front of the supply store and did such a good job that I began a month of painting my way around the ten-acre plant.

These were good days for me. I was nineteen years old and this was the hardest work I had ever done. The days were stunning, starting hot and growing insistently hotter. My first week two of the days had been 116. The heat was a pure physical thing, magnified by the steel and pavement of the plant, and in that first week, I learned what not to touch, where not to stand, and I found the powerhouse heat simply bracing. I lost some of the winter dormitory fat and could feel myself browning and getting into shape. It felt good to pull on my Levi's and work-shoes every morning (I'd tossed my tennies after the nail inci-dent), and not to have any papers due for any class.

Of course, during this time I was living at home, that is arriv-ing home from work sometime after six and then leaving for work sometime before seven the next morning. My parents and I had little use for each other. They were in their mid-forties then, an age I've since found out that can be oddly taxing, and besides they were in the middle of a huge career decision which would make their fortune and allow them to live the way they live now. I was nineteen, as I said, which in this country is not a real age at all, and effectively disqualifies a person for one year from meaningful relationship with any other human being.

I was having a hard ride through the one relationship I had begun during the school year. Her name was Linda Enright, a classmate, and we had made the mistake of sleeping together that spring, just once, but it wrecked absolutely everything. We were dreamy beforehand, the kind of couple who walked real close, bumping foreheads. We read each other's papers. I'm not making this up: we read poetry on the library lawn under a tree. I had met her in a huge section of Western Civilization taught by a young firebrand named Whisner, whose credo was "West-ern civilization is what you personally are doing." He'd defined it that way the first day of class and some wit had called out, "Then Western Civ is watching television." But Linda and I had taken it seriously, the way we took all things I guess, and we joined the Democratic Student Alliance and worked on a grape boycott, though it didn't seem that there were that many grapes to begin with in Montana that chilly spring.

And then one night in her dorm room we went ahead with it, squirming out of our clothes on her hard bed, and we did something for about a minute that changed everything. After that we weren't even the same people. She wasn't she and I wasn't I; we were two young citizens in the wrong country. I see now that a great deal of it was double-and triple-think, that is I thought she thought it was my fault and I thought that she might be right with that thought and I should be sorry and that I was sure she didn't know how sorry I was already, regret like a big burning house on the hill of my conscience, or something like that, and besides all I could think through all my sorrow and compunction was that I wanted it to happen again, soon. It was confusing. All I could remember from the incident itself was Linda stopping once and undoing my belt and saying, "Here, I'll get it."

The coolness of that practical phrase repeated in my mind after I'd said goodbye to Linda and she'd gone off to Boulder, where her summer job was working in her parents' cookie shop. I called her every Sunday from a pay phone at an Exxon Station on Indian School Road, and we'd fight and if you asked me what we fought about I couldn't tell you. We both felt misunderstood. I knew I was misunderstood, because I didn't understand myself. It was a glass booth, the standard phone booth, and at five in the afternoon on a late-June Sunday the sun torched the little space into a furnace. The steel tray was too hot to fry eggs on, you'd have ruined them. It gave me little burns along my forearms. I'd slump outside the door as far as the steel cord allowed, my skin running to chills in the heat, and we'd argue until the operator came on and then I'd dump eight dollars of quarters into the blistering mechanism and go home.

The radio that summer played a strange mix, "Little Red Riding Hood," by Sam the Sham and the Pharaohs, over and over, along with songs by the Animals, even "Sky Pilot." This was not great music and I knew it at the time, but it all set me on edge. After work I'd shower and throw myself on the couch in my parents' dark and cool living room and read and sleep and watch the late movies, making a list of the titles eventually in the one notebook I was keeping.

About the third week of June, I burned myself. I'd graduated to the paint sprayer and was coating the caustic towers in the oxygen plant. These were two narrow, four-story tanks that stood beside the metal building where the oxygen was bottled. The towers were full of a viscous caustic material that air was forced through to remove nitrogen and other elements until the gas that emerged was 99 percent oxygen. I was forty feet up an extension ladder reaching right and left to spray the tops of the tanks. Beneath me was the pump station that ran the operation, a nasty tangle of motors, belts, and valving. The mistake I made was to spray where the ladder arms met the curved surface of the tank, and as I reached out then to hit the last and farthest spot, I felt the ladder slide in the new paint. Involuntarily I threw my arms straight out in a terrific hug against the superheated steel. Oddly I didn't feel the burn at first nor did I drop the spray gun. I looked down at what seemed now to be the wicked machinery of my death. It certainly would have killed me to fall. After a moment, and that's the right span here, a moment, seconds or a minute, long enough to stablilize my heartbeat and sear my cheekbone and the inside of both elbows, I slid one foot down one rung and began to descend.

RON CARLSON

All the burns were the shapes of little footballs, the one on my
face a three-inch oval below my left eye, but after an hour with
the doctor that afternoon, I didn't miss a day of work. They've
all healed extraordinarily well, though they darken first if I'm
not careful with the sun. That summer I was proud of them, the
way I was proud not to have dropped the spray gun, and proud
of my growing strength, of the way I'd broken in my workshoes,
and proud in a strange way of my loneliness.

Where does loneliness live in the body? How many kinds of
loneliness are there? Mine was the loneliness of the college student in a summer job at once very far from and very close to the
thing he will become. I thought my parents were hopelessly
bourgeois, my girlfriend a separate race, my body a thing of
wonder and terror, and as I went through the days, my loneliness built. Where? In my heart? It didn't feel like my heart. The
loneliness in me was a dryness in the back of my mouth that
could not be slaked.

And what about lust, that thing that seemed to have defeated
me that spring, undermined my sense of the good boy I'd been,
and rinsed the sweetness from my relationship with Linda? Lust
felt related to the loneliness, part of the dry, bittersweet taste in
the lava-hot air. It went with me like an aura as I strode with my
three burns across the paved yard of Ayr Oxygen Company, and
I felt it as a certain tension in the tendons in my legs, behind the
knees, a tight, wired feeling that I knew to be sexual.

THE LOADING DOCK at Ayr Oxygen was a huge rotting concrete slab under an old corrugated-metal roof. Mr. Mac Bonner
ran the dock with two Hispanic guys that I got to know pretty
well, Victor and Jesse, and they kept the place clean and well organized in a kind of military way. Industrial and medical trucks

were always delivering full or empty cylinders or taking them away, and the tanks had to be lodged in neat squadrons which would not be in the way. Victor, who was the older man, taught me how to roll two cylinders at once while I walked, turning my hands on the caps and kick-turning the bottom of the rear one. As soon as I could do that, briskly moving two at a time, I was accepted there and fell into a week of work with them, loading and unloading trucks. They were quiet men who knew the code and didn't have to speak or call instructions when a truck backed in. I followed their lead.

The fascinating thing about Victor and Jesse was their lunches. I had been eating my lunch at a little patio behind the main building, alone, not talking to the five or six other employees who sat in groups at the other metal tables. I was the college kid and they were afraid of me because they knew my dad knew one of the bosses. It seemed there had been some trouble in previous summers, and so I just ate my tuna sandwiches and drank my iced tea while the sweat dried on my forehead and I pulled my wet T-shirt away from my shoulders. After I burned my face, people were friendlier, but then I was transferred up to the dock.

There were dozens of little alcoves amid the gas cylinders standing on the platform, and that is where I ate my lunches now. Victor and Jesse had milk crates and they found one for me and we'd sit out of sight up there from eleven-thirty to noon and eat. There was a certain uneasiness at first, as if they weren't sure if I should be joining them, but then Victor saw it was essentially a necessity. I wasn't going to get my lunch out of the old fridge on the dock and walk across the yard to eat with the supply people. On the dock was where I learned the meaning of *whitebread,* the way it's used now. I'd open my little bag, two tuna sandwiches and a baggie of chips, and then I'd watch the two men open their huge sacks of burritos and tacos and other items I didn't know the names of and which I've never seen since. I mean these were huge lunches that their wives had prepared, everything wrapped in white paper. No baggies. Jesse and I traded a little bit; he liked my mother's tuna. And I loved the big burritos. I was hungry and thirsty all the time and the hefty food seemed to make me well for a while. The burritos were packed with roast beef and onions and a fiery salsa rich with cilantro. During these lunches Victor would talk a little, telling me where to keep my gloves so that the drivers didn't pick them up, and where not to sit even on break.

"There was a kid here last year," he said. "Used to take his breaks right over there." He shook his head. "Right in front of the boss's window." It was cool and private sitting behind the walls of cylinders.

"He didn't stay," Jesse said. "The boss don't know you're on break."

"Come back in here," Victor said. "Or don't sit down." He smiled at me. I looked at Jesse and he shrugged and smiled too. They hadn't told the other kid where not to sit. Jesse handed me a burrito rolled in white paper. I was on the inside now; they'd taken me in.

That afternoon there was a big Linde Oxygen semi backed against the dock and we were rolling the hot cylinders off when I heard a crash. Jesse yelled from back in the dock and I saw his arms flash and Victor, who was in front of me, laid the two tanks he was rolling on the deck of the truck and jumped off the side and ran into the open yard. I saw the first rows of tanks start to tumble wildly, a chain reaction, a murderous thundering domino chase. As the cylinders fell off the dock, they cartwheeled into the air crazily, heavily tearing clods from the cement dock ledge and thudding into the tarry asphalt. A dozen plummeted onto somebody's Dodge rental car parked too close to the action. It was crushed. The noise was ponderous, painful, and the session continued through a minute until there was only one lone bank of brown nitrogen cylinders standing like a little jury on the back corner of the loading dock. The space looked strange that empty.

The yard was full of people standing back in a crescent. Then I saw Victor step forward and walk toward where I stood on the back of the semi. I still had my hands on the tanks.

He looked what? Scared, disgusted, and a little amused. "Mi amigo," he said, climbing back on the truck. "When they go like that, run away." He pointed back to where all of the employees of Ayr Oxygen Company were watching us. "Away, get it?"

"Yes, sir," I told him. "I do."

"Now you can park those," he said, tapping the cylinders in my hand. "And we'll go pick up all these others."

It took the rest of the day and still stands as the afternoon during which I lifted more weight than any other in this life. It felt a little funny setting the hundreds of cylinders back on the old pitted concrete. "They should repour this," I said to Victor as we were finishing.

"They should," he said. "But if accidents are going to follow you, a new floor won't help." I wondered if he meant that I'd been responsible for the catastrophe. I had rolled and parked a dozen tanks when things blew, but I never considered that it might have been my fault, one cockeyed tank left wobbling.

"I'm through with accidents," I told him. "Don't worry. This is my third. I'm finished."

The next day I was drafted to drive one of the two medical

oxygen trucks. One of the drivers had quit and our foreman, Mac Bonner, came out onto the dock in the morning and told me to see Nadine, who ran Medical, in her little office building out front. She was a large woman who had one speed: gruff. I was instructed in a three-minute speech to go get my commercial driver's license that afternoon and then stop by the uniform shop on Bethany Home Road and get two sets of the brown trousers and short-sleeved yellow shirts worn by the delivery people. On my way out I went by and got my lunch and saw Victor. "They want me to drive the truck. Dennis quit, I guess." This was new to me and I was still working it over in my mind; I mean, it seemed like good news.

"Dennis wouldn't last," Victor said. "We'll have the Ford loaded for you by nine."

The yellow shirt had a name oval over the heart pocket: David. And the brown pants had a crease that will outlast us all. It felt funny going to work in those clothes and when I came up to the loading dock after picking up the truck keys and my delivery list, Jesse and Victor came out of the forest of cylinders grinning. Jesse saluted. I was embarrassed and uneasy. "One of you guys take the truck," I said.

"No way, David." Victor stepped up and pulled my collar straight. "You look too good. Besides, this job needs a white guy." I looked helplessly at Jesse.

"Better you than me," he said. They had the truck loaded: two groups of ten medical blue cylinders chain-hitched into the front of the bed. They'd used the special cardboard sleeves we had for medical gas on all the tanks; these kept them from getting too beat up. These tanks were going to be in people's bedrooms. Inside each was the same oxygen as in the dinged-up green cylinders that the welding shops used.

I climbed in the truck and started it up. Victor had already told me about allowing a little more stopping time because of the load. "Here he comes, ladies," Jesse called. I could see his hand raised in the rearview mirror as I pulled onto McDowell and headed for Sun City.

At that time, Sun City was set alone in the desert, a weird theme park for retired white people, and from the beginning it gave me an eerie feeling. The streets were like toy streets, narrow and clean, running in huge circles. No cars, no garage doors open, and, of course, in the heat, no pedestrians. As I made my rounds, wheeling the hot blue tanks up the driveways and through the carpeted houses to the bedroom, uncoupling the old tank, connecting the new one, I felt peculiar. In the houses I was met by the wife or the husband and was escorted along the way. Whoever was sick was in the other room. It was all very proper. These people had come here from the midwest and the east. They had been doctors and professors and lawyers and wanted to live among their own kind. No one under twenty could reside in Sun City. When I'd made my six calls, I fled that town, heading east on old Bell Road, which in those days was miles and miles of desert and orchards, not two traffic lights all the way to Scottsdale Road.

Mr. Rensdale was the first of my customers I ever saw in bed. He lived in one of the many blocks of townhouses they were building in Scottsdale. These were compact units with two stories and a pool in the small private yard. All of Scottsdale shuddered under bulldozers that year; it was dust and construction delays, as the little town began to see the future. I rang the bell and was met by a young woman in a long silk shirt who saw me and said, "Oh, yeah. Come on in. Where's Dennis?"

I had the hot blue cylinder on the single dolly and pulled it up the step and into the dark, cool space. I had my pocket rag and wiped the wheels as soon as she shut the door. I could see her knees and they seemed to glow in the near dark. "I'm taking his route for a while," I said, standing up. I couldn't see her face, but she had a hand on one hip.

"Right," she said. "He got fired."

"I don't know about that," I said. I pointed down the hall. "Is it this way?"

"No, upstairs, first door on your right. He's awake, David." She said my name just the way you read names off shirts. Then she put her hand on my sleeve and said, "Who hit you?" My burn was still raw across my cheekbone.

"I got burned."

"Cute," she said. "They're going to love that back at . . . where?"

"University of Montana," I said.

"University of what?" she said. "There's a university there?" She cocked her head at me. I couldn't tell what she was wearing under that shirt. She smiled. "I'm kidding. I'm a snob, but I'm kidding. What year are you?"

"I'll be a junior," I said.

"I'm a senior at Penn," she said. I nodded, my mind whipping around for something clever. I didn't even know where Penn was.

"Great," I said. I started up the stairs.

"Yeah," she said, turning. "Great."

I drew the dolly up the carpeted stair carefully, my first second story, and entered the bedroom. It was dim in there, but I could see the other cylinder beside the bed and a man in the bed, awake. He was wearing pajamas, and immediately upon seeing me, he said, "Good. Open the blinds, will you?"

"Sure thing," I said, and I went around the bed and turned the miniblind wand. The Arizona day fell into the room. The young woman I'd spoken to walked out to the pool beneath me. She took her shirt off and hung it on one of the chairs. Her breasts were white in the sunlight. She set out her magazine and drink by one of the lounges and lay facedown in a shiny green bikini bottom. I only looked down for a second or less, but I could feel the image in my body.

While I was disconnecting the regulator from the old tank and setting up the new one, Mr. Rensdale introduced himself. He was a thin, handsome man with dark hair and mustache and he looked like about three or four of the actors I was seeing those nights in late movies after my parents went to bed. He wore an aspirator with the two small nostril tubes, which he removed while I changed tanks. I liked him immediately. "Yeah," he went on, "it's good you're going back to college. Though there's a future, believe me, in this stuff." He knocked the oxygen tank with his knuckle.

"What field are you in?" I asked him. He seemed so absolutely worldly there, his wry eyes and his East Coast accent, and he seemed old the way people did then, but I realize now he wasn't fifty.

"I, lad, am the owner of Rensdale Foundations, which my father founded," his whisper was rich with humor, "and which supplies me with more money than my fine daughters will ever be able to spend." He turned his head toward me. "We make ladies' undergarments, lots of them."

The dolly was loaded and I was ready to go. "Do you enjoy it? Has it been a good thing to do?"

"Oh, for chrissakes," he wheezed a kind of laugh, "give me a week on that, will you? I didn't know this was going to be an interview. Come after four and it's worth a martini to you, kid, and we'll do some career counseling."

"You all set?" I said as I moved to the door.

"Set," he whispered now, rearranging his aspirator. "Oh absolutely. Go get them, champ." He gave me a thin smile and I left. Letting myself out of the dark downstairs, I did an odd thing. I stood still in the house. I had talked to her right here. I saw her breasts again in the bright light. No one knew where I was.

Of course, Elizabeth Rensdale, seeing her at the pool that way, so casually naked, made me think of Linda and the fact that I had no idea of what was going on. I couldn't remember her body, though, that summer, I gave it some thought. It was worse not being a virgin, because I should have then had some information to fuel my struggles with loneliness. I had none, except Linda's face and her voice, *"Here, let me get it."*

From the truck I called Nadine, telling her I was finished with Scottsdale and was heading—on schedule—to Mesa. "Did you pick up Mr. Rensdale's walker? Over."

"No, ma'am. Over." We had to say "Over."

"Why not? You were supposed to. Over."

The heat in the early afternoon as I dropped through the river bottom and headed out to Mesa was gigantic, an enormous, unrelenting thing, and I took a kind of perverse pleasure from it. I could feel a heartbeat in my healing burns. My truck was not air-conditioned, a thing that wouldn't fly now, but then I drove with my arm out the window through the traffic of these desert towns. "I'm sorry. I didn't know. Should I go back? Over." I could see going back, surprising the girl. I wanted to see that girl again.

"It was on your sheet. Let it go this week. But let's read the sheet from now on. Over and out."

"Over and out," I said into the air, hanging up the handset.

Half the streets in Mesa were dirt, freshly bladed into the huge grid which now is paved wall to wall. I made several deliveries and ended up at the torn edge of the known world, the road just a track, a year maybe two at most from the first ripples of the growth which would swallow hundreds of miles of the desert. The house was an old block home gone to seed, the lawn dirt, the shrubs dead, the windows brown with dust and cobwebs. From the front yard I had a clear view of the Santan Mountains to the south. I was fairly sure I had a wrong address and that the property was abandoned. I knocked on the greasy door and after five minutes a stooped, red-haired old man answered. This was Gil, and I have no idea how old he was that summer, but it was as old as you get. Plus he was sick with the emphysema and liver disease. His skin, stretched tight and translucent on his gaunt body, was splattered with brown spots. On his hands several had been picked raw.

I didn't want to go into the house. This was the oddest call of my first day driving oxygen. There had been something regular about the rest of it, even the sanitized houses in Sun City, the upscale apartments in Scottsdale so new the paint hadn't dried, and the other houses I'd been to, magazines on a coffee table, a wife paying bills in the kitchen.

I pulled my dolly into the house, dark inside against the crushing daylight, and was hit by the roiling smell of dog hair and urine. I didn't kneel to wipe the wheels. "Right in here," the old man said, leading me back into the house toward a yellow light in the small kitchen, where I could hear a radio chattering.

He had his oxygen set up in the corner of the kitchen; it looked like he lived in the one room. There was a fur of fine red dust on everything, the range, the sink, except half the kitchen table where he had his things arranged, some brown vials of prescription medicine, two decks of cards, a pencil or two on a small pad, a warped issue of *Field & Stream,* a little red Bible, and a box of cough drops. In the middle of the table was a fancy painted plate, maybe a seascape, with a line of Oreos on it. I got busy changing out the tanks. You take the cardboard sleeve off, unhook the regulator, open the valve on the new tank for one second, blasting dust from the mouth, screw the regulator on it, open the pressure so it reads the same as you came, sleeve the old tank, load it up, and go. The new tank was always hot, too hot to touch from being in the sun, and it seemed wrong to leave such a hot thing in someone's bedroom. Nadine handled all the paperwork.

The cookies had scared me and I was trying to get out. Meanwhile the old man sat down at the kitchen table and started talking. "I'm Gil Benson," his speech began, "and I'm glad to see you, David. My lungs got burned in France in 1919 and it took them all these years to buckle." He spoke like so many of my customers in a hoarse whisper. "I've lived all over the world, including the three A's: Africa, Cairo, Australia, Burberry, and Alaska, Point Barrow. My favorite place was Montreal, Canada, because I was in love there and married the woman, had children. She's dead. My least favorite place is right here because of this. One of my closest friends was young Jack Kramer, the tennis player. That was many years ago. I've flown almost every plane made between the years 1938 and 1958. I don't fly anymore with all this." He indicated the oxygen equipment. "Sit down. Have a cookie."

I had my dolly ready. "I shouldn't, sir," I said. "I've got a schedule and better keep it."

"Grab that pitcher out of the fridge before you sit down. I made us some Kool-Aid. It's good."

I opened his refrigerator. Except for the Tupperware pitcher, it was empty. Nothing. I put the pitcher on the table. "I really have to go," I said. "I'll be late.

Gil lifted the container of Kool-Aid and raised it into a jittery hover above the two plastic glasses. There was going to be an accident. His hands were covered with purple scabs. I took the pitcher from him and filled the glasses.

"Sit down," he said. "I'm glad you're here, young fella." When I didn't move he said, "Really. Nadine said you were a good-looking kid." He smiled, and leaning on both hands, he sat hard into the kitchen chair. "This is your last stop today. Have a snack."

So began my visits with old Gil Benson. He was my last delivery every fourth day that summer, and as far as could tell, I was the only one to visit his wretched house. On one occasion I placed one of the Oreos he gave me on the corner of my chair as I left and it was right there next time when I returned. Our visits became little three-part dramas: my arrival and the bustle of intrusion; the snack and his monologue; his hysteria and weeping.

The first time he reached for my wrist across the table as I was standing to get up, it scared me. Things had been going fine. He'd told me stories in an urgent voice, one story spilling into the other without a seam, because he didn't want me to interrupt. I had *I've got to go* all over my face, but he wouldn't read it. He spoke as if placing each word in the record, as if I were going to write it all down when I got home. It always started with a story of long ago, an airplane, a homemade repair, an emergency landing, a special cargo, an odd coincidence, each part told with pride, but his voice would gradually change, slide into a kind of whine as he began an escalating series of complaints about his doctors, the insurance, his children—naming each of the four and relating their indifference, petty greed, or cruelty. I nodded through all of this: I've got to go. He leaned forward and picked at the back of his hands. When he tired after forty minutes, I'd slide my chair back and he'd grab my wrist. By then I could understand his children pushing him away and moving out of state. I wanted out. But I'd stand—while he still held me—and say, "That's interesting. Save some of these cookies for next time." And then I'd move to the door, hurrying the dolly, but never fast enough to escape. Crying softly and carrying his little walker bottle of oxygen, he'd see me to the door and then out into the numbing heat to the big white pickup. He'd continue his monologue while I chained the old tank in the back and while I climbed in the cab and started the engine and then while I'd start to pull away. I cannot describe how despicable I felt doing that, gradually moving away from old Gil on that dirt lane, and when I hit the corner and turned west for the shop, I tromped it: forty-five, fifty, fifty-five, raising a thick red dust train along what would someday be Chandler Boulevard.

Backing up to the loading dock late on those days with a truck of empties, I was full of animal happiness. The sun was at its worst, blasting the sides of everything, and I moved with the measured deliberation the full day had given me. My shirt was crusted with salt, but I wasn't sweating anymore. When I bent to the metal fountain beside the dock, gulping the water, I could feel it bloom on my back and chest and come out along my hairline. Jesse or Victor would help me sort the cylinders and reload for tomorrow, or many days, everyone would be gone already except Gene, the swing man, who'd talk to me while I finished up. His comments were always about overtime, which I'd be getting if I saw him, and what was I going to do with all my money.

What I was doing was banking it all, except for pocket money and the eight dollars I spent every Sunday calling Linda Enright. I became tight and fit, my burns finally scabbed up so that by mid-July I looked like a young boxer, and I tried not to think about anything.

A terrible thing happened in my phone correspondence with Linda. We stopped fighting. We'd talk about her family; the cookie business was taking off, but her father wouldn't let her take the car. He was stingy. I told her about my deliveries, the heat. She was looking forward to getting the fall bulletin. Was I going to major in geology as I'd planned? As I listened to us talk, I stood and wondered: Who are these people? The other me wanted to interrupt, to ask: Hey, didn't we have sex? I mean, was that sexual intercourse? Isn't the world a little different for you now? But I chatted with her. Neither one of us mentioned other people, that is boys she might have met, and I didn't mention Elizabeth Rensdale. I shifted my feet in the baking phone booth and chatted. When the operator came on, I was crazy with Linda's indifference, but unable to say anything but "Take care, I'll call."

Meanwhile the summer assumed a regularity that was nothing but comfort. I drove my routes: hospitals Mondays, rest homes Tuesdays, residences the rest of the week. Sun City, Scottsdale, Mesa. Nights I'd stay up and watch the old movies, keeping a list of titles and great lines. It was as much of a life of the mind as I wanted. Then it would be six a.m. and I'd have Sun City, Scottsdale, Mesa. I was hard and brown and lost in the routine.

I was used to sitting with Gil Benson and hearing his stories, pocketing the Oreos secretly to throw them from the truck later; I was used to the new-carpet smell of all the little homes in Sun City, everything clean, quiet, and polite; I was used to Elizabeth Rensdale showing me her white breasts, posturing by the pool whenever she knew I was upstairs with her father. By the end of July I had three or four of her little moves memorized, the way she rolled on her back, the way she kneaded them with oil sitting with her long legs on each side of the lounge chair. Driving the valley those long summer days, each window of the truck a furnace, listening to "Paperback Writer" and "Last Train to Clarksville," I delivered oxygen to the paralyzed and dying, and I felt so alive and on edge at every moment that I could have burst. I liked the truck, hopping up unloading the hot cylinders at each address and then driving to the next stop. I knew what I was doing and wanted no more.

Rain broke the summer. The second week in August I woke to the first clouds in ninety days. They massed and thickened and by the time I left Sun City, it had begun, a crashing downpour. It never rains lightly in the desert. The wipers on the truck were shot with sun rot and I had to stop and charge a set at a Chevron station on the Black Canyon Freeway and then continue east toward Scottsdale, crawling along in the stunned traffic, water everywhere over the highway.

I didn't want to be late at the Rensdales'. I liked the way Elizabeth looked at me when she let me in, and I liked looking at her naked by the pool. It didn't occur to me that today would be any different until I pulled my dolly toward their door through the warm rain. I was wiping down the tank in the covered entry when she opened the door and disappeared back into the dark house. I was wet and coming into the air-conditioned house ran a chill along my sides. The blue light of the television pulsed against the darkness. When my eyes adjusted and I started backing up the stairway with the new cylinder, I saw Elizabeth sitting on the couch in the den, her knees together up under her chin, watching me. She was looking right at me. I'd never seen her like this, and she'd never looked at me before.

"This is the worst summer of my entire life," she said.

"Sorry," I said, coming down a step. "What'd you say?"

"David! Is that you?" Mr. Rensdale called from his room. His voice was a ghost. I liked him very much and it had become clear over the summer that he was not going back to Pennsylvania. He'd lost weight. His face had become even more angular and his eyes had sunken. "David."

Elizabeth Rensdale whispered across the room to me, "I don't want to be here." She closed her eyes and rocked her head. I stood the cylinder on the dolly and went over to her. I didn't like leaving it there on the carpet. It wasn't what I wanted to do. She was sitting in her underpants on the couch. "He's dying," she said to me.

"Oh," I said, trying to make it simply a place holder, let her know that I'd heard her. It was the wrong thing, but anything, even silence, would have been wrong. She put her face in her hands and lay over on the couch. I dropped to a knee and, putting my hand on her shoulder, I said, "What can I do?"

This was the secret side that I suspected from this summer. Elizabeth Rensdale put her hand on mine and turned her face to mine so slowly that I felt my heart drop a gear, grinding now heavily uphill in my chest. The rain was like a pressure on the roof.

Mr. Rensdale called my name again. Elizabeth's face on mine so close and open made it possible for me to move my hand around her back and pull her to me. It was like I knew what I was doing. I didn't take my eyes from hers when she rolled onto her back and guided me onto her. It was different in every way from what I had imagined. The dark room closed around us. Her mouth came to mine and stayed there. This wasn't education; this was need. And later, when I felt her hand on my bare ass, her heels rolling in the back of my knees, I knew it was the mirror of my cradling her in both my arms as we rocked along the edge of the couch, moving it finally halfway across the den as I pushed into her. I wish I could get this right here, but there is no chance. We stayed together for a moment afterward and my eyes opened and focused. She was still looking at me, holding me, and her look was simply serious. Her father called, "David?" from upstairs again, and I realized he must have been calling steadily. Still, we were slow to move. I stood without embarrassment and dressed, tucking my shirt in. That we were intent, that we were still rapt, made me confident in a way I'd never been. I grabbed the dolly and ascended the stairs.

Mr. Rensdale lay white and twisted in the bed. He looked the way the dying look, his face parched and sunken, the mouth a dry orifice, his eyes little spots of water. I saw him acknowledge me with a withering look, more power than you'd think could rise from such a body. I felt it a cruel scolding, and I moved in the room deliberate with shame, avoiding his eyes. The rain drummed against the window in waves. After I had changed out the tanks, I turned to him and said, "There you go."

He rolled his hand in a little flip toward the bedtable and his glass of water. His chalky mouth was in the shape of an O, and I could hear him breathing, a thin rasp. Who knows what happened in me then, because I stood in the little bedroom with Mr. Rensdale and then I just rolled the dolly and the expired tank out and down the stairs. I didn't go to him; I didn't hand him the glass of water. I burned; who would ever know what I had done?

When I opened the door downstairs on the world of rain, Elizabeth came out of the dark again, naked, to stand a foot or two away. I took her not speaking as just part of the intensity I felt and the way she stood with her arms easy at her sides was the way I felt when I'd been naked before her. We looked at each other for a moment; the rain was already at my head and the dolly and tank was between us in the narrow entry, and then something happened that sealed the way I feel about myself even today. She came up and we met beside the tank and there was no question about the way we went for each other what was going on. I pushed by the oxygen equipment and followed her onto the entry tile, then a moment later turning in adjustment so that she could climb me, get her bare back off the floor.

So the last month of that summer I began seeing Elizabeth Rensdale every day. My weekly visits to the Rensdale townhouse continued, but then I started driving out to Scottsdale nights. I told my parents I was at the library, because I wanted it to sound like a lie and have them know it was a lie. I came in after midnight; the library closed at nine. After work I'd shower and put on a clean shirt, something without my name on it, and I'd call back from the door, "Going to the library." And I knew they knew I was up to something. It was like I wanted them to challenge me, to have it out.

Elizabeth and I were hardy and focused lovers. I relished the

way every night she'd meet my knock at the door and pull me
into the room and then, having touched, we didn't stop. Knowing we had two hours, we used every minute of it and we became experts at each other. For me these nights were the first
nights in my new life, I mean, I could tell then that there was no
going back, that I had changed my life forever and I could not
stop it. We never went out for a Coke, we never took a break for
a glass of water, we rarely spoke. There was admiration and curiosity in my touch and affection and gratitude in hers or so I assumed, and I was pleased, even proud, at the time that there was
so little need to speak. There was one time when I arrived a little
early when Mr. Rensdale's nurse was still there and Elizabeth
and I sat in the den watching television two feet apart on the
couch, and even then we didn't speak. I forget what program
was on, but Elizabeth asked me if it was okay, and I said fine
and that was all we said while we waited for the nurse to leave.

On the way home with my arm out in the hot night, I drove
like the young king of the desert. Looking into my car at a traffic
light, other drivers could read it all on my face and the way I
held my head cocked back. I was young those nights, but I was
getting over it.

Meanwhile Gil Benson had begun clinging to me worse than
ever and those prolonged visits were full of agony and desperation. As the Arizona monsoon season continued toward Labor
Day, the rains played hell with his old red road, and many times
I pulled up in the same tracks I'd left the week before. He
stopped putting cookies out, which at first I took as a good sign,
but then I realized that he now considered me so familiar that
cookies weren't necessary. A kind of terror had inhabited him,
and it was fed by the weather. Now most days I had to go west
to cross the flooded Salt River at the old Mill Avenue Bridge to

get to Mesa late and by the time I arrived, Gil would be on the porch, frantic. Not because of oxygen deprivation; he only needed to use the stuff nights. But I was his oxygen now, his only visitor, his only companion. I'd never had such a thing happen before and until it did I'd thought of myself as a compassionate person. I watched myself arrive at his terrible house and wheel the tank toward the door and I searched myself for compassion, the smallest shred of fellow feeling, kindness, affection, pity, but all I found was repulsion, impatience. I thought, surely I would be kind, but that was a joke, and I saw that compassion was a joke too along with fidelity and chastity and all the other notions I'd run over this summer. Words, I thought, big words. Give me the truck keys and a job to do, and the words can look out for themselves. I had no compassion for Gil Benson and that diminished over the summer. His scabby hands, the dried spittle in the ruined corners of his mouth, his crummy weeping in his stinking house. He always grabbed my wrist with both hands, and I shuffled back toward the truck. His voice, already a whisper, broke and he cried, his face a twisted ugliness which he wiped at with one hand while holding me with the other. I tried to nod and say, "You bet," and "That's too bad. I'll see you next week." But he wouldn't hear me any more than I was listening to him. His voice was so nakedly plaintive it embarrassed me. I wanted to push him down in the mud and weeds of his yard and drive away, but I never did that. What I finally did was worse.

The summer already felt nothing but old as Labor Day approached, the shadows in the afternoon gathering reach although the temperature was always 105. I could see it when I backed into the dock late every day, the banks of cylinders stark in the slanted sunlight, Victor and Jesse emerging from a world which was only black and white, sun and long shadow. The change gave me a feeling that I can only describe as anxiety. Birds flew overhead, three and four at a time, headed somewhere. There were huge banks of clouds in the sky every afternoon and after such a long season of blanched white heat, the shadows beside things seemed ominous. The cars and buildings and the massive tin roof of the loading dock were just things, but their shadows seemed like meanings. Summer, whatever it had meant, was ending. The fact that I would be going back to Montana and college in three weeks became tangible. It all felt complicated.

I sensed this all through a growing curtain of fatigue. The long hot days and the sharp extended nights with Elizabeth began to shave my energy. At first it took all the extra that I had being nineteen, and then I started to cut into the principal. I couldn't feel it mornings, which passed in a flurry, but afternoons, my back solid sweat against the seat of my truck, I felt it as a weight, my body going leaden as I drove the streets of Phoenix. Unloading became an absolute drag. I stopped jumping off the truck and started climbing down, stopped skipping up onto the dock, started walking, and every few minutes would put my hands on my waist and lean against something, the tailgate, the dock, a pillar.

"Oy, amigo," Jesse said one day late in August as I rested against the shipping desk in back of the dock. "Qué pasa?"

"Nothing but good things," I said. "How're you doing?"

He came closer and looked at my face, concerned. "You sick?"

"No, I'm great. Long day."

Victor appeared with the cargo sheet and handed me the clipboard to sign. He and Jesse exchanged glances. I looked up at them. Victor put his hand on my chin and let it drop. "Too

much tail." He was speaking to Jesse. "He got the truck and forgot what I told him. Remember?" He turned to me. "Remember? Watch what you're doing." Victor took the clipboard back
and tapped it against his leg. "When the tanks start to fall, run
the *other* way."

A moment later as I was getting ready to move the truck,
Jesse came out with his white lunch bag and gave me his leftover
burrito. It was as heavy as a book and I ate it like a lesson.

But it was a hot heedless summer and I showered every night
like some animal born of it, heedless and hot, and I pulled a cotton T-shirt over my ribs, combed my wet hair back, and without
a word to my parents, who were wary of me now it seemed,
drove to Scottsdale and buried myself in Elizabeth Rensdale.

The Sunday before Labor Day, I didn't call Linda Enright.
This had been my custom all these many weeks and now I was
breaking it. I rousted around the house, finally raking the yard,
sweeping the garage, and washing all three of the cars, before
rolling onto the couch in the den and watching some of the sad,
throwaway television of a summer Sunday. In each minute of
the day, Linda Enright, sitting in her father's home office, which
she'd described to me on the telephone many times (we always
talked about where we were; I told her about my phone booth,
the heat, graffiti, and passing traffic), was in my mind. I saw her
there in her green sweater by her father's rolltop. We always
talked about what we were wearing and she always said the
green sweater, saying it innocently as if wearing the sweater that
I'd helped pull over her head that night in her dorm room was
of little note, a coincidence, and not the most important thing
that she'd say in the whole eight-dollar call, and I'd say just
Levi's and a T-shirt, hoping she'd imagine the belt, the buckle,

the trouble it could all be in the dark. I saw her sitting still in the afternoon shadow, maybe writing some notes in her calendar or reading, and right over there, the telephone. I lay there in my stocking feet knowing I could get up and hit the phone booth in less than ten minutes and make that phone ring, have her reach for it, but I didn't. I stared at the television screen as if this was some kind of work and I had to do it. It was the most vivid that Linda had appeared before me the entire summer. Green sweater in the study through the endless day. I let her sit there until the last sunlight rocked through the den, broke, and disappeared. I hated the television, the couch, my body which would not move. I finally got up sometime after nine and went to bed.

Elizabeth Rensdale and I kept at it. Over the Labor Day weekend, I stayed with her overnight and we worked and reworked ourselves long past satiation. She was ravenous and my appetite for her was relentless. That was how I felt it all: relentless. Moments after coming hard into her, I would begin to palm her bare hip as if dreaming and then still dreaming begin to mouth her ear and her hand would play over my genitals lightly and then move in dreamily sorting me around in the dark and we would shift to begin again. I woke from a brief nap sometime after four in the morning with Elizabeth across me, a leg between mine, her face in my neck, and I felt a heaviness in my arm as I slid it down her tight back that reminded me of what Victor had said. I was tired in a way I'd never known. My blood stilled and I could feel a pressure running in my head like sand, and still my hand descended in the dark. There was no stopping. Soon I felt her hand, as I had every night for a month, and we labored toward dawn.

In the morning, Sunday, I didn't go home, but drove way down by Ayr Oxygen Company to the Roadrunner, the truck stop there on McDowell adjacent to the freeway. It was the first day I'd ever been sore and I walked carefully to the coffee shop. I sat alone at the counter, eating eggs and bacon and toast and coffee, feeling the night tick away in every sinew the way a car cools after a long drive. It was an effort to breathe and at times I had to stop and gulp some air, adjusting myself on the counter stool. Around me it was only truck drivers who had driven all night from Los Angeles, Sacramento, Albuquerque, Salt Lake City. There was only one woman in the place, a large woman in a white waitress dress who moved up and down the counter pouring coffee. When she poured mine, I looked up at her and our eyes locked, I mean her head tipped and her face registered something I'd never seen before. If I used such words I'd call it *horror,* but I don't. My old heart bucked. I thought of my Professor Whisner and Western Civ; if it was what I was personally doing, then it was in tough shape. The gravity of the moment between the waitress and myself was such that I was certain to my toenails I'd been seen: she knew all about me.

THAT WEEK I GAVE Nadine my notice, reminding her that I would be leaving in ten days, mid-September, to go back to school. "Well, sonnyboy, I hope we didn't work your wheels off." She leaned back, letting me know there was more to say.

"No, ma'am. It's been a good summer."

"We think so too," she said. "Come by and I'll have your last check cut early, so we don't have to mail it."

"Thanks, Nadine." I moved to the door; I had a full day of deliveries.

"Old Gil Benson is going to miss you, I think."

"I've met a lot of nice people," I said. I wanted to deflect this and get going.

"No," she said, "you've been good to him; it's important. Some of these old guys don't have much to look forward to. He's called several times. I might as well tell you. Mr. Ayr heard about it and is writing you a little bonus."

I stepped back toward her. "What?"

"Congratulations." She smiled. "Drive carefully."

I walked slowly out to the truck. I cinched the chain hitches in the back of my Ford, securing the cylinders, climbed wearily down to the asphalt, which was already baking at half past eight, and pulled myself into the driver's seat. In the rearview mirror I could see Victor and Jesse standing in the shadows. I was tired.

Some of my customers knew I was leaving and made kind remarks or shook my hand or had their wife hand me an envelope with a twenty in it. I smiled and nodded gratefully and then turned businesslike to the dolly and left. These were strange goodbyes, because there was no question that we would ever see each other again. It had been a summer and I had been their oxygen guy. But there was more: I was young and they were ill. I stood in the bedroom doors in Sun City and said, "Take care," and I moved to the truck and felt something, but I couldn't even today tell you what it was. The people who didn't know, who said, "See you next week, David," I didn't correct them. I said, "See you," and I left their homes too. It all had me on edge.

The last day of my job in the summer of 1967, I drove to work under a cloud cover as thick as twilight in winter and still massing. It began to rain early and I made the quick decision to beat the Salt River flooding by hitting Mesa first and Scottsdale in the afternoon. I had known for a week that I did not want Gil Benson to be my last call for the summer, and this rain, steady but light, gave me the excuse I wanted. Of course, it was nuts to think I could get out to Mesa before the crossings were flooded. And by now, mid-September, all the drivers were wise to the monsoon and headed for the Tempe Bridge as soon as they saw overcast. The traffic was colossal, and I crept in a huge column of cars east across the river, noting it was twice as bad coming back, everyone trying to get to Phoenix for the day. My heart was only heavy, not fearful or nervous, as I edged forward. What I am saying is that I had time to think about it all, this summer, myself, and it was a powerful stew. The radio wouldn't finish a song, "Young Girl," by Gary Puckett and the Union Gap or "Cherish," by the Association without interrupting with a traffic bulletin about crossing the river.

I imagined it raining in the hills of Boulder, Colorado, Linda Enright selling cookies in her apron in a shop with curtains, a Victorian tearoom, ten years ahead of itself as it turned out, her sturdy face with no expression telling she wasn't a virgin anymore, and that now she had been for thirty days betrayed. I thought, and this is the truth, I thought for the first time of what I was going to say *last* to Elizabeth Rensdale. I tried to imagine it, and my imagination failed. I tried again, I mean, I really tried to picture us there in the entry of the Scottsdale townhouse speaking to each other, which we had never, ever done. When I climbed from her bed the nights I'd gone to her, it was just that, climbing out, dressing, and crossing to the door. She didn't get up. This wasn't *Casablanca* or *High Noon,* or *Captain Blood,* which I had seen this summer, this was getting laid in a hot summer desert town by your father's oxygen deliveryman. There was no way to make it anything else, and it was too late as I moved through Tempe toward Mesa and Gil Benson's outpost to make it anything else. We were not going to hold each other's faces in our hands and whisper; we were not going to stand speechless in the shadows. I was going to try to get her pants off one more time and let her see me. That was it. I shifted in my truck seat and drove.

Even driving slowly, I fishtailed through the red clay along Gil's road. The rain had moved in for the day, persistent and even, and the temperature stalled and hovered at about a hundred. I thought Gil would be pleased to see me so soon in the day, because he was always glad to see me, welcomed me, but I surprised him this last Friday knocking at the door for five full minutes before he unlocked the door, looking scared. Though I had told him I would eventually be going back to college, I hadn't told him this was my last day. I didn't want any this or that, just the little visit and the drive away. I wanted to get to Scottsdale.

Shaken up like he was, things went differently. There was no chatter right off the bat, no sitting down at the table. He just moved things out of the way as I wheeled the oxygen in and changed tanks. He stood to one side, leaning against the counter. When I finished, he made no move to keep me there, so I just kept going. I wondered for a moment if he knew who I was or if he was just waking up. At the front door, I said, "There you go, good luck, Gil." His name quickened him and he came after me with short steps in his slippers.

"Well, yes," he started as always, "I wouldn't need this stuff at all if I'd stayed out of the war." And he was off and cranking. But when I went outside, he followed me into the rain. "Of course, I was strong as a horse and came back and got right with it. I mean, there wasn't any sue-the-government then. We were happy to be home. I was happy." He went on, the rain pelting us both. His slippers were all muddy.

"You gotta go," I told him. "It's wet out here." His wet skin in the flat light looked raw, the spots on his forehead brown and liquid; under his eyes the skin was purple. I'd let him get too close to the truck and he'd grabbed the door handle.

"I wasn't sick a day in my life," he said. "Not as a kid, not in the army. Ask my wife. When this came on," he patted his chest, "it came on bang! Just like that and here I am. Somewhere." His eyes, which had been looking everywhere past me, found mine and took hold. "This place!" He pointed at his ruined house. "This place!" I put my hand on his on the door handle and I knew that I wasn't going to be able to pry it off without breaking it.

Then there was a hitch in the rain, a gust of wet wind, and hail began to rattle through the yard, bouncing up from the mud, bouncing off the truck and our heads. "Let me take you back inside," I said. "Quick, Gil, let's get out of this weather." The hail stepped up a notch, a million mothballs ringing every surface. Gil Benson pulled the truck door open, and with surprising dexterity, he stepped up into the vehicle, sitting on all my paperwork. He wasn't going to budge and I hated pleading with him. I wouldn't do it. Now the hail had tripled, quadrupled, in a crashfest off the hood. I looked at Gil, shrunken and purple in the darkness of the cab; he looked like the victim of a fire.

"Well, at least we're dry in here, right?" I said. "We'll give it a minute." And that's what it took, about sixty seconds for the hail to abate, and after a couple of heavy curtains of the rain ripped across the hood as if they'd been thrown from somewhere, the world went silent and we could hear only the patter of the last faint drops. "Gil," I said. "I'm late. Let's go in." I looked at him but he did not look at me. "I've got to go." He sat still, his eyes timid, frightened, smug. It was an expression you use when you want someone to hit you.

I started the truck, hoping that would scare him, but he did not move. His eyes were still floating and it looked like he was grinning, but it wasn't a grin. I crammed the truck into gear and began to fishtail along the road. I didn't care for that second if we went off the road; the wheels roared mud. At the corner, we slid in the wet clay across the street and stopped.

I kicked my door open and jumped down into the red mud and went around the front of the truck. When I opened his door, he did not turn or look at me, which was fine with me. I lifted Gil like a bride and he clutched me, his wet face against my face. I carried him to the weedy corner lot. He was light and bony like an old bird and I was strong and I felt strong, but I could tell this was an insult the old man didn't need. When I stood him there he would not let go, his hands clasped around my neck, and I peeled his hands apart carefully, easily, and I folded them back toward him so he wouldn't snag me again. "Goodbye, Gil," I said. He was an old wet man alone in the desert. He did not acknowledge me.

I ran to the truck and eased ahead for traction and when I had traction, I floored it, throwing mud behind me like a rocket.

By the time I lined up for the Tempe Bridge, the sky was torn with blue vents. The Salt River was nothing but muscle, a brown torrent four feet over the river-bottom roadway. The traffic was thick. I merged and merged again and finally funneled onto the bridge and across toward Scottsdale. A ten-mile rainbow had emerged over the McDowell Mountains.

I radioed Nadine that the rain had slowed me up and I wouldn't make it back before five.

"No problem, sonnyboy," she said. "I'll leave your checks on my desk. Have you been to Scottsdale yet? Over."

"Just now," I said. "I'll hit the Rensdales' and on in. Over."

"Sonnyboy," she said. "Just pick up there. Mr. Rensdale died yesterday. Remember the portable unit, okay? And good luck at school. Stop in if you're down for Christmas break. Over."

I waited a minute to over and out to Nadine while the news subsided in me. I was on Scottsdale Road at Camelback, where I turned right. That corner will always be that radio call. "Copy. Over," I said.

I just drove. Now the sky was ripped apart the way I've learned only a western sky can be, the glacial cloud cover broken and the shreds gathering against the Superstition Mountains, the blue air a color you don't see twice a summer in the desert, icy and clear, no dust or smoke. All the construction crews in Scottsdale had given it up and the bright lumber on the sites sat dripping in the afternoon sun. They had taken the day off from changing this place.

In front of the Rensdales' townhouse I felt odd going to the door with the empty dolly. I rang the bell, and after a moment Elizabeth appeared. She was barefoot in jeans and a T-shirt, and she just looked at me. "I'm sorry about your father," I said. "This is tough." She stared at me and I held the gaze. "I mean it. I'm sorry."

She drifted back into the house. It felt for the first time strange and cumbersome to be in the dark little townhouse. She had the air conditioning cranked way up so that I could feel the edge of a chill on my arms and neck as I pulled the dolly up the stairs to Mr. Rensdale's room. It had been taken apart a little bit, the bed stripped, our gear all standing in the corner. With Mr. Rensdale gone you could see what the room was, just a little box in the desert. Looking out the window over the pool and the two dozen tiled roofs before the edge of the Indian reservation and the sage and creosote bushes, it seemed clearly someplace to come and die. The mountains, now all rinsed by rain, were red and purple, a pretty lie.

"I'm going back Friday." Elizabeth had come into the room. "I guess I'll go back to school."

"Good," I said. "Good idea." I didn't know what I was saying. The space in my heart about returning to school was nothing but dread.

"They're going to bury him tomorrow." She sat on the bed. "Out here somewhere."

I started to say something about that, but she pointed at me. "Don't come. Just do what you do, but don't come to the funeral. You don't have to."

"I want to," I said. Her tone had hurt, made me mad.

"My mother and sister will be here tonight," she said.

"I want to," I said. I walked to the bed and put my hands on her shoulders.

"Don't."

I bent and looked into her face.

"Don't."

I went to pull her toward me to kiss her and she leaned away sharply. "Don't, David." But I followed her over onto the bed, and though she squirmed, tight as a knot, I held her beside me, adjusting her, drawing her back against me. We'd struggled in every manner, but not this. Her arms were tight cords and it took more strength than I'd ever used to pin them both against her chest while I opened my mouth on her neck and ran my other hand flat inside the front of her pants. I reached deep and she drew a sharp breath and stretched her legs out along mine, bumping at my ankles with her heels. Then she gave way and I knew I could let go of her arms. We lay still that way, nothing moving but my finger. She rocked her head back.

About a minute later she said, "What are you doing?"

"It's okay," I said.

Then she put her hand on my wrist, stopping it. "Don't," she said. "What are you doing?"

"Elizabeth," I said, kissing at her nape. "This is what we do. Don't you like it?"

She rose to an elbow and looked at me, her face rock-hard, unfamiliar. "This is what we do?" Our eyes were locked. "Is this what you came for?" She lay back and thumbed off her pants until she was naked from the waist down. "Is it?"

"Yes," I said. It was the truth and there was pleasure in saying it.

"Then go ahead. Here." She moved to the edge of the bed, a clear display. The moment had fused and I held her look and I felt seen. I felt known. I stood and undid my belt and went at her, the whole time neither of us changing expression, eyes open, though I studied her as I moved looking for a signal of the old ways, the pleasure, a lowered eyelid, the opening mouth, but none came. Her mouth was open but as a challenge to me, and her fists gripped the mattress but simply so she didn't give ground. She didn't move when I pulled away, just lay there looking at me. I remember it as the moment in this life when I was farthest from any of my feelings. I gathered the empty cylinder and the portable gear with the strangest thought: *It's going to take me twenty years to figure out who I am now.*

I could feel Elizabeth Rensdale's hatred, as I would feel it dozens of times a season for many years. It's a kind of dread for me that has become a rudder and kept me out of other troubles. That next year at school, I used it to treat Linda Enright correctly, as a gentleman, and keep my distance, though I came to know I was in love with her and had been all along. I had the

chance to win her back and I did not take it. We worked together several times with the Democratic Student Alliance, and
it is public record that our organization brought Robert
Kennedy to the Houck Center on campus that March. Professor
Whisner introduced him that night, and at the reception I shook
Robert Kennedy's hand. It felt, for one beat, like Western Civilization.

THAT BAD DAY at the Rensdales' I descended the stair, carefully, not looking back, and I let myself out of the townhouse for
the last time. The mud on the truck had dried in brown fans
along the sides and rear. The late afternoon in Scottsdale had
been scrubbed and hung out to dry, the air glassy and quick,
the color of everything distinct, and the brown folds of the Mc-
Dowell Mountains magnified and looming. It was fresh, the
temperature had dropped twenty degrees, and the elongated
shadows of the short new imported palms along the street
printed themselves eerily in the wet lawns. Today those trees are
as tall as those weird shadows. I just wanted to close this whole
show down.

But as I drove through Scottsdale, block by block, west
toward Camelback Mountain, I was torn by a nagging thought
of Gil Benson. I shouldn't have left him out there. At a dead end
by the Indian School canal I stopped and turned off the truck.
The grapefruit grove there was being bladed under. Summer
was over; I was supposed to be happy.

Back at Ayr Oxygen, I told Gene, the swing man, to forget
it and I unloaded the truck myself. It was the one good hour
of that day, one hour of straight work, lifting and rolling my
empties into the ranks at the far end of the old structure. Victor
and Jesse would find them tomorrow. They would be the last

gas cylinders I would ever handle. I locked the truck and walked to the office in my worn-out workshoes. I found two envelopes on Nadine's desk: my check and the bonus check. It was two hundred and fifty dollars. I put them in my pocket and left my keys, pulling the door locked behind me.

I left for my junior year of college at Missoula three days later. The evening before my flight, my parents took me to dinner at a steakhouse on a mesa, a western place where they cut your tie off if you wear one. The barn-plank walls were covered with the clipped ends of ties. It was a good dinner, hearty, the baked potatoes big as melons and the charred edges of the steaks dropping off the plates. My parents were giddy, ebullient, because their business plans which had so consumed them were looking good. Every loan they'd positioned was ready; the world was right. They were proud of me, they said, working hard like this all summer away from my friends. I was changing, they said, and they could tell it was for the better.

After dinner we went back to the house and had a drink on the back terrace, which was a new thing in our lives. I didn't drink very much and I had never had a drink with my parents. My father made a toast to my success at school and then my mother made a toast to my success at school and to my success with Linda Enright, and she smiled at me, a little friendly joke, and she clinked her scotch and water against my bottle of Bud and tossed it back. "I'm serious," she said. Then she stood and threw her glass out back and we heard it shatter against the stucco wall. A moment later she hugged me and she and my father went in to bed.

I cupped my car keys and went outside. I drove the dark streets. The radio played a steady rotation of exactly the same songs heard today on every fifty-thousand-watt station in this country; every fifth song was the Supremes. I knew where I was going. Beyond the bright rough edge of the lights of Mesa I drove until the pavement ended, and then I dropped onto the red clay roads and found Gil Benson's house. It was as dark as some final place, and there was no disturbance in the dust on the front walk or in the network of spiderwebs inside the broken storm door. I knocked and called for minutes. Out back, I kicked through the debris and weeds until I found one of the back bedroom windows unlocked and I slid it open and climbed inside. In the stale heat, I knew immediately that the house was abandoned. I called Gil's name and picked my way carefully to the hall. The lights did not work, and in the kitchen when I opened the fridge, the light was out and the humid stench hit me and I closed the door. I wasn't scared, but I was something else. Standing in that dark room where I had palmed old Oreos all summer long, I now had proof, hard proof, that I had lost Gil Benson. He hadn't made it back and I couldn't wish him back.

Outside, the cooked air filled my lungs and the bright dish of Phoenix glittered to the west. I drove toward it carefully. Nothing had cooled down. In every direction the desert was being torn up, and I let the raw night rip through the open car window. At home my suitcases were packed. Some big thing was closing down in me; I'd spent the summer as someone else, someone I knew I didn't care for and I would be glad when he left town. We would see each other from time to time, but I also knew he was no friend of mine. I eased along the empty roadways trying simply to gather what was left, to think, but it was like trying to fold a big blanket alone. I kept having to start over.

LARSTAN's THE BLACK BOOK™ ON PERSONAL FINANCE

Todd Bauerle, Cheryl Burbano, Paul Capuzziello, Brian Evans,
Avery Kanfer, Luke R. Reinhard, Scott B. Rose, Stan Sklenar,
Stuart J. Spivak, Lori Watt, Greg Werlinich

Published by:
Larstan Publishing Inc.
10604 Outpost Dr., N. Potomac, MD 20878
301-637-4591
orders@blackbookfinance.com   www.larstan.com

© 2005, Larstan Publishing Inc. All rights reserved.
Reproduction of any portion of this book is permitted for individual use if credit is given to Larstan's The Black Book™ on Personal Finance. Systematic or multiple reproduction or distribution of any part of this book or inclusion of material in publications for sale is permitted only with prior written permission of Larstan Publishing, Inc.

The Black Book on is a registered trademark of Larstan Publishing, Inc.

PRINTED IN THE UNITED STATES OF AMERICA

Design by Rob Hudgins & 5050Design.com

This book is designed to provide accurate and authoritative information on the topic of personal finance. It is sold with the understanding that neither the Authors nor the Publisher are engaged in rendering any professional or consulting services by publishing this book. As each individual situation is unique, questions relevant to personal finance should be addressed to an appropriate professional to ensure that the situation has been evaluated carefully and appropriately. The Authors and Publisher specifically disclaim any liability, loss or risk which is incurred as a consequence, directly or indirectly, of the use and application of any of the contents of this work.

ISBN, Print Edition 0-9764266-6-8
First Edition

LARSTAN'S THE BLACK BOOK ON

PERSONAL FINANCE

- TODD BAUERLE
- CHERYL BURBANO
- PAUL CAPUZZIELLO
- BRIAN EVANS
- AVERY KANFER
- LUKE R. REINHARD

- SCOTT B. ROSE
- STAN SKLENAR
- STUART J. SPIVAK
- LORI WATT
- GREG WERLINICH

LARSTAN
PUBLISHING

WASHINGTON D.C. ■ PHILADELPHIA

TABLE OF CONTENTS

6 THE HIDDEN POWER OF LIFE INSURANCE.............................153
By Stuart J. Spivak

Shrewd investors understand life insurance can play a unique role in pre-serving and protecting their wealth. Learn advanced life insurance tactics for maximum tax, retirement and investment benefits.

7 LIFE INSURANCE PREMIUM FINANCING 177
By Scott B. Rose

Smart investors are leveraging their portfolios through life insurance premium financing, a little-known method for "borrowing" your premiums to achieve your investment goals.

8 FINANCIAL PLANNING FOR WOMEN.............................211
By Cheryl Burbano

Far too many women have relinquished control of their financial destinies to the men in their lives, leaving them unprepared for major life events. Learn a step-by-step process for becoming the chief financial officer of your family's finances.

9 THE ENTREPRENEUR'S WAY TO WEALTH BUILDING.............................235
By Luke R. Reinhard

Your small business can provide strong tax, retirement and income benefits when integrated with your personal finances, but only with proper planning and management.

10 MACRO STRATEGIC PLANNING® 267
By Paul Capuzziello

You could follow your financial roadmap flawlessly, but what if it's the wrong map? This proprietary process will help you identify, prioritize and, most importantly, align your personal goals and your financial plan.

11 MANIFESTING WEALTH 293
By Avery Kanfer

Every person who's ever become rich has deliberately (or accidentally) employed a set of universal wealth creation laws. Like gravity, these laws work all the time and give those who act on them the ability to create abundant wealth.

ACKNOWLEDGEMENTS

Without a doubt, the quality of this book is a testament to its excellent authors. As with each book in **Larstan's The Black Book Series™**, this book was co-authored by professional practitioners with active practices — emphasis on active! Fitting a demanding writing schedule into their very busy professional lives was no easy feat, but they all got the job done, on time (with, er, one or two exceptions!) and in tip-top shape (zero exceptions!).

The 11 authors for **Larstan's The Black Book™ on Personal Finance** were chosen not only for their financial experience and credentials, but also, most importantly, their ability and passion for sharing their expertise with their clients — and our readers. Also, we hoped for, sought and, actually lucked out and found, authors with a good sense of humor and a good amount of patience — both necessary components of any publishing endeavor, but especially so for a book.

As I told many of our authors before they agreed to work on the project: "Publishing a book is like giving birth — except not as easy." As a non-female, this, of course, was pure speculation on my part, designed to be mildly amusing. As the process continued, though, our authors and the entire Larstan team came to see the truth of this statement — and to blame me whenever anything went wrong. But that is, well, okay. I can — and should — take the heat; as anyone will tell you, it was my fault!

Over the past year, I have learned from and laughed with each of our authors as we've endeavored to "get it all down on paper." The Black Book™ on Personal Finance had 11 babies (i.e., Chapters) to deliver, with their parents (i.e., Authors) scattered all across the United States — or the Lower 48, at least. All our authors were, and continue to be, extremely busy with their financial planning practices. Getting their chapters researched, written, polished and fact-checked took many a late night and many a weekend. Their desire to share their professional expertise and experience has resulted in the book that you are now reading. As a group,

I'd like to congratulate them on their hard work, their ideas and their contribution to the literature on personal finance. Individually, I'd like to tell them what I really think!

To **Cheryl Burbano**, of Tampa, I am grateful for your passion — and clearly defined action plan — for helping women better their financial fortunes.

Also from Florida, my hat's off to **Todd Bauerle** for your investing wisdom, sharp wit and strong desire to share your insights with our readers.

In the Northeast, I'd like to thank New York's own **Greg Werlinich**. A regular guest analyst on FoxNews, your investing expertise — and writing ability — impressed us throughout.

To fellow New Yorker, **Scott B. Rose**, my thanks for your innovative strategies on life insurance premium financing — and for hitting every deadline.

Up north, in Rhode Island, I'd like to thank **Paul Capuzziello** for your clear vision and actionable ideas about financial plans and goal-setting.

Representing the Midwest, **Luke Reinhard**, of Minnesota, I greatly appreciate your bringing the small business perspective to the book through compelling anecdotes and case histories.

To **Stuart Spivak**, who splits his time between Arizona and Pennsylvania, my thanks for your delivering the goods on life insurance — on deadline and right on the money.

In Washington State, I want to thank **Brian Evans**, for your easygoing personality and sharp intellect as well as your innovative — and lively — approach to asset allocation.

Also from the Northwest, in Oregon, my thanks to **Lori Watt** for your excellent chapter on estate planning — and for being so accessible and a real pleasure to work with.

To **Stan Sklenar**, a native Czechoslovakian who found his way to great success as an investment manager in San Francisco, I thank you for your incredible patience, vision and determination to get every detail exactly right.

And, closer to home, **Avery Kanfer**, less than 10 minutes away from Larstan headquarters in Potomac, Md., thanks for your positive energy and innovative approach to helping clients, and our readers, adopt the necessary mindset for wealth creation.

The Black Book™ on Personal Finance would not have been possible without the commitment and publishing expertise of the many people associated with it. Our editorial team benefited from the contributions of **Lane Cooper, Christine Avallone** and **Tom Moore**. Larstan's production manager, **Sherrie Saldana**, I thank for your patience, dedication and hard work. To **Eric Green**, publisher of **The Black Book™ on Corporate Security**, congratulations on putting together a fabulous book that we're all proud of. Your energy and ability to make things happen are an inspiration for all of us. And to **Jennifer O'Grady**, I thank for your friendship, your organizational acumen, and for being the publisher of what I know will be the next great book in the series, **The Black Book™ on Supply Chain**.

Larstan's creative director, **Rob Hudgins**, has proven to be an invaluable contributor — and a creative force — behind the book's look and feel. Whether it's brainstorming ideas, or inputting corrections late on a Friday night, we can always count on him to be calm, cool and collected — even when others, er, are not! My thanks, Rob, for your talent and professionalism — and making me laugh at least five times every day.

In publishing this book, I've had the rare pleasure of working with my former (and continuing!) mentor and close friend, **John Persinos**. Back when John hired me as a reporter at a political magazine 10 years ago, I doubt either of us thought we'd still be in the trenches together. Hiring John as editorial director of this book was one of the happiest, proudest and, well, luckiest moments in my career. My sincere thanks, John, for bringing me into the publishing business (and making me want to stay) when I didn't know nobody, or nothing — and for bringing your editorial wit, style and energy

(**The Persinos Treatment**™) to the book, **The Black Book Series**™, Larstan, our clients...and back to me, personally, in my day-to-day work life.

Most importantly, I want to thank the true visionary behind the book, **Larry Genkin**. When this book was merely one of his (many!) ideas, Larry invited me, then a freelance writer with way too much "down" time, to The Silver Diner in Rockville, Md. Three hours and two notepads full of scribbling later, an idea was born: The Black Book Series™, a series of advanced insider guides on business topics. I came out of that lunch excited, invigorated and with a new direction for my career. Larry has proven to be a tremendous business mentor, collaborator and boss, besides being a great friend. Thank you, Larry, for never wavering in your belief in the project — or me, personally or professionally.

Lastly, I want to thank my mother, **Coleen Wiebner**. She's an incredible woman, a great friend, and a role model who, along with my late father, **Howard Wiebner**, instilled in me a love of learning, a love of books, and the self-confidence to take chances and pursue my dreams. My work on this book, and all the books that are to come, is a testament to their love, self-sacrifice and support for me, through good times and bad. Thank you.

Mike Wiebner
Publisher, The Black Book™ on Personal Finance

THE TEAM

LARSTAN
PUBLISHING

Editorial Director | John Persinos
Publisher, The Black Book™ on Personal Finance | Mike Wiebner
Editors | Lane Cooper, Christine Avallone and Tom Moore
Creative Director | Rob Hudgins
Production Manager | Sherrie Saldana

COO | Stan Genkin
CEO | Larry Genkin

DEDICATIONS

I dedicate this to my supportive wife and children for always standing by me. Many thanks to the Bauerle Financial staff for all their assistance with this project. Above all, thanks to God for blessing me with the support, words and opportunity. —*Todd Bauerle*

This chapter is dedicated first and foremost to my spouse, Juan — my rock and support for over 34 years, and to my family, Philip, Valentina, and granddaughter, Anika — the joys of my life. A special note of gratitude to Ian Staples and Mike Rearden for their support and advocacy through the legal review process; a sincere note of appreciation to Bobbie Carlino for her assistance with all the re-writes; and finally, a special dedication to all my clients who allow me through their trust to assist them in achieving their financial planning goals. — *Cheryl Burbano*

First, I would like to thank my friend and mentor Bruce Wright for his help with this book, and for teaching me Macro Strategic Planning®. I would also like to thank my wife Tracey for her love, support and encouragement that never fails. Also, my father, Tom, who without his support over the years, I would not be the person I am today. Finally, to all the clients, friends, and professionals that I have learned so much from — I thank you for teaching me and letting me be a part of your lives. — *Paul T. Capuzziello*

I want to thank my wife, Tracie, and my sons, Samuel and Benjamin, for their sacrifices and support. I'd also like to thank my parents, Al and Naomi, for being such wonderful mentors. — *Brian Evans*

I dedicate this to my wife, Moselle, for her support and understanding of my beliefs about life. — *Avery Kanfer*

I would like to thank Joyce B. Johnson, my wife and partner, whose understanding and support has allowed me to prosper and flourish. I would like to express my gratitude to my colleagues at Reinhard &

Associates who have lent their critical eyes and encouragement, and especially, Ben Daigle, for his tolerance and doggedness. And of course, a special thanks to my clients for their trust and friendship and Larstan Publishing for their tenacity. — *Luke R. Reinhard*

I would like to dedicate this to my wife Jennifer and my children, Jacob and Maya. Without their unconditional love and support, I could not achieve my greatest success...my family. Additional thanks to my colleagues at ECG and PCG for the lessons learned that inspired me to achieve more than anyone believed possible. — *Scott B. Rose*

I'd like to dedicate my chapter to my children: David and Patrik. I also want to thank the other professionals I have worked with in my field, who have provided me with invaluable support and guidance. — *Stan Sklenar*

To my father, Richard Spivak, who unfortunately I never got the opportunity to work with in this wonderful, noble and rewarding business. Thank you, Dad, for instilling in me the principles with which I conduct my business and personal life: honesty, integrity, pride and conviction. — *Stuart J. Spivak*

This chapter is dedicated to the entire staff of Investors Advisory Group. Their commitment to our clients, our firm, and to me continues to be an inspiration in all I do. I especially want to thank my family — Dick & Tony, Mom & Dad — for always believing in me and encouraging me to accomplish more than I ever dreamed possible. Also, a special thanks to Susan Kuhlenbeck for her encouragement and support over the years — keep pedaling! — *Lori Watt*

I would like to thank my mother, Lucille Werlinich, for her love and support of not only this project, but of everything that I do in life. I would also like to acknowledge everyone at Larstan publishing for all of their hard work in making this book the very best that it could be. Finally, I'd like to express my love for the three most important people in my life, my beautiful children — Nola, Lily and Ezra. — *Greg Werlinich*

[1]

MARKET MYTHS EXPOSED

When it comes to investing, the conventional wisdom is usually right — about as often as it is wrong. Most investors, besieged by contradictory advice from self-anointed experts, find themselves dazed and confused. Learn the specific tactics and strategies you should know — and the market myths you should avoid — to be a better investor, across all market conditions.

"OFTEN, THE LESS THERE IS TO JUSTIFY A TRADITIONAL CUSTOM, THE HARDER IT IS TO GET RID OF IT."

- Mark Twain

by TODD BAUERLE

Too many investors subscribe to rules and methods that are either outdated or never made much sense from the start. A bit of received "wisdom" gains currency through repetition. Over time, this wisdom becomes enshrined as myth. The most profitable investors learn how to pinpoint market myths and go against the crowd.

The recent stock market crash has challenged virtually every general rule of thumb and long-standing tactic for successful investing. In fact, many hard-and-fast market strategies trusted for decades can be considered myths now, due to the market fallout over the past three years.

This chapter is about debunking investment myths, so you can make investment decisions based not on the herd mentality, but on clear-eyed, rational analysis. Never be swayed by traditional customs unless those customs hold up to reality. When left unchallenged, the conventional wisdom about the market contributes greatly to investor dissatisfaction. These myths anesthetize investors' anxiety and delude them into thinking they've eliminated risk. Wall Street and financial academics use myths to confuse investors into believing they have the magic remedy. When investors feel pain, investment professionals try to sell them a cure-all for whatever ails them.

Unfortunately, regardless of how well planned any investment strategy is, it is impossible — repeat impossible — to protect a portfolio from an unknowable number of variables. Events like those of the past three years, although painful, can provide instruction for those seeking to discern good advice from the bad. Just looking at what worked and what didn't is a good way to start. In the words of the great Oracle of Omaha, Warren Buffet: "It's just not necessary to do extraordinary things to produce extraordinary results."

In this chapter, I will apply a cold, contrarian eye to several market myths, and debunk them one by one. What they all have in common is the aim to provide a single, infallible solution to every possible variable. It's so tempting, though, to provide the perfect "one size-fits-all" solution to an increasingly eager (and gullible) investing public.

Here are four of the most egregious myths out there now:
❶ Diversification is the perfect plan.
❷ You can and should manage your own money.
❸ You can't time the market.
❹ Mutual funds are perfect for the individual investor.

There's a lot of conflicting advice out there, and the best way to sort through the "white noise" is to first conduct a sincere self-evaluation of who you really are as an investor. First answer these questions about yourself: Are you a younger, growth investor who can afford to take some risks? Are you nearing retirement and need to be more conservative? Are you saving for a specific goal such as college tuition or buying a home?

When you understand your investing preferences, you are better-equipped to discern fact from fiction as it pertains to your unique situation and investing style. By emulating the strategies that I present in this chapter, you can better position your portfolio in the event of a long-term bear market.

Consider what I like to call my AH-HAH! moment. In July 2002, as the market plummeted lower and lower, my research analyst and I sequestered ourselves in a conference room for three days. The result was a new investment process that provides for tactical adjustments to a portfolio based on macroeconomic, geopolitical, interest rates, global currency, market valuation, and many other key factors that, when analyzed, are likely to affect portfolio performance to a significant degree. The result led us in late 2003 to short the market and buy un-hedged institutional international bond funds; non-public, non-leveraged real estate investments; individual church bonds; and small-cap value international stock funds. All of these actions created portfolio returns of 8-12%, with a Beta of less than 0.25% and an expense ratio of 0.5% or less.

Risk can be better managed by taking a more active approach to asset allocation. Most investors want to obtain the returns they need with the least possible risk. Passive indexing can often lead to excess risks; I'll show you how to achieve success by being a proactive investor. But first, let's discard some intellectual baggage that could be holding you back.

Insider Notes: Risk can be better managed by taking a more active approach to asset allocation. Passive indexing can often lead to excess risks.

MYTH #1: DIVERSIFICATION IS THE PERFECT PLAN

The old expression, "don't put all of your eggs in one basket," is often used to justify this very popular myth. However, don't confuse solving a problem with managing a process. Unfortunately, the premise of this commonly held belief — that diversification protects you from all woes — is deeply flawed.

When it comes to investing, there is no perfect investment plan. For example, anyone who had money in the market during 2000-2002, even if invested in a well-diversified asset allocation, probably lost money. In a discipline as variable as investing, it is foolish to ever think a perfect solution can be found.

That said, there is good news and bad news about diversification. The bad news is that, even with a thoroughly diversified portfolio, investors are still subject to the possible loss of some or all of their money. But the good news is powerful indeed: diversification provides the highest degree of protection possible for investors.

Let's start with the bad news first and debunk the myth. Then we can look at how diversification really does minimize risk.

EXPECT THE UNEXPECTED

The myth is rooted in the general desire for clear answers to every dilemma. People prefer unambiguous, conflict-free solutions — hence, the prevalence of militant ideology around the world. But as we see in the newspapers every day, blind adherence to ideology is dangerous.

Investing is as much an art as it is a science. We'd like to believe that, with the proper analysis and effort, we could implement a portfolio diversification plan that will eliminate all anxiety, fear, confusion, uncertainty, doubt, discomfort, and loss. The truth: it's just not possible. The unpleasant aspects of being an investor can be managed and minimized, but never eliminated.

Why not? First, an almost infinite number of variables affect the financial world. Because of economic globalization, an incident in Indonesia can affect companies in Silicon Valley. Economies of countries halfway across the globe can influence our own. Look at the impact 9/11 had on not just the United States but the entire world economy. As devastating as it was, what will happen when a much worse terrorist incident occurs? Like most people, I believe it's only a matter of time before an even more horrific terrorist attack occurs on American soil, and I guarantee you it will affect all investors, probably in totally unexpected ways. In the face of so many unpredictable, unlimited variables, it is impossible to develop a "perfect" diversification plan. You must plan on the unexpected.

Secondly, it is impossible to know all the variables now, or what they will be in the future. In Colonial America, lamps and even factory machinery burned whale oil. Many "experts" predicted that, once the whale population was decimated by over-hunting, the world would collapse for the lack of fuel. Low and behold! An alternate source of fuel was found at the world's first working oil well in Titusville, Pennsylvania, and the Hydrocarbon Age was born. The world did not end; it merely changed, radically and forever. Who could have foretold that fossil fuel would render whale oil obsolete?

More recent history provides another compelling example of the unknowable. The turn of the last century, or "Y2K" as it's popularly known, gave investors reason to believe that life as they knew it would end on January 1, 2000 — the doomsday for all computer-dependent functioning. In the end, Y2K brought only minor inconveniences, but no major disasters. No matter how hard we try, we are limited in our abilities to predict what will affect our world and how.

Too often, investors mistake portfolio diversification for risk elimination, rather than using it as a tool to manage the continual process of risk reduction. They build a diversified portfolio, and think their job is done. It's not. The world continues to change and evolve, so the process always

Insider Notes: Be forewarned: investors are much more likely to sell stocks that have risen in value than those that fall. It's an unfortunate law of investor behavior.

continues. Too much effort? If you want to be successful, roll up your sleeves and get over it.

My approach toward diversification differs from most other advisors. I tell clients up-front that it is impossible to invest without accepting some degree of risk, anxiety and discomfort. A lot of advisors avoid speaking frankly with their clients about risk because they fear scaring the client away. The relationship that ensues is not one of mutual understanding, but of misunderstanding and, sooner or later, conflict due to unmet expectations. As an advisor, I attempt to avoid such unfulfilling relationships by addressing these issues with investors in a forthright and candid manner, right from the get-go. Setting realistic expectations reduces the possibility of misunderstandings later in the advisory relationship.

All forms of handling money create risk. Even digging a hole in the back yard and burying your money subjects you to risk — the risk of inflation. Because your buried funds earn no interest or dividend while inflation accrues over time, the value of the currency in the ground decreases.

Some people look to an advisor to quell their fears about risk, which is why some clients don't appreciate my frank approach. Eventually, however, their denial wears off, they appreciate the truth and seek to invest in a way that manages unavoidable risks.

To avoid dissatisfaction with your investment plan, you must accept that diversification is a risk management strategy; it is carried out as part of an ongoing process that considers several factors and implements various strategies. It is not a one-time event wherein you simply diversify your portfolio. Know yourself; don't take risk you can't handle. Realize that, no matter how hard you or your advisor works at managing your money, the unexpected can and often does happen. A diversification plan will result in losses from time to time, but over the long haul, it should provide the returns you desire.

EIGHT INVESTMENT FACTORS TO CONSIDER

In addition to risk management through diversification, there are eight factors to consider when developing an investment plan:

❶ **Time Horizon** — Investment holding period or length of time in which a specific goal is to be achieved.

❷ **Liquidity/Marketability** — Accessibility of cash when you want it; ability to readily convert an asset into cash, independent of changes in the economy, without risking loss of principal.

❸ **Risk Tolerance** — Willingness to accept investment risk. The level of risk an investor is willing to assume affects the types of returns expected. The objective of rational investment management is to select investment vehicles that maximize expected return for a given level of risk, or minimize risk for a given level of expected return.

❹ **Tax Consequences** — Expected or realized performance of all investments should be calculated on an after-tax basis, thus comparing returns for both taxable and non-taxable investments on an equal basis.

❺ **Diversification** — Risk-reducing strategy that can produce greater realized returns than a single-asset-class portfolio. The major purpose of diversification is to reduce the risk exposure by building a portfolio with assets whose risks or returns are not influenced by the same variable factors. Therefore, the type of risk associated with each investment must be evaluated.

❻ **Personal Management Efforts** — Degree to which you desire, and are able, to manage your own assets.

❼ **Market Cycle** — Since 1802, there have been 15 major market cycles: seven secular (long-term) bull markets and eight secular bear markets. Identifying and adjusting to the market cycle can have a major impact on investment returns over the subsequent 10 to 20 years.

❽ **Interest Rate Cycle** — Interest rates on U.S. Treasury securities have fluctuated within very specific ranges over the years, allowing astute investors to determine whether owning long- or short-term bonds provides the best risk-adjusted return.

CASE STUDY: FITTING FACTORS TO GOALS

 Once you define the major investment factors and tailor them to your portfolio goals, you may discover that how you thought you should invest is not at all accurate.

An 81-year-old retiree named Thomas recently asked my firm to review his existing $500,000 portfolio, managed at the time by a large bank trust department. His portfolio was invested 50% in U.S. stock mutual funds and 50% in bonds. Thomas' three main objectives were: 1) increase income from principal without endangering it; 2) avoid repetition of 2000-2003 shrinkage, while maintaining principal; and 3) achieve modest growth. We assisted him in allocating his portfolio based on his investment factors, as follows:

- **Time Horizon** — Based on his age of 81, his life expectancy is 7.6 years. His portfolio must provide income for the remainder of his life, so his investments should be made with a short to moderate time horizon.

- **Liquidity/Marketability** — Because he does maintain an emergency reserve but requires monthly income, the need for liquidity in his investment portfolio is moderate.

- **Risk Tolerance** — He characterized himself as a moderate risk-taker. His existing portfolio subjects him to moderate to high risk; that (coupled with his short time horizon of 7-10 years) meant that he should consider reducing his portfolio risk to be more aligned with his moderate risk tolerance.

- **Tax Consequences** — Since he is in the 15% Marginal Federal Income Tax bracket, and his Effective Tax Rate is somewhat lower, income taxes should be of minor concern in the design and management of his portfolio.

- **Diversification** — Adequate portfolio diversification is always advisable as a risk-reduction strategy. His existing portfolio lacks diversification; therefore, he should attempt to increase diversification by adding asset classes that he does not currently hold.

- **Personal Management Efforts** — He has indicated a desire for assistance in the selection, monitoring and maintenance of his portfolio. Therefore, he needs an investment portfolio requiring a low to moderate level of personal management.

- **Market Cycle** — We are currently in a secular (long-term) bear market. This cycle began in March 2000 and has had five cyclical (short-term) bull market rallies. Right now, we're seeing a bull market rally that may last several weeks or months. He should keep this in mind as he and his advisors monitor and manage his portfolio.
- **Interest Rate Cycle** — Interest rates on long-term U.S. Bonds at press time in 2004 were at 50-year lows; they can go a little lower and will eventually cycle back to historical averages.

After analyzing his income and expenses, we determined that he could live to age 95 without running out of money, if he obtained at least a 4.5% rate of return on his portfolio. We informed him that he could avoid all stock market risk by buying 100% U.S. government securities yielding 4.5% or higher and still have plenty to live on. He didn't choose to be that conservative, but he did greatly reduce the percentage of stock in his portfolio.

As Thomas did by following our advice, you too should accurately define your objectives and coordinate them with an investment strategy that meets all your objectives. (For assistance, see my contact info at the end of this chapter.) I also suggest that you take my Risk Tolerance Test, in this chapter, to determine your general Risk Profile as an investor.

MYTH #2: YOU CAN AND SHOULD MANAGE YOUR OWN MONEY

The root of this myth is twofold. First, there's pride. We all like to think that we have the smarts and "know-how" to decide for ourselves what to do with our own money. However, the truly wise set aside their pride and seek help from the experts in making their money grow. Many others hold tight to their pride and attempt to manage their own money, but as the Bible teaches us, pride comes before a fall.

Secondly, thousands of investment businesses promote this myth because they cater to the individual investor. These self-serving businesses want the individual to feel empowered to make their own decisions about which investments to buy. Their hefty direct-marketing budgets reinforce this notion.

Why isn't this myth true? The relatively new field of behavioral finance provides the answer. Study after study reveals that, psychologically, people are very poorly suited to make day-to-day decisions regarding investments.

Daniel Kahnman, the 2002 Nobel Prize winner in economics, has shown that investors use overconfident, highly emotional logic in making investment decisions. Kahnman and his research partner, Amos Tvesky, considered by many the fathers of modern behavioral finance, found that instincts are the enemy of sound investing. An investor's biggest obstacle to sound investing is his own ego. He thinks he knows more than he does and acts upon that false belief.

Prospect Theory, developed by Kahnman and Tversky, states that investors hate to accept losses because they trigger emotional pain. This results in holding on to poorly performing investments longer than they should and in selling well performing investments when they should hold on to them. Investors make decisions based on their aversion to loss because the pain of a loss is perceived twice as strongly as the pleasure of a gain. Kahnman and Tversky's research has shown that emotional pain increases as losses are realized.

As stated above, overconfidence is a real problem for the individual investor. Researchers in behavioral finance have found that individual investors hurt themselves by making investments with a confidence not supported by adequate information. Investors have an "illusion of control" over all kinds of events that affect the market, which no one can predict with any degree of certainty. Kahnman observed that, over the three years leading up to the stock market bubble, many investors knew it was a bubble but thought they could get out in time, so they invested anyway. Rather than trying to determine the meaning of day-to-day market gyrations, Kahman suggests investors focus on long-term investing and make fewer investment decisions on their own.

HOW DO YOU RATE?

Not convinced yet? Then take the "Test Your Basic Knowledge" challenge on the following page, to illustrate that none of us are as smart as we think. Answer the questions to assure a 90% probability that the range you chose will include the correct answer.

TEST YOUR BASIC KNOWELDGE

For each of the following, provide a low and high guess, so you are 90% sure the correct answer is within your low-high range. Your challenge is to set a range that is neither too narrow nor too wide, but try to make the ranges as narrow as possible. To meet this challenge, the correct answer should fall within your low-high range for nine out of the 10 questions. The test's purpose is to show that none of us is as informed as we think.

	90% Confidence Range	
	Low	**High**
1. Martin Luther King's age at death.	____	____
2. Length of the Nile River, in miles.	____	____
3. Number of OPEC member countries.	____	____
4. Number of books in the Old Testament.	____	____
5. Diameter of the moon, in miles.	____	____
6. Weight of an empty Boeing 747, in pounds.	____	____
7. Birth year of Wolfgang Amadeus Mozart.	____	____
8. Gestation period of an Asian elephant, in days.	____	____
9. Air distance from London to Tokyo, in miles.	____	____
10. Deepest known point in the oceans, in feet.	____	____

Answers on the next page.

If you've taken this test and are still not convinced that everyone has their limits, consider the study by Professor Terrance Odean of U.C. Berkeley. Odean looked at the trading habits of 10,000 investors at a large discount brokerage firm from 1987 to 1993, and he identified two incredible facts: Investors were much more likely to sell stocks that had risen in value rather than those that fell.

■ The stocks that were sold outperformed those kept by 3.4% over the succeeding 12 months. In other words, investors sold the stocks they should have kept and kept the stocks they should have sold.

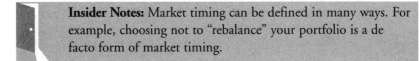

Insider Notes: Market timing can be defined in many ways. For example, choosing not to "rebalance" your portfolio is a de facto form of market timing.

BAUERLE'S ROCK-SOLID INVESTMENT RULES

- There is no risk-free investment. Even Money Market Funds, CDs, government bonds, and first mortgages have risk.
- There is no perfect investment. You may accomplish a particular goal with one investment, but through its use, you may ignore or neglect other investment goals.
- Every decision is a compromise.
- Even though history indicates that stocks outperformed most other asset classes over long periods of time, there have been long periods that they have not.
- There are no guarantees that any portfolio, regardless of how it is allocated, will provide your target return.
- Never hurry a financial decision.
- Never make a financial move without both spouses being in agreement.
- Always seek qualified counsel.
- Diversify, diversify, diversify.
- Portfolio management is a process, not a one-time event.
- Never invest in something you don't completely understand.
- Never pay a load for a mutal fund.

Use the following guidelines when selecting and managing a professional:

- Chose a fee-only Certified Financial Planner who practices comprehensive planning. Under a fee-only arrangement, all expectations are clearly understood within defined parameters. Conduct a personal interview, scrutinize credentials, and check references from clients and other professionals. Really want to blow them away? Ask for a copy of their net-worth statement and personal trading records for the past five years. You don't want to be advised by Joe Thousandaire!
- Hold your advisor accountable, by executing a written Investment Advisory Agreement that outlines client and advisor responsibilities, as well as investment performance benchmarks. Contact me for a sample of an Advisory Agreement. Meetings should occur at

Quiz Answers: 1: 39, 2: 4,187; 3: 13; 4: 39; 5: 2,160; 6: 390,000; 7: 1756; 8: 645; 9: 5,959; 10: 36,198

least semi-annually and, depending on circumstances, as often as bimonthly.
- If things don't work out, and you need to change advisors, repeat the process listed above for selecting an advisor. Don't burn any bridges; the investment community is close-knit.

MYTH #3: YOU CAN'T TIME THE MARKET

Many academics and advisors say you can't time the market, but that's simply not true. They promulgate this myth because they have their own axes and investment theories to grind.

Investors should question three of the anti-timing community's key arguments:
- Is passive indexing truly a better way to invest? Passive indexing is hitching your portfolio to the general trends of a broader index such as the S&P 500.
- Does dollar-cost averaging really reduce risk and improve returns? Dollar-cost averaging is a program of investing a set amount on a regular schedule, regardless of the price of shares at the time. The theory is that you buy more shares at low prices than at high prices.
- Does buy-and-hold investing work best? This is buying securities and just holding them for a long period of time, without any allocation adjustments.

None of these three rules-of-thumb make sense in secular bear markets. The strategies I use during a long-term bull market are not the same as those for a severe bear market. The strategies and investments I use during a falling interest-rate environment are not the same as those I use in a rising interest-rate environment. Being flexible reduces portfolio risk and enhances returns.

 Insider Notes: Even though history indicates that stocks outperformed most other asset classes over long periods of time, there have been long periods that they have not.

ANECDOTE: WHY EVEN THE SMARTEST INVESTORS NEED ADVISORS

A middle-aged man with Bachelors degrees in Electronic Engineering and Quantitative Methods and an MBA approached my firm after watching his account lose $1 million (50% of its value) from 2000 to 2004. If anyone ever had the mental capability to manage money it was this man, but psychologically he was unable to pull the trigger during the crash to stop the losses. His portfolio had no real estate, small company stocks, or bonds. No tax-loss selling was executed to reduce income taxes. The portfolio was full of high-cost mutual funds. It takes more than brains to manage money.

MARKET TIMING DEFINED

Market timing is commonly defined as being either fully invested in the market or fully invested in cash. But this approach is not intelligent because it's "all-or-nothing" and lacks nuance. Any strategy that attempts to identify those variables that significantly affect portfolio performance and - through analysis of macroeconomic conditions, geopolitical issues and market conditions — chooses to invest or not invest, or determines the degree to which to invest in various asset classes should be considered market timing.

Consider the professional advisor who, after conducting his analysis of the market in late 1999, decided that the valuations of stocks in the three major indexes — the Dow, the S&P500 and the NASDAQ — were grossly overvalued and exposed his clients to undo risk. He sold all his clients' equity holdings and completely avoided the ensuing crash that saw those same indexes fall 37%, 54%, and 78%, respectively, over the following three years. Did he market time? Is it unwise to do so? The mantra from those who counsel against market timing is that it can't be done. The bottom line: this mantra is simply not true. You can, and should, use good common sense and any quantitative or technical tools possible to assist in making all investment decisions.

MARKET TIMING (RE)DEFINED

The myth that investors can't time the market also lies in misconceptions about the meaning of "timing." Historically, market timing has been defined as the practice of deciding either to be 100% invested in the stock market or cash. Frequent short-term trading is assumed as part of this definition. Most rational people would agree that it is impossible to successfully buy and sell stocks on a short-term basis. No one can guess right all the time.

The 2000 crash forced professionals and private investors to think about their investing beliefs. First, very few (if any) invest 100% in the stock market. If they don't, any type of trading behavior they may exhibit could not be classified as market timing based on the traditional definition. Second, even die-hard buy-and-hold investors began to question the efficacy of maintaining their allocations in equities over the three-year downturn. Appropriate "rebalancing" enhances returns.

Does rebalancing annually make the investor a timer? Not by the traditional definition. But many investment advisors and academics would probably say it was. I propose that choosing not to rebalance is a form of timing. I would further assert that not buying stocks with P/Es above 35 is timing. I suggest not buying long-term bonds right now is market timing. Making investment decisions based on macroeconomic data, geopolitical trends, monetary policy, interest rates, or any other variable that affects the market is a form of timing and is done regularly by many investment professionals quite successfully.

Peter Bernstein, prominent strategist and editor of the prestigious *Journal of Portfolio Management,* set the investment world on its ear in January 2004 when he said, "What if we can no longer be so confident that stocks are necessarily the best place to be in the long run? What if moving around more frequently is now a necessity rather than a matter of choice? I am talking about market timing — dirty words."

Even Roger Ibbotson, the Yale University purveyor of financial data supporting the buy-and-hold passive investing style, concedes frequent imbalances in the market means investors could benefit from responding with short-term strategies, such as selling technology stocks when valuations reach unjustifiable heights.

So what is an investor to do? Even though Ibbotson concedes that market inefficiencies do exist, he went on to say, "Maybe a hedge fund might be

THE DOT-COM BUST: A CAUTIONARY TALE

The dot-com bust that began in 2000 ended up costing investors trillions in losses. The Dow Jones, S&P 500, and NASDAQ fell from highs of 11,722.98, 1,527.46, and 4,048.62, respectively, to lows of 7,286.27, 776.76, and 1,114,11. Percentage losses were 37.85 for the Dow Jones, 49.15 for the S&P 500, and 77.93 for the NASDAQ. Ouch!

How much did you lose from 2000 to 2002? On average, our clients lost approximately 1% to 4% in 2000, 2% to 4% in 2001, and 4% to 7% in 2002. Unfortunately many investors who were managing their own money during this time lost 50% or more of their portfolio. Based on the index losses, it was easy to do if not properly diversified.

The reason for our success was primarily having listened to our clients and accurately identifying their risk tolerance. Based on that information, we allocated assets between stocks, bonds, and real estate in proportions that didn't overexpose our clients to risks they were unwilling to take. The second reason for our success was adequately diversifying within the asset allocation. Large stocks, small stocks, growth stocks, value stocks, international, and domestic stocks were utilized. Church bonds and both U.S. and international bonds were utilized as well. Lastly, we kept investment costs very low, by using institutional index funds as well as exchange-traded funds. Expense ratios of our portfolios were a low 0.40 to 0.60 basis points.

Unfortunately two of our clients refused to heed our advice to diversify and chased the dot-com frenzy, largely by utilizing technology funds. Each investor lost over 70% and learned a very expensive lesson. Interestingly, both clients admit to having been unrealistic about their true risk tolerance during the financial planning process. This illustrates how crucially important it is for both client and advisor to seek truth in developing the initial plan.

able to do this sort of thing and make some money, but I think it's a more dangerous policy for individuals. Most individuals, and even most institutional investors, shouldn't get involved in markets this way."

If you're not a serious investor spending 20 hours or more per week managing your portfolio, then get a professional money manager to do this for you. The approach currently used in my practice was adopted as a result of the crash of 2000. Richard Nixon's Attorney General, John Mitchell, once famously said, "Don't listen to what we say; watch what we do." Instead of listening to Wall Street and governmental pronouncements, I watched what traders and the government did, and I observed 180-degree differences.

While Wall Street was saying buy, it was selling short. While the government was espousing the benefits of a strong dollar, it let the dollar plummet against foreign currencies. I identify investment factors in respect to major worldwide macroeconomic and geopolitical issues and base asset allocations on these facts. My approach has never led to daily trading, but rather more active management.

MARKET TIMING TRUTHS:

- Market timing has nothing to do with forecasting the market's future direction.
- Market timing assumes that stock prices are not random and that the stock market is not efficient.
- Market timing should be a mechanical, emotionless approach to investing.
- With market timing, you'll probably under-perform in a sustained bull market.
- Market timing provides the buy-and-sell signals to tell you when to go long and when to short the market.
- Market timing isn't magic, 100% accurate, or for everyone.

MYTH #4: MUTUAL FUNDS ARE PERFECT FOR THE INDIVIDUAL INVESTOR

Here's another myth that supposedly began with the individual investor's best interest in mind. Historically, individuals have found it virtually impossible to adequately diversify an investment portfolio of individual

Insider Notes: Very few mutual fund managers meet or beat their benchmark annually, simply because front-end, back-end, or 12b-1 fees reduce return.

RISK TOLERANCE QUIZ

1. Just 60 days after you put money into an investment, its price fell 20%. If none of the fundamentals have changed, what would you do?
   - [ ] Sell to avoid further worry and try something else.
   - [ ] Do nothing and wait for the investment to come back.
   - [ ] Buy more. It was a good investment before; now it's a cheap.

2. Now look again at the first question. Your investment fell 20%, but it's being used to meet investment goals with three different time spans.

What would you do if the goal were five years away?
   - [ ] Sell   [ ] Do nothing   [ ] Buy more

What would you do if the goal were 15 years away?
   - [ ] Sell   [ ] Do nothing   [ ] Buy more

What would you do if the goal were 30 years away?
   - [ ] Sell   [ ] Do nothing   [ ] Buy more

3. The price of your retirement investment jumps 25% a month after you buy it. The fundamentals haven't changed. What do you do?
   - [ ] Sell it and lock in your gains.
   - [ ] Stay put and hope for more gain.
   - [ ] Buy more; it could go higher.

4. You're investing for retirement, which is 15 years away. What do you do?
   - [ ] Invest in a money-market fund or guaranteed investment contract, forgoing major gains, but virtually assuring the safety of your principal.
   - [ ] Invest in a 50-50 mix of bond and stock funds, in hopes of getting

stocks or bonds because stocks and bonds cost so much. Mutual funds provide the small investor the opportunity to own hundreds or even thousands of stocks as individual investments, for as little as $250. However, the fact that mutual funds solve this major issue of cost doesn't make them the perfect investment, only a better option than individual stocks for

some growth, but also giving some protection in the form of income.
- ☐ Invest in aggressive growth mutual funds whose value will probably fluctuate significantly during the year, but have the potential for impressive gains over the five or 10 years.

5. You just won a big prize! But which one do you choose?
   - ☐ $2,000 in cash
   - ☐ 50% chance to win $5,000
   - ☐ 20% chance to win $15,000

6. A good investment opportunity just came along. But you have to borrow money to get in. Would you take out a loan?
   - ☐ Definitely not ☐ Perhaps ☐ Yes

7. Your company is selling stock to its employees. In three years, management plans to take the company public. Until then, you won't be able to sell your shares and you will get no dividends. But your investment could multiply as much as 10 times when the company goes public. How much money would you invest?
   - ☐ None ☐ Two months' salary ☐ Four months' salary

To score the quiz, add up the number of answers you gave in each category a-c, then multiply as shown to find your score.
(a) Answers _____ x 1 = _____ points
(b) Answers _____ x 2 = _____ points
(c) Answers _____ x 3 = _____ points
YOUR SCORE: _____ points

If you scored: 9-14 points, you are a conservative investor, **15-21** points, you are a moderate investor, **22-27** points, you are an aggressive investor.

small investors. Recent and highly publicized mutual fund scandals underscore the falseness of the myth.

MUTUAL FUND "MINI MYTHS"
Our fourth myth is buttressed by the following falsehoods:

RELIABLE SOURCES OF MUTUAL FUND DATA

Before picking a fund, do your homework. The following guides are well-respected sources of fund data:

- **Value Line Mutual Fund Survey** — Biweekly publication analyzing the performance of more than 2,000 funds (800-535-8760; www.valueline.com)
- **Directory of Mutual Funds** — A guide to nearly 4,000 funds; updated annually (202-326-5800; www.ici.org)
- **Morningstar Mutual Funds** — Mutual fund analysis updated biweekly (800-735-0700; www.morningstar.net)

- Mutual funds are long-term investments — unfortunately, they are often not managed that way by the fund manager.
- Mutual fund managers are long-term investors — they often aren't.
- Mutual fund owners are long-term owners —again, they often aren't.
- Mutual fund costs will decline as fund assets increase — in most funds, this has not happened.
- Mutual fund returns are meeting the expectations of investors — most do not even equal their benchmark index.

Mutual funds should be evaluated by the following criteria:

- Fund performance over one year, five years, since inception, etc.
- Fund expense ratio, as stated in the fund prospectus.
- Strategy used by the manager, also stated in prospectus.
- Long-term commitment to your investment style; e.g., if you're a retirement investor, the fund must be truly conservative.
- Portfolio turnover, risk adjusted returns, and after-tax returns, also stated in the prospectus.

According to Morningstar, in 1999 fund managers had an all-fund average turnover of 103%, meaning that managers sold every share they owned at the beginning of the year plus an additional 3% of stocks purchased throughout the year. Heavy trading such as this subjects fund investors to two deadly foes, trading expenses and income taxes. Industry experts estimate that these expenses cost investors between 0.7% and 2.0% annually. Income taxes can easily range from 0.7% to 2.7%, depending on an investor's tax bracket. If you consider adding these costs together, you can see how difficult it is for investors to win.

If you think things couldn't get worse, you're wrong. Individual investor behavior is often worse than that of fund managers. Investors often buy and sell funds as a market timing strategy. The new, no-transaction fee fund platforms only encourage this behavior.

In addition to often buying high and selling low, investors incur trading costs just as portfolio managers do. Individual investors also create income tax consequences for themselves as well. Can you imagine the devastating affect that occurs when both fund managers and investors trade aggressively?

MUTUAL FUND COSTS DEFY GRAVITY

Let's start with the basic expense ratio of funds. The investment industry has preached the gospel that the law of large numbers will benefit the individual investor. They said that as a fund's assets grew, each individual would be responsible for a smaller percentage of the fixed costs of managing the fund. What actually happened in most cases is that fund expenses went up.

Next, let's look at the infamous 12b-1 fee to help smaller funds compete with larger funds. The 12b-1 fee originated in 1980 under the SEC's authorization. The fee's alphanumeric name refers to the section in the Investment Company Act of 1940 that allows funds to pay distribution and marketing expenses out of the fund's assets. The 12b-1 fee was intended to assist investors. Here's the theory: through marketing, a fund's assets will increase, and as assets grow, the fund can reap better economies of

Insider Notes: Screen all funds for turnover ratio. If a fund has turnover of 50% or more, determine whether its returns are better than funds with lower turnover, and if so, over what time periods. Any manager can be lucky for a year or two, maybe even three, but luck is a less likely factor over 5, 10 or 15 years. You don't invest for just 12 months; you invest for longer periods of time. There are plenty of low turnover funds available if you look for them.

scale, giving investors lower annual operational expenses. This has not happened. In reality, 12b-1 fees have been used as a hidden, and quite insidious, way to funnel money to brokers for using the fund. In essence, the 12b-1 fee is tantamount to a hidden load.

Initially, these expenses were never intended to be entitlements to the fund industry. But they have been. In fact, some funds have closed and continue to charge 12b-1 fees. The chart below provided by Lipper Research provides evidence that 12b-1 fees are alive and well.

THE RISE OF THE 12B-1 FEES

	1980	1986	1990	1996	2002
YEAR END FUND ASSETS (BILLIONS)	$135	$716	$1,067	$3,539	$6,391
ANNUAL 12B-1 FEES (BILLIONS)	$0	$0.37	$1.2	$4.4	$7.5

Now let's look at fund trading costs. Fund managers aren't required to include trading costs in the calculation of their expense ratio. With today's high turnover, it is very likely that trading costs have averaged investors between 1-2% annually — which adds up to big money over time.

GREAT EXPECTATIONS

Mutual fund returns are supposed to meet the reasonable expectations of investors, right? Well, here's the most shocking information yet: very few fund managers meet or beat their benchmark annually, simply because front end, back end, or 12b-1 fees reduce return. Beating a benchmark is important; it tells you whether the manager is actually meeting the promised goals of the fund. Active trading increases trading costs; it also creates tax consequences. Even if the fund beats its benchmark, the individual investor's after-tax return is below the benchmark. Avoid this "mutual fund trap" by avoiding high fund turnover.

Now for a tough question: how do you protect yourself from yourself? As indicated above, you probably shouldn't manage your own money. But if you do, commit yourself to specific trading criteria. If you can't write that criteria down, you probably shouldn't manage your own money. If you do create your criteria and then break them, hire a professional advisor.

With over 16,000 mutual funds in operation, it is highly unlikely that a layperson can successfully select appropriate funds for the various asset classes without falling victim to the many traps I've just described. The cost of a quality advisor is easily paid for in reduced expense ratios alone. However, only put your faith in talented, hard-working professionals who are passionate about your financial well being. When choosing and monitoring an advisor, you should adhere to a philosophy once expressed by Vince Lombardi: "If you are not fired with enthusiasm, you will be fired with enthusiasm."

■ ■ ■

Todd A. Bauerle is a Certified Financial Planner with 20 years of industry experience. He is a member of the National Association of Personal Financial Advisors (NAPFA) and the Financial Planners Association (FPA). Todd earned a B.S. degree in Aviation Management from Embry-Riddle Aeronautical University. As a certified trainer for the A.A.R.P. "Think of Your Future" Retirement Planning Program, he has taught continuing education courses at Stetson University and has been a featured speaker at Florida Power Corporation Retirement Preparation seminars.

Todd is president of Bauerle Financial, Inc., a "Fee-Only" investment advisory firm that is registered with the Securities & Exchange Commission. Bauerle Financial, Inc. manages client assets in excess of $50 million and provides comprehensive financial planning and investment management services throughout the United States. He can be contacted at 386-734-4548 or todd@bauerlefinancial.com.

[2]
ASSET ALLOCATION
A FINANCIAL FLIGHT PLAN

What goes up must come down, so you'd better diversify. This mantra makes sense, but few know exactly what it means — and fewer yet how to properly put it to work. Learn your financial dashboard to map out your asset allocation flight plan — and avoid an investment crash-and-burn.

"DON'T JUDGE EACH DAY BY THE **HARVEST** YOU REAP, BUT BY THE **SEEDS YOU PLANT**"

- Robert Louis Stevenson

by Brian Evans

We've all heard this familiar aphorism: "The only things certain in life are death and taxes." Well, for those with a financial plan, there's another certainty: someday, we'll have to make decisions about how to allocate our investments.

For some of us, that means choosing among stock market

WE CAN EASILY GET CAUGHT UP IN THE "IRRATIONAL EXUBERANCE" OF THE MARKET WHILE IT'S GOING UP. CONVERSELY, WE CAN EQUALLY DAMAGE OUR PORTFOLIO'S GROWTH BY GETTING CAUGHT UP IN THE IRRATIONAL FEAR THAT A DOWN MARKET CAN CREATE.

alternatives in our employer 401(k) plan. For others, it may involve an inheritance, appointment as a trustee, helping a parent invest for income, or implementing a personal investment plan for retirement or our children's education.

There is a wealth of information out there on how to invest in the market. The problem is, much of this information is contradictory. One brokerage firm's "strong buy" is another's "strong sell." One TV business channel tells you to buy stocks, while the other says to sell stocks and buy bonds.

Wouldn't it be nice to have a working knowledge of how to invest your money, combined with a commonsense approach that allows you to ignore most of the informational overload?

In this chapter, I will describe my unique strategy for investing that can help you in almost any planning situation. I will discuss what I mean by "true asset allocation," a method you can use as a template regardless of your age or investment goals.

Asset allocation is a continual process, not a one-time event. It is the process of selecting among disparate investment choices and combining them to achieve adequate returns while reducing volatility.

Reducing volatility is important because you never know when you may need to cash out some of your portfolio. Moreover, unexpected catastrophe can suddenly strike an ostensibly secure investment. I only need to broach such once-mighty names as Enron, MCI WorldCom, Adelphia and Tyco to illustrate the importance of asset allocation.

MARKET MISCONCEPTIONS

Chances are you were taught that if you own the S&P 500 index, you're diversified. The index holds 500 of the largest U.S. companies, so why wouldn't you believe it? In reality, the much-vaunted S&P 500 index is just one piece of a much bigger investment pie.

Another misconception is that you must "time the market" to succeed with your investment goals. Not so. In fact, most investors who try to invest at "just the right time" do the opposite. They buy when the market has increased and is all the talk around the office, and they sell when the market falls due to world events and other fears.

Here's a sure-fire contrarian indicator: when a cab driver or shoe-shine guy starts giving you stock tips, the market is frothy and due for a correction.

Human beings are given to fads and crowd behavior. Charles Mackay, in his 19th century classic, *Memoirs of Extraordinary Popular Delusions and the Madness of Crowds,* described it best when recounting "tulip mania":

"In 1593, no Dutchman had ever seen a tulip. Their beauty and rarity caught the national fancy. In no time, they became 'the rage' as aristocrats flaunted the exotic flowers as symbols of power and prestige...Though supplies could be increased only as fast as nature allowed, demand for tulip bulbs accelerated at a fevered pitch. Soon all tiers of Dutch society were swept up in a tulip-trading craze that peaked in the 1630s, selling 'futures' on crops not yet grown or harvested. In the end, crops of bulbs still in the ground were bought and sold so many times that the sales were called the 'Wind Trade' (as the speculative prices were being made up out of thin air). After the market crashed in 1637, bankrupting many, the era came to be known as 'Tulipmania' or 'Tulipomania.' "

Insider Notes: Reducing volatility is important because you never know when you may need to cash out some of your portfolio. Moreover, unexpected catastrophe can suddenly strike an ostensibly secure investment.

In the last paragraph, substitute "tulip" for "dot-com," and you realize that nothing has changed in more than 400 years.

Today, we are experiencing a volatile stock market and historically low interest rates. Investments in CDs and bonds have very low yields, and it is increasingly risky to lock up our money in such fixed income investments. There's an alternative to these fixed-income investments that offers both a higher average yield and a much higher appreciation. They're called REITs (Real Estate Investment Trusts), and they essentially place the investor in the position of being a commercial landlord, without any of the hassles typically associated with leasing property.

Why did so many people do so poorly in the stock market in the last few years? One primary reason is that they lacked a plan and lost discipline-two elements of successful investing that go hand in hand. In this chapter, I will review the overall stock market experience of the last several years and common fears about the market. Then, I will present my Asset Allocation Dashboard strategy: a "flight plan" for successful long-term investing in the stock market.

ASSET ALLOCATION DASHBOARD

Question: From the end of 1999 through the end of 2002, was there a stock market crash?

The typical answer: What a silly question! With the S&P losing over a third its value and the NASDAQ losing more than half of its value, of course there was a crash!

Not so fast. Before we come to this conclusion, let's examine the question in terms of asset allocation. Specifically, let's analyze the behavior of the market using an approach that I have developed, called the Asset Allocation Dashboard.

When flying an airplane, a pilot uses various gauges in the cockpit to help make appropriate decisions to fly the plane safely. The gauges on the dashboard indicate direction, altitude, wind speed, fuel levels, etc. If one of the indicators is not within its proper tolerance level, the pilot makes corrections to normalize the situation. Without these dashboard gauges, it would be impossible to fly the plane safely. No one would even think of flying an airplane through turbulent skies or trying to land in the fog without checking the dashboard gauges. When it comes to investing, however, people often fly blindly, unable to see where they are going or deal with the turbulence of the markets to land safely in achieving their goals.

The good news is that managing an investment portfolio can be done in much the same way as piloting a plane with gauges on a dashboard. It requires a plan and discipline. The process of developing your investment dashboard will clarify your goals and methods for reaching them.

STEPS TO CREATING THE DASHBOARD

To illustrate how it's done, let's create a sample asset allocation for ourselves. First we need to figure out which classification of investments we would like to include in our overall mix of assets. Each of these classifications will act as a gauge in our dashboard. Once we have determined all of our gauges, we must then decide what percentages of our assets we want allocated to each of the gauges and which specific investment choices we will use in each gauge. With our dashboard in place, we can then implement our plan.

Here are the four steps to creating a customized dashboard:
❶ Define which investment classifications you want or need to gauge.
❷ Determine the percentage of your assets that you want allocated to each gauge.
❸ Make the appropriate specific investment selections to implement this plan.
❹ Monitor the readings on your gauges and make adjustments to ensure that your readings remain within your tolerance level.

It is vitally important to have a solid plan for investing in the stock market and the discipline to implement the plan. You probably know people who

Insider Notes: Greed can be your enemy; identifying when to sell an investment is every bit as important as knowing when to buy.

CASE STUDY: JOHN DOE

Let's assume I am selecting an allocation plan for the retirement account of Mr. John Doe. He is a fairly seasoned stock market investor, relatively aggressive with his investment choices, and at least 10 years will pass before there is any reasonable chance that any of her invested funds will need to be liquidated.

The returns on John's porfolio have not been adjusted for amounts held in cash or for any fees associated with the investments or paid to the investment advisor.

Given John's particular investment goals, I have allocated his portfolio in the percentages indicated by the dials on the gauges shown in Dashboard #1. Along with each classification I have inserted an arrow indicating the percentage of the portfolio invested in the particular gauge.

DASHBOARD #1

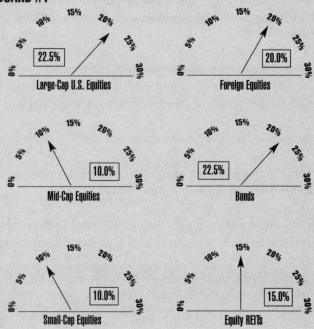

Now, using index mutual funds in the percentages shown in Dashboard #1, I have structured the investment allocation as seen below. For each gauge, I have included the index used, the amount invested at the end of 1999 and the approximate amount this investment was worth at the end of 2002.

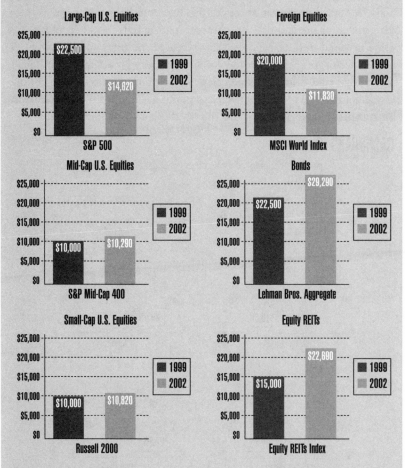

As you can see, in this three-year time frame ending December 31, 2002, two of the gauges decreased substantially in value; two of them stayed about the same; and two of them increased substantially in value for the three years ending December 31, 2002. John's investment of $100,000 at the end of 1999 dropped to $99,500, a loss of less than 1%.

From the end of 1999 through the end of 2002, the stock market experienced its biggest three-year decline since the Great Depression, yet John hardly noticed any change.

Continuing with John's portfolio analysis, it's now apparent that the dials are significantly out of range with his intended percentages as determined at the end of 1999. Human nature tells us to keep a lot more invested in the categories that increased the most and leave the poorly performing classes at low levels. John must resist this urge! This is where logic and discipline are critical to maintain our desire for genuine asset allocation. As John continues to guide her investment vehicle, let's look at his gauge readings at the end of 2002:

DASHBOARD #2

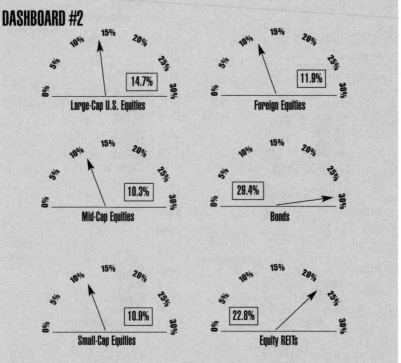

If John had re-balanced to the percentages in Dashboard #1 at the end of 2002, how would he have come out? During the impressive year of 2003, all six gauges gained ground. In fact five of the six gauges gained in excess of 20% during 2003. At the end of 2003, John's original investment of $100,000 would have grown to approximately $123,600! Now let's make final selections on John's investment plan using our asset allocation dashboard. As you recall, we had created six different classifications to gauge on our dashboard. For us to further define exactly which type of investment we desire in each classification, additional gauges must be added. Dashboard #3 represents how John's investments will be allocated and gauged.

DASHBOARD #3

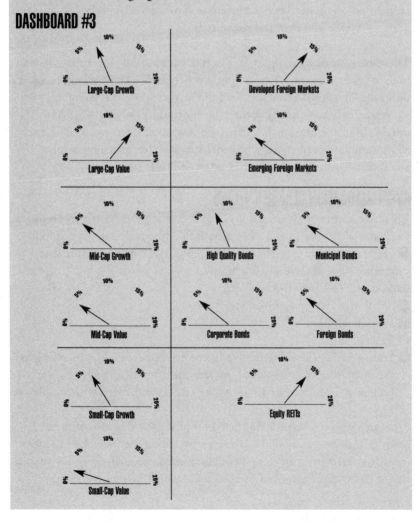

WHEN INTEREST RATES ARE RISING, THE VALUE OF YOUR BONDS DECREASES. SIMILARLY, WHEN INTEREST RATES ARE DECREASING, THE VALUE OF YOUR BONDS INCREASES. THE LATTER SCENARIO IS WHAT WE HAVE BEEN EXPERIENCING IN RECENT YEARS.

let their emotions dictate their investment process during the last four years — maybe you even did so yourself.

There are countless examples of investors who lost 50, 75 or even 90% or more of their account values during this period. We can easily get caught up in the "irrational exuberance" of the market while it is going up. Conversely, we can equally damage our portfolio's growth by getting caught up in the irrational fear that a down market can create. The asset allocation dashboard strategy provides structure for managing your account successfully in both good times and bad.

ASSET ALLOCATION CLASSIFICATIONS

There are six major classifications or gauges that I commonly recommend to clients when creating an asset allocation dashboard. They are as follows:

❶ Large caps (large capitalization U.S. equities), companies with a total market value exceeding $5 billion.

❷ Mid caps ($1 billion-$5 billion).

❸ Small caps (less than $1 billion).

❹ Foreign equities.

❺ Bonds.

❻ Equity REITs (Real Estate Investment Trusts), companies investing in the ownership of commercial property held for lease, such as office buildings, industrial parks, shopping centers and apartment complexes.

As an investor, you've probably had a lot of exposure to two of these gauges: large caps and bonds. However, including the lesser-known areas in your investment plan can potentially increase your diversity, lower your risk of short-term losses and increase your overall investment returns.

CHOOSING YOUR GAUGES

Careful consideration in choosing your gauges is the critical first step to creating your dashboard. The exclusion of the proper gauges is a primary reason why most individual investors' investment plans failed during the bear market of the early 2000s.

Many asset allocation strategies propose some kind of mix between large caps and bonds. Large cap U.S. equities account for 70-80% of the total value of the U.S. stock market, and bonds are viewed as the major source of investment diversification to equities.

LARGE CAPS

Large caps are the primary component of the S&P 500, which approximates an average of most of the largest 500 companies in the U.S. The 70-year average annual rate of return of large cap equities approximates 10% per year. It should be apparent to every investor that this rate of return is not achieved in a straight line!

Large cap equities exist in many different industries; some of the largest and best known include Microsoft, Wal-Mart, General Electric, Exxon, and Pfeizer. One of your gauges must be devoted to this category, as a core holding.

MID-CAPS AND SMALL-CAPS

Mid-cap and small-cap equities each comprise another classification important to a long-term asset allocation plan, and I generally attribute a gauge to each of them. Although these two categories are made up of over 6,000 publicly traded stocks, they account for only 20-30% of the total value of the U.S. stock market.

Small caps are typically less-known companies. Because these companies aren't industry leaders, they tend to exhibit greater volatility than their large-cap counterparts Nonetheless, small caps sometimes possess more

Insider Notes: The 20-year average rate of return of equity REITs exceeds the average of both the S&P 500 and the bond market.

flexibility and are better able to adapt to changes in the market. As a result, they confer higher up-side potential. Many asset allocation plans ignore small caps as an important classification, but the 70-year average annual rate of return of this asset class approximates 12% per year, exceeding its large-cap counterpart.

FOREIGN STOCKS

Foreign stocks are another asset class I like to gauge in the dashboard. In a global and increasingly integrated economy, only a parochial and fool-hardy-investor restricts his investments to the U.S. Well-known foreign equities include such companies as Sony, Nokia and Nestle. However, as with small and mid-cap stocks, foreign investing can be volatile.

During the bear market of this decade, foreign equities showed poor returns, even poorer than large-cap U.S. equities. But what goes down often comes up. During 2003, foreign stock returns on investment exceeded large-cap U.S. stock returns. When foreign stocks are in favor, the returns can be dramatic.

If you had invested in a foreign equity index at the end of 1984, you would have more than quadrupled your money over the next four years. I prefer to place a greater investment in U.S. equities as compared to foreign equities in the portfolios that I manage, but don't ignore this classification as an investment option.

BONDS

When you and I want to borrow money, we typically go to our bank or mortgage company. When the U.S. government, a large corporation or a city wants to borrow money, they usually do not walk down to the local bank and fill out a loan request. Instead they "borrow" money from the investment community in the form of a bond.

They do this because they usually can pay a lower interest rate through the issuance of a bond than they can by borrowing from a bank. When you buy a bond, you have essentially replaced the bank and have become the lender to whoever issued that bond.

Most bonds are issued with a very long repayment term. Some can be as long as 30 years. Even though the bond may promise to pay six percent for 30 years, bondholders often end up selling the bond before that time.

I often hear people say that bonds act much like a certificate of deposit, but that is not the case. Let's briefly review the nature of bond values. Say you buy a bond for $10,000, paying six percent interest for 30 years. If you hold the bond for the full 30 years, you should receive your $10,000, and your average rate of return on your investment was obviously six percent.

What if you decided to sell your bond after five years instead of waiting the full 30 years? The issuer of the bond does not buy it back; you need to find another investor to buy it from you. This is not hard to do, but let's assume that during the five years you held the bond, interest rates increased and people buying new bonds could receive nine percent instead of the six percent your bond is paying. As I said, you can easily sell your bond, but you will not receive your $10,000. Instead, you will be offered an amount at a significant discount to what you paid, and your overall rate of return for holding the bond could be negative.

We can summarize the value of bonds in this way. When interest rates are rising, the value of your bonds decreases, as illustrated in the example above. Similarly, when interest rates are decreasing, the value of your bonds increases. The latter scenario is what we have been experiencing in recent years. The value of bonds increased substantially from 2000 through 2003, due to the lowering of overall interest rates. If you had a large amount of bonds in your portfolio during this time, you probably feel quite fortunate and are very happy owning a large percentage of bonds.

However, with interest rates at or near their all-time lows, we have learned that bond prices are accordingly at or near their all-time highs. For bond prices to continue to increase, interest rates would have to fall further than they already have. This is possible, but do you think it is likely to happen?

Insider Notes: Mutual funds charge sales loads from 0.0% to 5.75% and annual fees from 0.1% to over 2.0% per year. Pay attention to fees before buying a fund.

If interest rates rise in the coming years, the value of most of our bond portfolios will decrease if we sell them. Interest is still paid to you as the owner of your bond, but the value of your bond could decrease.

Bonds have always been a great diversification tool to use in conjunction with the stock market and should always be a component of a well-diversified portfolio. However, if you believe that interest rates are on the rise, then you may consider allocating less to bonds than you have in the past. Even so, bonds are an important classification to gauge in the dashboard.

EQUITY REITS

We know from experience that the large-cap stock market can be very volatile. As I stated above, the small-cap, mid-cap and foreign markets can have very high returns but are, historically, even more volatile than the large caps. In today's market, we must be careful not to allocate too much to bonds, a strategy that, in the past, had served as our primary tool to reduce the volatility of our portfolio.

The question we're left with: "Is there any other investment classification offering not only high potential returns but also a way to potentially decrease the volatility of my portfolio?" There is, and that asset class is called equity REITs.

First of all, what's a REIT? It stands for Real Estate Investment Trust and refers to stocks in companies investing in the ownership of commercial property held for lease, such as office buildings, industrial parks, shopping centers and apartment complexes. These are not the limited partnerships of the 1980s. Those partnerships were riddled with syndication, organization and management fees and were illiquid. REITs are NYSE-traded stocks just like any other stock. They come in many forms, but when I refer to REITs in this chapter, I solely mean "equity REITs".

An equity REIT is a company whose primary focus is the net rental income from owning and operating commercial real estate. Essentially, they operate as landlords. For example, a company such as Equity Office Properties, symbol EOP on the NYSE, is the largest REIT of them all and primarily owns and leases out large office buildings across the country. It is the largest operator of office property in Seattle, Boston, Chicago, Atlanta, and San Francisco. When you own a share of stock in EOP, you own a share of each of the more than 700 buildings they own, leasing out over 120 million square feet of office space.

REITs have proven to be an excellent diversification tool. During the difficult equity market since the end of 1999, REITs have averaged a total return of over 15% per year. The 10 and 20 year average total returns of equity REITs each exceeds 12% per year. They have a very low correlation to both the equity market and to bond investments, and for these reasons I generally include them as a major gauge on any dashboard.

Before implementing your asset allocation plan, it is important to learn more about what REITs really are and how they can be an important investment given the low interest rate environment today.

MANAGING THE DASHBOARD

Why is it hard to stay allocated? Intellectually, we all know to buy low and sell high. In reality, we rarely do this. The stock market is the only industry where we buy more when prices rise, and we don't want to buy when there's a sale.

When stock values are rising, we all want to get in on the action and buy stocks, regardless of the increased purchase price. When stock values fall and buying them costs less, no one wants to buy. Hence the Wall Street expression, "Buy winter coats in July." During the summer, winter clothing is on sale, because demand for it is low. Makes sense. But in practice, almost none of us show this sort of foresight and patience.

As an investment advisor, this phenomenon is clear to see. Whenever the markets perform well for a sustained period and the prices of many stocks begin to exceed their values based on standard valuation measures, I get large amounts of new money to invest. Conversely, when the markets are

Insider Notes: When buying individual stocks, make sure you cover different industries. Owning Microsoft, Cisco, Intel and Dell does not mean you are diversified!

at multi-year lows, as they were during March 2003, I get very little new money. Indeed, several clients liquidate their accounts because they grow worried that "the end is near" for the stock market.

When certain areas of the market increase, you end up with a high weighting of that particular sector or category of investment. The returns on investments by category are often cyclical. Last year's loser is often this year's winner, and vice versa.

Here is a hypothetical conversation between an investment advisor and his or her client:

Trusted Advisor:	You know that investment that you like so much because it went up 50%?
Happy Client:	Oh yes, hasn't that been wonderful?
Trusted Advisor:	Yes, it has. It's been so wonderful that it's now overpriced and too heavily weighted in your portfolio. We need to sell some of it.
Client:	We do? What are we buying instead?
Advisor:	I'm glad you asked. You know that investment we had that went down 10 percent each of the last two years?
Client [now confused]:	Yes??
Advisor:	Well, we need to buy more of it because, based on its fundamentals, it's undervalued to the market and underweighted in your portfolio.
Soon-to-be Former Client:	You don't say?
Soon-to-be Fired Advisor:	Yes, I do....

Another example comes from a real life situation. A young couple, with two very young children, asked for my advice on the exercise of stock options. At the time, they were renting a modest house. She stayed home with the kids, and he worked in shipping at Amazon.com, so he didn't make a lot of income. However, he had been at the company almost from the start and had over $1 million worth of stock options in Amazon stock, based on the fair market value of the stock-about $80 per share at the time.

I suggested he consider exercising the options and then diversify his assets, buy a house, put money away for the kids' education, etc. He told me he didn't want to do that because Amazon was the best company in the world and the wave of the future. I told him he may be right, but that, at a minimum, he should exercise half of the options, just in case he was wrong, and still keep over $500,000 in the Amazon stock options. He informed me about the "new economy" and told me that I didn't understand what was happening in the world.

Months later, I saw him at a party. At that time, the stock had dropped to below $15 a share. I knew that his potential $1 million nest egg was now completely worthless because his stock options had value only if the share price were above about $40 per share. He couldn't even look at me all night.

CHOOSING YOUR GAUGES

Earlier in this chapter, I introduced the concept of the asset allocation dashboard. It is important to understand that each classification includes investments dissimilar from each other. Let's more closely dissect the classifications, to help you make the final investment selections that are right for your portfolio.

GROWTH STOCKS VS. VALUE STOCKS

A common way to divide investments in the U.S. stock market is "growth stocks vs. value stocks." Growth stocks typically are defined as stocks with lower current earnings but higher earnings growth prospects than their value stock counterparts. Growth stocks tend to be more "aggressive" in nature, simply meaning they increase more rapidly in a robust stock market.

Conversely, in a declining market, growth stocks often do worse than value stocks. The NASDAQ index is made up almost exclusively of stocks considered as growth stocks. Companies in the technology and telecommunication sectors make up a large portion of the NASDAQ. As we know, this

Insider Notes: Foreign funds are smart places to invest when the value of the dollar is falling, because their holdings tend to be denominated in foreign currencies and investors profit from the favorable exchange rates.

THE REIT STUFF

I'm emphasizing equity REITs in this chapter, because they are a little understood and often overlooked investment class.

REITs typically focus on ownership in office buildings, industrial parks, large apartment complexes, shopping centers, regional malls, hotels and self-storage facilities. They are very easy to own and easy to sell.

Let's review some of the advantages of owning real estate through REITs. First, if you own stock in a REIT, I can promise you that you will not receive a phone call in the middle of the night because your tenant has a leaky faucet. These companies have a staff to take care of that. REITs have a preferential income tax treatment benefiting their shareholders in two ways.

Pay attention to this point: REITs do not pay federal income tax! Corporate America pays 34% of its taxable income in federal income tax, thereby reducing the amount available to shareholders.

To be classified as a REIT, the real estate company agrees to pay out at least 90% of the net accounting income in the form of a dividend to its shareholders, thereby acting as a pass-through entity. If the company does this, they can obtain the desired classification of REIT and they do NOT owe any federal income tax at the corporate level.

As a result, REITs are the highest-paying dividend stocks of any class of stock. Recently, the dividend payout of the average REIT stock was six percent and has averaged over eight percent for the last 20 years. Their rate of dividend growth has consistently outpaced inflation. For the ten years ending 2002, the rate of equity REIT dividend growth has averaged over six percent per year, while the CPI has averaged an increase of 2.5% per year.

For years, much of the investment advisory community has preached that a diversified portfolio should be allocated roughly 60% to equities (common stocks) and 40% to bonds. The reasoning for this is sound:

bonds and stocks do not have a high correlation, so if one is down, it does not mean that the other is down, too.

This relationship is measured with a statistic called beta. Beta measures how closely an investment follows the movement of the S&P 500 index. If a mutual fund is invested similarly to the S&P 500, its beta will be close to 1.00. If there is no real correlation to the index at all, the beta will be 0.0.

Finally, if an investment typically moves opposite the S&P 500 index, its beta will be negative. For the five years ending in 2002, the beta for the equity REIT index was .22, meaning that it is only 22% correlated to the movement in the S&P 500 index. During the same period, the bond index had a beta close to that of the REIT index at about 0.0.

This is not to say the bonds and REITs move hand in hand; they do not. In fact, REITs and bonds have a negative correlation with each other. By increasing your holdings to include REITs along with stocks and bonds, you add another area of diversity, while maintaining a historically strong-performing investment class.

Depending on your source, interest rates are near a 45-year low, which conversely means that bond prices are near a 45-year high. As I mentioned, bond prices primarily only rise when interest rates decrease. I have my doubts that interest rates have much room to decrease at the present time. I think they have a very good chance of increasing or staying in the current range, which does not bode well for an increase in bond values.

Your next question is probably, "Given the fact that I want diversification in my portfolio and something that yields a reasonable income, what could I substitute for some of my bond component?"

REITs appreciate and depreciate in value based on factors other than the change in interest rates. At the time of this writing, the typical dividend from REITs exceeds the typical interest received from indexed bond funds. In addition, REITs can appreciate due to increasing real estate prices, an improving economy and increases in the demand for rental space.

In this era of low interest rates, investors should consider replacing some of their bond component, as well as some of their stock component, with equity REITs.

REITS AND RISK

As with any stock, REITs come with risk. For instance, in 1998 and 1999, when everybody wanted to buy large-cap stocks, dot-coms and Initial Public Offerings, REITs decreased in value by over 20% over this two-year time period.

Nonetheless, REITs represent large portions of the economy. To answer whether they are a substantial asset classification, consider the value of all of the commercial real estate in the U.S. and the huge part it plays in our economy. Given the immense value of U.S. commercial real estate, how can investors claim to be truly diversified if they don't own real estate in their portfolios?

index posted huge gains in the 1990s and huge losses during the recession of the early 2000s.

Common sectors considered as growth sectors include computer hardware, computer software, biotechnology, and health care stocks. Sectors considered to be made up primarily of value stocks include utilities, banks and financial institutions, REITs, energy and industrials.

The next chart illustrates how differently these classifications performed. Next to the asset classifications, I have listed the index used and the annual average rate of return of this index during the three-year bear market in first column, followed by the one-year return of the subsequent bull market.

	1999 - 2002	2003
LARGE-CAP GROWTH (RUSSELL 1000 GROWTH)	-19.2%	29.8%
LARGE-CAP VALUE (RUSSELL 1000 VALUE)	-3.6	30.0
MID-CAP GROWTH (RUSSELL MID-CAP GROWTH)	-13.9	42.7
MID-CAP VALUE (RUSSELL MID-CAP VALUE)	5.0	38.1
SMALL-CAP GROWTH (RUSSELL 2000 GROWTH)	-14.7	48.5
SMALL-CAP VALUE (RUSSELL 2000 VALUE)	10.1	46.0

The debate as to whether investors should have more money in growth stocks or more in value stocks has been around for years. It is my opinion that true asset allocation should have components of each, since it is difficult to predict the short-term movement of any single classification of the market.

That said, investments weighted heavily in the growth classification tend to have higher volatility in the short term. Investors are a bit more on the aggressive side as they increase their overall holdings of growth stocks and a bit more on the conservative side as their value component increases.

GROWTH AND VALUE IN FOREIGN MARKETS

The foreign markets share many of the same characteristics of the U.S. markets when referring to large-cap vs. small-cap stocks and value vs. growth characteristics. However, foreign markets do have distinctions. In particular, we need to consider the differences between companies operating in the industrialized countries of Western Europe, and their competitors in countries such as India, China, Brazil and Indonesia.

I further divide foreign investments into the two general classifications of "developed markets" and "emerging markets." Developed markets include many countries in Europe, and in the Far East such as Japan. For Jane's dashboard (see sidebar), when we refer to this classification of investment, we will use the MSCI Europe/Asia/Far East (EAFE) index.

Insider Notes: Save up to 20% on incomes taxes by waiting to sell gain positions until you have held them at least one year, to qualify for the lower capital gains tax rate.

THE DEBATE AS TO WHETHER INVESTORS SHOULD HAVE MORE MONEY IN GROWTH STOCKS OR MORE IN VALUE STOCKS HAS BEEN AROUND FOR YEARS. IT IS MY OPINION THAT TRUE ASSET ALLOCATION SHOULD HAVE COMPONENTS OF EACH, SINCE IT IS DIFFICULT TO PREDICT THE SHORT-TERM MOVEMENT OF ANY SINGLE CLASSIFICATION OF THE MARKET.

Some of the largest populations in the world live within countries considered "emerging markets." These countries often have the highest potential, due to their large populations and low labor costs, but also tend to carry more risk due to their unstable political climates and inexperience in the financial marketplace. When referring to this classification, we will use the MSCI Emerging Markets index.

THE BOND CLASSIFICATION

The bond market has many sub-classification possibilities. As I discussed earlier, the number of years to maturity of a bond can have a pronounced effect on the interest rate received on that bond and on the price of the bond if interest rates are moving. Generally, we can divide bonds into maturity time frames as follows:

Short-term	0-3 years
Intermediate-term	3-7 years
Long-term	7-30 years

Every bond that is issued also comes with a rating. The rating is an indication of the "quality" of the issuer of that bond. Remember that a bond is just a promise to repay the investor both interest and the bond principal at a stated future date. If the issuer of the bond is no longer solvent when the bond matures, the investor loses their investment.

The highest rated bonds are those issued by the biggest issuer of bonds in the world: Uncle Sam. If the U.S. government goes out of business before your bond matures, we are all in big trouble, and I will most certainly have to rewrite this chapter! But don't bet on it. These bonds receive a rating of AAA and are called high quality bonds.

So why would anybody buy a bond that isn't of the highest rating? Bonds with the highest ratings also carry the lowest yields, meaning they pay less interest to the investor than do lower rated bonds. The most common form of lower rated bonds is called corporate bonds. These are also known as high yield bonds and, if the rating is too low, they're referred to as junk bonds. Bonds in this category often receive a rating of B, BB or BBB.

Another large classification of bonds derives from the area of taxation. Usually, the interest received from a bond is taxable to the investor at ordinary income tax rates at the federal level, and also at the state level for those of you with a state income tax. That is not the case with municipal bonds.

Cities and other non-profit entities issue municipal bonds. When a city needs to build a new stadium or sewer-treatment facility costing hundreds of millions of dollars, it can raise the money from investors by issuing a bond. Because there is no federal income tax owed by the investor on interest received, these bonds can be very attractive to investors in a high income tax bracket. They are also attractive to people in states that have an income tax; state income tax is not owed on interest paid on these bonds if the bond is issued by an entity from the same state as the investor.

As with stocks, bonds can be purchased from issuers in foreign countries. These bonds carry additional risk and potential returns due to factors such as foreign currency fluctuations.

MUTUAL FUNDS

Several important points govern our expanded asset allocation dashboard. First, it is unnecessary to split each category between value and growth investment styles. You can accomplish a mixture of both styles by adding indexed mutual funds, referred to as blend funds. However, if you want to place more assets into only one style (value or growth), you should not buy indexed funds.

Insider Notes: The cash flows per dollar invested in the average foreign security has improved more than three-fold over the last four years. Foreign investments may now be worth a closer look.

Second, better asset allocation can be achieved by using mutual funds instead of individual company stocks or individual bonds. Many of my clients, and maybe you as well, own individual stocks or bonds and do not wish to sell them at this time. You do not have to. I suggest that, if you own stocks or bonds that fall within one of your desired gauges, you reduce the amount of new purchases in that gauge.

When selecting the actual mutual funds to buy, there are several criteria to keep in mind. All mutual funds charge an internal fee to operate the fund, but these fees can vary from less than a quarter percent per year for an index fund to over two percent for some managed funds. In addition, many funds charge a sales commission of over five percent when you purchase their fund.

Funds charging sales fees are called load funds. Many mutual funds are offered without a sales charge; these are called no load funds. As you research managed funds, find out how long the fund manager has been running the fund and how the fund did compared to its peers in both bull and bear markets. In my practice, it is my job to do this research for my clients as I allocate their investments using the asset allocation dashboard.

One thing to remember regarding true asset allocation is that if everything you own is going up or going down, it's a good sign you are not diversified. You should not expect everything to go up or down every year. Nobody can predict the timing of the markets and individual sectors consistently over time. Money typically moves from one area of the investment markets to another. One asset is often increasing just as another is decreasing, as the money merely moves from one investment vehicle to another.

I do not suggest that you go out and invest in the market using the sample portfolio we created for John Doe (see sidebar). Each individual investor must consider his or her own unique set of circumstances, risk tolerance and goals.

THE SEVENTH GAUGE: MEASURING "FUN"
We now have explored the six major gauges of asset allocation, but something may still be missing for you; the element of fun.

Achieving a diversified investment portfolio is like going on a diet: We may understand the need for it, know how to implement it and initially do a good job following it. However, as time passes, our desire to binge on a box of Double Stuffed Oreos may overtake us. Likewise, we get tempted by "hot stock tips" or high-flying sectors, as many people did during the dot-com era.

I can't tell you how to resist the urge for a box of Oreos, but I can tell you that you don't have to completely resist your temptation for fun when building an asset allocation plan.

I often meet with clients whose portfolios include stocks that are not the type I would recommend they keep. I also frequently meet couples in conflict over investing styles. Spouse A, for instance, enjoys the fun of buying and selling stocks, but has performed so poorly that Spouse B has arranged the meeting with me, to stop any further damage to their portfolio.

That's why you should split your total investment portfolio into two pieces: your serious money and your play money. Gauges one through six are designed to help you achieve good long-term returns on your investments and to reduce losses when certain areas of the investment markets are doing poorly.

The seventh gauge is for those who need to have some fun with investments. This is your chance for excitement and the adrenaline rush you crave. For example, after reading this chapter you might decide that 95% of your investment portfolio should follow the strategy I have outlined using gauges one through six, and that 5% of your money will be invested in a much riskier manner.

Maybe you want to buy some small local company you've heard about, or a biotech company working on a cure for AIDS, or a small computer

Insider Notes: Economics 101 — If the demand for certain investments increases, their prices increase. Currently, there is more than $3 trillion in money market funds. You want to own what this money eventually buys.

company that thinks it can someday overtake Microsoft as the software marketplace leader. Whatever you decide, make sure that you have selected an amount that you are willing and able to lose.

Very often, risky investing results in a worthless stock on somebody's tax return years later. Conversely, sound investing can bring enormously successful long-term results. Early in my career, I worked less than a mile from a start-up company whose product was something called DOS, made by a company called Microsoft.

Today, the early owners of Microsoft stock are very happy with their risk capital decision. Gauge seven allows you to indulge your desire to play the stock market. When selecting how much of our portfolio to allocate to high-risk investments, you stand a greater chance of remaining disciplined with your serious money asset allocation.

LESSONS LEARNED

Let's recap what you've learned:
- The principles of building a diversified investment plan, using the asset allocation dashboard.
- How to break the investment market into six major categories. Each category can be further split into smaller sub-categories, increasing diversification.
- How to analyze your long-term investment objectives, your time frame for holding the investments, and your risk tolerance, all of which you then use to determine what percentage of your overall portfolio should be allocated to each investment classification.
- Once you have selected your percentage allocation to each classification and the specific investments to hold within each classification, you've learned to monitor how much you hold within each investment classification.
- If a particular classification has increased or decreased in value too much over time, you've learned to recognize that it no longer represents your desired target. Whenever you determine that you are no longer at your targeted investment percentages, you can rebalance your portfolio to ensure that you stay with your asset allocation plan.

■ The ins-and-outs of a little-used asset class called REITs and how they can diversify your portfolio without exposing your bond component to as much risk, in the event that interest rates begin to rise.

And, of course, you've learned that it's possible to remain a disciplined investor, and still have fun playing the market.

■ ■ ■

Brian Evans, CPA/PFS is the president of Bauer Evans, Inc., P.S., a Certified Public Accounting firm, and Bauer Evans Wealth Management, LLC located in Everett, WA. He holds a B.A. in Accounting, graduating Summa Cum Laude from Washington State University. Brian oversees 14 staff members on the CPA side and manages over $40 million of client money himself. In 2001, he earned the prestigious Personal Financial Specialist designation for his breadth of skills in the areas of investments, income taxes, retirement and estate planning. He can be reached at 425-252-6909, brian@bauerevans.com or at www.bauerevans.com.

Brian has developed 19 different model portfolios to use to invest his clients' money. Each model is patterned using the principles of the Asset Allocation Dashboard as outlined in this chapter. Individual investors vary in age, goals, portfolio size, and risk tolerance. After matching an investor to the proper model portfolio, it becomes his job to monitor and execute the investment allocations and specific investment choices. Brian successfully serves clients across the country and is currently accepting new clients.

[3]

SMART INVESTMENT MANAGEMENT

Playing stock tips is like playing the slot machines: you might hit it big, but in the long run, you're more likely to get hit yourself, in your wallet. To be a successful investor, not even industry and market knowledge is enough; you need a sound process that reflects your risk tolerance, helps you hire the appropriate investment managers, and effectively monitor your growing portfolio. Learn this 11-step, easy-to-implement investment management process to dramatically tilt the odds — in your favor.

"THERE IS NOTHING IS MORE TERRIBLE THAN IGNORANCE IN ACTION."

- Johann Wolfgang von Goethe

by STAN SKLENAR

Snap quiz: Do you invest with a clear strategy? Have you established sound risk management parameters? Do you perform due diligence before hiring an investment advisor? Is your portfolio tax efficient?

If you answered "no" to any of these questions, it's time for a thorough examination of your invest-

WITH A THOROUGH UNDERSTANDING OF YOUR CURRENT POSITION,
YOU CAN BEGIN LOOKING INTO THE FUTURE.

ment approach. Adopt an investment management process, and you'll take charge of your money—for life.

This process is crucial for wealth creation (or accumulation) and preservation because:

- It conveys an understanding of your risk tolerance;
- It allows you to avoid the insidious cycle of market emotions and resist temptations to put money into investments when the market may be peaking or to take money out at the wrong time;
- It helps you hire the appropriate investment managers;
- It helps you monitor and evaluate your portfolio objectively;
- It guides you as to when and how to rebalance; and, perhaps most importantly,
- It prevents unrealistic, illogical, and inconsistent goals.

An investment management process is necessary to deal with risks that arise from uncertainty and from scarce investment capital. One of the things you do not know is what the future will bring. This process is a management tool on one hand, but it is also a framework that helps you to understand scarcity and helps you to understand uncertainty because managing what you do not know is as important as managing what you know.

You can't invest in everything because you have limited resources; this process allows you to prioritize the best opportunities to pursue. Also, you need to have a basis for handling losses in a controllable manner and this process provides a trigger for you to adjust those loses before they become a crisis.

Most investors don't have an investment management process. They often give lip service to the idea, but very often, it falls by the wayside because of emotional or irrational decisions.

BEWARE OF THE LATEST FAD

Generally, most investors associate managing money with looking for a good investment idea, as opposed to having a rational and disciplined investment process. With an idea, what investors are really getting is just a false sense of security, because they are largely basing their decision on hindsight, on the opinion of someone they know, intuition, a guess, or a hunch.

Many retail investors also love to pour money into every investment idea that is hitting new highs, whether it's the NASDAQ, the bond market, the S&P 500, or real estate. These investors project what has happened in the past into the future, and they think that this evaluation amounts to enough research.

However, investors do not ask why the fund, portfolio or program has produced a certain track record. They must ask, is this track record sustainable going into the future? How does the world look today as opposed to yesterday when the track record was established?

People sell for all the wrong reasons, and usually at the worst time. In an up market, investors sell the winners to take profits. They keep the losers, which are usually down for a reason. Instead, they should keep the winners, let the profits grow, and weed out the losers.

Most investors also follow what is known as the "cycle of market emotions," which means they invest in times of optimism and euphoria, and sell out at the point of panic, capitulation or despondency. They buy at the point of maximum financial risk and sell out at the point of maximum financial opportunity.

Implementing an investment management process helps prevent all of the aforementioned investor syndromes. The process keeps you on track and pointed toward your goals.

> **Insider Notes:** People sell for all the wrong reasons, and usually at the worst time. In an up market, investors sell the winners to take profits. They keep the losers, which are usually down for a reason. Instead, they should keep the winners, let the profits grow, and weed out the losers.

YOU SHOULD LOOK AT THE ECONOMIC BIG PICTURE, NOT THE QUARTER-TO-QUARTER OR EVEN YEAR-TO-YEAR.

Undesirable outcomes result from not following a disciplined process:
- Ending up somewhere else than where you want to be;
- Discovering mistakes when it is too late to correct them;
- Letting emotions drive investment management decisions;
- Making knee-jerk reactions or reacting to incorrect or extraneous information;
- Ending up with a non-diversified portfolio;
- Mismatching appropriate and suitable investment assets without considering current or future liabilities;
- Chasing the hottest idea of the day — or even worse — of yesterday, which results in buying at the peak and eventually selling out at the bottom;
- Sustaining losses greater than you can tolerate; and
- Following the crowd or becoming seduced by media frenzy or hype.

In the passages that follow, you will learn how an investment management process helps you understand your current situation and investment opportunities—and ultimately help you reach your goals.

You also will understand how an investment management process helps you manage your portfolio, in a pro-active way.

The investment management process is NOT based on the "best investment idea of the day" or on how well an investment or an investment manager is performing today or, even worse, yesterday. The overall approach is focused on the future; it is a pro-active approach, as opposed to reactive. The focus is on risk management, on controlling the downside risk of investing, and on addressing controllable factors. Also, it is about how the pieces fit together

SKLENAR'S ELEVEN

To get your investment management process into place, follow my 11-step program:

❶ Analyze your current position. List all your assets and liabilities in an easy-to-understand way. Assign value, to the best of your knowledge, to all assets: real estate, U.S stocks, non-U.S./international stocks, U.S. fixed income securities, non-U.S./international fixed-income securities, cash and cash equivalents (regardless if held directly, through mutual funds, exchange traded funds, annuities, etc.). Include your qualified retirement plan assets and your non-qualified retirement assets. Do not count stock options—neither "incentive stock options" (qualified) nor non-qualified stock options—unless they have been exercised. For liabilities, record amount and terms (short- and long-term, fixed rate, variable rate, pre-payment penalties, etc.).

❷ Document how assets were acquired or accumulated. You should have documentation or a thorough understanding of how you have accumulated assets, and how each of your individual assets reached its current status or value. For complex situations, create a flow chart.

Documenting your assets thoroughly at a granular level provides you with a greater understanding. Also, it helps you to develop your instincts better than, say, analysis based only on advice from a financial magazine.

Often investors understand the dollar amount of assets, but they do not understand the disposition and/or characteristics of their assets; they do not have the mastery of what to expect the assets to do under various global economic scenario, and the dynamics involved in globalization.

Taking a thorough inventory of your assets entails understanding the risk-reward dynamic, and judging whether an asset is likely to go up or down. In other words, someone will look at a statement and say, "My house is worth $1.2 million and my house in Malibu is worth $2 million." They'll give you the dollar numbers and that gives them the sense of knowing of

Insider Notes: Documenting your assets thoroughly at a granular level provides you with a greater understanding. Also, it helps you to develop your instincts better than, say, analysis based only on advice from a financial magazine.

THE DUMB MONEY

Major reasons why the investment management process is either not used or is misused by the investing public include the following:

- **Lack of knowledge among the general investing public.** There is an extraordinary range of options, so it is very difficult for the average investor to fully understand all of the variables and make good decisions. Consequently, most investors make decisions on a very narrow or superficial basis.

- **Investors' natural urge to join in bull markets and run away from market downturns.** There is some magic to how the "up" markets attract investors; it has nothing to do with the investors' need to have their money invested and allocated to meet their needs.

  Powerful messages from the media, Internet, friends, and colleagues play an important part in this irrational behavior. Part of human nature is the difficulty of overcoming the "herd mentality." However, an investment management process can provide you with a vehicle to give you the perspective to resist following the herd when its direction conflicts with your process.

  As the investment professor Jimmy Rodgers once said: "Everybody does well in a bull market. But don't confuse a bull market for brains."

- **Most investors are long-term investors with a strong appetite for short-term profits (causing uncontrollable losses).** On the one hand, man is a social animal whose natural inclination is to follow the crowd. But men also are very greedy, and it is very difficult to overcome the desire to collect money quickly.

  There is a difference between wealth created as a result of a disciplined investment management process, and somebody who tries to get rich quick. The former has accumulated wealth almost inevitably over time, while the latter is much more of a random occurrence based on good fortune.

■ **Investors are influenced by very recent experiences.** Here is a story of a client who had an investment management process in place, but broke the commitment because of very short-term experiences.

The client, with a $2 million portfolio, had an appropriate assets allocation and portfolio structure in place. The portfolio had been actually exceeding our targeted rates of return. One day, in the very late '90s, the client called and told me that based on a conversation with some of his friends, he decided to transfer all of his money and securities to two of the investment managers that we had in the overall portfolio. Obviously, those were managers showing the highest returns. The investor told me, "It's all about the new economy. I can judge for myself which manager is doing a good job, and volatility does not matter to me."

The investor had lost more than 55% of the value of his portfolio.

■ **Public distrust of professional services.** The financial services industry is not completely regulated or licensed. As a result, there are very few easy ways to objectively tell the difference between good advisors and bad advisors.

Even among the largest and most well known organizations, investors can be exposed to unethical behavior. Also, many financial institutions have been more interested in selling high-profit-margin proprietary or non-proprietary financial products.

The nature of how we share information in a western democracy is such that bad news tends to be the news. The nature of how the media works is to report on aberrations. The problem with this is that most of the news stories are not the same as analytical reports.

Consequently, news stories about investment professionals tend to be negative. A good outcome of this is that it can lead investors to approach their prospective financial service provider with skepticism. You should be skeptical; people should prove themselves to you. But don't let skepticism lapse into cynicism.

- **Most investors aren't willing to allocate enough time to the investment management process.** Whether you are trying to build a business or prepare for an athletic event, consistent application of time, money, and resources is required to achieve success. People who revisit their financial strategy only once every year, twice a year, or every two years are by definition not consistent or disciplined.

- **Many investors micro-manage their investments, as opposed to macro-managing them.** These investors focus on less-important details and lose sight of the big picture. The purpose of the investment management process is to provide context that will help you understand that the day-to-day move of 30 points in the marketplace that may seem like big dollars actually is really a minor development in the context of long-term trends and plans.

  An understanding of context will help you understand what has a big impact on the performance and volatility of your portfolio,

what they own, but they do not understand that the house might be sitting on a mudslide.

The goal is to have a three-dimensional, rather than two-dimensional, picture of your portfolio. A two-dimensional picture is just a snapshot that allows you to look at what is occurring at a point in time. The three-dimensional view provides insight into the reasons for changes and also facilitates predictions of likely future changes. Investors buy an investment not for the money it can make them today, but for the money they hope it will make for them tomorrow.

❸ **Evaluate your relationship with your assets.** Ask what you like and do not like about your assets. Consider whether or not you are happy with your assets and whether or not you believe you are on track to reach your goals. Evaluate critically the performance of your assets.

and what has a small impact, so you can avoid micro-managing.

- **There is a mistaken belief that investment management can be "commoditized."** Some cookie-cutter approaches, often using Internet-based processes, are based on historical capital markets assumptions. However, the methods give very little consideration to how the world looks today and to the investors' current position. Consequently, these processes have been misused.

Wealth management is very personal issue, and people have very unique needs — and emotions. Emotions and personal outlooks must be addressed, as investors will face uncertainties, risks and downturns that test will or nerve.

- **Investors confuse short-term tactics with long-term strategies.** People may have a plan, but often can't resist short-term opportunities. Investors need to be committed to a strategy and then use tactics flexibly in response to changing marketplace conditions. You want to create a framework to which you are committed.

Keep in mind that performance must be evaluated in the context of the purpose of an investment. People usually focus on performance, but there also is a purpose behind investments.

For example, a hedged investment is designed to protect against the downside; it is supposed to protect you when everything else goes bad. Consequently, do not simply give assets that performed well a high grade, and assets that performed poorly a low grade. Measure assets' performance against their purpose, or within the context of the purpose and their performance.

With a thorough understanding of your current position, you can begin looking into the future. Then you can determine how to best allocate your resources, the different options, and how to organize your resources for best use.

From your asset base you can go in many different directions. Within those many directions you have to pick and choose among them. Do that in the context of your station in life, magnitude of wealth, your job income, and whatever might affect your current and/or future cash flow and expenses. In this vein, you should determine your cash flow.

❹ **Formulate investment goals.** To formulate your investment goals, consider how much you want to include your family and its next generation into your goal setting, and/or into the decision making process. What are your resources? Look at the titling of the assets that you have listed. Does the title of the assets make sense? Is the title of the assets offering you the benefits that you expect during your lifetime, in case of incapacity of the grantor or death of the grantor?

Other questions to check off:
- Do you own these assets or do you control the assets on behalf of someone else?
- Who is the ultimate beneficiary?
- What are your lifetime goals?
- What is your biggest financial fear in life?
- How much minimum income do you need?
- Are you at a point in life at which you are creating and growing wealth? Or do you just want to protect and preserve what you have?
- How much wealth do you have?
- Do you have any concentrated positions?
- Are the assets in a taxable account, a tax-deferred qualified retirement plan, an IRA, or a combination of two or more of them?
- Are there any considerations like planning for distribution of the wealth during retirement in the most tax-advantageous way, or planning for the distribution of assets at death in the most tax-advantageous way?
- How important is tax-management or at least tax efficiency in this case?
- What are our preferences and feelings? Are there any other issues relevant to us that we feel should be raised?

❺ **State the purpose of the investing.** Keep a focus on the purpose of the assets. Will the assets under management include capital for lifetime needs? Is there a need for assets management of wealth surplus? Is the purpose or multiple purposes to grow assets for retirement, to generate cash flow and preserve the assets during retirement, to preserve family estate for next generations, to park cash reserves for a future business opportunity, to fund a future liability, or any other goal?

❻ **State the objective(s).** Ask whether you need growth, tax-managed growth, growth and income, growth consistent with preservation of principal, taxable income, tax-exempt income, and/or liquidity. Do you need or want only a U.S. portfolio, or a global portfolio?

What is the minimum rate of return that I need to achieve, to build or maintain the size of the portfolio that can be reasonably expected to generate the cash flow that I need during my retirement? Also, do I want to grow the assets to provide for my family's next generation or two, and for our family charitable purposes?

What are your liquidity and cash flow needs: How liquid do you need to stay? Do you expect any major expenditures during the foreseeable future? Do we need the portfolio to generate some predictable and reliable income? And how much? When? Now, or later?

Do you have any future liabilities that need to be funded? If you have, do they need to be funded at a certain point in time or on regular basis?

Determine the minimum rate of return that you need to achieve to have the correct cash flow and distributions from your portfolio, now and later.

> **Insider Notes:** To formulate your investment goals, consider how much you want to include your family and its next generation into your goal setting, and/or into the decision making process.

RECOMMENDED STRATEGIES FOR CERTAIN HORIZONS:

1-3 years: Do not invest for growth; appropriate assets are cash, cash equivalents, bonds with short term duration;
3-5 years: Invest in cash, bonds & stocks;
5+ years: Stocks, bonds & real estate.

For retirement, most financial professionals suggest distributions of about 4%, which should leave earnings for reinvestment while not excessively eating into the principal during adverse market conditions.

❼ **Evaluate your risk tolerance.** How much risk and volatility are you willing and able to tolerate over your stated time horizon? How much risk and volatility are you willing to tolerate within a year or any other given time period?

What is your risk tolerance? Are you:
- Conservative (preferring little risk and low volatility in return for accepting potentially lower returns);
- Moderately Conservative (willing to take some risk to seek enhanced returns);
- Moderate (willing to assume an average amount of market risk and volatility or loss of principal to achieve higher returns);
- Moderately Aggressive (willing to accept an above-average amount of risk and volatility or loss of principal to realize potentially higher returns); or
- Aggressive (willing to accept substantial volatility or loss of principal to pursue potentially higher returns).

For all of your assets, rate the degree of risk you are willing to accept on a scale from 1 to 10, with 1 being the least amount of risk and 10 being the greatest.

IMPORTANT INSTRUCTIONS

Asset classes have inherent, or generally accepted risk levels, that can be expressed as a range, on a scale of 1-10. Investors can use this scale as a guide to stay within their risk profile.

Income 1-3, Growth & Income 3-7, Growth U.S. Equity 4-10, Growth Global Equity 4-9, Growth International Equity 5-10

Which risks are your primary concern? Prioritize among the following:
- The possibility that my investment may not grow enough to meet my future needs.
- A sharp decline in value in a short period of time.
- My portfolio may not grow enough to keep pace with inflation.
- Not earning a rate of return greater than the stock market.
- My portfolio will not generate enough current income.

❽ **Determine your time horizon.** Ask yourself, "What is the time horizon for my goals? When do I need the money?" An even better question is, "How long you are willing to wait for these assets to reach your investment objective? Is it one to three years? Three to five years? Ten years? Longer?"

If you are expecting to retire in 25 years, your investment strategy will be very different from someone whose short-term goal is to save a down payment for a house, or who invests wealth surplus for the next two-to-three generations.

Time horizons are a crucial element in designing your optimal portfolio. They can help you to narrow down the appropriate type of assets to use. Time horizons must be matched to goals and to appropriate assets.

Otherwise it is only a question of time when you will encounter a major problem. Time also has a moderating effect on risk.

❾ **Determine special needs, considerations, and limitations.** Some investors have very particular needs, e.g.:

Insider Notes: Determine the minimum rate of return that you need to achieve to have the correct cash flow and distributions from your portfolio, now and later.

THE CLASSIC INVESTMENT PITFALLS

Most investors focus on wrong things when investing. For example, investors often sell winners and keep losers, as opposed to keeping winners and selling losers.

Another typical mistake is to buy a packaged investment vehicle that appealed to them for some reason. Very seldom would these investors ask if it is an appropriate investment for their situation. Other times, a decision is made to buy, but there has been no optimization of the portfolio and no investment policy statement.

Classic examples of inappropriate investments:
- The investment vehicle is too aggressive because of the type of securities in it, or the investment strategies and style used by the portfolio managers;
- The investment has an inappropriate structure, such as lack of full or partial liquidity;
- The investment has not historically offered returns high enough to provide for retirement in 20 years;
- The investment has unreliable cash flow; or
- The investment has no compatibility with the rest of the investor's overall portfolio.

International residents. Those living in multiple jurisdictions or having assets in multiple jurisdictions may need to have more exposure to global assets.

The "suddenly" wealthy. Professional athletes or others who suddenly become wealthy usually need access to their retirement cash flow or income much sooner than the average person. They may go from nothing to the "grow and protect" stage—skipping the growth stage entirely.

Those with a disabled or ill minor. These investors must plan to secure the future of their dependent after their deaths.

⑩ **Evaluate regulatory issues.** When investing, consider regulations, such as tax rules, that limit investment or withdrawal amounts. Other regulations may limit the types of investments or ownership of certain assets.

⓫ Develop a thorough understanding of your "current position." The first 10 steps have led you to this conclusion. This is the only way that you can make sure that your investments are compatible with the purpose(s) for holding the investment. Determine whether the purpose/goal is to maintain a standard of living in retirement, to pass on a legacy to loved ones, to launch a new business, some combination of those, or something else. You might need to segregate and/or prioritize some of the variables.

All decisions must be compatible with your time horizon, cash flow needs, and taxes. (At times, the compatibility issues warrant bringing additional advisors such as an attorney, CPA, or others onto the team.) All-inclusive understanding of your current position will help you to determine in what proportions your portfolio parts should be one to another, and what the inter-relationships of the pieces should be.

When it comes to current position, common mistakes made by investors include:

- When they analyze their current position they are not totally objective;
- They let their questions and answers be influenced by preconceptions about the financial markets, by information from the media, their recent experiences or those of a friend, and the natural tendency to do what everyone else is doing;
- Their whole approach to investing is reactive as opposed to proactive; and
- They generally spend enormous time analyzing individual investment ideas, but unfortunately focusing on the wrong issues.

Also, many times investors analyze and tweak numbers to get results that prove they were right all along.

 Insider Notes: If you are expecting to retire in 25 years, your investment strategy will be very different from someone whose short-term goal is to save a down payment for a house, or who invests wealth surplus for the next two-to-three generations.

DUE DILIGENCE IS AN IMPORTANT PART OF HIRING THE RIGHT PORTFOLIO/INVESTMENT MANAGER.

DESIGNING THE OPTIMAL PORTFOLIO

Now that you've finished the 11 steps, you're ready for the next major phase: designing the optimal portfolio.

With the right asset allocation and investment manager structure, you can design the optimal portfolio that has a reasonably high probability of achieving the investor's objectives without undue risk.

You need to develop something what will guide the investment management activity. The overall strategy begins with asset allocation guidelines. This focuses on the two steps that will have the biggest impact on the portfolio's performance and volatility: asset class allocation and sub-asset class allocation.

- Start by developing policy guidelines. These are rules, essentially, for the investment management activity. The guidelines determine the boundaries and parameters within which portfolio(s) will be managed as a whole and as individual investments. The guidelines help the investor to achieve his or her objectives without undue risk. Your current position (your profile as an investor), and regulatory issues are at the center of developing investment policy guidelines.
- Set an asset allocation policy, which entails dividing a portfolio's investments among different asset classes. The most common classes are stocks, bonds, cash and cash equivalents, real estate, natural resources, collectibles, and derivatives.

Asset allocation is the most important decision in investing. Probably no other decision will have a greater impact on your portfolio performance and volatility than asset allocation. Virtually all industry studies have suggested that upwards of 80% of performance and volatility is associated with asset allocation.

Use the following checklist of criteria when setting the assets allocation:

■ What is the purpose of this fund? Is it to grow money to build the future cash flow in retirement; to grow family estate for next generation; to park cash reserves for business opportunity; etc.?

■ At what station in life are you? Is that station capital growth; growth and preservation; retirement in the next 10 years; preservation and growth; etc.?

■ How much wealth do you have?

■ What is your risk tolerance?

■ Is there a minimum rate of return requirement?

■ Will your financial situation likely improve, worsen, or stay the same?

■ Will there be any withdrawals? If yes, how much and when?

■ Are there any regulatory requirements?

■ Is this an IRA? Are there any mandatory distribution requirements?

■ Is this money managed for the benefit of someone else?

■ What is the investor's time horizon?

Take note: time horizon will help you to narrow down the appropriate type of assets to use. You must match the time horizon of your goals (you might look at them as liabilities) with the appropriate assets; otherwise it is only a question of time when you will encounter a major problem.

Time has a moderating effect on risk (standard deviation), and with a longer time horizon, you may increase your probabilities of a positive rate of return on your investments and meet your long-term investment objectives. A longer time horizon allows for investment gains to compound and for losses to recoup. History does show that the ranges of stocks' and bonds' annualized returns narrow over time.

Insider Notes: Asset allocation is the most important decision in investing. Probably no other decision will have a greater impact on your portfolio performance and volatility than asset allocation. Virtually all industry studies have suggested that upwards of 80% of performance and volatility is associated with asset allocation.

THE WOODSTOCK GENERATION TURNS GRAY

Demographic and other socioeconomic trends are making it very difficult for the U.S. government to fund retirement and other social benefits. Governments and employers are shifting the responsibility for planning, funding, and managing retirement savings to individuals. At the same time, people are living longer, so retirees' money must last longer.

In the U.S., the government has been passing legislation to create new company-sponsored retirement savings plans and new individual retirement plans, and to increase retirement plan contribution limits. More employers are sponsoring retirement plans for employees, but their role and financial contribution are kept to a minimum. Moreover, many of these plans favor employer stock, which introduces portfolio risk.

In this challenging environment, one of your portfolio's goals should be to provide future cash flows during retirement years. This may begin at age 65, but it could begin much sooner. Your portfolio must allow you to maintain your standard of living. You should not expect your cost of living to drop.

Expected/targeted ranges of rates of returns will among other things depend on the percentages of the proposed asset mix. The greater the bond percentage of the asset mix, the lower the expected volatility of the asset mix. The converse is true as well: the smaller the bond percentage of the asset mix, the greater the volatility of the asset mix. Obviously, this is what the history has shown over a meaningful period of time (assuming only stocks and bonds are included in the asset mix).

The expected ranges of rates of returns are based on a mathematical model that takes into account the historical risk measurements of certain indices from 1926-2001 as well as the current interest rate environment. Based on the model, the return of the proposed asset allocation would have fallen within the range shown for each time 95% of the time.

Expected and targeted ranges of rates of return will depend on the percentages of the proposed asset mix, among other things. The greater the bond percentage of the asset mix, the lower the expected volatility of the asset mix. The smaller the percentage of bonds within the asset mix, the greater the volatility of the asset mix.

VOLATILITY OF RETURNS OVER TIME

Since 1930, over rolling five-year periods, stocks have been a better-performing asset class than bonds about 75% of the time. The following are percentage returns by decade, compared to the S&P 500:

1930s: 4.3%
1940s: 9.6%
1950s: 20.9%
1960s: 8.6%
1970s: 7.5%
1980s: 18.2%
1990s: 19%

Determine manager or portfolio structure. Manager structure refers to the sub-categories — also called sub-asset classes — within the individual asset classes, and money management styles. Sub-asset classes include: domestic or international stocks; large, medium or small capitalization stocks; growth, value, or core money management style; long-term, intermediate-term, and/or short-term bond portfolio duration; high quality (low credit risk) or low quality (high credit risk); total return; and enhanced cash.

The appropriate percentage blend of the individual parts of the portfolio's structure depends on the individual. It also is tied to our assessment of the economy and the financial markets.

You should look at the economic big picture, not the quarter-to-quarter or even year-to-year. (Example of some of the underlying economic issues is globalization, 45 year-low interest rates, demographics, etc.)

Insider Notes: I am not aware of a study that says there is evidence that someone or something can pinpoint when it is the appropriate time to switch from one money management style to another one, and to continue to do it reliably over a meaningful period.

From 1926-2002, large capitalization stocks have posted an annualized return of 10%. For small cap stocks during the same period, the figure is 12%. This might indicate that it is best to invest in small cap stocks for long-term growth; however, it does not tell us how long it took for small cap stocks to recover when they fell out of favor during those times. Consequently, it goes back to the current position of the client, because not everyone has the appetite or endurance for such volatility.

How much U.S. equities versus international equities do you need in your portfolio? There is no doubt that an investor investing some portion of his or her assets in equities needs some exposure to the international markets in one form or another.

One can argue that by investing in U.S. multinational companies, investors are already getting exposure to international markets since many of the multinational companies operate in more than 200 countries, and they manage the currency and other risks associated with these markets. In the very long run, this probably is true.

For the time being, there should be some exposure to direct investing in international equities. Hedged and not hedged international equity portfolios seem to have similar levels of risk. I prefer not hedged international equities.

As far as money management styles, there are two major schools of money management, growth and value money management. Obviously, other money management styles have evolved over the years that are classified somewhere between these styles or as an extreme of these styles. Examples would be growth at a reasonable price money management style (GARP); core style; or deep value style. These money management styles go in and out of favor.

These investment management style cycles are unpredictable. The individual cycles vary in length, and in magnitude. The variability of returns of the individual styles has varied substantially.

The money management style (growth or value) that has been dominating during one cycle, in other words has had higher returns, has not had necessarily greater variability of returns, as one might expect. Of course, studies regarding money management styles differ as to exactly when a particular cycle started, the magnitude of one style against another one, and in other respects.

I am not aware of a study that says there is evidence that someone or something can pinpoint when it is the appropriate time to switch from one money management style to another one, and to continue to do it reliably over a meaningful period. With respect to what the appropriate investment money management percentage blend is, it is still and will probably stay a controversial subject. I believe the appropriate blend percentage depends on individual factors and relates to the investor's/fund's current position.

Companies are usually classified as either large capitalization companies, medium cap, small cap, and micro cap, depending on their market capitalization, but the dividing lines are somewhat arbitrary. As a general guideline, the market capitalization is $5 billion or more for large caps, $1 billion to $5 billion for medium caps, $250 million to $1 billion for small caps, and less than $250 million for micro caps.

As far as bonds, at a very minimum the following should be addressed, and analyzed: taxable bonds vs. tax-free bonds; the duration of the portfolio (exposure to interest rate risk); and default free vs. non-default free bonds (the credit risk).

Duration of the bonds or bond portfolio can be used by the bond investor to implement his bond investment strategy. If the investor believes that market yields will decline, he may wish to change his/her bond mix to include bonds carrying higher durations in order to leverage the increase in bond value. If an increase in yields is expected, he/she may elect to

Insider Notes: Whether investing in a mutual fund or buying the services of an institutional portfolio manager, the biggest difference between disciplined implementation and ad hoc implementation is the attitude that you bring when you make those decisions.

change the mix to include bonds with lower duration to minimize the negative effect on his/her portfolio.

Credit risk is risk associated with the likelihood of a default in paying interest, or original principal back to the investors upon the bond's maturity. Credit rating is an estimate that illustrates the credit quality. Diversification is about spreading your investments among different classes of assets (stocks, bonds, cash & cash equivalents), different sub-asset classes (U.S. & international, large, medium, small capitalization of companies, money management styles, bonds' credit quality, maturities, maybe even between private and public sector issuers), different economic sectors, and industries.

Diversification also is about spreading money so that the above mentioned parts work together to help build your wealth while giving you some protection from downturns in any specific asset class. There are two kinds of risks: "specific" or diversifiable risk, and "systematic risk" or market risk. Diversification does not eliminate market risk, which is risk associated with the overall financial markets.

FORMALIZE A PERSONAL INVESTMENT POLICY

Create an investment policy statement outlining the goals, objectives, and guidelines of your portfolio. This document generally includes:

Statement of purpose:
- Your objectives: What is the portfolio designed to accomplished? And how?
- Guidelines for asset allocation; for expected rate of return; for the minimum returns required to meet overall goals;
- Risk tolerance: your willingness to tolerate volatility in the short- and long-run;
- Cash flow and liquidity needs: how much cash does the investor expect to withdraw and how often?
- Time horizon for achieving objectives; and
- Limitations (types of securities, capitalization, credit risk, duration, etc.).

Restrictions:
- Use of derivatives like futures, options, borrowing money or investing on margin, short sales, etc; and
- Requirements for monitoring, supervising and reviewing, to establish the grounds for measuring progress.

There are several reasons to use an investment policy statement:
- It formalizes the intended purposes of the portfolio or fund;
- It takes emotions out of the investment decisions;
- It helps maintain continuity in uncertain times; and
- It establishes the criteria by which to measure progress.

IMPLEMENT POLICY

When implementing your policy, consider active money management versus passive management, indexing or a combination of them. If you use a combination, use active management for less-efficient asset classes.

It is easy to get caught up in the Wall Street hype about which approach is better. Since active management is appropriate for most situations, this chapter will cover active money management.

Individual investment managers that you hire will implement tactical strategies. For instance, a U.S. bond manager with an intermediate bond duration portfolio might still reduce or increase duration of the bond portfolio within the strategic constrains. Other examples would be global or international investment managers perhaps implementing tactical country rotation strategies, or a U.S. equity manager changing a weighting within a sector, or an industry.

By implementing the policy, I mean hiring the right investment managers who in turn invest the money in accordance with the "investment policy

Insider Notes: Once you select a manager and decide to put your wealth in the hands of money management companies, you should structure the compensation in a way that you and your investment professional share the risks and the rewards.

statement," negotiating investment manager fees, and reviewing the lending program (using securities as a collateral for loans, if needed).

Whether investing in a mutual fund or buying the services of an institutional portfolio manager, the biggest difference between disciplined implementation and ad hoc implementation is the attitude that you bring when you make those decisions.

If you make these decisions as if you were buying a commodity such as a mutual fund, then you will take a more tactical approach. If you take the approach of hiring a mutual fund manager, then you are hiring the manager who operates that mutual fund and that changes your mindset and the nature of your relationship with the financial professionals executing your investment policy. Whether it is a broker, financial advisor, or mutual funds manager, you must look at the people, their philosophy, their track record, and their plans for the future. You need to map all of those to the investment strategy that you have outlined in the previous sections (see the next sub-step, below).

ISSUES TO ADDRESS

- **Ownership of securities (stocks, bonds, etc.).** For whatever reason, do you want to own the securities directly or via an investment vehicle (mutual fund, annuity, exchange traded fund, etc.)? Some structures of ownership might limit your financial benefits; other structures offer additional characteristics and consequently additional benefits (mentioned bellow).

- **Transparency of the investments.** What level of scrutiny do you want and your guidelines require? To what level must you take "ongoing due diligence" (as explained bellow)?

  A higher level of transparency allows you to control the pre-determined and appropriate percentage blend of the individual parts of the portfolio. Also, it allows you to scrutinize the risks taken by the individual managers. One example: aggressive hedging strategies, which might be unsuitable for your current position.

■ **Tax-efficiency.** How important is it to establish your own cost basis? To what degree do you want the flexibility to manage tax liability?

Are you transferring securities into the new accounts as opposed to only cash? Are these securities already held by the portfolio managers that you are considering? Do you wish to stretch out tax liability for your beneficiaries?

Mutual fund shareholders usually buy into "embedded capital gains," which are securities purchased by the fund years ago that have since risen in price and will generate taxable capital gains when those securities are one day sold.

In individually managed accounts, investors have some flexibility to manage their tax liability. They can "harvest" losses in their accounts to offset gains that the investors might have from even unrelated transactions. Some investment structures allow you to stretch out tax liability for your beneficiaries. Regardless of the options you choose, ALWAYS consult your tax and legal advisors.

■ **Fees.** Once you select a manager and decide to put your wealth in the hands of money management companies, you should structure the compensation in a way that you and your investment professional share the risks and the rewards. Also, do it based on the consolidated asset size and not on individual accounts. The pricing structure should minimize any potential for conflicts of interest.

Ask yourself: What do I want to delegate and what do I want to do by myself? How do I want to pay fees associated with investment management? Does a certain fee structure provide me with tax-deductibility?

The typical fees associated with investment management are some of the combinations of the following: investment management advisory; portfolio management; transaction costs; operating expenses, possibly including 12-b1 fees; front-end load; back-end charge; etc.

Investors in mutual funds are subject to annual fees that are deducted from the fund's net asset value (NAV) and are not seen by investors as a line item on their statements. Mutual fund investors also might be paying a "front-end" load, or back-end charge.

In individually managed accounts, investors often pay a single "wrap fee" that covers portfolio management, trading costs, investment consultation, and any other operating expenses.

Fees might have a visible disclosure and be a one line item on your statement, hidden, or a combination of both.

- **Continuity of your wealth management.** This relates to potential changes due to the investment managers and to changes in your circumstances. These may include changes with respect to the key people involved in your investment managment and/or changes related to your own circumstances.

GETTING THE RIGHT HELP

Manager search and selection is primarily driven by asset allocation and manager structure. Look at the portfolio as a whole, and select each portfolio manager based on both a quantitative and qualitative analysis. Pay attention to how one manager fits with other managers in the portfolio.

Find and get access to as many money managers as you can (a few high quality computerized databases are on the market).

Objectively monitor a universe of managers, according to quantitative analysis. You must evaluate:
- Past returns, absolute returns and returns on a risk-adjusted basis, as well as variability and consistency of returns;
- The managers in the context of their asset class universe, and in the context of their peer group universe;
- The managers' performance relative to the appropriate benchmark(s)—e.g., up and down market capture ratio (how much of the positive or negative rates of returns the portfolio manager is capturing);

- The sharp ratio, which indicates how much excess return was achieved per unit of total risk;
- Money management style and sub-style; and
- The profile of the manager in terms of the amount of assets under management; number of years needed to establish a favorable track record; and investment strategy (bottom-up, earning surprise, emphasis on internal research, etc.).

Now, you must apply qualitative analysis:

- What has been the reason for the portfolio managers' successful rates of returns? Can they repeat the success?
- Who are the key people on the portfolio management team? Are they the same people that are responsible for the historical track record?
- How committed are the key employees?
- Have there been any changes in their portfolio management processes? Are their results luck or skill? How do they fit with the other managers in the portfolio?
- How quickly has the firm grown? Has the firm grown its research and analytical capabilities, and operational capabilities, to accommodate the additional business?
- What steps has the firm taken to assure continuity of high quality of their portfolio management?

The following are examples of issues that might come up if a very thorough analysis, as described above, was not conducted. Investors must analyze the considered investment managers for their money management style discipline. More then a few managers wander outside their advertised money management style area to gain competitive advantage in a short

Insider Notes: Manager search and selection is primarily driven by asset allocation and manager structure. Look at the portfolio as a whole, and select each portfolio manager based on both a quantitative and qualitative analysis. Pay attention to how one manager fits with other managers in the portfolio.

run. They might be chasing the momentum—hot stocks, a hot industry, or a hot sector. This approach might temporarily improve their returns; this is known as "style drift." This causes investors to have significantly higher risk exposure than they might think they have. They are actually overexposed to today's hot style and underexposed to what might be tomorrow's money management style. I have not seen one study that would suggest that someone can successfully "time switch" among money management styles over a meaningful period of time.

Investors must also analyze the considered investment managers for their discipline, when it comes to the capitalization of the companies that they buy for their portfolio. Some managers, again, stray from their expertise and chase the momentum, whether it's large cap stocks, mid cap, or small cap stocks, or even a few hot stocks.

One example would be a small cap manager buying a small cap stock, and keeping the winners after their market value rises above $1 billion. They hold onto the stock because it goes up in value, even though the company has grown in capitalization, and it has become a large cap company.

A similar issue arises when a large cap manager holds onto small spin-offs from large cap companies that he owns in the portfolio because he likes the spin-offs. This approach might improve the manager's returns in the short-run, but it causes investors to have significantly higher risk exposure then they might realize.

The majority of your emphasis should be given to qualitative analysis, as opposed to quantitative analysis. It is crucial to successful implementation of policy to hire managers who really do what they advertise. Any wandering outside of the advertised area can significantly increase investor's undue risk exposure.

Due diligence is an important part of hiring the right portfolio/investment manager. The process needs to be a third party, independent, objective evaluation of how portfolio managers are carrying out your investment policies.

MONITOR, SUPERVISE, REVIEW AND REBALANCE

Now that your process is in place, you must conduct "performance reviews" of your portfolio in the broad context of your current position, your policies and the market. Consider questions such as:

- What market conditions existed during the review period?
- Did fund results meet your objectives?
- What was the performance of the individual managers?
- How much risk did the manager take in achieving results?
- Are you getting closer to your objectives or further away? Have there been any changes in your current position in terms of goals, stage in life, risk tolerance, time horizon, cash flow needs, magnitude of wealth, inheritance?
- What adjustments or changes need to be made to bring the portfolio in line with any changes above? Should any re-balancing be done now, over a period of time, or combination of both?

A formal performance measurement is a report that quantifies the underlying investment activity. It quantifies it in terms of performance that is related to returns and to risk. It establishes the groundwork for evaluating the managers' activity and comparing it against the investor's investment objectives.

Investors should be able to see all performance measurement analysis at the family level as well as at the level of each separate entity that they own or control.

Reporting of performance should be on a composite basis and on an individual manager basis. Reporting also should allow for varying levels of analysis along each asset class and each asset style, and on a gross and net-of-fee basis.

Returns should be calculated on a dollar-weighted and time-weighted basis. Dollar-weighted rate-of-returns measure the portfolio's total growth. The time-weighted rate of return is an excellent measure to evaluate the money manager's performance, because it minimizes the effects of cash flows.

For those investors who choose to take a hands-on approach to their financial life, this monitoring and review process is critical; it should be what comprises 90% of your activity.

Many people feel that they are not managing their portfolio unless they are buying and selling stocks or moving assets around. In fact, pro-active monitoring of advisors keeps you engaged, without unnecessary investment decisions on your part.

Monitoring must be done not only in the context of what is happening in the market today, but also in the context of all the work that you have done up until now to establish your objectives. Without this framework for monitoring, you will be tempted to impulsively respond to market forces. Your investment management process will help you stay the course.

■ ■ ■

Stan Sklenar, MBA, CIMA, has been providing investment management services to clients in the U.S. and many other countries since 1984. Born in Europe and educated in both Europe and the U.S., he earned the Certified Investment Management Analyst (CIMA) designation from the Investment Management Consultants Association, after completing the educational requirements held at the Wharton School of Business at the University of Pennsylvania.

His international education and experience give him a distinctive, multi-cultural understanding of the global financial marketplace. His articles on wealth management and personal investing have been published in a variety of publications, and he has recently co-authored a book on these subjects. He is fluent in Czech and Slovak. He can be reached at 925-963-2421 or at lavka2002@yahoo.com.

[4]
SECTOR ROTATION INVESTING

Here's an investment strategy that can protect your principal and make money for you in good times and bad.

> "STATIC ASSET ALLOCATION ONLY MAKES SENSE IN A WORLD WHERE ASSET CLASS RETURN EXPECTATIONS DO NOT VARY WITH TIME...IT'S TIME FOR THE FINANCIAL PLANNING COMMUNITY TO DUMP STATIC ASSET ALLOCATION."
>
> - William Jahnke

by GREG WERLINICH

Set aside your pre-conceived notions of investing for the long run through traditional asset allocation models. As we have learned since the end of 1999, stocks don't always go up. Strategies like "buy on the dips" that worked for the prior 25 years are not appropriate in today's dynamic and volatile market. It's time for a new approach.

Below, I'll show you how to preserve your capital and make money in bull or bear markets by using a technique called "sector rotation investing."

The majority of what you read in the popular press, from "authorities" like Smart Money and Money magazines or CNBC and Fox News, trumpet strategies to profit from the latest investment fad or purport to show you how to *make money now.*

You've seen the headlines: Ten Stocks To Buy Now! or What You Need To Know To Make Money Today! While these stories help to sell magazines or increase viewers, they do a great disservice to investors looking to build an investment portfolio that can prosper in good times and bad.

Rather than focusing on the hot trend or trying just to "beat the market," investors should concentrate their efforts on crafting an investment strategy that can yield appropriate real, or "absolute" returns, year in and year out.

Too often, investment professionals talk about their performance in relative terms. The mutual fund industry is the most glaring example. All mutual funds measure their success or failure by comparing their results to a relevant benchmark, like the S&P 500 or Russell 2000. Fund managers are judged on their ability to "beat the index." The managers who do so consistently can become very wealthy. Those who don't are soon looking for new jobs.

Even financial planners or investment advisors (like me), who try to focus more on long-term goals and objectives, are often judged by our clients on our short-term performance relative to a particular benchmark.

MEDIOCRE METHODOLOGY

The problem is that this methodology rewards relative, not absolute, performance, and this can lead to mediocrity. I have often seen on television, or read about, a fund manager defending his record of outperforming his benchmark, even though his fund lost money. Even though he lost money for his investors, he is praised for doing a good job. Ultimately, it doesn't matter if a fund manager makes or loses money; what matters is that he beats his benchmark. The problem is that the money lost was yours, not his!

I don't mean to flay that fund manager. He's just doing his job. He is conforming to the rules of the game as they have been laid out. He works in a specific investment style box, like "large-cap growth" or "small-cap value." He is told to invest according to that style, and beat his relevant index, regardless of its merits at any particular time.

For example, when the bubble burst in March 2000 and the market began its three-year decline, mutual fund managers in the technology sector were forced, by investment style mandate, to continue to invest in over-priced tech stocks, even though it was the worst performing sector in the market. According to industry standards, as long as a fund manager beats his index, he could claim to have done a good job, no matter how much money he lost.

While that mentality can work for the mutual fund industry, it isn't appropriate for individual investors. At the end of the year, when you review the performance of your portfolio, you probably just want to know how much money you made or lost, not how the performance of your portfolio compared to the S&P 500.

At the end of the day, you should be more concerned with the absolute return on your investments, the real return, not whether you were able to beat some index that may or may not have any real bearing on your investment philosophy.

It's time to develop a new outlook and a new investment strategy that can make real money in good years and protect you from large losses in bad times. That strategy is dynamic sector rotation investing. Here's how you can put it to work for you.

SECTOR ROTATION INVESTING DEFINED

So what is sector rotation investing, and how can investing through sectors preserve your wealth and create positive returns, regardless of market con-

Insider Notes: You should be more concerned with the absolute return on your investments, the real return, not whether you were able to beat some index that may or may not have any real bearing on your investment philosophy.

ditions? First, I'll explain what sectors are, then I'll review how you can invest in them.

Broadly speaking, a sector is an industry classification. It describes the industry or country in which a particular company operates. Sectors can be country specific (like investing in China) or industry specific (like investing in oil and gas companies). Every publicly traded security (and all privately held securities too) can be slotted into a sector.

For example, Pfizer operates in the pharmaceutical sector while ExxonMobil can be found in the energy sector. Unlike the style boxes used by the mutual fund industry, sectors don't care about the size of the company, only the industry in which it operates. For instance, ExxonMobil, with a market capitalization over $300 billion, is in the same sector as Marathon Oil, which has a market cap of about $13 billion-yet they are in different styles: large-cap value versus mid-cap value, respectively.

When you are ready to develop a sector-based investment strategy, you must first choose the sectors in which to invest, then select the investments that will populate those sectors. This is different from traditional asset allocation theories, whereby you assign a certain percentage of your investments to each of a number of asset classes (large-cap, mid-cap, small-cap, growth, value, fixed income, international, etc.) and then maintain or change those weights as market conditions dictate. With a sector-based approach, rather than maintain prearranged asset class weightings, you will invest the majority of your assets in those sectors of the market that you believe will generate positive results given the current market conditions.

Most investors today employ some form of asset allocation strategy because that's how they've been taught by the general media, and because, quite frankly, it's less work. It is much easier to pick one investment from each of a prescribed number of styles and sit back and wait for the results, than it is to create a dynamic investment strategy that requires constant monitoring and adjusting.

For accounts like 401(k)s and 403(b)s, in which you often have a limited palette of options from which to choose, traditional asset allocation is the appropriate action, assuming that you have sufficient knowledge to make the best choices from the available styles. But for the majority of investment accounts, whether self-directed or professionally managed, there is a better way. That way is dynamic sector rotation.

This crucial distinction of style versus sector underpins the philosophy of sector rotation investing. Rather than allocate investments by style, which if done broadly enough, will generate returns that mimic the broad market averages, be they positive or negative, people are better off investing in those sectors of the market that are more likely to generate positive returns at a given time.

Done properly, sector rotation investing should allow you to beat the markets in good times and bad and do so while taking less market risk than following a broad allocation strategy, because you aren't investing in the broad market, just certain sectors of it. You will certainly have investment risk, but your overall market risk should be minimized.

The key to this form of investing is doing it properly. As with any strategy, be it market timing, indexing or classic asset allocation, if it isn't done well, your returns will suffer. Sector rotation investing requires the investor to be aware of the economic and political forces that shape the current and future investment climate and invest accordingly. These forces are dynamic. Therefore, the investment strategy must be similarly dynamic.

For example, the price of oil today is relatively high at $45-$50 per barrel. Therefore, the stocks of companies in the oil and gas sector have been doing very well. Should the price of oil fall back to $30 per barrel or below for a sustained period, or if you believe such an event is likely to happen in the near future, then you may want to avoid the stocks of companies that are sensitive to the movements in the price of oil.

Insider Notes: Invest in those sectors of the market that have the greatest chance of yielding positive returns at any given time and also invest in other sectors that will offer the greatest protection during difficult times.

WHY THIS METHOD WORKS

Why is this important to you? To be honest, in good times, it might not be so important. When the stock market is going up, a rising tide tends to lift all boats. On the other hand, this strategy gains in importance during the tough times that we face today and possibly for the next few years. We are talking about your money here. This is neither an abstract concept nor a theoretical discussion. These are the funds you are setting aside to pay for college, weddings, homes, vacations, health care, retirement, or future generations.

Let me be very clear: losses on paper are real losses. If you buy a stock at $50 and hold it while it drops to $25, you have lost 50% of your money, regardless of whether or not you sold that stock. You will still need to double your money just to get back to break-even.

Therefore, you need to take the steps necessary to avoid big losses whenever possible. One way to do that is to invest in those sectors of the market that have the greatest chance of yielding positive returns at any given time and to also invest in other sectors that will offer the greatest protection during difficult times.

The key to any investment strategy is gauging its potential for success in good and bad stock market environments. The real strength to dynamic sector investing is that it allows the diligent investor to rotate investment dollars from weaker areas of the market to stronger ones and thereby create positive returns regardless of the direction of the overall market.

On the other hand, many analysts and scholars argue that you can't beat the market over time and that it's a waste of time to try. They maintain that your best option is to invest in a basket of inexpensive index funds that will closely mimic the returns of the broad market, which in the long run, will provide you with the best returns possible.

The biggest problem with that theory is with the definition of "long run." Every person has a different investment time horizon. And everyone has a different starting point. I assure you that someone who invested for 10 years begininng on January 2, 1990 will have had a very different experience (and a much happier one) than someone who invested for 10 years beginning on January 2, 2000. Similarly, the person who invested for 20 years beginning on January 2, 1980 will likely have far greater returns than investors who also had a 20-year horizon and started anytime after 1990. Remember, a passive investment approach is guaranteed to lose money in down market cycles.

Besides, "beating the market" is not the goal. The goal is simply to make money every year. Being down 10% while the market is down 15% may be a relatively good result, but it still means you lost money, and that is to be avoided whenever possible.

WHY THIS MATTERS TO YOU

Let's put my abstract discussion of sector investing into a real-life context. As I write this chapter, I manage about $35 million of client and family money. Those funds today are heavily concentrated in the following key sectors: commodities/natural resources; diversified financial; metals/mining; specialty retail; pharmaceutical; defense; energy; dollar hedge; and a basket of micro-caps.

On the whole, these sectors are fairly defensive. The majority of them pay above-average dividend yields. The ones with little or no dividends offer the potential for positive returns even in a down market. I will review these sectors in greater detail later in this chapter, when I present a real-life case study.

This uncommon approach puts me in the minority of professional investment advisors, most of whom adhere to the traditional asset allocation methodology. It is my experience that most individual investors do too. As I mention above, there is nothing inherently wrong with a general asset allocation strategy because it's certainly better than no strategy at all and it can work fairly well in a bull market.

Insider Notes: The key to making money in the stock market over the long haul is to avoid the big losses. It is far better to make a little less money in the good years while losing less in the bad years.

So why am I recommending a different approach? First, after experiencing relatively good years for my clients in 2000 through 2002 (meaning I lost less money than the broad market averages, so I seemed to do a good job), I decided to adopt a new investment strategy that would give my clients the best chance to earn positive returns every year, regardless of the direction of the overall market.

The key to making money in the stock market over the long haul is to avoid the big losses. It is far better to make a little less money in the good years while losing less in the bad years. The buy and hold approach used by many investors for the past 30 years is doomed to fail in a prolonged bear market. Unfortunately, I believe we are approaching the second phase of a potentially long and painful bear market.

The good news is that if I am wrong about the length and breadth of the coming bear market, or even about there being a bear market on the horizon at all, this strategy can be very effective and make money every year. And if I am right about the coming bear market, this strategy can shelter you from incurring large losses, or possibly even make you a few bucks. To paraphrase Richard Russell, the author of The Dow Theory Letters, everyone loses in a bear market; the person who loses the least wins.

At its core, sector rotation investing is about being aware of the factors that shape the direction of the economy and the stock market, forming an opinion about the near- and long-term direction of the general market, forecasting sectors that will outperform during that period of time, then devising a strategy to profit from that anticipated movement. Simple, right? Not really; the devil is in the details.

I imagine if you were sitting in front of me right now, you would probably ask the following question: "OK, I understand what sector rotation investing is, but tell me, what does that really mean to me right now?!"

I would say that's a great question and answer it in the following way: I believe that our economy, and our stock market, is heading towards a crisis. We are faced with massive federal trade and budget deficits, an unsustainably low, but rising, interest rate environment, a surprisingly low number of highly-paid jobs being created, an increasingly devalued dollar, rising oil and commodity prices and a frighteningly high personal debt load.

Moreover, we face a possible escalation of the war in Iraq, or even just an extended occupation, as well as further terrorist attacks in this country and around the world. I'm obviously not alone in that fear. There's a "terror premium" in the price of oil of as much as $8 per barrel, as worried traders bid up the price of oil. Every time insurgents blow up an Iraqi pipeline, the price of oil spikes in frantic trading. A terrorist attack on the vast Saudi oil complex would drive oil prices to new heights. Additionally, worries about the nationalization of Yukos in Russia and political problems in Venezuela and other oil producing countries adds fuel to price speculation.

Oil is one of the most important commodities in the modern world. In fact, 80 million barrels of oil are consumed every day worldwide. The United States accounts for 25% of that usage. According to the International Energy Agency, oil usage is now growing at a 3.2% annual rate, up from 2%. And this problem is not going away. Supplies are tight around the globe as many of the reliable sources of oil are embroiled in political turmoil and violence. While oil exploration and production may have reached its peak, demand for petroleum products continues to grow unabated. Demand from China alone will likely keep oil prices high for the foreseeable future.

With all this being said, it should be no surprise that energy is one of my core sector holdings, and should continue to be for years to come.

Another factor that has aided us in the short run, but will be a problem at some point in the future, is that foreign governments (especially China and Japan) have been buying billions of dollars worth of our Treasury debt every month. They've been scooping up debt as part of an effort to prop

Insider Notes: Before choosing a sector fund, call each fund to get its prospectus. Compare funds on past performance over several years; check each fund's volatility score; compare annual expense and turnover ratios; and make sure that the managers who compiled a good record still run the fund.

up the value of the dollar. This is turn lowers the relative value of their currency which makes their goods cheaper for us to buy.

In the first quarter of 2004, the net increase in U.S. government debt held by foreign countries was almost $150 billion! Roughly another $100 billion was added in the second quarter. By September 2004, the amount of U.S. debt held by foreign countries was more than $1.25 trillion! Japan alone purchased over $360 billion in debt in the first half of the year, for a net increase of almost $130 billion.

At some point, these debt holders may tire of the poor return on their investments due to our low interest rates or the falling value of the dollar. Should that happen, and there was evidence in October that this may have begun, and they sell or just slow the purchase of our bonds, our interest rates will soar and the value of our bonds will plummet, taking the housing and financial sectors down with them.

To mitigate as many of these problems as possible, the Bush administration and the Federal Reserve have been doing everything in their power to stimulate the economy, and by extension, the stock market. The rally we enjoyed in 2003 and the first quarter of 2004 was due in large part to the fiscal and monetary stimulus provided by tax cuts, historically low interest rates and billions of new dollars being printed and circulated every week.

The stock market was bound to go up, thanks to all of this money looking for a place to go. The government, by keeping interest rates artificially low, forced you to either invest your money or spend it, because you couldn't make any money by putting it in the bank, where you earned less than one percent in interest. The problem is that this policy has created a nation of debtors, not a nation of savers.

Unfortunately, it appears that the easy money has been made and that the stimulus has run its course. Rates have begun to rise. Oil and commodity prices are still going up. In the face of generally strong corporate earnings reports and positive economic news, the stock market has been drifting lower. Notwithstanding a strong post-election surge, I think the risks of an overall downturn in the market are greater than the chances of another sustained upswing.

For investors, these are precarious times indeed. I don't mean to depress you or frighten you, but forewarned is forearmed. I would finish answering your question by saying that, while I don't know when the market is going to turn down again, I prefer to be ahead of the curve.

While attempting to capture some of the gains in the broader market, I have been investing primarily in sectors that pay a high current income and have the best chance of achieving positive returns in a bear market environment. I also remain vigilant for changes in the political, economic and international climates that might dictate a major change in my investment strategy. If such a change occurs, I am ready to reduce or eliminate my positions in a given sector if market conditions dictate that move.

Remember, this is a dynamic process. If you don't have the time, energy or interest to actively manage your portfolio, then either find an advisor who will do it for you or stick to a more traditional buy-and-hold approach with broad asset allocation. That is still better than no strategy at all.

ASSET ALLOCATION vs. SECTOR ROTATION

Traditional Asset Allocation. In a traditional asset allocation approach to investing, there is relatively little consideration given to the current market environment. Instead, you just manage allocation percentages. Your first step is to decide what percentage of your portfolio to invest in equities and what percentage will go to bonds.

For example, if you are about 40 years old, married with one child, you might allocate 70% of your portfolio to stocks, 20% to bonds and 10% to cash. Then you would choose the securities, either individual stocks, mutual funds or a combination of the two, that would satisfy that allocation.

Insider Notes: If you don't have the time, energy or interest to actively manage your portfolio, then either find an advisor who will do it for you or stick to a more traditional buy-and-hold approach with broad asset allocation.

If you took this methodology a step further, you might break down your 70% equity allocation into certain percentages of large-cap, medium-cap and small-cap, plus maybe some international, along with a cross-section of growth versus value.

Then, at some regular interval (quarterly, semi-annually or annually), you would be expected to rebalance your portfolio to adjust for the results of that period. For example, if the market was up during that time, and your equity allocation had grown to 75%, you would sell enough of your equities to reduce that exposure back to the original 70% and allocate the proceeds to your diminished bond position.

The process of rebalancing forces you to take some profit off the table and buy more of your poorly performing asset. The theory behind this is that eventually, the under-performing asset class will strengthen and outperform for a period of time.

By following this approach you should achieve results that, on a pre-tax basis, roughly parallel the results of the broader markets. Remember, the net return on your investments each year will be negatively impacted by your trading costs and possibly by taxes.

The biggest variable affecting your return would be the percent that you allocated to equities and bonds. If you allocated more to equities during a period in which bonds outperformed, your return would suffer.

Conversely, if you had a large weighting in growth stocks, and the technology market boomed, your results would outpace the general market. Over a period of years, if you diligently rebalance your portfolio each year, these ups and downs will smooth out and you will likely achieve returns that mimic the broad markets.

Achieving average market returns may be just fine for many people. In fact, for 401(k) and 403(b) accounts, which offer a limited selection of choices, this is probably the best methodology that you can employ. On the other hand, when you have total control over your investment choices you can utilize a sector rotation strategy.

Sector Rotation Investing. The first step is to develop a point of view for the overall direction of the market. Then you must determine which sectors of the market will likely produce positive returns in that environment. The next step is to choose what types of securities (stocks, funds, bonds, etc.) you want in your portfolio. You must then choose an appropriate brokerage/advisory relationship (traditional full-service broker, self-directed discount broker or fee-based advisor) and purchase your securities. Finally, once the portfolio has been created, you must monitor its performance against your present and future expectations and be prepared to make adjustments when circumstances dictate a change.

Implemented properly, you should be able to earn consistently positive returns, regardless of the direction of the broad market. For example:
- In a strong bull market, you might want to own securities in the technology, small-cap growth, biotech, and manufacturing sectors.
- In a low interest rate environment, you might want to own securities in the banking, brokerage and home building sectors.
- During poor economic times, you may want to own discount retailers and drugstore chains.
- In a severe bear market, precious metals, certain foreign securities and cash are probably your best bets.

In each example, you should experience positive absolute returns regardless of the direction of the overall market. And you control your investment methodology, taxes, expenses and, to some extent, your returns.

That control, though, comes at a cost: your time, energy and attention. This strategy is not a long-term buy-and-hold approach. If times and conditions change, you must change with them.

For example, if you invested in the energy sector because of high oil prices and you expected the price of oil to drop for an extended period of time,

Insider Notes: Being able to identify the dominant trends in the economy and the stock market is the most critical factor for successfully implementing a dynamic sector rotation investment strategy.

CASE STUDY: ZACH PUTS HIS CASH TO WORK

I will now provide a real-life illustration of a portfolio designed and implemented by a sector rotation investment strategy. I took on a new client last November. This client (we'll call him "Zach") is married, around 40 years old, and has no children. Zach came to me with $300,000 in cash. That was what remained from a portfolio that had been self-managed and had at one time been worth more than $500,000.

He had been sitting on that cash for more than two years because he was nervous about going back into the market, but was unhappy with the paltry returns offered by his bank. After many meetings and conversations, we agreed upon a sector rotation strategy that would seek first and foremost to preserve his capital while offering the opportunity to realize strong positive returns.

I explained to Zach that it might take a few months to invest all the money. In fact, it took me almost a year to create the portfolio that exists today. Since November, I have sold only two positions and was taken out of another when the company was purchased (at a substantial profit for Zach) for cash. As of this writing, October 31, 2004, his portfolio looks like this:

- Commodities/natural resources 7.6%
- Diversified financial 6.80%
- Small/micro cap stocks 14.50%
- Metals/Mining 11.30%
- Specialty retail 5.20%
- Pharmaceutical 5.80%
- Defense 6.70%
- Oil and gas 18.00%
- Dollar hedge investments 6.00%
- Fixed income instruments 10.10%
- Cash 8.00%

Zach's portfolio was up about 9.20% for the year through October, whereas the S&P 500 was up 1.4% and the Dow Jones Industrial Averages was down 4.08%. The best results were in the micro cap, energy and natural resources sectors, while the precious metal and pharma-ceutical sectors were the laggards.

Part of my reason for holding the precious metals sector is "portfolio insurance". I'm perfectly happy holding a 10% position in something that is likely to do well if the broader market does poorly. This is one of the ways that I can actually make money during market declines. My dollar hedge investments perform the same function, with the added benefit of yielding significant current income.

The phrase "past performance is no guarantee of future results" has become a cliché on Wall Street, but like many clichés, there's a lot of truth behind it. While a sector rotation strategy is unlikely to produce super-heated results, you should sleep better at night knowing that your investments are likely to grow year in and year out.

you may want to reduce or eliminate this sector holding. If your forecast came to pass and you had not taken the appropriate action, you would be left with losses that could have been avoided.

You cannot afford to "fall in love" with your investments; if something has to go, get rid of it and move on to the next idea. Don't be sentimental; look at each investment coldly and dispassionately.

MONITORING A SECTOR ROTATION INVESTMENT STRATEGY

Now that you have devised and implemented your sector rotation invest-ment strategy, you must monitor its results and make changes as necessary. As mentioned above, with a traditional asset allocation strategy, the major-ity of the implementation involves periodically rebalancing your holdings so that your allocation percentages remain steady.

Insider Notes: Never allow taxes to become the key factor when deciding whether or not to sell something. If something needs to be sold, sell it now and worry about the tax implica-tions later.

On the other hand, a sector rotation investment strategy will require a great deal more diligence, oversight and thought. You must perform a constant risk/reward analysis on your sectors and the securities you hold within your sectors. If the economic, political or market conditions shift in such a way that your potential risk is greater then the potential reward, you must make the appropriate changes. For example, when the Federal Reserve signaled that it would begin a measured, but steady increase in the short-term lending rates, I reduced my holdings in my most interest-rate sensitive securities. Then, when Merck announced its Vioxx recall, I reduced my exposure to the pharmaceutical sector.

Outside of your retirement accounts (401(k), IRA, etc.) there will be tax consequences from the sale of a security, whether it be for a gain or a loss. While this is certainly an important consideration, never allow taxes to become the key factor when deciding whether or not to sell something. If something needs to be sold, sell it now and worry about the tax implications later. It is far better to pay the taxes on a gain then to incur a loss.

Once you have sold something, don't look back. Too many investors agonize over the money that they "could have made" had they held onto something. If you had a good reason for selling something but it still went up after you sold it, don't worry about it. We rarely have the good fortune of selling at the top or buying at the bottom. If your research and experience tells you that it's time to sell, then do so and move on to the next thing. You can always buy something back at a later date if conditions warrant such a move.

CRITICAL FACTORS FOR SUCCESS AND FAILURE

Factors for Success: Being able to identify the dominant trends in the economy and the stock market is the most critical factor for successfully implementing a dynamic sector rotation investment strategy. There are many ways to do this: technical analysis (charts), fundamental analysis (earnings), various micro- and macro-economic indicators, understanding the national and international political landscapes, following the historical trends of the presidential cycle, astrological charts, hem-lines, the winner of the Super Bowl and the dartboard, just to name a few. There are people out there who employ each one of these methodologies to varying degrees of success. Personally, I'll stick with the first four items. I've never been very good at forecasting hem-lines. You don't have to be a trained technical geek, a Certified Financial Analyst (CFA), an economist or an expert political pundit to be a successful sector investor. However, it is important to be widely read, to have some understanding of fundamental and technical market analysis and to be able to absorb a lot of different information and opinions and channel that data into your own outlook.

I probably read about a dozen weekly or monthly magazines that relate to business and investing, plus at least a half a dozen fee-based newsletters and a few free ones. Add to that the newspapers, research and internet resources that I read every day, and you get an idea of how much information I attempt to synthesize on a regular basis. Being able to absorb all of these disparate sources of information, ideas and opinions and then formulate your own strategy, is critical to being a successful investor over the long haul.

Once you have formulated the overall strategy, which in this case means picking your sectors, you then have to choose the components of those sectors. That means knowing which securities to buy. That will require a lot of research on your part. You should approach picking your individual investments with the same care and diligence that you gave to your sector choices.

Although it is important to know what to buy and when to buy it, it is equally important to know what and when to sell. Sooner or later every sector goes out of favor, as do the individual components of that sector. When that happens, you must be ready, willing and able to get out. The problem is that selling is probably the most difficult part of investing.

There are numerous psychological and emotional reasons that prevent people from selling: falling in love with a stock, holding onto a stock for senti-

Insider Notes: You cannot afford to "fall in love" with your investments; if something has to go, get rid of it and move on to the next idea. Don't be sentimental; look at each investment coldly and dispassionately.

mental reasons and the simple fact that it's easier to celebrate a profit than accept a loss.

How do you know when it's time to sell an individual security? Some people use a strict discipline of stop-losses (which sets a specific price or percentage below the current price that triggers the automatic stock sale.) Others set a general percentage loss that they would accept before they would sell. Still others use their gut instincts to tell them when to get out.

There is no hard and fast rule except that you must avoid the big losses. Whatever discipline you choose to employ, make sure you follow it. On the flip side, don't be in a hurry to sell your winners. Many people in the business will encourage you to "let your winners run." As a general rule, I agree, as long as that winner is in a sector whose trend remains positive, and the fundamental reason for owning that security hasn't changed.

Another factor critical to your success is resolve. Will you stick to your guns in the face of opinions that differ from your own? For example, for the past two years, the consensus expert opinion was that oil and gas prices could never get or stay this high, and would eventually fall. I have been steadfast in my belief that the experts were wrong and that oil and gas prices would stay high and even rise. So far, I have been proven correct, and my investments in that sector have done very well.

Similarly, the consensus opinion has been that gold has little value as an investment because, from 1980 to 2001, gold prices slid steadily from about $850 to about $270. So when the price of gold turned and began to move up, its potential growth was discounted. I disagreed with the conventional wisdom and started to buy gold stocks in early 2003, and I continue to add to my positions today. I believe that gold and other precious metals are in a bull market and will continue to hit new highs for a few more years.

Factors for Failure: I alluded earlier to one factor that contributes to failure: falling in love with your stocks. We all have at least one of those in our portfolios. For some of us, it was a stock gifted to us by a parent or grandparent. For others, it might be the stock of a current or former employer. Still others may just be reluctant to part with a stock that they have owned for a long time. Whatever the reason, being unwilling to part with a stock when logic and circumstances dictate otherwise will surely have a negative impact on a sector rotation strategy, or any investment strategy for that matter.

As I indicated previoulsy, every sector goes in and out of favor. The key is to avoid the sectors that go way out of favor. For example, look what happened to investors who lost billions in the telecom sector after the Internet Bubble burst. Rather than recognizing that the entire telecom sector was crumbling, too many investors held onto their various telecom positions, hoping in vain that the stocks would recover their losses. Similar losses were suffered by investors in the travel sector when people stopped flying after 9/11.

Another contributor to failure is not paying close attention to the local, national or international events that shape the economy and the stock market. Whether it's fighting in Iraq, outsourcing in India, an economic policy statement from China, a shift in interest rate policy by our Federal Reserve, or a major change in domestic policy by our elected leaders, these events must all be factored into your investment decision-making.

A third contributor to failure in any investment scenario, not just sector investing, is not being able to pull the trigger on a trade. Too often, rather than place a trade, investors miss out by trying to buy at the bottom or sell at the top. Don't be greedy. And don't take things personally. When you make a decision, execute the order and move on.

There are many other reasons why you may hesitate before making a necessary trade. Regardless, if your reasons are well thought-out and valid, then that hesitation could cost you dearly, regardless of whether you are attempting to buy or sell a security. It's just like taking a test back in school — stick with your first answer because your first instinct is usually correct.

ACTION ITEM CHECKLIST

The most important action you can take after reading this chapter is to immediately pull out your most recent brokerage, pension and retirement account statements. Some of you may not have looked at them for months, or years. Now, evaluate your investment methodology and your results.

First of all, do you have a clear, well-thought-out plan that governs the investment strategy for all of your accounts? Or are you just implementing random ideas on an account-by-account basis? Are your returns meeting your financial goals and objectives? If you don't have an overall strategy or if the strategy that you have isn't working as well as you'd like, you should consider the following checklist:

- For what period of time are these funds to be invested?
- What is the anticipated use of these funds?
- What is your expected annual return on these funds for the next 10 years?
- How much risk are you willing to take to achieve that expected return?
- What is the maximum amount of money that you would be willing to lose in any one year during that 10 year period?
- Do you feel that your current investment plan is sufficient to achieve your stated goals and objectives?
- Do you feel comfortable with your ability to create, implement and monitor a plan on your own or with your current advisor? If not, maybe you should consider finding a new advisor.

■ ■ ■

Greg Werlinich is President of Werlinich Asset Management, LLC (www.waminvest.com). Greg can be reached at 800-746-6926 or at greg@waminvest.com. He has been giving financial advice to individuals for more than seven years. He holds a B.A. in politics from Princeton University and an MBA in finance from the Stern School at New York University. For more than a year he has authored a free monthly newsletter on personal finance called "News and Views." (If you would like to receive this newsletter, simply send an e-mail to Greg with your full name and you will be added to the distribution list.) Greg also appears regularly as a guest stock market analsyt on the FoxNews channel.

Take note: as with all investment advice, timeliness is a crucial factor. The advice offered in this chapter may be affected by changing conditions. You can receive Greg's latest opinions in his newsletter. To subscribe, go to www.waminvest.com.

[5]
ESTATE PLANNING:
HOW TO PRESERVE WEALTH FOR YOUR SURVIVORS

In our complex modern world, nothing is simple anymore, not even dying. The issues affecting estate planning have never been more challenging. Not only tax laws, but also social norms are evolving at an ever-quickening pace.

"YOU CAN'T TAKE IT WITH YOU WHEN YOU GO."
- Popular Saying

by LORI WATT

As the old saying goes, you can't take it with you. However, you can at least bequeath a substantial legacy to your heirs, instead of leaving your estate in the clutches of Uncle Sam.

Let's start by putting aside one misconception, right now: Estate planning is not just for the rich. This chapter will provide you with innovative but often overlooked methods for preserving your hard-earned wealth for future generations.

HERE'S ANOTHER COMMON MISCONCEPTION ABOUT ESTATE PLANNING: IT'S ONLY ABOUT PLANNING FOR YOUR DEMISE. WHILE PLANNING FOR DEATH IS CRITICAL, THERE ARE MANY INVESTMENT AND PLANNING CHOICES THAT CAN EXERT A HUGELY FAVORABLE EFFECT ON YOUR LIFETIME ESTATE.

In previous generations, the husband made most financial decisions. In today's culture, there's considerably more dialogue between spouses. Most decisions are made after much discussion, and often with differing viewpoints. As life expectancies lengthen, a well-designed and mutually agreeable plan is crucial to the long-term well being of the surviving spouse.

Therein lies the challenge. Effective estate planning must pull off a "trifecta" of perfectly balanced goals:
- provide flexibility for the surviving spouse;
- assure the family assets remain in the family; and
- incur the lowest possible tax impact.

To accomplish this balancing act, it's important to have a solid understanding of the options available and the ultimate decisions.

WHY YOU SHOULD ACT NOW
You must act now, proactively. The decisions you make (or don't make) can substantially affect your family, not only upon your death, but during your life as well.

Here's another common misconception about estate planning: it's only about planning for your demise. While planning for death is critical, there are many investment and planning choices that can exert a hugely favorable effect on your lifetime estate.

The increasing number of blended families makes proactive estate planning even more urgent. Open communication among the generations can lead to the best plan for your family, while minimizing future conflict and misunderstanding. Parents must discuss how to handle divorces in the family. Moreover, grown children may need to have a frank discussion about money with a parent who has remarried. These discussions are never easy and they're all too easily postponed. But if you don't communicate now, you're setting yourself up for a nasty battle when someone dies.

Gone are the days when a "simple will" could accomplish all your goals. With the rapid growth of blended families, difficult dilemmas have multiplied: How should the assets be divided? Should all children be treated equally? What if older children from a first marriage are already financially well established? Should the primary consideration be the surviving spouse? How would a potential divorce or lawsuit affect your children? What provisions should be made to care for an elderly parent? The questions are many, as are the planning opportunities and consequences.

The overly litigious nature of society also makes it imperative to protect your assets against lawsuits and creditors. It's crucial that planning take place prior to a claim against your assets. Many of the concepts and strategies that are typically associated with estate planning also can be used to protect assets against legal assault during your lifetime.

NEW SOURCES OF WEALTH CREATION

Over the years, we have seen an increasing complexity in HOW wealth is created, as well as HOW it can be protected, and HOW it will be managed upon death. In previous generations, most people just went to work, brought home a paycheck, paid their expenses, and saved what was left over. Savings accounts, stocks, bonds, and occasionally real estate were the basic investments used to accumulate wealth. Retirement income was provided through pensions, over which the worker had no control. Upon death, the retirement income stopped, and what was left in savings was passed on to the family.

Insider Notes: Family Limited Partnerships can be used to maximize the value of assets transferred to the next generation, without losing control of the assets during your lifetime.

IF YOU'LL PARDON THE PUN, EACH OF THESE "HIGH WATTAGE" METHODS CAN REAP SUBSTANTIAL REWARDS FOR YOUR ESTATE, DEPENDING OF COURSE ON YOUR PARTICULAR SITUATION.

Nowadays, it's hardly that simple! The Information Age has added great complexity to our individual financial lives. Society is more entrepreneurial, with substantial amounts of wealth created through small, privately owned businesses. The planning opportunities available to small businesses are numerous, and provide wealth creation potential beyond the business itself.

To maximize the value of a small business, you must be aware of the planning opportunities that are available, and how they can impact your overall estate. While small businesses provide many opportunities to create wealth, they also can increase the exposure of your personal assets to creditors and lawsuits. With proper planning, you can minimize that exposure, as well as maximize the ultimate value of your business to your estate. Even those who have built their wealth through employment with a large, public firm often have more complexity in their financial lives than just a decade ago. The transition from pension plans to other types of retirement plans—i.e., 401(k), 403(b), SEP, SARSEP, or SIMPLE—has resulted in more flexibility for employees, but has also increased the number of financial decisions required.

Many employees work two, three, or more jobs in a lifetime, accumulating retirement plan assets at each employer. While the easiest decision is often to leave an old plan with the employer, or possibly roll it into a new plan, that may not always be the best choice. Rolling the assets to an IRA rollover account can provide you and your heirs with more planning flexibility.

In addition to retirement plan assets, there are many corporate benefits that can create wealth-planning opportunities. Stock options, executive benefit plans, corporate stock held in a retirement plan, and split dollar insurance are examples of corporate benefits that should be evaluated as part of an overall financial plan.

ABOVE ALL...THINK!

As I unveil my how-to strategies for estate planning, think about how they can be used to maximize your personal wealth.

Think beyond the traditional concept of estate planning (who gets what and when). Think about protecting your wealth, not only from taxes, but also from creditors and outside claims. Think about the wealth you have accumulated so far: retirement plans, investments, your home, personal property, etc. Think about the wealth you will continue to create through earnings and other sources. And finally, think about the wealth that will be created upon your death, through insurance.

In most situations, you should work with an attorney to draft the necessary documents and assure that they are tailored to your individual needs. This chapter is not intended to be a legal textbook, but rather a thought-provoking glimpse of proven strategies that can be used to reduce taxes and maximize wealth.

Let's start with an overview of basic estate planning concepts (see "Black Book Primer," this chapter). Once you have a good understanding of the basics, study my "Seven Simple Strategies" below. If you'll pardon the pun, each of these "high Wattage" methods can reap substantial rewards for your estate, depending of course on your particular situation.

LORI WATT'S "SEVEN SIMPLE STRATEGIES" FOR ESTATE PLANNING

STRATEGY #1. FAMILY LIMITED PARTNERSHIPS

One of the continuing challenges many people face as they evaluate estate planning alternatives is the balancing of two sometimes conflicting goals: minimizing the tax impact of transfers while maintaining control of their

> **Insider Notes:** Assets that have a high potential for future appreciation are ideal transfers to a Family Limited Partnership. In addition to maximizing the current after-tax transfer value, all future appreciation will occur outside the taxable estate of the donor.

assets during their lifetime. A Family Limited Partnership, often referred to as a FLP, provides a unique balance between those two goals.

WHAT IS A FAMILY LIMITED PARTNERSHIP?

Let's start with a broad overview. A Family Limited Partnership is a legal entity created by a family member for the primary benefit of the family. Assets are transferred to the FLP in exchange for FLP interests. Those interests are subsequently gifted to other family members.

There are many advantages to this strategy--consolidation of assets, potential to shift income among family members, flexibility in gifting, reduced income taxes, reduced gift and estate taxes, maintaining control of the assets, and protection against creditors, to name just a few. It's very important to obtain competent legal counsel to implement this strategy.

WHAT ARE THE GOALS OF THIS STRATEGY?

The primary goal of this strategy is often to reduce income and transfer taxes paid by your family. However, it's important that there be a valid business purpose for the FLP to achieve those tax savings. There are several other important features of an FLP that should be considered as part of your decision whether to implement this strategy:

- FLPs allow an individual to transfer assets to the next generation, while retaining control of those assets.
- Asset protection features in an FLP provide protection against creditors, lawsuits, divorces, etc.
- Consolidation of family assets into one entity can simplify the transfer of assets from one generation to the next, through lifetime gifting or transfer upon death.
- Continuous family ownership of the assets is assured through the proper structuring of the FLP.

WHO ARE THE PLAYERS?

When structuring an FLP, two or more family members serve as general and/or limited partners. Generally, the senior generation becomes the general partner, and the younger generation family members are the limited partners. The senior generation often forms the FLP and gifts assets to the new entity.

The General Partner is responsible for managing the FLP. This includes day to day operations, as well as major decisions such as the sale or purchase of assets, and the amount of any partnership distributions to family members. Although the General Partners typically only hold 1-2% of the total ownership in the FLP, they maintain total control over the underlying assets. The General Partner can be one or more individuals or even a separate entity (such as a corporation), created to serve in this capacity.

The Limited Partners are generally members of the younger generations, including children and grandchildren. When the FLP is first formed, the senior generation typically will own a major portion of the Limited Partner interests, as well as all of the General Partner interests. The goal is to transfer the Limited Partner interests to the younger generations through annual and lifetime gift tax exclusions. The FLP is usually structured with 98-99% of the interests owned by Limited Partners.

In summary, the General Partner owns a small percentage of the FLP (1-2%), but controls 100% of the assets. The Limited Partners own the majority of the FLP (98-99%), but have no control over the assets.

WHAT TYPES OF ASSETS CAN BE OWNED BY AN FLP?

FLPs are often used to hold closely held "C" corporation stock, publicly traded stocks and bonds, mutual funds, bank accounts, real estate, and life insurance policies. It is also appropriate to hold more unusual assets in an FLP, such as precious metals, promissory notes, collectibles, art, copyrights, and patents.

There are several asset types that are not appropriate for FLPs. These include personal residences, "S" corporation stock, professional corporation stock, stock options received as part of a compensation package, and retirement plan assets. While annuity contracts can be owned by an FLP, they will not obtain the benefit of tax-deferred growth.

Insider Notes: Consider establishing several Family Limited Partnerships if you own high-risk assets, or if you are employed in a high-risk profession. This strategy can provide maximum protection against lawsuits and other claims.

A BLACK BOOK PRIMER: THE BASICS OF ESTATE PLANNING

With all the changes that have taken place in the last few years, it's important to understand where we are today, and what will be different in the years to come.

- **Estate Taxes**. Under current law, every individual is eligible for an estate tax exemption of $1.5 million. That amount increases gradually to $3.5 million in 2009, after which the estate tax is scheduled for repeal in 2010. However, beginning in 2011, unless Congress takes action, the estate tax returns with only a $1 million exemption. Any amount over the exemption is currently taxed at a top rate of 48%.

  Rising exemptions allow larger estates to transfer without estate taxes, but they also create a potential problem. Many estate plans were designed with a "credit shelter trust" (also known as a "bypass trust") which is to be funded based on a formula. That formula could unintentionally transfer a much larger portion of the estate than was intended, leaving the surviving spouse with little or no assets. It's important to have your will reviewed by an attorney after any major tax law change.

- **Gift Taxes**. The gift tax exemption (for gifts made during life) is locked in at $1 million, with no repeal or increase scheduled. Previously, the gift and estate tax exemptions were identical, creating more opportunities for lifetime gifts. Under current law, gifts should generally be limited to the $1 million exclusion.

  In addition to the $1 million lifetime exemption, every individual may give up to $11,000 per year to an unlimited number of people. A husband and wife together could give up to $22,000 per year. Assuming three married children and six grandchildren, up to $264,000 per year could be gifted.

  An unlimited amount may be paid directly to medical or educational institutions on behalf of your children or grandchildren.

Gifts and transfers upon death to a surviving spouse are exempt from taxes. While this would seem like the simplest approach, it could end up generating substantial estate taxes for your heirs. A common solution is to transfer an amount up to the exclusion amount (currently $1.5 million) outright to the spouse, while putting the balance into a Credit Shelter Trust. This strategy allows a husband and wife to transfer up to $3 million without estate taxes (based on current exemptions).

■ **Income Taxes.** An often-overlooked tax upon death is income taxes. Income taxes are generally due on distributions from retirement plans. A surviving spouse has the ability to rollover the plan assets into an IRA account, thus deferring taxes. However, other beneficiaries do not have that flexibility. Income taxes must be paid as the distributions are made.

■ **Life Insurance.** Although life insurance is generally not subject to income taxes, it is subject to estate taxes. If life insurance is owned by the insured, the proceeds will be included in the taxable estate upon death. This can create a significant unplanned tax liability. A common solution is to have the policy owned by an irrevocable life insurance trust, with the trust also being the beneficiary. It's important to work with an attorney to establish this trust to assure all the requirements are being met.

High-risk assets such as airplanes and boats can be owned by an FLP, but it is preferable to set up several entities to separate the high-risk assets from the low risk assets.

WHEN SHOULD YOU CONSIDER AN FLP?

There are many reasons unrelated to taxes for considering an FLP, making it an appropriate tool for many individuals to consider. The consolidation of family assets can help simplify continuing management and the ultimate transfer to future generations. Rather than gifting specific assets on an annual basis, interests in the FLP are transferred, which results in a simplified and consistent approach to gifting.

Because the General Partner can retain control of the assets being transferred, this is an ideal approach to use when the senior generation is not ready to transfer control to the younger generation. Even with as little as 1% ownership, the General Partner has total control over management decisions, investment of assets, and distribution of income. If desired, control can be transferred gradually to one or more of the individuals over a period of time. While the percentage owned by each limited partner can remain equal, control can be given to selected individuals.

A common challenge for small business owners is the fair treatment of children who are not involved in the family business. They often would like all children to share equally in the value of the business, but only want those children actively involved to have decision-making authority. An FLP is an ideal tool to balance those objectives.

Many people find the asset protection features available in an FLP to be of significant importance. Because the partners do not personally own the assets contributed to the partnership, it is much more difficult for creditors to reach those assets. The asset that is actually owned by the partner is the partnership interest. A court order is generally required for partnership interests, and even then, only the income from the FLP is paid to the creditor.

The creditor can't demand distribution or become a partner. The General Partner continues to have control over the timing and amounts to be distributed. General Partners don't receive the same level of protection as Limited Partners. Often a corporation or Limited Liability Company is used as the General Partner to provide further protection.

The FLP is commonly used in situations where the senior generation has accumulated significant net worth. Through 2005, assets transferred to someone other than a spouse are subject to estate taxes, to the extent they exceed $1.5 million. Using an FLP can allow a greater amount to be transferred to the next generation free of estate taxes.

It is very important to work with an attorney specializing in this area to assure that the FLP is structured properly to obtain all the desired benefits.

HOW ARE TAX SAVINGS ACHIEVED?

The FLP structure imposes significant restrictions on Limited Partners with regard to their voting rights, ability to transfer their interests, and control over distributions. As a result, "valuation discounts" are typically applied when calculating the value of a gift. To determine the appropriate value for gift tax purposes, a written opinion on valuation should be obtained from a qualified business appraiser. Discounts in the range of 30-40% are common.

If assets were gifted directly, without using an FLP, a husband and wife can transfer $22,000/year to each of their children. If there are three children, this amounts to $66,000/year. By using an FLP, and assuming a 30% discount, $94,286 can be transferred every year. The savings can compound rapidly depending on the number of children and grandchildren, particularly over a number of years.

In addition, the lifetime gift tax exclusion of $1 million can also be transferred using the applicable discount. This would result in over $1.4 million of assets transferred free of gift tax.

Income tax advantages also are obtainable through the use of an FLP. Income distributions can be spread among other family members, who may be in a lower income tax bracket. Income distributions are an effective way of further transferring value to the next generation, over and above the allowed annual and lifetime gift tax exclusions.

One final tax advantage can result from transferring assets to the next generation, prior to significant growth occurring in the value of those assets. All future appreciation will occur in the estates of the younger generation, and will not be subject to estate taxes until their death, hopefully much further in the future. There will be no estate tax due on that appreciation upon the death of the senior family member.

The combination of these tax benefits can generate tremendous tax savings. However, I can't emphasize this enough: there MUST be a legitimate business purpose for structuring the FLP, beyond the tax savings.

PERHAPS THE MOST IMPORTANT GOAL FOR MANY INDIVIDUALS IS THE ABILITY TO CREATE A LASTING LEGACY, BY ULTIMATELY GIVING A MAJOR GIFT TO A FAVORITE CHARITY.

THE FLP CHECKLIST

Before implementing an FLP, first consider this checklist of challenges:

- Expert legal advice is critical.
- Laws can vary considerably from state to state.
- A written valuation of the assets to be transferred, obtained from a qualified appraiser, is absolutely necessary
- Ongoing valuations are needed if gifting continues to occur
- Since the General Partner will continue to have liability exposure, consider the use of a corporation or limited liability company to serve in this role.
- The FLP is a separate business entity, requiring the maintenance of certain business formalities.
- Separate tax forms and other reporting requirements will be necessary.

STRATEGY #2. CHARITABLE REMAINDER TRUSTS

An increasingly popular estate planning tool is the Charitable Remainder Unitrust (CRUT). The CRUT can provide significant advantages to individuals, including increased income, reduced taxes and the ability to create a lasting legacy.

WHAT IS A CHARITABLE REMAINDER UNITRUST?

A Charitable Remainder Unitrust is established to ultimately pass assets to a charity. However, during the term of the trust, those assets provide tax and income benefits to the person who established the trust.

Many people own investments that are worth significantly more today than when they originally purchased them. At some point, they may want to sell a highly appreciated asset, and reinvest the proceeds elsewhere. They may need to generate more income, or create more diversification, or they may feel there are better investment alternatives available. However, they often feel "locked-in," because of the taxes that would be due if they were to sell the assets outright. One solution to that dilemma can be found in the CRUT.

WHAT ARE THE GOALS OF THIS STRATEGY?

Perhaps the most important goal for many individuals is the ability to create a lasting legacy, by ultimately giving a major gift to a favorite charity.

A valuable strategy is the ability to sell a highly appreciated asset without paying capital gains tax on the profits. This creates several additional advantages, such as the ability to diversify an investment portfolio, and also increased income. In addition, immediate tax savings can be achieved through a charitable deduction.

CRUT's also can be structured to generate retirement income, or to provide for the educational needs of children or grandchildren. When combined with insurance, they can significantly boost the value passed to the next generation.

WHO ARE THE PLAYERS?

The Donor is an individual(s) currently owning a highly appreciated asset, desiring to achieve the goals mentioned above.

The Charitable Beneficiary is the charity who will ultimately receive the value remaining in the trust at the end of the term. The Charitable Beneficiary can be changed at any time, as long as it is always an IRS-approved charity. One option that provides a great degree of flexibility is to name a Donor Advised Fund as the charitable beneficiary. This allows the remaining family members to distribute gifts to individual charities over a long-term period. Donor Advised Funds are offered through a number of investment firms.

 Insider Notes: The Alternative Minimum Tax impacts many taxpayers and can come as an unexpected surprise. Be sure to calculate the AMT when evaluating the use of a CRUT.

The Trustee of the CRUT can be the Donor, a charity, an independent trust company or another person.

HOW IS THE TRUST STRUCTURED?

With the help of a qualified attorney, a Charitable Remainder Trust is established. The trust must name the Trustee, the Charitable Beneficiary, the percentage to be paid to the Donor (or selected individuals chosen by the donor), and the term of the trust.

The trust must specify the annual percentage to be paid out to the donor. This amount must be a minimum of 5% and a maximum of 50% per year. The percentage calculated must also provide for a minimum charitable deduction of 10% of the amount transferred to the CRUT. Because the length of the projected payout is a factor in the deduction, it sometimes makes it more difficult for a younger person to use as high a payout percentage as a much older person.

The term of the trust can be for the life of the donor, or for the life of the donor and another individual, such as a spouse. It can also be for a term of years, up to 20 years.

The trust also can be structured to accumulate distributions if the annual income is not sufficient to cover the distribution. This is an excellent planning tool if the goal is for income in future years, since an even higher amount can be paid out at that time. This strategy is often used when the CRUT is being structured to provide retirement income or to provide educational funds for grandchildren.

CRUTs allow for continuing contributions, which make them an excellent vehicle for long term planning goals.

HOW DOES THIS STRATEGY WORK?

Prior to any sale, the Donor transfers an asset, generally one that is highly appreciated, into the trust. Then the trustee (who can also be the Donor) sells the asset, reinvesting the proceeds. The trustee continues to manage the trust throughout its term, making investment choices and making distributions to the income beneficiaries. Upon the death of the income beneficiaries, or reaching the end of the term, whatever is remaining in the trust is paid out to the charitable beneficiary.

HOW ARE TAX SAVINGS ACHIEVED?

There are two levels of tax savings. First of all, there's an immediate income tax deduction for the present value of the future gift. While this sounds confusing, the IRS provides guidelines for calculating this amount. The deduction varies based on the term of the trust, the monthly AFR rate published by the IRS, the distributions being paid out to the donor during the term, the frequency of the distributions, and the amount contributed. This deduction must equal 10% of the value contributed to the CRUT.

It's important to realize that the donor will not receive a deduction for the full value of the amount being transferred into the CRUT. This is because the gift is a future gift, and the charity may not receive it for many years. A future gift does not have the same value to the charity as an outright gift received today. In addition, the ongoing distributions to the donor further reduce the ultimate value to the charity.

The second level of tax savings is the bypass of capital gains taxes. Because the CRUT is tax-exempt, there are no taxes due upon the sale of the asset. This allows reinvestment of 100% of the proceeds. Since that is the base upon which distributions to the donor are calculated, a higher income level can be achieved than would be available through an outright taxable sale.

WHAT TYPES OF ASSETS CAN YOU CONTRIBUTE TO A CRUT?

A wide variety of assets can be contributed to a CRUT. However, the tax consequences can vary considerably. Perhaps the simplest and most common asset is highly appreciated, publicly traded stock. It is also possible to use stock in a small, closely held company, although it is somewhat more complicated.

Insider Notes: Charitable Remainder Trusts can be an excellent tool to convert a highly appreciated, non-income producing asset (i.e., undeveloped land, stock, closely held business, etc.) into a diversified portfolio of income producing investments.

BILL AND JOAN: A CRUT CASE STUDY

Bill and Joan, both age 65, own publicly traded stock with a value of $500,000. Their original purchase price is $50,000, resulting in a potential capital gain of $450,000. If they were to sell the stock outright, they would have state and federal capital gains taxes totaling $81,000, leaving them $419,000 to invest.

Instead, they establish a Charitable Remainder Unitrust, transferring the stock into the trust prior to sale. The trust is structured to pay an 8% annual distribution for as long as either spouse is living. They receive an immediate income tax deduction totaling $182,000.

In addition, they establish a Life Insurance Trust and obtain a $500,000 life insurance policy that pays upon the death of the second spouse. They plan to use a portion of the income from the trust to pay the annual premium.

Once the stock is in the trust, they sell the stock, paying no capital gains taxes. The trust now has the full $500,000 proceeds to invest. The 6% distribution rate generates $30,000 of income to Bill and Joan. Assuming an 8% rate of return on the CRUT investments, their income will actually increase over their joint life expectancy of 21.3 years. If they lived to their life expectancy, they would have received a total of $772,000 in income distributions. After their death, $734,000 would be remaining in the trust to be transferred to charity. In addition, the $500,000 in the Life Insurance Trust would transfer free of all taxes to their heirs.

Another common asset used is real estate. Not only has the real estate appreciated in value, but also if depreciation has been taken, there is the potential for even further taxable gain. Real estate subject to a mortgage should not be transferred to a CRUT.

Other more unusual types of assets (i.e., art, collectibles, personal property, intangibles, etc.) can also be contributed to a CRUT, but are more complicated.

WHEN SHOULD A CRUT BE CONSIDERED?

A CRUT should be considered when selling highly appreciated assets with a value in excess of $250,000. It is especially effective when there is a desire for increased income, reduced taxes, and a major future gift to charity.

One of the major obstacles in actually implementing a CRUT is the fact that the balance remaining in the trust at the end of the term must be distributed to a charity. This means the assets will not be distributed to your heirs. One solution to this obstacle is the use of a Wealth Replacement Trust.

As part of the initial set up, a life insurance policy is obtained on the life of the donor (and possibly the spouse), equal to the amount transferred to the CRUT. Ideally, the policy should be owned by a separate life insurance trust. To ensure that the proceeds avoid all taxes upon death, the insurance trust must be irrevocable, meaning it cannot be changed. A portion of the increased income coming from the CRUT can be used to pay the insurance premium.

CRUT CHECKLIST

Consider these challenges:
- Significant legal and tax considerations are involved, making it vital to secure the services of an attorney and accountant.
- If the donated asset is not publicly traded, an appraisal is necessary to establish the value.
- The gain bypassed by selling the asset through the CRUT is considered a preference item for Alternative Minimum Tax. Proper tax planning is necessary to take this into consideration.
- Income distributions are subject to a complicated four-tier schedule to determine the tax treatment. It will be necessary to have a qualified CPA complete the tax return on an annual basis.
- The costs associated with establishing and maintaining the trust typically make this inappropriate for gifts of less than $250,000. Some advisors recommend limitations in the range of $100,000 to $500,000.

Insider Notes: Charitable remainder trusts can be used for many different types of assets. Less traditional assets (i.e., art, collectibles, personal property, intangibles, etc.) are allowed, but are somewhat more complicated.

ESTATE PLANNING WORKSHEET

Before you even start your estate planning, you first need to calculate the total value of your estate. Bring this completed worksheet with you to your initial meeting with an attorney, CPA or financial planner.

■ **Ownership of liquid assets:**
Bank account(s) _____ Average balance $_____
In whose name? □ Mine □ Spouse □ Jointly with spouse
                □ Jointly with someone else
If jointly owned, is there a right of survivorship? Yes □ No □

■ **Savings account(s)** _____ Average balance $_____
In whose name? □ Mine □ Spouse □ Jointly with spouse
                □ Jointly with someone else
If jointly owned, is there a right of survivorship? Yes □ No □

■ **Money market account(s)**_____ Average balance $_____
In whose name? □ Mine □ Spouse □ Jointly with spouse
                □ Jointly with someone else
If jointly owned, is there a right of survivorship? Yes □ No □

■ **Certificate(s) of deposit**_____Average balance $_____
In whose name? □ Mine □ Spouse □ Jointly with spouse
                □ Jointly with someone else
If jointly owned, is there a right of survivorship? Yes □ No □

■ **Stocks:**
Fair market value: $_____
In whose name? □ Mine □ Spouse □ Jointly with spouse
                □ Jointly with someone else
If jointly owned, is there a right of survivorship? Yes □ No □

■ **Bonds:**
Fair market value: $_____
In whose name? □ Mine □ Spouse □ Jointly with spouse
                □ Jointly with someone else
If jointly owned, is there a right of survivorship? Yes □ No □

■ **U.S. Savings Bonds**

Fair market value: $_____

In whose name? □ Mine □ Spouse □ Jointly with spouse
□ Jointly with someone else

If jointly owned, is there a right of survivorship? Yes □ No □

■ **Real Property owned (Complete all that apply):**

Personal residence.

Fair market value: $_____

In whose name? □ Mine □ Spouse □ Jointly with spouse
□ Jointly with someone else

Amount of mortgage owed: $_____

Date acquired: _____

Vacation home.

Fair market value: $_____

In whose name? □ Mine □ Spouse □ Jointly with spouse
□ Jointly with someone else

Amount of mortgage owed: $_____

Date acquired: _____

Rental property.

Fair market value: $_____

In whose name? □ Mine □ Spouse □ Jointly with spouse
□ Jointly with someone else

Amount of mortgage owed: $_____

Date acquired: _____

Other real property.

Fair market value: $_____

In whose name? □ Mine □ Spouse □ Jointly with spouse
□ Jointly with someone else

Amount of mortgage owed: $_____

Date acquired: _____

Miscellaneous assets *(Fill in all that apply):*
Automobile #1. Estimated value: $_____
Automobile #2. Estimated value: $_____
Automobile #3. Estimated value: $_____
Automobile #4. Estimated value: $_____

Boats. Estimated value: $_____
Trailers/Mobile homes. Estimated value: $_____
RV. Estimated value: $_____
Motorcycle. Estimated value: $_____

Home furnishings. Estimated value: $_____
Jewelry. Estimated value: $_____
Jewelry owned by spouse. Estimated value: $_____
Stamp collections. Estimated value: $_____
Coin collections. Estimated value: $_____
Antiques. Estimated value: $_____
Gun collections. Estimated value: $_____
Art collection. Estimated value: $_____
Computer/electronics. Estimated value: $_____

Livestock. Estimated value: $_____
Business machinery. Estimated value: $_____
Crop inventory. Estimated value: $_____
Business inventory. Estimated value: $_____

■ Employee benefit plans *(Fill in where applicable):*
Pension plan. Estimated value: $_____
Profit sharing plan. Estimated value: $_____
Employee stock plan. Estimated value: $_____
IRA. Estimated value: $_____

■ Liabilities *(Where applicable):*
Car loans. Amount owed: $_____
Credit card debt. Amount owed: $_____
Personal loans. Amount owed: $_____
Business loans. Amount owed: $_____

State income taxes. Amount owed: $_____

Federal income taxes. Amount owed: $_____

Property taxes. Amount owed: $_____

Other taxes. Amount owed: $_____

Other loans. Amount owed: $_____

■ **Insurance on your life** *(Where applicable):*

Whole life insurance. Face amount: $_____

Beneficiaries: _____

Owner of policy: _____

Term life insurance. Face amount: $_____

Beneficiaries: _____

Owner of policy: _____

■ **Trusts** *(Where applicable):*

I am beneficiary of a trust. Value of trust: $_____

I am trustee or co-trustee of a trust. Value of trust: $_____

I have created a trust. Value of trust: $_____

■ **Income** *(Where applicable):*

Your gross income for the current year: $_____

Spouse's income for the current year: $_____

Bonuses: $_____

Dividends per year: $_____

Interest per year: $_____

Social Security per month: $_____

Disability benefits per month: $_____

Pension benefits per month: $_____

Rental income per year: $_____

Capital gains per year: $_____

TOTAL VALUE OF ESTATE: $_____

THE USE OF A CHARITABLE REMAINDER UNITRUST CAN RESULT IN A WIN-WIN-WIN STRATEGY. THE DONOR ACHIEVES DIVERSIFICATION AND INCREASED INCOME. THE HEIRS RECEIVE A TAX-FREE INHERITANCE. PERHAPS MOST IMPORTANTLY, A LASTING LEGACY IS CREATED THOUGH A MAJOR GIFT TO A FAVORITE CHARITY.

The use of a Charitable Remainder Unitrust can result in a win-win-win strategy. The donor achieves diversification and increased income. The heirs receive a tax-free inheritance. Perhaps most importantly, a lasting legacy is created though a major gift to a favorite charity.

STRATEGY #3. STRETCH IRAS

You may not think of this next strategy as an estate planning technique, but think again! It has all the necessary characteristics.

Structured properly, a Stretch IRA can save significant income and estate taxes, and maximize the inheritance passed on for several generations. One of the key differences between this strategy and others discussed in this chapter is that you do not need the services of an attorney to implement a Stretch IRA. However, this can be a complex area that still requires the expertise of a qualified financial professional to assure that all the details are considered.

WHAT IS A STRETCH IRA?

A Stretch IRA is not a specific type of IRA. Rather it is a term given to a method of structuring the beneficiaries of your IRA to maximize the after-tax value for generations to come.

Many people focus all their investment efforts on accumulating assets in tax deferred accounts, such as 401(k)s, IRAs and profit sharing plans. During the accumulation phase, very little attention is given to how those assets will ultimately be distributed, and what the tax impact will be. That oversight can cost you and your estate substantial, unnecessary tax dollars.

IRAs and other retirement plans provide wonderful tax benefits in the early years. Perhaps the most valuable benefit is obtained through the ability to invest pre-tax dollars, allowing a greater amount to be compounded over the years. The compounding of earnings also grows on a tax-deferred basis, often resulting in substantial amounts accumulated at the time of retirement.

The challenge occurs when an individual decides to take money out of an IRA account that has never been subject to tax. At that point, all distributions are subject to ordinary income tax rates. If assets are not withdrawn during the contributor's lifetime, they will be subject to the tax rates of the individual ultimately receiving the distributions.

The tax laws become very complicated with regard to when distributions must be made after an individual's death, and that is beyond the scope of this discussion. The bottom line is that the distribution of IRA assets will generate taxable income, either for the person originally making the contribution, or for the heirs.

By structuring the beneficiaries of an IRA properly, the distributions can be "stretched" over the lives of your children and grandchildren. Because the major portion of IRA assets will continue to grow tax deferred, this strategy provides a substantial increase in the amount ultimately distributed to your heirs.

WHAT IS THE GOAL OF THIS STRATEGY?

The primary goal of this strategy is to maximize the after-tax value of assets held in tax-deferred investment vehicles (IRAs, annuities, retirement plans, etc.). Retirement assets that will likely not be used during the contributor's lifetime are structured to stretch the taxable distributions over multiple generations.

Insider Notes: Qualified Personal Residence Trusts can be an excellent tool to transfer a vacation home that will likely stay in the family for many years. Many of the disadvantages of a QPRT are reduced when transferring a vacation home, as opposed to a primary residence.

IRAS CAN RESULT IN EITHER ONE OF THE MOST HEAVILY TAXED ASSETS IN AN ESTATE, OR ONE THAT PROVIDES THE GREATEST LEGACY FOR GENERATIONS TO COME.

WHO ARE THE PLAYERS?

The owner is the individual who has contributed pre-tax dollars to an investment account over a period of years. The beneficiary is very often the spouse, with the children listed as contingent (secondary) beneficiaries.

HOW ARE IRAS TYPICALLY TAXED?

The tax laws in this area can be very complex, although recent changes have simplified them somewhat. Generally, individuals must begin taking required minimum distributions (RMDs) from their IRA accounts once they reach age 70 1/2. The IRS has published guidelines to determine the correct amount.

Upon the owner's death, the rules become more complex. There are different options available to a surviving spouse than there are for non-spousal beneficiaries. Generally, surviving spouses have more flexibility to continue tax deferral throughout the remainder of their life. A surviving spouse can transfer the IRA into her own name, or leave it in the name of the deceased spouse, or disclaim the asset, allowing it to pass to the contingent beneficiaries. The option chosen will determine when distributions must be taken.

When the beneficiary is not a spouse, minimum distributions must begin in the year following the death of the IRA owner. The minimum distribution is based on the life expectancy of the beneficiary. If the IRA owner was under age 70 1/2, the beneficiary also has the option to totally liquidate the account within five years.

A major problem can occur if a large portion of an individual's net worth is tied up in IRAs or other retirement plans. Upon death, IRA distributions may be required to pay the final expenses and estate taxes due. This can create a huge tax bill of 80% or more, since these assets are subject to both income and estate taxes.

HOW DOES A STRETCH IRA WORK?

Prior to implementing this strategy, retirement cash flow projections should be completed to determine the annual cash flow needs and the potential estate value that may be passed to future generations. Estate tax projections should also be completed to assure that there is sufficient liquidity in the estate to pay final expenses and estate taxes without tapping into the retirement plan assets.

If there is not enough liquidity, life insurance can be purchased to take maximum advantage of this strategy. Very often, it makes sense to take additional distributions from an IRA account to pay the life insurance premium. By paying a small additional amount of tax every year, a portion of the IRA assets can be transferred to a much larger life insurance policy that will be totally free of income taxes at death. If structured properly and owned by a life insurance trust, it could be free of estate taxes as well. This strategy deserves careful consideration by anyone with substantial retirement assets.

Once retirement cash flow needs are determined, a plan should be established to take funds from the best available source. There are many factors that influence WHERE retirement income is best derived, and the services of a financial planner can be extremely valuable in this area.

Providing your heirs with the flexibility to "stretch" their distributions over their life expectancies is achieved through the proper balancing of several factors during your lifetime. Cash flow projections, annual income tax brackets, and estimated estate taxes must all be taken into consideration. Beneficiary designations are a critical part of the plan. If a surviving spouse is named as primary beneficiary, children can be named as contingent beneficiaries. This gives the spouse the flexibility to "disclaim" the assets, passing them to the younger generation. Distributions are then based on a longer life expectancy, resulting in lower annual taxes and longer tax deferred growth.

Insider Notes: IRAs and other retirement plan assets can be subject to significant taxes upon death. Proper beneficiary planning can allow tax deferral to be stretched over many tax years.

JOHN AND MARY: A "STRETCH IRA" CASE STUDY

 John, age 65, owns an IRA valued at $1.5 million. Mary, age 60, is the beneficiary of the IRA. Their son, Bill, is 40 and is the contingent beneficiary of the IRA. John and Mary's total net worth is $5 million, with about $1 million in taxable CDs and stocks, $2.5 million in illiquid real estate and business assets, and $1.5 million in the IRA. They also invested in a $1 million second-to-die life insurance policy, which is held in an irrevocable life insurance trust. This was purchased to provide the necessary liquidity to allow the IRA account to grow tax deferred for as long as possible.

Upon John's death, it is determined that the $1 million of liquid, taxable assets will be sufficient to take care of Mary for her remaining life expectancy. Mary decides to disclaim the $1.5 million IRA, allowing it to pass to their son, Bill. Based on IRS tables, Bill has a life expectancy of 43.6 years. Assuming an 8% growth rate and annual withdrawals of his required minimum distribution, he will withdraw close to $12 million over his lifetime.

Without proper planning, it may have been necessary to liquidate over half of the IRA upon Mary's death. Over his 43 year life expectancy, this would result in almost $7 million LESS in distributions.

IRA owners often find it desirable to separate assets into separate accounts to allow for the greatest degree of flexibility for each beneficiary. This way, some funds can be left directly to a surviving spouse, while others can go directly to the children. Upon the IRA owner's death, each beneficiary can then manage their individual assets according to their specific needs.

HOW ARE TAX SAVINGS ACHIEVED?

Tax savings are achieved through the continued deferral of taxable distributions from a retirement account after the owner's death. By stretching those distributions across multiple generations, the assets continue to grow tax deferred for many years to come.

STRETCH IRA CHECKLIST

The Challenges:
- Special rules apply when naming a trust as beneficiary. Work with a qualified attorney if this is desired.
- Naming your estate as beneficiary should generally be avoided. This will force your IRA to go through probate, which can be avoided by naming an individual instead.
- Cash flow projections are necessary to assure that both the IRA owner and the surviving spouse have sufficient assets to last throughout their lifetimes.
- Estate tax projections must be done to ensure there is sufficient liquidity in the estate to pay final expenses and estate taxes, without tapping into the retirement plan assets.

IRAs can result in either one of the most heavily taxed assets in an estate, or one that provides the greatest legacy for generations to come.

WHEN SHOULD A STRETCH IRA BE CONSIDERED?

A Stretch IRA should be considered whenever an individual's total investment portfolio exceeds what will be needed to support their financial needs during their lifetime. This strategy can also be used with tax-deferred annuities, whether held in an IRA account or not.

OTHER CREATIVE STRATEGIES

The three ideas above are advanced, time-tested strategies for estate planning. However, there are many other opportunities that are ideal in different circumstances. This final section will give a brief overview of several of these strategies, along with the circumstances in which they are most effective.

Insider Notes: If retirement plan or IRA assets make up the major portion of your net worth, consider taking annual distributions to fund a life insurance policy. Small distributions can create a substantial amount of tax-free liquidity upon death, allowing for maximum "stretching" of IRA assets.

To keep illustrations simple, we will assume that property is initially owned by a parent and is being transferred to children and/or grandchildren. Almost every strategy discussed can involve other parties, although this is much less common.

STRATEGY #4. QPRTS (QUALIFIED PERSONAL RESIDENCE TRUSTS)

This strategy is used to reduce estate and gift taxes on the transfer of a family home or other residence, such as a vacation home, to children or grandchildren, while retaining the right to live in the home for a number of years. The home is first transferred to a trust for a term of years. At the end of the term, the home is transferred out of the trust to be held directly by the children or grandchildren.

Tax savings are achieved because the value of the property is reduced for gift tax purposes, since the person making the gift is retaining the right to live in the home. That right has a financial value, thereby reducing the value of the gift. This value is determined according to IRS guidelines. It is based on IRS rates that are published monthly (Sec. 7520 rates). The number of years the donor may live there also influences this value. The value retained increases as the years increase.

There are several major challenges to this strategy. If the grantor (the person making the gift) dies prior to the end of the term, the home will end up back in his estate. Another draw back is that after the term has ended, the grantor will either have to move out or rent the home from his children. This can actually provide further benefits if the family is already maximizing the annual gift tax exclusion (currently $11,000/year), but would like to reduce their estate even further.

One additional consideration is the fact that the children will have to pay capital gains taxes when they ultimately sell the property. However, since the current capital gains taxes are much lower than the potential estate taxes, this is often a fair tradeoff.

For example: let's say mom and dad own a home valued at $500,000. If the value of the retained interest to live in the home is calculated to be $250,000, the value of their gift for gift tax purposes is only $250,000. After

10 years, the ownership of the home would transfer to the children. If it had appreciated at the rate of 7% per year for 10 years, it could be worth over $1 million at that time. The result is that a $1 million asset was transferred out of the estate, while only using $250,000 of the gift tax exclusion.

STRATEGY #5. PRIVATE ANNUITIES

A private annuity is often used to convert a business or piece of real estate into an income-producing asset, while potentially saving considerable estate taxes. This should not be confused with commercial annuities, which are issued through insurance companies.

The owner of an asset transfers that asset to someone else, often his children or grandchildren, in exchange for a fixed income stream for the rest of his life. This must be structured as an unsecured promise to pay on the part of the children.

The present value of the future annuity payments must equal the fair market value of the property being transferred. As monthly income is received, a portion is considered a non-taxable return of principal, and a portion is treated as taxable gain.

This technique can be especially appealing to the owner of a non-income producing asset, who would like to turn that asset into an income stream, while retaining the asset in the family. In addition, all future appreciation will be transferred to the children, outside the parent's taxable estate.

As with virtually all techniques, there are some potential challenges when considering a private annuity. The annuity payments made by the children are not deductible, although a portion is taxable to the parent receiving the income. If the parent lives too long, the annuity payments made by the children could exceed the value of the property being transferred. An additional risk that should not be ignored is that the annuity is unsecured.

Insider Notes: Private annuities can be especially valuable if the owner of an asset has a reduced life expectancy. Substantial value can often be transferred to the next generation, at a fraction of the normal tax cost.

THERE ARE VIRTUALLY LIMITLESS POSSIBILITIES WHEN IT COMES TO MAXIMIZING THE VALUE OF ESTATES PASSED TO FUTURE GENERATIONS.

Although this strategy can work well regardless of the health of the parents, it can be extremely valuable if one parent has a reduced life expectancy. Some advisors also consider this a useful tool when planning for nursing home care and Medicaid. This can vary considerably on a state-by-state basis and should only be implemented after receiving qualified professional advice.

STRATEGY #6. GRANTOR RETAINED TRUSTS: GRATS, GRUTS AND GRITS

Grantor Retained Trusts are often used to transfer assets to family members at reduced gift tax values, while retaining an interest of some type for the use of the parents. There are several variations of Grantor Retained Trusts; the most common are GRATs (Grantor Retained Annuity Trusts), GRUTs (Grantor Retained UniTrusts), and GRITs (Grantor Retained Interest Trusts).

All of these variations have some aspects in common. For instance, they are all irrevocable trusts, meaning the gift cannot be reversed and the trust cannot be changed. They are structured for a term of years, during which time the parent retains an ownership interest. At the end of the term, the assets pass to the children. All appreciation that has occurred during that period will occur outside the parent's estate, for further benefit to the children.

One drawback to all grantor retained trusts is that the children will not receive a "step-up in basis" when they ultimately sell the asset. This means that they will have to pay capital gains tax on the difference between the selling price and the parent's original cost basis. This is often offset by the fact that estate tax savings are generally higher than the capital gains tax cost, but it must be taken into consideration.

In addition, when the asset being transferred is a family home or other asset that will likely stay in the family for generations, the capital gains tax may not be realized for many, many years. It should also be noted that this "step up in basis" is actually scheduled to disappear in 2010 when the estate tax is repealed. At that time, heirs would be required to pay capital gains taxes on any gains earned during the life of the original owner.

The most common type of GRIT is actually the Qualified Personal Residence Trust, which was described above. These can also be used to transfer artwork, raw land and collectibles.

GRATs and GRUTs are ideal tools to transfer future appreciation to the next generation, while receiving a stream of income for a period of years. GRATs pay out annually a portion of the asset's initial value during the term of the trust. An asset that is expected to appreciate rapidly is transferred into the trust. The value for gift tax purposes is the fair market value, reduced by the present value of the future income stream that will be paid to the parents. At the end of the trust term, the assets pass to the children and the income stream stops.

GRUTs are very similar to GRATs. The main difference is that with GRUTs, the income stream that is paid to the parents is based on a percentage of the value of the trust calculated on an annual basis. GRATs calculate the income stream up front, based on the value of the asset at the time of the gift to the trust. GRUTs are the better choice when parents want the potential for increasing income over the years. GRATs are preferable when the goal is to maximize the transfer out of the parent's estate.

STRATEGY #7. DYNASTY TRUSTS

As we discuss the numerous possibilities of reducing estate taxes upon the transfer of assets to the next generation, a common question is: "Why don't we just skip a generation and save the estate taxes generated each time assets are transferred to the next generation?"

Insider Notes: Life insurance is often used to fund a Dynasty Trust, since there will be no tax due on the "appreciation"— either annually, or upon death.

Unfortunately, Congress saw this loophole, too, and created the Generation Skipping Transfer Tax (GSTT). The law currently allows an exemption of up to $1.5 million. Anything over that amount will be taxed at the rate of 48%. This is in addition to the regular estate taxes that are due, which again can be up to 48%. These amounts adjust on an annual basis, as the overall estate tax brackets change. This exclusion allows a grandparent to transfer up to $1.5 million to grandchildren, or a trust set up for grandchildren.

Dynasty Trusts are often used to accomplish this goal. A Dynasty Trust is actually an irrevocable life insurance trust that is designed to continue for several generations. It can be structured to provide for the specific needs of each generation, such as health, education, maintenance, and support. Structured properly, it will avoid estate taxes as it is passed through the generations.

There are virtually limitless possibilities when it comes to maximizing the value of estates passed to future generations. The examples given here are intended to open your mind to how those possibilities can work in your personal situation.

It's true, you can't take it with you. But you can make sure that after you're gone, the greatest value has been preserved for those you love.

■ ■ ■

Lori A. Watt, CFP is the president of Investors Advisory Group, Inc., a full-service financial planning firm in Pewaukee, Wisconsin. For almost 25 years, Lori has been a financial advisor and is one of a select few planners around the country who specialize in advanced financial planning techniques.

In addition, Lori is currently serving on a number of boards and committees, including Executive Director at St. Paul's Lutheran Church and School in Oconomowoc, WI, the Christian Stewardship Foundation, and the University Lake School Endowment Fund. Past service has also included the Board of Trustees at University Lake School, Hartland, WI and the Board of Directors at the Lutheran Church-Missouri Synod, South Wisconsin District. She can be reached at 262-523-5750, or via Lori@Watt.org.

[6]

THE HIDDEN POWER OF LIFE INSURANCE

There's more to life insurance than you think. A lot more! It's one of the most versatile financial tools you'll ever use to create, preserve and distribute wealth.

"LIFE IS SHORT AND SO IS MONEY."

- Bertolt Brecht

by STUART J. SPIVAK, LUTCF

Savvy investors know that life insurance is an amazingly powerful way to create, protect, preserve and distribute wealth. Few people realize this fact. However, after you read this chapter, you'll be in on the secret.

Life insurance is a complex integration of legal, tax and economic elements. As such, when used optimally, it is an excellent wealth accumulation and preservation tool that addresses the three eventualities that each and every one of us, regardless of our affluence, could one day face: living too long, dying too soon, or becoming disabled.

Despite the distinctive wealth creation and preservation features and tax advantages of life insurance, most people do not want to think about it. Why? Because many people think that life insurance only provides value if they die, a consideration most people would rather avoid contemplating. Many high net worth individuals, who have the most to gain from life insurance, often don't understand it well.

If more people understood what the world's top financial experts understand about life insurance, they would line up to buy it. They would understand that the acquisition of cash value life insurance is not an expenditure, but rather a new, beneficial reallocation of assets. Life insurance provides tremendous advantages whether you live, die or become disabled and is the cornerstone of a financial portfolio.

In this chapter, we'll examine the conventional wisdom about the role life insurance plays in your financial plan. We'll discuss why investors tend to think long term but act short term. We'll then look at how life insurance should be viewed — specifically, how it is valuable in the three most likely outcomes in one's financial lifetime.

Next, we'll go through the steps you must take to effectively implement a life insurance policy in your financial portfolio and how these steps are best managed. Detailed, realistic case studies illustrating how affluent individuals have benefited having life insurance in their financial portfolios should help make these points more relevant.

I want to inspire you to have the same confidence and passion in life insurance shared by my most successful clients and me. I want to remove the misunderstandings and misconceptions that surround life insurance and help you understand its importance as a financial planning instrument. Most importantly, I want to help you create and pass along your wealth to the people and organizations for whom you care most deeply. The bottom line is that many people view life insurance as purely transactional: you die, it pays. However, successful investors know that life insurance is a multifaceted financial tool. In fact, it's the Swiss Army knife of your financial plan!

THE EVOLUTION OF LIFE INSURANCE

To understand why life insurance is so misunderstood, it is important to first understand its evolution.

In its infancy, life insurance was purchased to have funds for burial expenses. Early in the 1900s, Dr. Solomon Huebner of the University of Pennsylvania introduced the concept of human life value. Human life value recognizes that a lost life represents a lost stream of income to an individual's family and business.

For example, a 40-year-old earning $100,000 annually would have a human life value of $2.5 million, assuming retirement at age 65, and no increase in income. This premise determined that not only do you have to worry about burial costs and final expenses, but also the impact of dying prematurely.

The concept of human life value continues to have strong relevance today. Case in point: On the Internet, you can find the matrix developed by the federal government to calculate payments for the September 11 Victim's Compensation Fund (www.usdoj.gov/victimcompensation). The government relied on Solomon Huebner's human life value concept to determine the payment that would be made to the families of the victims of the horrendous terrorist attacks on September 11, 2001. The calculations were based on the present value of the victim's future income, as well as in factors such as marital status and number of dependents.

While calculating human life value is far from an exact science, it is clear that it still remains a critical dynamic in any discussion of life insurance.

Insider Notes: The predominant fear facing Americans today is not dying too soon, but living too long and outliving their assets.

What would your family do to maintain their standard of living and lifestyle if you died yesterday? How would your income be replaced? How would debts/liabilities be paid?

In the early 1970s, there was another shift in the utilization and value of life insurance. As a result of medical advances, people were living significantly longer lives than they had in the past. Suddenly, the predominant fear facing Americans was not dying too soon, but living too long and outliving their assets.

Compounding that fear was increasing concern about the future of the Social Security system in America, and the reduction of employer funded Pension plans. The insurance industry responded by introducing "universal" life insurance products. Universal life lets you decide how much of the premium to use for insurance and how much for the investment/savings component. These plans offered death benefit protection, for those who died prematurely, as well as a new way to accumulate tax deferred cash value for long-term needs such as retirement income.

In the 1980s, life insurance evolved once again, this time adapting to a baby boomer generation with renewed interest in investing in the stock market. This generation was fascinated by the big profits being made and wanted more control as to how their cash value dollars were being invested by insurance companies.

The insurance industry responded by introducing "variable" life insurance. Variable life is similar to universal life, because it has an investment component. However, with variable life, the underlying cash values are invested in sub-accounts (equities, fixed income, real estate, etc.) selected by the policyowner, giving them the most control over how their money is invested. The need for a trusted financial advisor when purchasing universal or variable life insurance became even more important.

In tandem with life insurance's rapid evolution, there was a tendency by many unethical or uninformed financial professionals to portray life insurance as purely an investment. Sophisticated software programs also made it very easy to produce overly attractive, yet unrealistic, insurance proposals.

Most of these illustrations were more sizzle than steak, and often were nothing more than overly ambitious projections based on unreasonable assumptions. These assumptions included sustained high interest rates over a very long period of time and projected improvements in operating expenses and mortality costs.

Unfortunately, the consumer was too often led to believe that what was on paper was guaranteed. It was not! When interest rates declined or mortality demographics were not as favorable (i.e. AIDS claims), these projections could not be met. The policyowner was offered unappealing options, such as paying a higher premium or taking a reduced death benefit and did not have the cash accumulation they expected.

Many attorneys, accountants and other financial advisors focus solely on the most inexpensive products and don't have the expertise to analyze the risk components found in life insurance contracts. It is essential that you select a trusted advisor who has the knowledge, experience and wisdom to help you appropriately integrate life insurance into your comprehensive financial plan and design an insurance product with realistic projections.

COMMON MYTHS

- **Myth: Life insurance is a necessary evil.** Nobody likes to think about death. Therefore, people who readily insure their homes, their cars and their personal possessions often do not insure their most valuable asset-their lives. Or, when they do, they often choose an amount of protection with little planning or thought.

  Successful individuals realize that life insurance is a very effective solution to the problems created by death, especially premature death, and choosing the appropriate amount and type of policy is important.

Insider Notes: Select a trusted advisor who has the knowledge, experience and wisdom to help you appropriately integrate life insurance into your comprehensive financial plan and design an insurance product with realistic projections.

CASE STUDY: JEFF'S FAMILY GETS STRANDED

Here's a cautionary tale of an ostensibly successful man who didn't give enough credence to the value of life insurance.

Jeff was an affluent individual in my community whose tremendous aptitude for stock investing allowed him to build a significant portfolio from scratch.

Jeff was the picture of success in many ways: 46 years old, a mid-six figure income, with a beautiful wife, two wonderful boys, a newborn daughter, a $700,000 suburban home and a stock portfolio valued at close to $1 million. He believed that these assets would be more than adequate to support his family if something happened to him, so he neglected to purchase any form of life insurance.

Unfortunately, like many of us, Jeff's stock portfolio dropped more than 60% during the fall of the dot.com industry in early 2000. Then, tragically, Jeff died suddenly of a heart attack in December 2001.

Unlike most of us who had time to ride out the bear market and eventually recover, Jeff and his family did not get that opportunity. Because of Jeff's failure to recognize life insurance as an integral component of his financial plan, his family was forced to sell their home and dramatically change their lifestyle at one of the most emotionally difficult times of their lives.

Jeff's grieving family learned an important lesson too late: **Life insurance is the one financial product that provides immediate tax-free dollars upon death, giving your survivors financial stability and the time necessary to sell assets on a favorable basis.**

- ■ **Myth: You have to die for life insurance to be a good deal.** Life insurance tends to be thought of one dimensionally — in other words, it is only effective if you die very soon after you buy it. This viewpoint fails to recognize the versatility of "permanent" life insurance. Later in this chapter I will review your *Four Financial*

Buckets. Every dollar we save falls into one of these buckets. You will see that life insurance, because of its flexibility, plays an important role in each bucket.

■ **Myth: It always makes sense to buy term insurance and invest the difference.** "Buying term and investing the difference," is based on the theory that term insurance premiums are initially less expensive than "permanent insurance" premiums. Therefore, you should buy term insurance and each year invest the difference in premium into some type of investment account. Based on current assumptions, the thinking is that you will have more money after say 20 or 30 years in this investment than if you had simply purchased permanent insurance from the beginning. This is a strategy often espoused by countless financial "experts" in the media. The theory is that all individuals, regardless of their age, objectives or financial status, should purchase term life insurance.

Term insurance is life insurance in its simplest form. You insure you life for a certain dollar amount for a fixed period of time, and pay an annual premium based on your age and the amount of coverage. Term insurance has no versatility beyond paying upon death. There is only one way to "win" with term insurance (to die) and you must die within the "term." Why? Because after the "term," the premiums are designed to become unaffordable.

In my opinion, a blanket recommendation such as this is irresponsible. How much confidence would you have in your physician if he prescribed the same thing, to all patients, regardless of their symptoms or medical history? Should you really accept less from your financial advisor?

Insider Notes: By providing financial security for the things that are most important to you, with life insurance in place, you have the opportunity to be more aggressive in other investment opportunities.

IF YOU TAKE NOTHING ELSE FROM THIS CHAPTER, IT IS MY SINCERE HOPE THAT YOU WILL REMEMBER THAT NO ONE PRODUCT OR STRATEGY IS RIGHT FOR EVERY SITUATION. YOU OWE IT TO YOURSELF TO UNDERGO A THOROUGH FINANCIAL ANALYSIS BEFORE SELECTING THE LIFE INSURANCE PRODUCT THAT IS OPTIMAL FOR YOUR NEEDS AND GOALS.

If you take nothing else from this chapter, it is my sincere hope that you will remember that no one product or strategy is right for every person. You owe it to yourself to undergo a thorough financial analysis before selecting the life insurance product that is optimal for your needs and goals.

THE REALITIES OF LIFE INSURANCE

- **Reality: Life insurance is the cornerstone of any financial plan.** Regardless of one's affluence, none of us can control the timing or outcome of life's three potential crises: living too long, dying too soon or becoming disabled.
- **Reality: Life insurance allows for more investment opportunities.** Financially successful individuals realize that a good defense can be the platform from which to build a strong offense. By providing financial security for the things that are most important to you, with life insurance in place, you have the opportunity to be more aggressive in other investment opportunities.
- **Reality: Life insurance plays a role in lifestyle protection during your life and for your family after your death.** We have predominantly discussed the advantages of life insurance provided at death. Life insurance can also play a big role in helping individuals achieve their dreams during their lives. Years ago, a young man had a grand idea for an amusement park. It was an adventure into the imagination unlike any envisioned before. To make his dream a reality, he needed capital. He went to his local bank, but unable to secure the appropriate collateral, his loan was denied. He called upon potential investors, but all needed more time than he had to raise the money.

Finally, he contacted his life insurance carrier and took a loan against his policy's cash value. Less than a week later, these monies were in hand. That individual went on to build the world's most famous amusement park, one that's still thriving today: Disneyland. From that day forward, Walt Disney considered life insurance as his most important financial instrument.

THE FOUR FINANCIAL BUCKETS

Now, we are ready to explore the "Four Financial Buckets." What exactly do these buckets represent, and how does life insurance play a role in each?

❶ **Short Term**. Your short-term bucket is best defined as your emergency fund-the money that you keep on hand for instant liquidity, should you need it. Financial planners typically define an adequate emergency fund as three to six months of living expenses. These dollars are most often placed in checking accounts, savings accounts and money markets. The existing cash value of mature life insurance policies also falls into this category.

❷ **Midterm**. Your midterm bucket is best described as money you are "saving to spend." Midterm financial goals are typically things that we are saving for and intend to purchase in one to five years (i.e., second homes, boats, remodeling projects, vacations). Financial planners tend to recommend investing midterm money in financial instruments such as CDs, Treasury bills, short-term bonds, balanced mutual funds and preferred stock.

❸ **Long Term**. Your long-term bucket is for those things that you are saving for and do not plan to need for at least ten years. These goals often focus on educational funding, long-term care and supplemental retirement funding, especially for individuals who plan to retire before age 59 1/2.

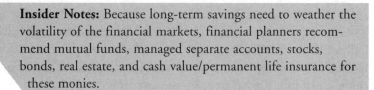

Insider Notes: Because long-term savings need to weather the volatility of the financial markets, financial planners recommend mutual funds, managed separate accounts, stocks, bonds, real estate, and cash value/permanent life insurance for these monies.

Because long-term savings need to weather the volatility of the financial markets, financial planners recommend mutual funds, managed separate accounts, stocks, bonds, real estate, and cash value/permanent life insurance for these monies.

❹ **Your Retirement Bucket**. Planning for a comfortable retirement is a high priority for most Americans, regardless of their economic status. The retirement bucket is, as its name implies, the bucket reserved to provide your standard of living during your retirement years.

Most individuals believe that their retirement buckets will be supported by Social Security and their employer's pension plans. However, the federal government estimates that Social Security and employer-funded pension plans will provide less than half of the pre-retirement income needed for many Americans.

As we mentioned earlier, people are living longer than ever before. In fact, the largest growing segment of our population is individuals over the age of 85. As a result, Non-Qualified Retirement Plans and employee funded plans (such as 401k plans and IRAs) have become increasingly popular in providing additional retirement dollars.

THE FLEXIBILITY OF LIFE INSURANCE

An overview of our buckets brings us back to the question: what role does life insurance play in each?

Permanent life insurance by design is a forced savings vehicle. Statistics indicate that even the most affluent among us have a tendency to not be good savers. According to financial expert John Savage, 98% of people "spend first and save last", while only 2% people have a dedicated savings program ("saving first, then spending"). These figures support the old adage that "people don't plan to fail, they simply fail to plan." Case in point: In my 18 years of business, I have yet to meet a 60 or 70 year old individual who had the discipline to actually "buy term and invest the difference." The reality is most people "spend the difference" and do not commit to a formal, systematic investment plan.

By simply paying the premiums for your permanent life insurance policy each year, you are automatically increasing the cash you are accumulating. Additionally, the provisions in your life insurance policy (if set up properly) allow you to access your cash value with no adverse tax consequences.

> *Why life insurance has a tax-free income stream —*
> *A life insurance policy has the ability to deliver a tax-free stream of income as long as the policy is not a Modified Endowment Contract (MEC), and policy values are accessed via surrenders to cost basis and loans. Income derived from this strategy will remain tax-free as long as the life insurance policy remains in force and therefore does not lapse.*

Life insurance plays an even more significant role in your long-term bucket. Not only does the cash value grow tax deferred, and is accessible tax free, but variable life insurance also allows you to "rebalance" your sub-account allocations without paying capital gains tax, which may be a significant advantage in protecting and maximizing your cash accumulation potential.

And don't forget, if you die while you are still in the funding stages, the life insurance death benefit provides needed funds to accomplish your goals for your survivors.

In recent years, life insurance has played an even greater role in funding the retirement bucket. Where else can you get an equity equivalent rate of return under a tax-advantaged umbrella? Successful business owners and executives have learned that while qualified retirement plans (IRAs, pensions, 401(k) plans) are great during the accumulation phase of retirement (savings), they can be terrible during the distribution phase (payout).

Affluent individuals often find themselves trying to delay taking distributions from their qualified plans as long as possible to avoid the income, estate and penalty taxes that may be imposed. Many companies are now

Insider Notes: Don't forget, if you die while you are still in the funding stages, the life insurance death benefit provides needed funds to accomplish your goals for your survivors.

LIFE INSURANCE PLANNING IS MOST SUCCESSFUL AFTER A COMPREHENSIVE STUDY OF YOUR NEEDS AND CONCERNS, A PROCESS OFTEN REFERRED TO AS GOALS-BASED PLANNING. THIS PROCESS MUST BEGIN AND END WITH YOUR GOALS IN MIND, NOT THE GOALS OF YOUR ADVISOR, OR A COOKIE CUTTER, GENERIC RECOMMENDATION.

using non-qualified retirement plans, which, are often funded using investment grade life insurance because this offers:

- Tax-preferred cash accumulation;
- Tax-preferred investment flexibility;
- Tax-preferred access to cash accumulation;
- Plan completion in the event of death or disability (with rider);
- Protection from personal creditors (varies by state); and
- No requirement to comply with ERISA restrictions.

ACTION PLAN: HOW TO BUILD AN EFFECTIVE LIFE INSURANCE PORTFOLIO

First, when planning your life insurance portfolio, you must choose an advisor that will help you assess your life insurance needs. How much life insurance you need, which product to choose and how it is owned depends on your goals and financial situation.

Calculating the value of your life to your family or business is difficult but must be considered. Life insurance planning is most successful after a comprehensive study of your needs and concerns, a process often referred to as goals-based planning. This process must begin and end with your goals in mind, not the goals of your advisor. A cookie cutter, generic recommendation is not a viable solution; you and your family deserve better.

It is also critical that you do a static and dynamic analysis. Static analysis bases the estimate of required insurance on the needs that must be funded if the insured were to die very soon after the coverage goes in force. A dynamic analysis looks at how your needs are expected to change over your lifetime and makes the necessary adjustments to cover as many of these contingencies as possible.

A dynamic analysis is, of course, based on many assumptions about how the future will unfold. For this reason, it is critical to periodically update and review your insurance plans, to make sure you stay on track.

Goal-based planning gives professionals like myself the opportunity to help both the "current you" and the "future you."

Here are some of the questions I ask clients to consider when planning their life insurance portfolios:
- What legacy would you like to leave behind in both your business and your personal life?
- What are the three biggest dangers, challenges and problems you see ahead?
- What is important about money to you?
- Do you want to be actively involved in the management of your money?
- Are you willing to accept large variations in annual returns as you seek higher long-term returns?
- When you make financial decisions, how do you make them?
- What financial strategies are you currently employing?
- How important is it for you to provide a college education for your children/grandchildren?
- Do you know exactly what would have happened to your family if you had died last night?
- If we were meeting here three years from today, and you were to look back on those three years, what has to happen both personally and professionally to make you feel happy about your progress?

The following checklist includes most of the key information required to customize a life insurance portfolio:
- Tax returns.
- Pension, 401(k) statements from employer-sponsored plans.

CASE STUDY: THE ROBERTS RETIRE IN STYLE

C.J. and Heather Roberts are both 45 years old and in good health. C.J. owns a successful and growing construction business. Heather left her full-time position as a nurse practitioner to stay home and raise their son Brett, a high school sophomore, and daughter Kelly, a high school freshman.

As a result of sustained low mortgage rates and a construction boom on the East Coast, C.J.'s business had grown by leaps and bounds. His was one of the most successful construction companies in the area. Due to the cost of covering rank and file employees, and IRS limits on benefits for executive level employees, C.J. had chosen not to have any company paid qualified retirement plans. He and Heather did, however, invest regularly into a carefully designed portfolio of mutual funds, stocks and bonds.

The Roberts were working hard and dreaming about what they would do when they reached their "golden years." They wanted to travel and spend time on hobbies, family and friends. Although they never sat down and calculated exactly what they would need to make their retirement dreams come true, they kept to a budget, rarely made extravagant purchases and were financially successful by any measure.

Yet C.J. and Heather were realizing what many Americans had already learned: with no pension plan and an increasingly shaky Social Security system, affording their dream retirement would require planning, building significant assets and preserving their wealth.

As an adjunct to their existing savings plan, insurance and investment portfolio, the Roberts decided to purchase a second to die variable universal life policy. They agreed to allocate $4,000 per month into this policy for 20 years, and then to start taking withdrawals from the policy in year 21 when both would be age 66.

Assuming a hypothetical net return of 8% per year (based on their moderately aggressive allocation), the cash value accumulation of the policy after 20 years will be over $2.1 million. Using the proper tax-preferenced distribution strategy, the Roberts project that they will be able to withdraw over $216,000 per year for 15 years, which would translate into a total of more than $3.2 million in tax-free retirement income. At that point, the policy would still have a net cash value (meaning a total cash value less any policy loans) of over $600,000 and a net death benefit (after repayment of the policy loans) of over $780,000. This remaining death benefit could be used to efficiently pay estate taxes and/or provide a legacy to their children upon their death.

The Roberts were hard workers and good investors, who knew they needed more than Social Security and investments to realize the retirement of their dreams. Unlike many Americans, however, the Roberts understood the dynamic versatility of life insurance, and the exciting role that it can play in retirement planning.

- All existing life insurance, long-term care and disability insurance policies.
- Latest investment related statements from trust companies, brokers, investment companies, insurance companies, and banks.
- Company benefit booklets and annual statement.
- Budget of personal living expenses.
- Latest mortgage and other loan statements.
- Latest will, trust and power of attorney, as well as any other estate and tax documentation.

Assumptions Necessary to Calculate Life Insurance Needs:
- Income
- Expenses
- Liabilities
- Family/business situation
- Special needs/elder care needs
- Your unique goals and objectives

Insider Notes: Term insurance is most often recommended for young married couples who can't afford to purchase the death benefit they need.

- Long-term inflation rate
- Current and projected tax brackets
- Rate of return assumptions
- Retirement age/life expectancy

WHAT TYPE OF LIFE INSURANCE DO YOU NEED?

The type of life insurance product that is utilized is as important as the amount of protection you need. Just as some individuals prefer to lease an automobile or rent an apartment, others choose to purchase a car or own a home.

You must consider the duration of the need, cash flow, risk tolerance, and, most importantly, your unique goals and objectives. When selecting the appropriate type of life insurance for your portfolio, it is crucial to match the appropriate product to the concern and goals.

The following are the most common types of life insurance for you to consider:

- **Term Insurance.** True to its name, term insurance provides a death benefit for a definable period of time, or a "term." Less than 20% of term insurance policies are still in force when the insured dies, and therefore never pay a claim. This product tends to be the least expensive insurance, initially. However, either the face amount decreases or the premiums increase as the insured gets older. Term insurance provides death benefit protection only, has no cash value and not much versatility.

  Term insurance premiums may increase annually, or remain level for periods of 10, 20 or 30 years. Term Insurance is most often recommended for young married couples who can't afford to purchase the death benefit they need. It can also be used to indemnify short-term debt obligations, such as a business loan and/or while children are in college, or for any other temporary need. While term insurance can provide the most insurance for the least amount of money initially, it could also be the most expensive option if it is needed for an extended period of time. Nevertheless, there is no excuse for anybody to underinsured, considering how inexpensive term insurance is today.

- **Whole Life Insurance.** In a traditional whole life policy, both the death benefit and the premium remain level throughout the life of the policy. To keep the premiums level, whole life insurance premiums are initially higher than term products in the early years (when mortality costs are low), and are lower than their term counterparts in later years (when mortality rates are higher).

These policies also build cash value and provide the peace of mind of knowing that they will never get more expensive and will be there whenever death occurs. Policyholders who terminate their policy prior to their death are entitled to this cash value and, as we demonstrated earlier with Mr. Disney, may borrow or withdraw from these cash values as well.

Typically the death benefit and premiums are guaranteed in a whole life policy, although dividends are not. Cash values are invested very conservatively by insurance companies and are considered "safe money."

The individuals who benefit most from whole life insurance tend to be individuals who have a death benefits need for ten or more years, those who foresee a series of evolving needs over their lifetimes, and people with a low risk tolerance regarding savings and investments.

- **Universal Life Insurance.** Universal life insurance offers permanent death benefit protection and cash value accumulation. However, unlike whole life insurance, universal life provides flexible premium payments, an adjustable death benefit, and cash values that are tied to current interest rates.

Most universal life policies pay a current interest rate that is comparable with rates available on long-term bonds. These current

Insider Notes: Don't forget that the purchasing power of the life insurance you buy today will be steadily eroded over the years by inflation. With the help of your adviser, always make an "inflation assumption" before buying life insurance of any type.

CASE STUDY: JACK "SETTLES" ON A BETTER WAY

Jack is 69 years old and formerly the CEO of a Fortune 500 company. Due to declining health, Jack retired and moved to California to spend more time with his children and grandchildren.

As part of his retirement package, Jack was given the choice of keeping a $15 million Key Executive Life Insurance policy, which the company had purchased on his life, or to surrender the policy and take $900,000 in cash value that had been accumulated.

After an initial meeting with his estate planning attorney, it was recommended to Jack that keeping the Key Executive policy would not be to his benefit since it would merely increase his taxable estate. It was then suggested that Jack surrender the policy and use the proceeds to purchase a "second to die" life insurance policy on himself and his wife, owned by an irrevocable life insurance trust, for the purpose of paying the inevitable, significant taxes that would eventually be due on their estate.

rates are subject to change and are not guaranteed for the lifetime of the contract, although there is a minimum guaranteed rate of return. The experience that is used to calculate the mortality costs of the contract is also based on current assumptions, and also is not guaranteed. Today, universal life policies provide for death benefit and premium guarantees.

When comparing whole life and universal life insurance policies, it's extremely important to make sure that you know exactly what is and what is not guaranteed in the contracts. Universal life insurance is appropriate for individuals who are able to (and are comfortable with) accepting a greater level of risk, in return for the opportunity to potentially receive higher current interest rates and lower mortality expenses.

■ **Variable Universal Life Insurance.** Variable universal life insurance differs from traditional universal life insurance, because the under-

This new policy would not increase Jack's estate, because he wouldn't own it; the Irrevocable Life Insurance Trust is the owner. Moreover, the proceeds would be payable at the deaths of Jack and his spouse.

This sounded good to Jack, until I told him about a concept called "life settlements" that would allow him to get more for his life insurance policy than simply the cash surrender value.

Life settlements give policyholders the opportunity to sell their existing life insurance policies versus surrendering them. If the insured is expected to die sooner, the "market value" will be higher. The market value is always in excess of the cash value in the policy to be sold.

Through a life settlement, which I arranged, Jack was able to sell his life insurance policy for $2 million (or $1.1 million more than if he had simply surrendered it). He deposited $1 million in a nine-year immediate annuity, which was used to pay the premiums for the $5 million survivorship (second to die) policy recommended by his attorney. The remaining $1 million became additional retirement assets for Jack and his wife to enjoy.

lying cash values can be invested at the direction of the policyowner into many sub-accounts, such as equity, fixed income and guaranteed account options. Each policyowner is given the opportunity to direct their cash value based on their own risk tolerance, investment objective and personal asset allocation model.

The policyowner assumes the most risk in a variable policy, but also has the potential for the highest return, and can integrate the policy most closely with their investment philosophy. Variable life insurance is typically recommended for longer-term needs, where cash accumulation, as well as death benefit protection, is a priority.

Insider Notes: You must always be guided by your goals, not the goals of your advisor. A cookie cutter, generic recommendation from an advisor is not a viable solution; you and your family deserve better.

CASE STUDY: THE COOPERS KEEP THE TAXMAN AT BAY

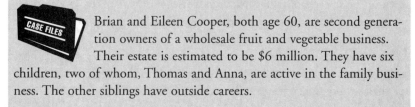 Brian and Eileen Cooper, both age 60, are second genera-
tion owners of a wholesale fruit and vegetable business.
Their estate is estimated to be $6 million. They have six
children, two of whom, Thomas and Anna, are active in the family business. The other siblings have outside careers.

When the Coopers sat down with their attorney to draft a business succession plan, Brian could not help but think about what had happened to his
favorite football team, the Miami Dolphins. Upon the death of the team's
owner, Joe Robbie, his family was torn apart by dissention and faced estate
taxes reportedly in excess of $46 million. Due to the lack of business suc-
cession planning, the Robbie family was forced to sell one of the most
valuable franchises in professional sports at a bargain basement price.
What could have been a dream inheritance or family legacy turned out to
be a disaster.

Brian also remembered reading about Malcolm Forbes in "The Wary
Capitalist" (Michael Cieply, 1989). In that book, Mr. Forbes was quoted
as saying "much of my company's income is being used to purchase enormous sums of life insurance, a device that can legally transfer millions of
dollars to my beneficiaries without an estate tax assessment." Brian's business thrived because of his astute financial acumen. But he was never a
believer in life insurance. I told him, if Malcolm Forbes bought enormous
sums of life insurance, shouldn't you at least consider it?

Utilizing a process that I call the Family Business Succession Analysis, we
determined that Brian and Eileen's children should purchase a $3 mil-
lion second to die life insurance policy on their parents' lives. To ensure
a successful plan, the family felt most comfortable with a guaranteed
policy design (guaranteed premium, guaranteed death benefit and guaranteed number of premium payments). The life insurance was structured
with an annual premium payment of approximately $65,000, guaran-
teed to be payable for 10 years only. This 10-year period coincides with
the Coopers' desire to pass control of the business to their children by
the time they reach age 70.

What the Coopers realized was the $650,000 of total premium payments ($65,000 per year for 10 years) represented approximately 23% of the $3 million life insurance. In effect, this translates into a 77% discount when compared to paying the full $3 million from the liquidation of estate assets.

At the death of their second parent, the policy would provide the funds to allow Thomas and Anna to purchase the business from the estate. The estate would then have the full worth of the business ($3 million) preserved and then equally divided among all six children after the estate taxes were paid.
The strength of this approach is that a non-liquid asset, such as a business, is converted into cash at a pre-established fair market value. The funds to make this purchase are readily available on a tax-favored basis.

Because they implemented this plan, Brian and Eileen's business would never have to be sold to an outsider or sold at a lesser amount to provide the liquidity needed for estate taxes. They also ensured that their company would remain a family business for future generations. Additionally, all six children will each receive their fair share of Brian and Eileen's hard-earned estate. Brian's open-mindedness allowed him to consider life insurance as a solution for his estate planning goals.

Case studies disclaimer —
The results demonstrated in the case studies are hypothetical and actual results may differ from those illustrated. The case studies include non-guaranteed life insurance values, premiums and death benefits. Actual results will depend on each individual's age and underwriting status. The account value and death benefit and premiums shown are based on current assumptions, which are not guaranteed. Actual results may be more or less favorable than shown.

SPECIALIZED LIFE INSURANCE PRODUCTS

In addition to the basic life insurance products described above, the insurance industry is constantly designing products to meet specific needs.

Survivorship life insurance, often referred to as "second to die" life insurance, insures two people's lives, paying a death benefit at the death of the second insured. These policies are extremely popular and effective tools to pay estate taxes that are currently due upon the second insured's death. Another variation is "first to die" life insurance, which insures two or more people. However, it pays a death benefit at the death of the first insured. This is an extremely efficient way to provide for business succession (buy-sell agreements) between partners or to insure the mortgage of a dual income couple. Regardless of the type of life insurance you select, it is important that you fully understand the policy illustration. This is the principle source of financial information for a newly issued policy.

Here are the critical questions you should ask when reviewing a life insurance policy illustration:

- What are the policy's death benefit, cash value and premium?
- Are the death benefit, cash value and premium guaranteed for the life of the policy, and if not, what portion is guaranteed?
- What interest assumptions are built into the proposal?
- Does the policy pay dividends, and, if so, is any portion of the proposal dependent on those dividend projections?
- What mortality assumptions are built into the proposal?
- Is improved mortality assumed in future years?

POLICY OWNERSHIP/DESIGN

Remember that selecting the amount and type of insurance that is appropriate for your portfolio is only half of the equation. I can't tell you how many times I have reviewed a client's existing insurance portfolio only to discover that their insurance policy will not accomplish their goals because of improper ownership, or beneficiary designations, or incorrect rider provisions. For your insurance portfolio to be most effective, it is imperative that you design it carefully with a knowledgeable financial professional, and that you review it annually to ensure that it is adaptable to any changes in your financial circumstances.

WHAT DOES THIS ALL MEAN TO YOU?

Planning for your future requires looking at your total financial picture and developing a comprehensive financial portfolio and wealth management plan, to help you achieve your goals. A crucial part of this plan must include a carefully designed insurance portfolio containing the desired type of product, the appropriate amount of coverage and the exact ownership and beneficiary structure.

Better than any other financial product available, a well-thought-out life insurance strategy will help you achieve your goals, such as a comfortable retirement or a college education for your children and grandchildren and provide a lasting legacy to those people and organizations that you care most about.

The case studies (names changed for privacy purposes) are real world examples that demonstrate how you can utilize life insurance in creative and innovative ways, to achieve your financial dreams.

After reading this chapter, I hope that you, too, have an open mind about the efficiency, versatility and power of life insurance. As I hope you saw from these case studies, life insurance is a strong and flexible way to create, preserve and pass along wealth to those people and organizations you care most deeply about.

■ ■ ■

Stuart J. Spivak, LUTCF is Founder and President of The Spivak Financial Group, an office of MetLife Financial Services, with offices in Scottsdale, Arizona and Bala Cynwyd, Pennsylvania. He has been a financial services professional for over 18 years and is a frequent and popular speaker for many civic and professional groups. He has been published in the Journal of Financial Service Professionals and he has an extensive background in tax and estate planning, with a special focus on wealth preservation and retirement planning.

Mr. Spivak's accomplishments have resulted in numerous accolades, including consistent membership as a Life and Qualifying Member in the prestigious Court of the Table division of The Million Dollar Round Table, as well as previously being named the youngest Hall of Fame member ever for the Phoenix Companies, Inc. (NYSE: PNX), a leading provider of wealth management products and services to individuals and institutions. He can be reached at 480-556-9931, 610-668-7682, or stu@spivakfinancial.com. Also go to: www.spivakfinancial.com.

[7]

LIFE INSURANCE PREMIUM FINANCING

Powerful yet poorly understood, life insurance premium financing is helping savvy investors leverage their portfolio for maximum returns. You can "borrow" your life insurance premiums to accomplish different investment goals, from gaining access to higher-yielding investments to increasing lack of cash flow or liquidity.

"GIVE ME A PLACE TO STAND, AND I CAN LEVERAGE THE WORLD."

- Archimedes

by SCOTT B. ROSE

At first glance, the term "life insurance premium financing" seems complicated, if not dull. But don't be dissuaded. Read this chapter, and I guarantee you'll be sold on a simple yet powerful concept that can greatly leverage your portfolio. It boils down to one elegant concept: using other people's money to pay for your life insurance premiums. The idea of financing life

LEVERAGING SHOULD NOT BE USED AS A MEANS TO BUY LIFE INSURANCE THAT YOU COULD NOT OTHERWISE AFFORD.

insurance premiums is counterintuitive for most people-a surprising fact, given how prevalent financing is for middle and upper income Americans. We finance our homes, our cars, our appliances, our investments, and even our everyday purchases when we use our credit cards. Nevertheless, very few people understand or even consider financing their purchase of life insurance.

Of course, whose money you can use and the advantages and disadvantages of using other people's money depend entirely on your particular financial and insurance objectives and means. This chapter will explore the little known, but rapidly emerging, concept of life insurance premium financing. I'll explain the steps necessary to enjoy the extraordinary benefits of building life insurance leverage into your portfolio.

But before we even begin, take a look at the box titled Caveat Emptor. Life insurance can be a treacherous path; this box will explain a few basic principals to consider at the outset.

TERM INSURANCE VS. PERMANENT INSURANCE

It's also important to understand the difference between two types of life insurance policies: term insurance and permanent insurance. It's very much like the difference between renting and owning a home. Term insurance is like "renting" the death benefit from an insurance company. You generally pay lower premiums (as compared to permanent insurance premiums) for the right to receive payment of a specified death benefit if you die during the term of the policy. If you stop paying the premiums on a term policy, the policy terminates, and you no longer have the right to receive a death benefit. It's just as if you stopped paying rent on your home-you only have the right to live there as long as the term covered by your last rent payment.

Term insurance is typically sold for periods of one, five, 10, and 20-year terms, with an annual, level premium payment for each year. If you choose not to make any given premium payment, the policy will terminate, regardless of the amount of time left in the original term.

In contrast, permanent insurance not only gives you the right to receive a specific death benefit, it also provides you with an investment vehicle, the value of which you can access. Permanent life insurance premiums are typically significantly higher than comparable term life insurance premiums. This excess premium is the source of the investment component of the permanent life insurance policy.

Just like homeowners who build equity in the value of their homes, permanent insurance policy owners can build value in their insurance policies and use it for virtually any reason they wish. Depending on the amount of "equity" in their permanent insurance policies, owners may or may not have to make additional premium payments, and the amount of benefit paid at death may vary as well. While it is possible to finance the purchase of term insurance, it is much more likely that you'll want to finance permanent insurance.

WHY FINANCE?

While there are many reasons to leverage the purchase of your life insurance, let me begin with one sure reason not to do it. Leveraging should not be used as a means to buy life insurance that you could not otherwise afford. In other words, if you can't afford to pay the life insurance premium in cash today, you should not use leverage on this element of your portfolio. This notion stands in stark contrast to our most basic concept of financing: I cannot afford to pay for the whole item today, but, over time, or at some later time, I will—so, let me enjoy use of the item today. The classic example of this concept is the purchase of a home. Few people pay 100% cash for their homes. Most people come up with a down payment and pay for the balance of the purchase price of their homes over extended

Insider Notes: Rather than putting your capital toward insurance premiums, you may want to put it into alternate, higher-yielding investment products. Generally, life insurance policies are not the best investments.

periods of time (e.g., 30 years). Life insurance premium financing, however, is only suitable for those who can pay for it with cash, but choose not to.

So, if you can pay for your life insurance, why would you finance it? There are two major reasons:
- To take advantage of higher-yielding investment products; and
- To address a lack of cash flow or liquidity.

First, rather than putting your capital toward insurance premiums, you may want to put it into alternate, higher-yielding investment products. Generally, life insurance policies are not the best investments. Many people measure the quality of their investments by the "return" on their investment, or the percentage by which the value of their investment increases over a specified period of time. For this discussion, let's consider the "return" on the investment in the life insurance policy to be the appreciation in the policy's account value, rather than the death benefit paid upon death. The "investment" in a life insurance policy would ordinarily be the premiums paid, but, as discussed below, when leveraged, the investment is the cost of financing (e.g., interest and fees).

Depending on the particular insurance product chosen, typical non-leveraged returns can range from three to nine percent per year on safer products (like whole life or universal life), and can range from significant losses to significant gains on the riskier variable and private placement products. Even though the gains (if any) building up inside an insurance policy grow tax-deferred, the ultimate investment returns on your insurance policy will lag the rest of the market. That's largely because a portion of the investment is absorbed as paid commissions, policy expenses and mortality costs of providing an insurance benefit. So, you may never see the returns go to work for you.

As a result, if you have $10,000 to make either a tax-deferred investment in a life insurance policy or a taxable investment in a more traditional market instrument (e.g., equities), most advisors will tell you to invest in the market. Despite the taxability of the investment, you can expect better performance in the long run from the market (historically, 10% average annual return).

Alternatively, you may want to put your funds into your own business, real estate or other less traditional investments with the potential for higher-than-normal returns. When you understand your investment options, you may logically choose to finance your insurance premiums so you can put your cash into non-insurance, higher yielding investment vehicles. You should not, however, opt not to buy insurance or to buy less insurance than you need to free up cash for investing. Use leverage to buy insurance, while still acquiring the insurance you need to fulfill your portfolio needs.

Of course, as with any other investment, if you fail to achieve returns in excess of your cost of borrowing, you will not see the benefits of leveraging this investment. Fortunately, as discussed later in this chapter, typical costs for implementing a life insurance premium financing are low enough to allow you to increase your chances of achieving this goal.

A second distinct, but related, reason for leveraging life insurance is to address a current lack of cash flow or liquidity. It is important to distinguish a lack of liquidity from the inability to afford life insurance. You may have sufficient cash to purchase the life insurance, but doing so could make you "life insurance poor" (all your disposable cash would be tied up in your life insurance), thereby depriving yourself of other assets or benefits more appropriately acquired with that cash. While you may be liquid, you really can't afford the life insurance.

Conversely, you may have substantial wealth, and consequently, great need for life insurance, but lack the cash on hand to purchase the insurance because, for example, your cash is tied up in relatively illiquid investments or other investments you prefer not to liquidate. As a result, you may be unable or unwilling to purchase the needed life insurance. Using life insurance premium financing techniques, you may be able to eliminate or significantly lower the cash needed to acquire the life insurance.

Insider Notes: Of course, as with any other investment, if you fail to achieve returns in excess of your cost of borrowing, you will not see the benefits of leveraging this investment.

CAVEAT EMPTOR: FINDING THE RIGHT COMPANY AND ADVISOR

Before you even make a move, always keep one crucial fact in mind: an insurance policy is a legal contract, and certain words carry legally binding meanings. These words not only specifically denote your rights but the insurance company's rights and obligations as well.

As with any investment, be sure to conduct thorough due diligence. Read the fine print. What the big print gives, the fine print taketh away. Unless your policy explicitly calls for the payout of a specific benefit initiated by a specific event, you may not get paid-regardless of what a smooth-talking insurance salesman told you!

Clever people work for insurance companies, and they're always trying to come up with new gimmicks. The fine print may seem eye-crossingly obscure, but make a big pot of coffee and wade through it, with the phone number of your agent next to you in case you have questions.

Another caveat: make sure the insurance company is safe. You don't want to conscientiously pay premiums for decades, only to see your insurance company go belly up. If you don't think that can happen, think again. Check the financial health of your prospective insurance company by looking up its standing in any major ratings service: Moody's Investor Services, Standard & Poors, or A.M. Best. The ratings vary greatly, but there's no reason why you should settle for any company that isn't rated at least an "A."

An essential step in putting together a premium financing transaction is identifying the appropriate professionals-advisor(s) who can help you design the insurance and financing programs to meet your specific needs and the right lender who can provide the appropriate loan. Clients often try to accomplish this task themselves and end up wasting significant time, energy and resources because they have neither the time nor the expertise to fully explore all of the options available and determine the one that is best.

The life insurance premium financing industry is developing rapidly and newer, more sophisticated and creative options continue to emerge in

the marketplace. You need an advisor with significant industry experience and reputation. You also need someone who works with different
lenders, uses a variety of programs, and maximizes your chances of success by tailoring a program to meet your specific needs.

There are several lenders in the life insurance premium finance marketplace, ranging from conservative established players, to more recent market entrants who tend to be more aggressive in pricing and other terms.
Within this range are a variety of lending options that can provide you
with the best program-if you know where to look and what to ask.

Primary premium finance lenders generally fall into one of three categories: (1) affiliates of insurance companies, (2) large commercial banks
with established private client groups, and (3) smaller private funds such
as hedge funds. When looking for the right lender, determine whether
your profile as a borrower is better suited to the insurance company affili-
ate, the private client banker, or the private investment fund.

If you have a very high net worth (usually $10 million or more), private
client groups will work very hard to get and keep your business. One of
these larger commercial banks is likely to be the lender that provides you
with the most flexibility and offers you the most attractive loan terms,
regardless of the particular insurance product or design you choose.

Conversely, if you are someone who is not necessarily the ideal "private
client," the insurance company affiliated lenders may be a better choice.
While these lenders are more accommodating with respect to you as a
borrower, they are less flexible when it comes to the particular insurance
product and design they are willing to finance. In choosing the right
lender, you must assess whether it is you (as a potential private client
coveted by many commercial banks) or your insurance program (i.e.,
policy and design) that drives the decision.

Finally, the recent development of hedge funds as premium financiers offers
a third alternative for premium finance programs. These funds are more
nimble and agile in their structure, like private banks, but do not require

any advisory relationship or promote any particular insurance products. In many respects, these lenders offer you the best of both worlds.

The information in this chapter should serve as a primer on how to assess whether you should explore life insurance premium financing and, if so, the considerations in properly structuring your own life insurance premium finance program. You'll need to perform a comprehensive analysis together with your advisor(s) on the specifics of your situation.

CHOOSING AN INSURANCE ADVISOR/PRODUCER

Typically, the person advising you on life insurance premium financing and the producer (or seller) of the life insurance policy will be one and the same. For the sake of simplicity, I will refer to that person as the "advisor." Look for an insurance advisor who has at least a working knowledge of life insurance premium financing.

Often, advisors conduct a thorough analysis of a client's life insurance needs and conclude that the client does need life insurance. Unfortunately, they usually stop short at that conclusion and are unable to fully advise on how to pay for the required life insurance. Because neither the advisor nor the client can formulate the best plan for paying for the insurance, the client often implements a less-than-optimum insurance program or fails to purchase life insurance at all.

Insurance advisors need to understand not only when financing life insurance makes sense, but also how to go about the life insurance financing process. Even though many people appreciate the power of leveraging life insurance, very few have access to the advisors and lenders specializing in structuring and implementing life insurance premium finance solutions. By familiarizing themselves with the life insurance premium finance marketplace and understanding the variety of financing options available to their clients, insurance advisors will be better positioned to advise you and differentiate themselves from other less versatile advisors.

After reading this chapter, I hope you will have a better appreciation of the rapidly developing life insurance premium finance phenomenon. You should understand how the principles of leverage make life insurance a more attractive, suitable and better performing investment than simply paying your premiums in cash.

Let's move on, and figure out whether life insurance premium financing is appropriate for you, and if so, how to go about implementing your ideal life insurance premium financing program.

UNDERSTANDING THE PHENOMENON

At this point, you may be asking, "What is so novel or interesting about life insurance premium financing? Haven't people been doing this for a long time?" While people may have borrowed money from their own sources and used those funds to purchase life insurance in the past, it is only in the last decade that life insurance premium financing has emerged as a distinct and rapidly developing industry. Industry experts estimate that, during the last five years alone, the amount of premiums financed has increased from approximately $100 million per year to as much as $800 million per year. Some predict that, in 2005, Americans will finance over $1 billion of life insurance premiums. How's that for a clear trend! How did this explosive growth in the life insurance premium financing industry come about? Not surprisingly, it was the insurance companies who made the earliest forays into the business of financing premiums. American International Group (AIG) and ING were the first market entrants. They established specific business programs for financing life insurance premiums, with the goal of promoting the sale of specific insurance companies' life insurance products.

By offering the opportunity to finance only certain products from certain insurance companies, AIG and ING hoped to increase sales of those products by driving insurance producers and their clients to select those insurance products over otherwise comparable choices.

Insider Notes: Check the financial health of your prospective insurance company by looking up its standing in any major ratings service: Moody's Investor Services, Standard & Poors, or A.M. Best. Don't settle for any company that isn't rated at least an "A."

DO YOU REALLY HAVE TO BE A HIGH NET-WORTH INDIVIDUAL TO TAKE ADVANTAGE OF LIFE INSURANCE PREMIUM FINANCING? THE ANSWER IS A RESOUNDING NO.

To make life insurance premium financing a safe and long-term business opportunity, however, these niche lenders had to do what no other financial institutions (other than the insurance companies themselves) had done. They had to take the time, energy and expense to learn about life insurance policies and how they operate; understand and manage their risks; and be willing to take the insurance policy itself as collateral for the loan. Before this "innovative" thinking, banks and other typical lenders refused to give any value to the insurance policy as an asset that can be pledged to secure such a loan.

During the mid to late 1990s, these lending companies created much greater market awareness of life insurance premium financing. The strength of these early programs was their relative simplicity (e.g., short loan documents and quick execution). Their ultimate weakness was their relative inflexibility in program structure. Because the programs' objectives were limited to promoting the sale of specific insurance products and maximizing the spread charged on the loan, the client had very limited options on which insurance to finance and how to structure the financing (e.g., term, interest rate, payment dates, collateral, valuation, etc.).

During the last three or four years, large commercial banks such as Citibank, Mellon, Wells Fargo, HSBC and others tried to capture some of the life insurance premium financing market by having their private bankers market through their private client groups. These banks made life insurance premium loans as an accommodation to their existing high net-worth clients.

In the wake of the repeal of the Depression Era Glass-Steagal Act, however, barriers between traditional banking services and insurance services began to crumble. These large banks then tried to capture market share as providers of insurance services and solutions to the coveted high net-worth individual market. While the banks were more flexible in structure and in loan terms, they were inflexible in their absolute demand for assets under management or other fee opportunities.

The banks were not interested in the sale of any particular insurance product or, for that matter, on making a meaningful profit on the loan itself. Rather, the loan was viewed as a loss leader to hook the high net-worth client and create an opportunity for the bank to make substantial fees off the client from other cross-selling opportunities (e.g., management of their assets or the sale of other "core" financial products). This fee-driven mentality, unfortunately, made these large banks the premium lenders of last resort, and their success depended heavily on the strength of the private client relationship.

THE INDUSTRY TODAY

In the last 18 months, a new twist appeared in the life insurance premium financing industry. A few large financial institutions have created structured programs that aggregate many loans made to various clients, package the loans together and "sell them off" to the investing community, similar to the way home mortgages are aggregated and sold to the public.

Unlike the private banking model, which focuses on serving the client and maintaining the bank's relationship with the client, the structured finance model is completely independent of the client and, instead, focuses on providing (selling) the financial instruments (the insurance policies) themselves. Lenders use these structured finance programs to maximize their profit from the insurance transaction with up-front fees and a portion of the death benefit at the insured's death. While these programs were often very attractive to the buyers of life insurance, they were often not as profitable to the client, because the structured lenders required a greater portion of the available transaction benefits for themselves.

 Insider Notes: In choosing the right lender, you must assess whether it is you (as a potential private client coveted by many commercial banks) or your insurance program (i.e., policy and design) that drives the decision.

Today, lenders are combining the best of all worlds. They're using the private client mentality of flexibility to meet the needs of the high net-worth individual, with a structure that provides insurance advisors and their clients with some reasonably consistent programs.

By creating formalized programs, rather than one-off, case-by-case transactions, these lenders are able to ease the learning curve for the industry and create synergies-relying on dedicated credit and underwriting teams to create consistency in program structures, manage the known risks and facilitate transaction analysis, documentation and administration.

One of the most current examples of this type of financing flexibility is the emergence of hedge funds as a source of premium financing. Their experience working with high net worth individuals, combined with the sophisticated financing structures often employed by hedge funds, makes hedge funds an ideal source of premium financing. Hedge funds have virtually limitless sources of capital and the flexibility to work with their clients in ways other institutions (such as large commercial banks) cannot.

As a result, the life insurance premium finance industry is rapidly developing to meet the growing demand for creative solutions to the life insurance needs for high net-worth individuals.

TO FINANCE OR NOT TO FINANCE?

While age is important, what really matters is life expectancy. Because there is such a strong negative correlation between a person's age and the actuarial estimate of a person's remaining time to live (i.e., life expectancy), using a person's age is a good gauge to determine the usefulness of premium financing alternatives. This is because a shorter life expectancy means a shorter expected duration of the premium loan and, in most premium finance structures, the shorter the expected loan duration, the more flexible it can be. There is no hard and fast rule of measure. Usually, the older the client, the more powerful life insurance premium financing will be.

Most premium finance loans are made for insured individuals age 70 and above, with very few going to persons below age 55. Not only do older individuals tend to have shorter life expectancies, but they also tend to have a higher net worth. As a result, lenders make a large percentage of premium finance loans to seniors.

Life insurance premium financing can work for younger individuals as well. I have seen one done for a 28 year-old. However, because their life expectancies are longer (generally more than 20 years), younger individuals will need to do additional planning and structuring to ensure that they do not defeat the advantages of premium financing by carrying too large a loan for too long.

The second essential element in evaluating the potential for financing a life insurance policy is the insurance underwriting class assigned to the insured. Most insurance companies "rate" the insured's health in one of the following types of ratings: preferred, standard, substandard, or uninsurable.

The preferred category often has subdivisions such as "ultra preferred" or "select preferred," and the substandard ratings often refer to a "table rating" such as "Table II" or "Table B," which relates to a table commonly used by insurance company actuaries to assess a particular individual's increased probability of death and the appropriate pricing for an insurance policy for such individuals (the higher table letter represents a more impaired health risk). In addition, insureds are categorized as "smoker" or "non-smoker."

The better your rating, the more likely that life insurance premium financing is an option for you. Obviously, if you're uninsurable, it is not an option at all. But you're a better candidate for premium financing if your rating is preferred than if it's standard or substandard. This is primarily due to the fact that the worse the rating, the more the insurance costs.

For example, the following table shows the annual premium for $10 million of universal life insurance issued by a top-rated life insurance compa-

Insider Notes: You're a better candidate for premium financing if your rating is preferred than if it's standard or substandard. This is primarily due to the fact that the worse the rating, the more the insurance costs.

ny on a male non-smoker living in New York at different ages and ratings. This table demonstrates how significantly the annual cost of the insurance policy differs based on age and on health.

	PREFERRED NON-SMOKER	STANDARD NON-SMOKER
AGE 70	$267,597	$348,383
AGE 75	$374,155	$491,953
AGE 80	$537,799	$756,461

A third factor in determining suitability of premium financing is the schedule of premium payments of your particular insurance policy. This is where universal life insurance policies come into play. Unlike term and whole life insurance policies, universal life insurance policies are flexible premium payment policies. Essentially, this means you have the flexibility (within certain prescribed limits) to pay more, less or, in some circumstances, no premiums in a given year. Due to this flexibility in the premium payment schedule, flexible premium payment policies are better for structuring life insurance loans. Not only does the freedom to modify the premium schedule afford the lender more options in the event of a loan default, but it gives you the ability to tailor the timing and amount of funds being borrowed to better suit your cash flow situation.

As shown in the table above, a 75-year-old male, preferred non-smoker would pay $374,155 a year, every year until age 100 for that particular $10 million policy. As an alternative, you could structure the premiums to be paid for a shorter period of time (known as a "short pay"). For example, the same policy could also be paid for in 10 equal installments of $563,494, in five equal installments of $937,229, or in one single premium of $4,017,767. This difference in premium schedules will have a significant effect on the interest cost, collateral required and loan structure for a life insurance premium loan.

Again, there are no hard-and-fast rules to follow. Generally, the shorter the period of payments, the larger the loan and therefore, the greater the interest cost-but the lower the collateral required by the lender. In contrast, longer pay policies require less funding and consequently, less interest cost.

However, you may be required to post more collateral than in other shorter pay structures.

Your advisor should evaluate age, insurance underwriting class and schedule of premium payments, together with many other elements such as your liquidity, net worth and insurance objectives, to structure the optimal premium financing program for you. Some elements can be structured to improve your options. Other elements, such as age, cannot be manipulated as easily or at all.

Hopefully, you now understand the basic factors and insurance policy features that increase your chances of finding a suitable financing option. Your advisor(s) should be able to conduct an exhaustive analysis of exactly what you need to do to create your best financing options. As a quick litmus test to assess whether or not yours is a suitable situation for financing, consider the following checklist:

- Are you age 65 or older?
- Is your net worth $10 million or greater?
- Are you insurable with a standard or better underwriting classification?
- Do you have flexible premium payment insurance policies from A-rated or better insurance companies?
- Do you have good credit?

If you can check all five boxes, then premium financing will work for you. But keep in mind, it even works for lower net-worth individuals, as I'll explain below.

BEWARE THE PERILS OF BORROWING

As you and your advisor(s) analyze whether or not premium financing makes sense for you, consider a few fundamental facts about life insurance premium financing. First and foremost, you are borrowing money. That

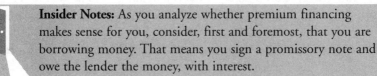

Insider Notes: As you analyze whether premium financing makes sense for you, consider, first and foremost, that you are borrowing money. That means you sign a promissory note and owe the lender the money, with interest.

BLACK BOOK CASE FILES

So far, we've covered some fairly complex concepts. Now, let's discuss life insurance premium financing in the context of actual situations that worked for my clients. Their names are protected, but the situations are real-life scenarios extracted from my case files.

■ Case #184: Mrs. U

Mrs. U is a 75-year-old woman who had recently lost her husband. As a result of her husband's death, Mrs. U became the sole owner of the family business, which was run by her son and worth approximately $125 million. Since the business' primary assets were commercial real estate holdings, a substantial portion of the family's wealth was tied up in relatively illiquid assets. As a result, the family would have a very difficult time creating the liquidity necessary to meet the estimated $40 million estate tax due after Mrs. U's death. To create the needed liquidity, the family's insurance, estate planning and financial advisors concurred that the business should own at least $40 million of life insurance on Mrs. U.

The family already owned a life insurance policy on Mrs. U's life in the amount of $25 million, but this coverage was costing the company approximately $700,000 a year, stressing the company's cash flow. The family's objective was to increase their insurance coverage using as little out-of-pocket money as possible. In addition, due to the nature of the family's assets, the only assets they could pledge as collateral for the loan (in addition to the life insurance policy itself) were the real estate holdings of the family business. The elements of limited cash flow and a large estate with illiquid assets made the family ideally suited for a life insurance premium financing transaction.

The family's advisors contacted me in April. By June, using life insurance premium financing, the family business was able to purchase a new policy in the gross (before loan repayment) amount of $40 million for an out-of-pocket cost below their current annual cost for only $25 million.

Because the family's net worth was almost exclusively in real estate, we determined they needed a loan from a premium finance lender that would accept their real estate as collateral. Moreover, because most of the real estate was already partially encumbered, we knew we had to find a lender comfortable with taking a junior (or second) position on prospective properties, as well as the cash-surrender value of the life insurance policy, as collateral for the loan.

Mrs. U was classified as a "preferred, non-smoker" risk by the top-rated insurance company we chose. We structured a life insurance policy that required three annual premium payments of approximately $4.2 million and a fourth, final premium payment of approximately $2.5 million, for an estimated aggregate loan after four years of approximately $15 million.

We used this four-year payment structure partly because the family believed that, due to Mrs. U's age and recent loss of her husband, she was not likely to live beyond the four-year premium period. Therefore, we structured a loan to coincide with this time frame. By doing so, we were able to keep the financing costs (e.g., the annual interest on the outstanding loan) down and take advantage of the then depressed interest rate environment.

The net result: The family obtained increased insurance coverage at a lower estimated out-of-pocket expense and, most importantly, the liquidity needed to meet their anticipated estate tax liability.

■ Case #952: Mr. M

Mr. M is a 78-year-old ultra-high net-worth individual with a complicated family situation. Mr. M's first wife had passed away and his sons were not happy about his subsequent marriage to a 45-year-old woman with no apparent independent means of support. Frankly, the children perceived her as a gold-digger and they wanted to block her access to their father's money.

The majority of Mr. M's net worth consisted of real estate and securities portfolios he had amassed over his lifetime. His sons felt strongly that their stepmother should not inherit any of these assets. However, Mr. M wanted his new wife to receive a significant amount of the assets. Mr. M was interested in purchasing a substantial amount of life insurance to provide his second wife with a cash death benefit upon his death.

Mr. M appreciated the tax-free nature of the death benefit proceeds, but he was concerned that, at his age and health, the large premiums he would have to pay for his wife to receive the death benefit would be a "bad investment." After all, Mr. M was a wealthy man because he was a shrewd investor. His determination was based on his substantial investment acumen and his belief that he could earn 10% returns on his own.
By conducting an IRR analysis for Mr. M, we calculated that, for a purchase of $45 million of life insurance with a single premium of approximately $21 million, the annualized IRR, while initially as high as 114+%, rapidly diminished to less than 10% by the eighth year. By the twentieth year, the IRR dropped to less than four percent. As do most insureds, Mr. M believed he was going to live a very long time. Therefore, he was not very attracted to the prospect of low, single digit returns on his investment.

Mr. M's insurance agent first contacted me in December. Given the complexity of Mr. M's financial picture and the need to obtain offers of insurance from 10 different life insurance companies and financing offers from four different lenders, it was not until the beginning of August that we were able to close Mr. M's life insurance premium finance loan. We did so for approximately $21 million.

While Mr. M had to post only a little over $1 million of cash collateral (in addition to pledging the substantial cash surrender value in the life insurance policies), we anticipated this collateral amount could go up gradually to approximately $10 million over the next 20 years. Fortunately, the IRRs for Mr. M on this financed transaction were substantially better than without financing.

The initial IRR was an incredible 7,491+%, and it did not fall below 10% until the sixteenth year, while still earning more than 5 percent in the twentieth year. Using leveraging, we were able to help Mr. M acquire the same $45 million of life insurance coverage at substantially improved IRRs.

means you sign a promissory note and owe the lender the money, with interest. If there are any reasons you can't or shouldn't borrow money (e.g., a recent bankruptcy, bad credit or contractual restrictions against additional borrowing), premium financing may not be an option at all, regardless of the elements discussed earlier in this chapter.

Second, premium lenders expect to be repaid from the death benefit paid under the insurance policy. Most non-premium finance loans have a set maturity with a defined date on which the loan must be fully repaid. Since most people do not know exactly when they will die, the imposition of a specified date for repayment or the expectation that repayment will come from sources other than the life insurance policy can severely limit your financing options. Moreover, these funding sources may not be available to you at death.

By using premium financing techniques for appropriate situations, many people are able to add life insurance to their portfolios or add more of it than otherwise possible. Today, there are many more lenders in the marketplace providing life insurance premium financing. More importantly, those lenders now have a greater understanding of insurance policies and are able to use those insurance policies to secure their loans. Until recently, individuals had to use their own liquidity to purchase their life insurance or, if they were able to use their own financing sources, they had to tie up their other assets to secure the typical bank loan.

Now, by looking for repayment from the life insurance policy when their clients die, the premium finance industry has created a loan structure that fits perfectly with their clients' timing and available cash to repay the loan. The clients not only know the funding source will be available, but precisely how much will be available.

The frequent emergence of new financing structures, new premium finance lenders and more insurance policies specifically designed for financing, reflects the continuing evolution of the life insurance premium finance industry toward a readily available and understood financial planning tool. The technique is no longer the sole province of the wealthy and the super-savvy.

THERE ARE MANY RULES OF THUMB USED BY LENDERS TO GAUGE HOW MUCH YOU CAN AFFORD TO BORROW, BUT YOUR NET WORTH OR, MORE IMPORTANTLY, YOUR LIQUID NET WORTH, AND YOUR HISTORICAL AND PROJECTED ANNUAL INCOME ARE THE MOST IMPORTANT FACTORS TO LIFE INSURANCE PREMIUM LENDERS.

ACTION PLAN: GETTING STARTED

To effectively implement a life insurance premium finance program, you must accomplish three things:

- Assess your needs and means for both life insurance and financing. If you have limited need or ability to obtain life insurance, there is no point in conducting a financing analysis.
- Once you have completed these initial assessments, design the insurance program in coordination with a financing structure to meet your objectives and fit within the lender's loan criteria.
- Choose a financing source and take the necessary steps to close an often complex financial transaction. There are several providers who can assist you with any of these implementation measures.

Begin the process by asking your insurance advisor to conduct a thorough insurance needs analysis for you, to determine how much insurance, if any, you need to purchase to fulfill your portfolio needs. By reviewing your current and projected future income needs and other related financial burdens as a result of death, your insurance advisor can help you assess how much and what type of life insurance to buy.

Just because you need life insurance, however, does not mean you can get it. For an insurance company to issue an insurance policy on your life, you need two things: insurability and insurable interest.

Insurability means the acceptability to an insurer of an applicant for insurance. Simply put, it is a question of whether the insurance company is willing to the take the risk of insuring you, based on a review of your health, lifestyle, and habits.

For example, late-stage cancer patients are not usually insurable because the likelihood of their death is too great for an insurer. Perfectly healthy individuals may also be uninsurable, however, due to their occupation, lifestyle, or habits. Let's face it: if you are a stunt person, private pilot, circus performer, or other "high-risk" professional, you will have great difficulty finding an insurer willing to insure your life.

To receive an insurance policy, not only must you be insurable, but also the proposed owner of the life insurance policy must have an insurable interest in the insured. A person (or entity) may have an insurable interest in your life if that person (or entity) will suffer a financial loss as a result of your death. The most obvious examples are immediate family members and other dependents. In addition, a corporation may have an insurable interest in your life if you are the president or other key executive due to the anticipated loss of income as a result of your death (known as "key person" insurance). The insurable interest concept is very important in premium financing transactions because the owner of the insurance policy on your life is often your spouse, trust, children or business-not you.

Once you have determined you need life insurance and can obtain it, you must then assess how to pay for it. As stated in the beginning of this chapter, if you cannot afford to pay the life insurance premiums in cash, do not consider financing them. Assuming you can afford to pay the premiums, the question of financing is twofold. First, does financing the premiums make economic sense for you? Second, can you structure financing that not only meets your objectives, but also is offered by a lender?

As a threshold matter, before conducting a financing, you must have an alternative need or higher-yielding use for the cash you would otherwise

Insider Notes: You should only borrow as much as you need. You can finance all of the amount of your insurance premiums or only part of the amount, but don't borrow more than the cost of the insurance policy.

FEEL CONFIDENT THAT YOUR DECISION MAKES ECONOMIC SENSE FOR YOU. EVEN IF YOU DETERMINE LIFE INSURANCE PREMIUM FINANCING IS SOMETHING YOU WANT, YOU MAY NOT HAVE THE MEANS TO OBTAIN IT.

use to pay your premiums. For example, if your premium is $10,000 a year, before borrowing $10,000 each year and paying interest on the borrowed amount, you must determine that you need to use your own money for something else, such as a college education, medical expenses, home improvement, you name it. Or, you want to use your own money in a better investment opportunity, such as reinvesting in your own business or another higher-than-average yield opportunity.

Either way, using other people's money to pay your insurance premiums has associated risks and costs, including interest, fees, and potential liability. Feel confident that your decision makes economic sense for you. Even if you determine life insurance premium financing is something you want, you may not have the means to obtain it.

THE "FIVE KEYS" TO FINANCING

Structuring a financing program that suits your needs and means and is available in the premium finance marketplace is the toughest step in the life insurance premium financing process. You need to quickly identify your financing limitations and build a program around them. Here are the five key questions you must first resolve:

KEY #1. HOW MUCH MONEY DO I WANT TO BORROW?

You might be tempted to answer, "As much as I can!" However, you should only borrow as much as you need. You can finance all of the amount of your insurance premiums or only part of the amount-but don't borrow more than the cost of the insurance policy. Many people pay some portion of the premiums and finance the rest, but the larger the percentage of the premium you finance, the greater your potential internal rate of return (IRR). While the investment return is more powerful when you borrow a higher percentage of the premiums, the loan is easier to structure and implement if you borrow a lower percentage. Generally, you should try to finance between 75 and 100% of the premiums.

KEY #2. HOW MUCH WOULD THE LENDER LET ME BORROW?

This is one of the most important questions and probably the most common limitation on a potential premium financing. Whether it's life insurance premium financing or any other type of financing, lenders will not lend unlimited amounts of money to you. It's primarily a function of your creditworthiness. A lender's analysis of your potential creditworthiness generally focuses on their assessment of your ability and willingness to pay the interest and principal due on the loan.

There are many rules of thumb used by lenders to gauge how much you can afford to borrow, but your net worth or, more importantly, your liquid net worth, and your historical and projected annual income are the most important factors to life insurance premium lenders.

As a general rule of premium financing, you should not expect to borrow more than 25 to 50% of your net worth (more, if we are using liquid net worth), and the annual interest cost should not be more than 50% of your annual income.

To evaluate these factors, lenders will require you to provide your tax returns and financial statements, usually for the past three years. Many premium finance transactions fail because the clients do not have the creditworthiness to warrant the loans they seek. Answering this question early in the process is vital to a smooth and successful premium finance transaction.

KEY #3. HOW MUCH INTEREST CAN I AFFORD?

Borrowing money comes at a cost: interest. One important factor to consider is the interest payments the lender requires for servicing the loan. Obviously, the amount of the interest rate is a major component-the higher the rate, the higher the cost. In addition to the rate, you need to consider the timing of the payments. Interest payments can be paid in advance (e.g., interest is paid on the first of the month for the entire month's balance), in arrears (e.g., on the last day of the month for the entire month's balance), or they may be deferred and capitalized. The latter scenario means the interest is borrowed too, and repaid at some later date, and then you pay interest on the unpaid interest.

If you choose to pay interest in advance, you can expect a lower interest rate on your loan. Conversely, if you pay in arrears, or even defer the interest payments, you will pay a higher interest rate and, consequently, your loan will cost more. You may also have some flexibility in structuring the frequency of the interest payments. Interest can be monthly, quarterly or annually, and in some instances, it can be specifically tailored for odd periods.

One of the most important determinants in your ability to meet interest costs on a premium finance loan is your amount of available income, or your liquid assets readily available to turn into cash to meet this expense. Your ability to meet the interest obligations may depend on other circumstances, such as the anticipated sale of a business, the payment of dividends, or the receipt of rental payments. These personal contingencies guide you toward selecting one interest payment structure over another.

Many potential financing transactions break down when even high networth clients realize too late that they can't meet the continuing cash flow needs of the scheduled interest payments. The timing and amount of their interest payments were not properly coordinated with expected available resources to meet their obligations.

KEY #4. HOW MUCH COLLATERAL CAN I AFFORD TO POST TO SECURE THE LOAN?

Most, but not all, premium finance loans use the life insurance policy as the primary form of collateral for the loan. Specifically, you assign the lender the right to the cash surrender value (CSV) and death benefit payable under the insurance policy.

The CSV is pledged as collateral to the lender if you default under the loan. In that case, the lender will surrender the policy to the insurer, and the lender will receive the CSV and apply it toward the balance of your loan.

The death benefit, usually paid only at the death of the insured, is assigned to the lender as the planned method of principal repayment of the loan. Upon death, the insurance company will send the death benefit equal to the outstanding loan balance to the lender and remit the excess death benefit to the beneficiaries under the policy.

Depending on your chosen loan structure, you might need to pledge additional collateral to secure the loan. The most common forms of additional collateral are cash, securities, letters of credit, guarantees, real estate, and other insurance policies. Whether or not you need to post additional collateral and how much you need to post are direct functions of the "design" of the insurance product you select.

As discussed earlier in this chapter, there are several factors, including amount, timing and frequency of premium payments, that affect the amount of CSV and death benefit for a given insurance policy. By altering these factors, you can engineer a policy design more likely to fit your desire and ability to post additional collateral.

Lenders usually want their loans to be fully secured. That is, they want the value of the collateral securing the loan to equal or exceed the amount of the outstanding loan balance. In the early years of a life insurance policy, the CSV is typically lower than the amount of premiums paid; unless you choose to finance a lesser percentage of the premiums, there will be additional collateral required to fully secure the loan.

How much additional collateral? Lenders typically advance (or lend) between 90 and 100% of the CSV of a universal life insurance policy (variable policies are treated like margin securities and you typically see advance rates of approximately 50% on variable products).

The additional collateral requirement for a hypothetical loan on a $5 million policy for a 55-year-old male, preferred non-smoker with 20 level premium payments might be calculated as follows:

Insider Notes: Whether or not you need to post additional collateral and how much you need to post are direct functions of the "design" of the insurance product you select.

YEAR	ANNUAL PREMIUM	OUTSTANDING LOAN BALANCE (100% OF PREMIUMS)	HYPOTHETICAL CSV	COLLATERAL VALUE @ 95% ADVANCE RATE	ADDITIONAL COLLATERAL REQUIRED
1	85,815	85,815	24,967	23,719	62,096
5	85,815	429,075	230,637	219,105	209,970
10	85,815	858,154	721,254	685,191	172,963
15	85,815	1,287,225	1,289,151	1,224,693	62,532
20	85,815	1,716,309	1,904,502	1,809,277	(92,968)*

At the point at which the Collateral Value exceeds the Outstanding Loan Balance, no additional collateral is required.

The table above demonstrates how the need for collateral changes over the life of the policy. By varying the policy design, you can structure a financing with collateral needs in terms of amount and timing that match your ability to provide additional collateral.

KEY #5. HOW LONG DO I NEED TO BORROW?

Life insurance premium finance loans can be structured with or without set maturity dates. The maturity date is the date on which the entire outstanding balance of the loan is due and payable. Premium financing lenders typically offer one, two, three, five, 10, and 15-year loan terms.

Some lenders even offer "loans for life" (i.e., the loan does not mature until you die). This alternative is often most attractive because most premium finance loans are repaid from the death benefit. The obvious uncertainty of when you will die and have the death benefit proceeds available to repay the loan can make it difficult to select a specific maturity date.

This loan-for-life structure, however, has certain disadvantages-it's more expensive, for one thing. Depending on the exact structure of the loan-and more importantly, your own time horizons-it may not be the best alternative. If you have a particularly short life expectancy, say, 10 years or less, it may be better to structure a loan with a set maturity and take advantage of a fixed interest rate option, an option not available on loans for life.

On the other hand, if you are relatively young and have a life expectancy of 20 years or more, over extended periods of time the costs of financing the loan for life can become exorbitant and erode any of the benefits of financing. Perhaps more effective would be a loan structure with a set maturity that provides you with a means to repay the loan before actually receiving the death benefit.

Knowing your maturity limitations helps structure the loan that works best for you. One potential pitfall in structuring the maturity of the loan is a mismatch between the due date of the loan and the client's means to repay the loan. If you know you will have the liquidity to repay the loan in five years, but not necessarily in 10 or 15, you should structure the loan to match your own ability to repay it. If you can't be sure if you will have the means to repay the loan, you should use the loan-for-life option to have the loan repaid from the death benefit.

MANAGING THE RISKS

Life insurance premium financing can be an effective solution only if you are properly advised of the risks of the financing and take the appropriate steps to assume or manage those risks. The two most serious risks in any premium finance loan involve the interest rate and the collateral.

■ Interest rate risk

There's the risk that interest rates will increase during the term of your loan and boost the cost of your transaction. When structuring your premium finance loan program, you need to model the expected results at various interest rate assumptions and "stress" the model to determine at what point (if any) you can no longer tolerate further increases in the interest rate.

Given recent historically low interest rates, it is prudent to anticipate increases over the life of your loan as interest rates return to normalized levels, especially as economic growth picks up and inflation starts to rear

Insider Notes: When structuring your premium finance loan program, model the expected results at various interest rate assumptions and "stress" the model to determine at what point (if any) you can no longer tolerate further rate increases.

THE EASIEST WAY FOR YOU TO AVOID A COLLATERAL CALL IS TO PROVIDE EXCESS COLLATERAL AS A BUFFER FOR UNANTICIPATED DECLINES IN THE PERFORMANCE OF YOUR COLLATERAL.

its ugly head. By using a combination of fixed rates and interest rate derivative instruments such as collars, caps and swaps, certain loan structures can protect against a majority, but not all, of the interest rate risk in a transaction.

Protecting yourself against interest rate risk, however, comes at a cost, and you may not necessarily want to pay for that protection. Instead, you may want to assume (or bear) that risk because other investments in your portfolio mitigate a interest rate increase, or the alternative investment you made with your money may earn a correspondingly higher interest rate to offset the premium loan's higher interest costs.

■ Collateral Risk

You could lose some or all of the collateral you provide to the lender to secure the transaction. If you are relying on the insurance policy death benefit to repay the loan, what happens if the insurance company goes into liquidation or otherwise fails to pay the death benefit? The lender will likely foreclose on the collateral you provided to secure the loan and, in many instances, look to you to make up the difference.

Fortunately, this risk is fairly remote. A more likely risk is that the cash surrender value of the life insurance policy may decline or not perform as well as originally projected. The premium lenders rely on the cash surrender value as collateral; to the extent the cash surrender value lags in performance or declines, the lender may initiate a collateral call (i.e., request additional collateral to make up for the shortfall). Under ordinary circumstances, the lender returns to you all of your collateral upon repayment of the loan. In the event of default, however, the lender will likely foreclose on the collateral.

The collateral's decline or inadequate performance causes most premium finance loan defaults. The lender becomes under-secured, makes a collateral call, and you may have to provide additional collateral to maintain the proper level of security.

The easiest way for you to avoid a collateral call is to provide excess collateral as a buffer for unanticipated declines in the performance of your collateral. Another common technique is to provide collateral with very little volatility (e.g., treasuries, cash, blue chip preferred stocks, or even a letter of credit).

Another common reason for default on a premium finance loan is the failure to pay interest. By making sure you fully appreciate the interest rate risk and are confident that you have adequately addressed it and can handle the fluctuations, you can minimize the likelihood of being unable to meet your interest obligations.

HOW TO CONDUCT A BOTTOM-LINE ANALYSIS

There are several reasons to finance the purchase of your life insurance, but, ultimately, you must determine if financing works for you by using a simple cost-benefit analysis. To do this, of course, we need to examine the potential costs and benefits of life insurance premium financing.

It's not as obvious as you might think. To make it easier, divide up the ledger in two halves: hard costs (out-of-pocket costs), compared to soft costs (intangible costs). The same distinction applies to the benefits of a financing transaction; there are hard benefits and soft benefits. After reviewing all of the costs and benefits, you can determine whether or not financing makes sense for you.

■ Hard Costs

With every financing structure, you pay interest. Whether this interest is advance, arrears or deferred, rest assured, you eventually pay it! The most

Insider Notes: The easiest way for you to avoid a collateral call is to provide excess collateral as a buffer for unanticipated declines in the performance of your collateral.

obvious hard cost is the interest you pay on the borrowed funds. Estimating this cost requires making certain assumptions about interest rates: The higher you project interest rates to reach during the term of the loan, the higher your out-of-pocket cost to maintain the loan.

The other most common hard cost in financing your premiums is the fees paid to advisors and the lender. Most advisors who help you put together a financing structure will charge a fee for their services. These one-time fees are typically a percentage of the amount of the loan you get and range from 20 basis points (0.2%) to 500 basis points (5%), depending on the size and complexity of your loan. Some lenders will charge origination and/or commitment fees to make the loan.

The origination fee is usually a relatively small, one-time fee for making the loan, while the commitment fee is a continuing, annual fee for committing to make further loans as needed in the future. Both fees typically range from 25 basis points to 100 basis points. It should be relatively simple to calculate these hard costs for a premium financing transaction.

■ Soft Costs

Borrowing money and pledging your assets to secure the loan have other non-monetary effects on your investment picture. These soft costs take several forms. For example, you may have to personally guarantee the loan, which may adversely affect your future creditworthiness and ability to obtain additional loans. In addition, if you pledge one or more assets to secure the loan (e.g., securities, cash, real estate, life insurance policies, etc.), you likely will be limited in your use and control of those pledged assets. Eventually, you have to repay the loan. Usually, this repayment will occur at death and be paid by the insurance company from the death benefit. However, this means your beneficiaries will receive less "net" death benefit than if you had not borrowed to pay the premiums. This does not necessarily mean borrowing is a bad idea. Remember, while you are getting less death benefit in a financed structure, you are also paying less since you are using someone else's money to pay the premiums.

INTERNAL RATE OF RETURN

TODAY (AGE 56)
*Premiums Paid Over Time
to the Insurance Company*

*If Your Aggregate Premiums
Paid Were...*

FUTURE (AGE 70)
*Death Benefits Paid
by Insurance Company*

*...and Your Net Death
Benefit was...*

Non-Financed	$975,000	Investment grows at 9.21% per year	$1,500,000
Financed	$610,000	Investment grows at 17.36% per year	$918,000

■ **Hard Benefits**

The hard benefits of using a life insurance premium financing program can be measured most easily in two ways. First, you can compare the estimated amount of premiums you will pay in a non-financed situation with the estimated amount of fees and interest you will pay if you choose to finance. For example, a 56-year-old male buying a $1,500,000 life insurance policy might expect to pay approximately $975,000 in premiums between ages 56 and 70. During that same period, however, using one particular financing structure, that person might spend as little as $610,000 in interest and fees, a savings of approximately $365,000. Unfortunately, this type of comparison, while simple, doesn't really address the question of whether or not financing will be a good investment. To make that determination, examine the transaction's internal rate of return, or IRR. Let's take a closer look at IRR, using the figure above.

The IRR tells you the percentage return earned on your investment(s), for a given set of cash inflows and outflows over a specified time period. In the example above, assuming death at age 70, under the non-financed program you would invest $975,000 and receive a return of $1,500,000 of death benefit, resulting in an IRR of 9.21%. This means your $975,000 insurance investment earned you 9.21% per year over that time period.

On the other hand, by financing the investment, your total investment would be approximately $610,000 and your return would be only about $918,000 (because some of the $1,500,000 death benefit was used to pay off the loan). Despite receiving less "net" death benefit, your IRR on the financed transaction would be 17.36% per year, nearly double the non-financed return on your investment. Therefore, when comparing a financed transaction to a non-financed transaction, it is important to measure not only the absolute cash flows, but also the internal rate of return of your investment.

■ Soft Benefits

The primary soft benefit of financing your life insurance premiums is the ability to use someone else's money to purchase your life insurance, allowing you to use your own money for other opportunities.

This benefit can be difficult to measure, because it depends on how much you value the alternative use of your funds. If freeing up your own funds allows you to give your daughter the wedding of her dreams, it may be impossible to place a dollar value on that use of your money.

However, if you use the funds to buy the stock your brother-in-law has been recommending and you double your money, it is very easy to value the alternative use of your money. Measuring this benefit of using a financed insurance program requires you to make certain assessments of how well you can use your money for other purposes.

Not every financing structure will result in a favorable cost-benefit conclusion. Make sure you thoroughly examine all of the costs and benefits for a variety of financing alternatives before concluding which financing structures, if any, will be ideal for you.

By now, you probably know more about life insurance premium financing than the average insurance advisor, but the industry is developing so rapidly and uses such cutting edge concepts, you really need to keep abreast of all the options available to you when considering the purchase of life insurance. I hope this chapter has given you a basic understanding of the important concepts and given you the tools necessary to begin an evaluation of whether or not premium financing may be right for you.

■ ■ ■

Scott Rose is an independent premium finance consultant and has been giving legal advice in the financial services industry for 10 years. He has specialized in life insurance financing for over five years. He earned his B.A. in pyschology from Cornell University with Distinction in all Subjects and received his J.D. from the University of Pennsylvania Law School, with cum laude and Order of the Coif honors.

Scott was managing partner of his own life insurance finance brokerage company and had been an assistant general counsel for American International Group, Inc., after leaving the corporate finance department at Weil, Gotshal & Manges. Scott can be reached at 914-656-8055 or at ScottBRose@aol.com.

[8]

FINANCIAL PLANNING
FOR WOMEN

The earnings gap has closed, to be sure, but the responsibility gap has not. Too many women have relinquished control of their finances to the men in their lives, leaving them wholly unprepared for major life events — divorce, widowhood, unemployment or retirement. Learn the specific strategies and tactics you'll need to know to take control of your investments, insurance, tax and retirement planning — and become the CFO of your family's finances.

"A WOMAN'S BEST PROTECTION IS A LITTLE MONEY OF HER OWN."

- Clare Boothe Luce

by CHERYL M. BURBANO

Despite the advancements of women in society, they still face many uphill battles. Notably, women are emerging as the poorest segment of America's senior population. According to the AARP Foundation,[1] women older than 65 are twice as likely to be poor than men over age 65. In fact, women make up 70% of all older people living in poverty. This trend has been dubbed "the feminization of poverty."

CALL IT THE FEMINIZATION OF POVERTY: WOMEN CONSTITUTE SLIGHTLY MORE THAN HALF THE WORLD'S POPULATION, PERFORM NEARLY TWO-THIRDS OF ITS WORK HOURS, RECEIVE ONE-TENTH OF THE WORLD'S INCOME AND OWN LESS THAN ONE ONE-HUNDREDTH OF THE WORLD'S ASSETS.

This chapter carefully examines the factors that adversely influence women's economic status and the resulting financial disparity between men and women. It also offers practical retirement planning tips to help women overcome these impediments and take charge of their financial destiny.

Facts on Aging: Experts indicate that 80 to 90% of American women will be solely and completely responsible for their finances at some time in their lives. Let's look at the reasons why: 1) Women outlive men by about 6 years — according to the U.S. Census Bureau, the average life expectancy for men is 73.4 years versus 79.5 for women; 2) The average age of widowhood is 55; and 3) Nearly 50% of all marriages in the United States end in divorce; about 63% of second marriages fail.

These data alone do not necessarily guarantee economic disparity between the sexes. However, when these demographic trends are examined along with various economic factors and social expectations, we see a clearer picture of today's negative financial realities for women.

Pension Plans: The old pension plans on which our parents retired are becoming a thing of the past. Less than 17% of positions in corporate America carry pension plans — employee contribution plans called 401(k)s have become the norm.[2] And, let's face it, older women often depended on a spouse's retirement pension income.

Although more women than ever have entered the labor force, they still earn less than their male counterparts. For every $1 earned by men, women earn 72 cents. In the year 2000, this meant that the median income for full-time women workers was $28,823, while men earned $39,230 on average.

Women are expected to and often do fulfill the role of unpaid caregiver and nurturer for the family. This means that women enter and exit the labor force more often than men to fulfill the demands of this important social role, whether to care for small children or aging parents.

Consequently, women have shortened careers, spending 14.7% less time in the workforce than men. Men miss out on just 1.6% of their working years.[3] Translated into economics, this means that women have less time to earn raises or contribute to retirement plans. And, sad to say, less than half (45%) of women ages 25-64 participate in a pension plan at work.

Call it the feminization of poverty: Women constitute slightly more than half the world's population, perform nearly two-thirds of its work hours, receive one-tenth of the world's income and own less than one one-hundredth of the world's assets.[4]

Although the women's movement has opened a lot of doors previously shut to women in the last three decades, older women, according to the AARP Foundation,[5] are still twice as likely to be poor than are men age 65 and older. In fact, women make up 70% of all older people living in poverty. Let's look at some of the reasons for this financial trend that economists call the "feminization of poverty."

From birth on, little girls and boys traditionally experience different gender role expectations from various key institutions of society: family, school, church, and the media. This has resulted in different types of socialization experiences and acceptable behavior for each gender.

Insider Notes: The old pension plans on which our parents retired are becoming a thing of the past. Less than 17% of positions in corporate America carry pension plans — employee contribution plans called 401(k)s have become the norm. And, let's face it, older women often depended on a spouse's retirement pension income.

As babies, girls are cuddled, talked to and nurtured more by both parents than are boys. Girls are encouraged to learn nurturing skills early with their first toy — often a baby doll. Other girl toys are meant for passive and quiet use. Meanwhile, boys' toys are often action or team oriented. Consequently, girls learn early in life that their expected social role is that of "nurturer." Unfortunately, they also learn that other stereotypical behaviors — passivity and dependency — are equally important.

This nurturer/caregiver role quite often emerges later in life as Mother, the first protector of the child. Over the years, unfortunately, it seems that we have abrogated part of our natural maternal instinct to the males in the family. The men are expected first and foremost to be the family protector and guardian. Meanwhile, our role as nurturer/caregiver has evolved to largely one of expected self-sacrifice. This is often misinterpreted by society to mean that, as a woman, you must always put yourself last.

However, as women, we are responsible for not only our children's welfare, but for all aspects of their lives, including the well being of their mothers' lives — that is, our own lives. Prince Charming may not show up! And if he does, he may not stick around or outlive us. Experts indicate that 80 to 90% of all American women will be solely and completely responsible for their finances at some time in their lives.

Therefore, as women, it is natural for us to become financially responsible adults by redefining and leveraging our protector/nurturer role. Assuming responsibility for our personal finances allows us to better take care of our families, and ourselves.

BECOMING CFO OF THE HOME

Becoming a financially responsible adult is a continual process, not a one-time exercise. Consider these steps:

❶ Visualize yourself as the chief financial officer (CFO) of "Your Family, Inc." Start by creating a vision for yourself. How do you see yourself financially? Totally dependent on someone else for income and investments, as well as family financial information? Or, independent and a co-equal with your mate, a woman who is fully aware of family income, expenses, assets, investments and liabilities?

As CFO of your family, make sure you know where every dime goes, and why. This means pursuing self-disciplined management of your family's cash flow, perhaps the most significant financial strategy that you can implement and your first step to achieving true financial freedom. The idea is to put you in a position where work is optional and retirement affordable — the true definition of financial freedom.

❷ Familiarize yourself with your household's economics. Learn your family's savings account numbers, where the accounts are located (bank, credit union, financial institution, etc.) and how they are titled (individually or jointly owned).

❸ Determine what retirement plans and retirement savings are in place and their balances, pay out options and beneficiaries. And be sure to know the location of other important family documents (updated wills, durable powers of attorney, healthcare surrogates and living wills).

❹ Have a serious family discussion about finances. If you are planning marriage, sit down and talk with your significant other about your new family finances. Although this recommendation is not considered very romantic, remember — there is nothing "sexy" about poverty.

❺ Create a household budget: your first step to financial freedom. Discuss expected total household income. Will you pool your incomes and have a joint checking account, or will you each contribute a portion of your income to pay the household expenses and maintain separate checking accounts?

Other critical items to discuss include:
- Deciding who will be responsible for paying the bills.
- How many credit cards will your household use and who will have possession of them;
- How much life insurance do you each have, who is the beneficiary, will you change it to your new mate;
- How much disability insurance does each of you have;
- What current investment and other assets do you each own? After

AS A FINANCIAL ADVISOR, I HAVE SEEN CLIENTS WITH HEALTHY SIX-FIGURE INCOMES WHO HAVE ALL THE "LOOKS" OF WEALTH — EXPENSIVE CARS, LARGE HOME, DESIGNER CLOTHES, CHILDREN IN PRIVATE SCHOOL, ETC. — BUT THEY'RE SPENDING MORE THAN THEY EARN AND ARE JUST A PAYCHECK AWAY FROM DISASTER.

marriage, will you jointly re-title these assets or continue to own them individually;

■ Who are the beneficiaries on your assets, will you change that to your new spouse; and

■ How will you make major spending decisions?

6 You may want to seriously consider a pre-nuptial agreement. This is especially true if you are about to marry a wealthy individual or if you will bring substantial financial assets to the new marriage yourself.

7 You may want to establish a marital trust. If this is to be a second marriage for you or your new mate and if either of you have children from a previous marriage, you may want to talk to an attorney about establishing a marital trust or a "Q tip" trust.

As the CFO of Your Family, Inc., you will establish a family budget that shows you all sources of income and household expenses. Once again, self-disciplined management of your family's cash flow is a significant financial strategy.

Insider Notes: As CFO of your family, make sure you know where every dime goes, and why. This means pursuing self-disciplined management of your family's cash flow, perhaps the most significant financial strategy that you can implement and your first step to achieving true financial freedom. The idea is to put you in a position where work is optional and retirement affordable — the true definition of financial freedom.

YES, VIRGINIA, YOU CAN RETIRE WEALTHY

Too many women, especially if they're divorced with kids, get caught in a trap of living paycheck to paycheck. They need to free themselves of this vicious cycle, and think of the future. Keep your eyes on the prize, by studying the following chart, which depicts how much your current investments will be worth in the future, assuming various annual rates of return.

Here's a hypothetical calculation to help you use this chart: Let's say you plan to retire in 25 years and expect your money to grow 8% a year from now until then. Find 25 years in the left-hand column and 8% in the middle of the chart. The two data points intersect at 6.85, which means $1,000 of your squirreled-away retirement money will be worth $6,850, assuming an 8% annualized return. This chart also helps you keep track of that insidious beast, inflation. It works this way: If you assume 4% inflation under the above scenario, you will require $2,670 (2.67 on the chart) in 25 years to match the buying power of $1,000 in today's dollars. Seeing the tangible potential effects of investing, in future years, should keep you motivated for the long haul!

YEARS	HYPOTHETICAL RATE OF RETURN*								
	4%	5%	6%	7%	8%	9%	10%	11%	12%
10	1.48	1.63	1.79	1.97	2.16	2.37	2.59	2.84	3.11
15	1.80	2.08	2.40	2.76	3.17	3.64	4.18	4.78	5.47
20	2.19	2.65	3.21	3.87	4.66	5.60	6.73	8.06	9.65
25	2.67	3.39	4.29	5.43	6.85	8.62	10.82	13.59	17.00

The numbers shown are for illustrative purposes only, are not guaranteed, do not represent any specific product or investment, do not take into consideration any taxes, fees or charges that may be assessed. All investments involve risk, and it is possible to lose money, including your principal investment.

Insider Notes: Get invested. Do not delay. Fill the bucket – the earlier the better. A woman saving $50 monthly for 30 years into an investment that averaged 8% annual return would have a total of $74,519!

BUDGET BLACK HOLES

You have discovered that a large part of successful budget management is learning where the mystery dollars go, to free up cash flow. Two common "black holes" in personal budgets are over-withholding of federal income taxes, which results in larger tax refunds, and maintaining very low deductibles on car and homeowner's insurance policies, which results in higher-than-necessary monthly insurance premiums.

The last two years have witnessed substantial federal income tax cuts.[6] Failure of workers to respond by making appropriate adjustments in their withholding amounts resulted in an average $2,000 income tax refund per household in 2002. Any tax refund is the equivalent of giving the federal government an interest-free loan for up to 15 months. When was the last time someone loaned you any amount of money interest-free for 15 months?

You only want to pay your fair share in taxes, nothing more and nothing less. Consider adjusting your withholding so the appropriate amount is withheld from your paycheck. This average $2,000 return is the equivalent of $166 monthly raise in an employee's paycheck, if the right amount had been withheld.

Insurance statistics show that if you increase your car insurance deductible from $100 to $250, you could lower your monthly premium by approximately 12%. Increase it to $500 and you could lower the premium by approximately 30%.[7]

Another black hole that can zap your household's cash flow is failing to understand the difference between "needs" and "wants." Unfortunately, the incessant barrage of advertising in our consumer culture has blurred the lines between these two concepts.

Too many of us believe Madison Avenue's insidious message: to be financially "successful" or "accepted," we must buy certain brand-name products or services, whether we really need them or not. We start viewing something that we would like to have (and for which we should save excess income), as something we can't do without. So, we buy it immediately on credit, with money we do not have. It's all too easy to get caught up in the never-ending, downward financial spiral of "keeping up with the Jones'."

PROPERLY DEFINING WEALTH

Wealth is defined not by what you buy — it's what you get to keep! If you're behind on payments for any purchase — home, car, appliance, or computer — the item can be repossessed or the bank can start foreclosure. As a financial advisor, I have seen clients with healthy six-figure incomes who have all the "looks" of wealth — expensive cars, large home, designer clothes, children in private school, etc. — but they're spending more than they earn and are just a paycheck away from disaster.

Your top priority should be to pay your credit card bill in full, before the grace period ends. This gives you an interest-free loan. Otherwise, your money is stuck in an investment that conveys "negative" returns of up to 18% or more.

Two university economic professors, Thomas J. Stanley and William D. Danko, studied common characteristics of millionaires and published their findings in a book called *The Millionaire Next Door.* What they learned was that the average millionaire probably lives next door to you in an unassuming home. The average annual income of the millionaire was $135,000 — not $400,000 or $500,000. They also found that the average millionaire buys a 1-3 year-old used car and always saves some money every month.

Wealth (what you get to keep) is not built overnight. Have you ever experienced a leaky roof either at home or at work? You can't call a roofer; it's raining outside. You'll probably get a bucket or wastebasket to catch the leaks. What's going into the bucket? One tiny drop of water at a time. After six to eight hours, we find our bucket or waste basket full of water; it

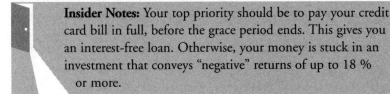

Insider Notes: Your top priority should be to pay your credit card bill in full, before the grace period ends. This gives you an interest-free loan. Otherwise, your money is stuck in an investment that conveys "negative" returns of up to 18 % or more.

CASE STUDY: "JANE DOE" *

Approximately four years ago, I met with a 34-year-old woman, who I will call "Jane Doe." Jane came to me looking for financial advice. She was a working professional and the mother of three young boys. She recently had been widowed when her 36-year-old husband died of a heart attack while playing golf.

Needless to say, Jane was devastated by her husband's death and was having a hard time in her grieving process. She had to take some unpaid leave from work to sort things out. Unfortunately, Jane and her husband never discussed family finances — she allowed her husband to fill that important role completely by himself.

Upon her husband's death, a significant household income source ended. Jane had no idea if her husband had any life insurance at all and, if so, where the policies were located or the designated beneficiaries. Subsequent meetings with Jane revealed that her husband had left the family with significant debt. Without her knowledge, Jane's husband had secured a home equity loan on their house to buy an interest in a new business with his brother and mother. This new liability together with the home's first mortgage left virtually no equity. Moreover, Jane's mother-in-law would not reveal the amount of her husband's interest in the business or its value.

Consequently, Jane's willingness to leave all the family financial business solely to her husband cost her dearly. Due to her lack of knowledge, Jane was forced to retain an attorney to sue her mother-in-law and brother-in-law for an unknown interest in a family business, with virtually no assets to pay for the counsel. Moreover, with her husband's income gone she had very few assets to continue her family's lifestyle and had to significantly cutback and downsize. Consider this a cautionary tale.

The names have been changed and the circumstances have been altered to protect the identity and confidentiality of the client.

may even be overflowing. That is how we build wealth: one dollar at a time, over time, consistently.

The biggest obstacle to creating wealth is procrastination — waiting until you feel that you can finally "save" some money. As a financial advisor, I hear this excuse all the time. At some point you are going to run out of time! As the CFO of Your Family, Inc., you need to learn to pay your most important creditor first: yourself! That means part of "Your Family, Inc.'s" budget includes a regular monthly savings line item, even if it is only $10 per week. Remember, the millionaire next door is in the habit of saving.

MANAGING RISK

Now that you have freed up cash flow and have discretionary monthly income, how and in what do you invest? The answer depends on your savings goal, the amount of time you have to save, and the amount of investment risk you are willing to take. As a general rule, the longer the time horizon to save, the more risk that you should be willing to take. Savings for a cash reserve "rainy day fund" should be in investments with no risk to your initial dollars invested (i.e., savings accounts, money markets, or certificates of deposit).

Studies have shown that women and men have distinctly different approaches to investing. Men tend to take more risks, and women tend to minimize risk and take very conservative investment approaches. The common reason offered for this difference is that, as women, we are accustomed to running very tight household budgets and literally living from paycheck to paycheck; we feel that we can't afford to lose even a nickel.

BUILDING WEALTH

To get a potentially higher return for your invested dollars, you must be willing to take a higher risk. Individual risk, however, is dictated by

Insider Notes: As a general rule, the longer the time horizon to save, the more risk that you should be willing to take. Savings for a cash reserve "rainy day fund" should be in investments with no risk to your initial dollars invested (i.e., savings accounts, money markets, or certificates of deposit).

CONTRARY TO FOLKLORE AND LATE NIGHT COMIC ROUTINES, A WOMAN'S FINANCIAL WELL BEING AFTER A DIVORCE TAKES A BIGGER HIT THAN THE MAN'S. TYPICALLY, AFTER A DIVORCE, A WOMAN'S STANDARD OF LIVING DECREASES BY 25 TO 45%, WHILE THAT OF HER EX-SPOUSE INCREASES BY 15%!

one's time horizon, goal and circumstances. There is no such animal as a guaranteed return of 10%, 15% or more without risk to your initially invested money.

There are no great mysteries to successful investing and wealth building.

❶ **Get invested.** Do not delay. Fill the bucket — the earlier the better. A woman saving $50 monthly for 30 years into an investment that averaged 8% annual return would have a total of $74,519! The average annual historical return over the entire history of the U.S. stock market, including the 1929 stock market collapse and the 1987 downturn, has been between 10.5% and 11% (large cap and small cap equities).[8]

❷ **Stay invested.** Market timing only contributes 2% to the overall investment returns.[9] Do not pull out your money. Do not get nervous with the ups and downs of the stock market.

❸ **Diversify your investment choices.** Have several buckets to modify your risk and help optimize your return.

MANAGING EXPENSES FOR "YOUR FAMILY, INC."

It is absolutely vital that you effectively manage your household budget. If you don't do it, no one else will. Some steps to get you started include:

❶ **Free up cash flow.** Do this by finding the "mystery" dollars in your budget.

❷ **As an example, initiate household purchasing rules.** For purchases of $100-$500, implement a 24-hour decision-time rule. For purchases over $500, implement a 7-day decision-time rule.

❸ **Fix your tax withholding.** If you received a tax refund last year, consult your tax advisor to consider adjusting your income tax withholding at work.

❹ **Review your insurance policies.** Get out your car and homeowner's insurance declaration pages. If you have very low deductibles, consider calling your insurance agent and ask to have them increased. In establishing your new deductibles, consider cash on hand to cover any out-of-pocket expenses (deductible).

❺ **Pay off credit cards.** With your new discretionary monthly income, pay off any high interest credit card debt.

❻ **Pay yourself first.** Start saving by arranging to have a certain dollar amount deducted automatically from your net paycheck and deposited into an investment (savings or money market for a cash reserve, or other investments) for future financial goals.

❼ **Diversify your portfolio.** For longer-term goals, diversify your investments to help optimize your investment portfolio returns.

DIVORCE SELF-DEFENSE FOR WOMEN

With approximately 50% of all marriages ending in divorce in the U.S., Prince Charming remains what he is: a fairy tale. We have already established that the wife usually abrogates financial responsibility to her husband and, after a divorce, often finds herself alone and responsible for budgeting and paying expenses for the first time in her life.

Contrary to folklore and late night comic routines, a woman's financial well being after a divorce takes a bigger hit than the man's. Typically, after a divorce, a woman's standard of living decreases by 25 — 45%, while that of her ex-spouse increases by 15%! Consequently, divorced women have less money to spend on basic living expenses, such as housing, transportation and food.[10]

Insider Notes: Use insurance to guard against death and disability of your ex-husband. In your divorce settlement, ask for a life insurance policy on your ex-spouse with you as the owner of the policy and your children as the beneficiaries.

MARIE GETS THE LAST LAUGH *

CASE FILES

One of my most illustrative — and inspiring — financial planning clients came to me while she was going through a messy divorce.

"Marie" was a mother of two small boys, both under the age of 5, and worked in the medical profession. Her ex-spouse, although a great father, was a spendthrift who was incapable of saving a dime.

Consequently, as a divorced woman, Marie's only assets included her ability to earn an income, a ten-year-old car and a settlement award of 50% of the equity in the marital home, equal to approximately $20,000. Marie first used her $20,000 equity settlement as a down payment on a new home for her and her children. She took advantage of locking in a low fixed-rate, 30-year mortgage to minimize her mortgage payments, making them almost equal to her current rent payments.

With Marie's modest income of under $40,000 and child support that was not guaranteed, her household budget was one of the tightest I had ever seen. She worked hard at developing a tight, but viable household budget by identifying and eliminating the traditional spending "black holes" — over-withholding of income taxes, low insurance deductibles,

How can this be? In the majority of divorce settlement cases, the woman is not only awarded child custody, but also child support and, sometimes either permanent or rehabilitative alimony. Well, the key to this seeming contradiction lies within the division of assets in divorce settlements themselves. Let's examine them.

Most divorce procedures resolve around highly charged emotional issues, especially when children are involved. Continuing income to the ex-wife is typically awarded in the form of alimony and child support, which usually ends when the child turns 18. Children increasingly are electing to remain in the home well beyond age 18.

Tangible and intangible assets are often divided equally between the spouses, or are awarded based upon a percentage of effort and longevity in the and confusing wants with needs. Her new budget included a "paying-her-self-first" line item among her expenses to create a cash reserve and to save for a new car.

Two years later, Marie called me, very excited to tell me that she had purchased a "new" used car for her family. She was pleased to announce that she had proudly written a check for $2,000 from her cash reserves as a down payment on the car and had successfully financed the rest through her credit union. She told me that, in her entire lifetime, this was the first time she was able to write a check for $2,000, and it felt great! She went on to tell me that her sons were excited to have a new car that's nice inside with air conditioning that works, and all they want-ed to do was ride around in it.

Now Marie is very proud of her new home, car and increased cash reserve savings. She indicated that she is in better financial shape than her ex-hus-band, even though he earns significantly more money than she does. She is now working on a retirement savings plan. It bears repeating: self-disciplined management of your cash flow is a simple but powerful financial strategy.

The names have been changed and the circumstances have been altered to protect the identity and confidentiality of the client.

workplace. As explained earlier, women spend less overall time in the labor force. As an example, consider a fictitious client:

In community property states, all assets that were attained during the mar-ital union are divided equally (regardless of who earned them). However, any asset brought into the marriage or inherited before or during the mar-riage is the sole property of that individual, is not subject to any settle-ment and is awarded back to that spouse.

Once again the maternal/protector instinct often emerges during the divorce settlement process. In an effort to minimize the disruption that divorce can bring to children's lives, the mother often insists on being awarded the marital home. Such an agreement is often at the expense of

PERSONAL ESTATE PAPERS MUST BE ACCESSIBLE, AND YOU SHOULD TELL LOVED ONES OF THEIR LOCATION.

other assets. In other words, besides a car, that is sometimes the only asset the woman gets in the divorce settlement.

After a few years of living on a substantially reduced household income, the house becomes a financial drain on the budget with increased maintenance expenses, taxes and insurance costs, to name a few. Consequently, some divorced mothers find themselves in the position of either finding additional income by entering the workforce or moonlighting, selling off the homestead and downsizing, or moving into a rental unit.

The sale of a real asset such as a home may often have significant capital gains tax consequences to be resolved. There is a capital gains tax exclusion, however, on home sales up to $250k per individual. With no other financial assets awarded in the divorce settlement, the woman may find herself at age 65 with little money saved for retirement, relying on Social Security to survive.

POST-DIVORCE FINANCES

Becoming the CFO of "Your Family, Inc." is an ongoing process, not a once-and-done exercise. Specific steps that you can consider include:

❶ **Immediately cancel all jointly held credit cards.** Check your credit record and make sure that you have credit reported in your name.

❷ **Unless court ordered, otherwise, change all your beneficiary designations.** This includes all your assets — checking, savings, money market, certificates, mutual funds, brokerage accounts, IRA accounts, 401(k)s, and other retirement savings.

❸ **Focus on finances, not emotion.** A divorce settlement should be approached from a financial/business point of view rather than from an emotional one. Try to analyze all assets with a long-term financial outlook rather than an immediate financial or emotional need.

❹ **Protect alimony and child support.** If your ex-spouse is injured and cannot work or is killed in an accident, your alimony and child support could either be reduced or stopped altogether. What will you do then?

❺ **Use insurance to guard against death and disability of your ex-husband.** In your divorce settlement, ask for a life insurance policy on your ex-spouse with you as the owner of the policy and your children as the beneficiaries. Also ensure that your ex-spouse carry long-term disability insurance and provide proof of the coverage on an annual basis. In both cases you may be able to negotiate so that your ex-spouse is responsible for paying the premiums on both policies.

❻ **Secure your share of retirement and pension plans.** If your spouse has either a pension program at work and/or other assets such as IRAs, 401(k)s, or other supplemental retirement plans, you may be entitled to a portion of up to half of those assets. If you live in a community property state, you are entitled to exactly half. This is achieved through a Qualified Domestic Relations Order (QDRO).

❼ **Consult with a financial planner.** This person should help you place these retirement assets in investments that have the potential to grow appropriately for your risk tolerance and time horizon.

ENSURING A FINANCIAL LIFE AFTER HIS DEATH

In the U.S., the average age of widowhood is 55.[11] This surprising fact, coupled with women's longer natural life expectancy of 79.5 years, means that it's possible a woman can expect to be a widow for as many as 20 plus years! Yet, as tragic as the death of a spouse may be, how many women are prepared for the financial transitions that such a tragedy brings? As a grieving widow, navigating the mire of the legal and financial systems can be overwhelming and challenging for an older woman whose spouse often dealt with the attorneys, courts and financial institutions.

Insider Notes: As a widow, you must start thinking about your own independence and self-reliance, even as your health begins to fail. I usually recommend applying for long-term care insurance with a home healthcare option that will allow you to remain in your home with as much dignity and independence as possible, for as long as possible.

SELF-DISCIPLINED MANAGEMENT OF YOUR FAMILY'S CASH FLOW IS A SIGNIFICANT FINANCIAL STRATEGY.

There is an old adage in the financial services business: Someone, some-where, is not coming home tonight. What if that someone was your spouse or significant other? Stop right now and ask yourself, "If an unex-pected disaster occurs, could I find all of the necessary documents integral to my family's needs?"

How many of your family's financial documents are literally scattered throughout your home or in someone else's possession? How easy (or diffi-cult) would it be for you or your personal representative to compile an inventory of your spouse's assets? Where are the wills, personal financial statements, deeds and titles to real estate, life insurance contracts, personal income tax returns, etc?

FINANCIAL CHECKLIST FOR WIDOWS

After finding some of these documents, where would you begin? Below are some steps you should consider doing:

- **Order 20 death certificates.** Get certified death certificates from the funeral home because each institution you notify will require an original copy.
- **Notify all income sources of spouse's death.** Contact everyone with the news, including: employer, pension fund, Social Security, insur-ance carriers, financial institutions, and health insurance carriers.
- **Check annuity pay-out options.** As a survivor, you may be entitled to continue receiving your spouse's pension income if he had chosen "joint annuity" pay out. However, it may be at a reduced rate.
- **Convert IRAs.** As the beneficiary on your spouse's IRAs, you have the opportunity to convert them to "spousal IRAs." Depending on your and your spouse's age and whether your spouse started to receive income from them, special IRS rules allow you to either continue receiving income payouts, or delay receiving payouts and creating a "stretch IRA," allowing potential tax-deferred growth to continue.
- **Invest life insurance proceeds.** Most death benefit payouts from life insurance are income tax free to the beneficiary and can become a significant source of income replacement for the survivor.

Find a financial advisor you trust to discuss how to potentially create additional income by investing these payouts.

■ **Get Social Security survivor benefits.** Immediately notify Social Security, which is, according to an article in the *Senior Journal* (2/27/04) the single most important financial resource for older women in the U.S. — to receive retirement or survivor's benefits to which you may be entitled.

■ **Visit Social Security website.** Social Security has set up a special website just for women. Social Security Online for Women at www.ssa.gov/women. It provides information on issues regarding survivor and disability benefits, as well as retirement and Supplemental Security Income.

■ **Determine age eligibility.** The earliest age you can receive Social Security survivor benefits is age 60, if you meet certain requirements per the Government Social Security website. However, you will not be entitled to Medicare benefits until age 65.

■ **Determine widow and orphan eligibility for children.** If you are a widow and have children under the age of 16 in the household, you may collect Social Security survivor benefits for both yourself and orphan benefits for your children, if you or your spouse earned the minimum credits to be deemed "fully insured".

■ **If there's no will, enter probate process for assets.** If your spouse made no will or you cannot find one; your spouse will have died "intestate" and all assets that are not jointly owned will be probated. Probate is the legal process of transferring assets in an estate that involves a court of law. It includes: creating an inventory of assets owned at death; paying final funeral expenses, as well as estate debts and taxes; and distributing remaining assets either to the beneficiaries named in a will or to the heirs specified by state law.

■ **Check beneficiary designations on assets.** Most people are unaware that beneficiary designations on financial assets (checking, savings, certificates, mutual funds, brokerage accounts, etc) supercede wills. This means that, upon proof of death (certified

Insider Notes: Most death benefit payouts from life insurance are income-tax free to the beneficiary and can become a significant source of income replacement for the survivor.

PLANNING IS THE PROCESS OF PREPARING FOR THE WORST AND HOPING FOR THE BEST.

death certificate), financial investments will automatically transfer assets to the designated beneficiary of record-even if the will states that all assets should be left to the spouse. The degree of court involvement in these activities varies, but the process nearly always incurs expenses, the greatest of which are attorney fees. Other fees include probate court costs and accountant fees.

- **Get health insurance.** Obtain health insurance for yourself if you are younger than 65. If your spouse was still in the workforce at time of death, you may be able to continue your husband's employer-sponsored health insurance through COBRA for up to 18 months.
- **Protect against identity theft.** Cancel all jointly held credit cards and secure all personal identification numbers from banks, computers, ATM cards and other security systems.
- **Consider delaying sale of home.** It is often recommended that the sale of the estate's largest asset, the marital home, be delayed for as long as possible. This will help ensure that a fair market value is obtained and that the buyer is not taking advantage of a new widow with little financial experience. IRS rules allow the net profits of up to $250,000 per individual or $500,000 per couple tax free from the sale of a residence, if you and your spouse lived in it for at least two of the years immediately prior to the sale of the home. Consult your tax advisor.
- **Consider obtaining long-term care insurance.** As a widow, you must start thinking about your own independence and self-reliance, even as your health begins to fail. I usually recommend applying for long-term care insurance with a home healthcare option that will allow you to remain in your home with as much dignity and independence as possible, for as long as possible.

PREPARING FOR DEATH

Planning is the process of preparing for the worst and hoping for the best. No one likes to think, much less talk, about what our families may go through upon our death. But you can take control of your financial future by considering these initial steps.

Life Insurance: Make sure that your spouse has the appropriate amount of life insurance coverage to take care of the needs of all survivor income needs upon death. This amount should be reviewed on an annual basis.

Pension Payouts: Understand the various pension payouts available to your spouse and the consequences upon death.
Social Security Payouts: Become familiar with Social Security payouts based upon the credits earned by your spouse or your own earnings.

Organize Key Documents: Organize you and your spouse's personal papers and documents so that, at death, you, your heirs and family will have all of the necessary information in an organized manner, at your fingertips. Personal estate papers must be accessible, and you should tell loved ones of their location. You can do this by placing them in a bank safety deposit box or a safe location within your home. The key documents include:

- Your most recent personal financial statements.
- Last will and testaments and life insurance contracts.
- Your most recent personal income tax returns.
- Passwords for computers and other security systems.
- Names, addresses and phone numbers of your bankers, attorneys, CPA, brokers, investment advisors, insurance, and financial planners and any other key people who would assist in the continuation of your business and financial legacy.
- Keys to all rental property and storage properties such as a safety deposit box (include inventory of any safety deposit box with a list of individuals who have authorized access).
- Instructions on how to find life insurance contracts, titles to motor vehicles, deeds to real estate and other valuable assets.
- Instructions with respect to any pre-arranged funeral contracts or other final instructions you want known.
- Updating all information as your family situation changes.

Women still face financial obstacles in society, which is why it's imperative for them to take control of their money now, before it's too late.

■ ■ ■

Cheryl M. Burbano, CFP, MBA is a senior financial advisor with American Express Financial Advisors Inc, Member NASD. She specializes in personal financial planning, including planning for asset allocation and preservation, estate preservation and tax reduction strategies. She holds an MBA from the University of South Florida and a Ph.D from the University of Florida. At American Express Financial Advisors, she earned the President's Recognition Award, 2001-2002, and was a member of the Advanced Advisor Group, Gold Team, in 2003 (phone: 813-994-1190, fax: 813-994-1336, email: cheryl.m.burbano@aexp.com).

This information is being provided only as a general source of information and is not intended to be the primary basis for investment, tax or legal decisions. It should not be construed as advice designed to meet the particular needs of an individual investor. Please seek the advice of a financial advisor regarding your particular financial concerns. Consult with your tax advisor or attorney regarding specific tax or legal issues.

■■■■■■

[1] *AARP Foundation and International Longevity Center "Unjust Desserts, 2003"*

[2] *Federal Interagency Forum 2000 Report*

[3] *Center for Retirement Research, 2002*

[4] *United Nations 2004 Womenwatch Website*

[5] *ibid*

[6] *Tax Relief Act of 2001; Growth Tax Relief Reconciliation Act of 2003*

[7] *Insurance Information Institute Website, 2004*

[8] *Ibbotson — Stocks, Bonds, Bills and Inflation 2000 Yearbook. (Past performance is no guarantee of future results)*

[9] *Brinson, Hood & Beebower, "Determinants of Portfolio Performance," Financial Analysts Journal, June, 1991*

[10] *National Center for Women and Retirement Research, U.S. Census Bureau, Current Population Survey, November, 2001*

[11] *U.S. Census Bureau, 2000*

[9]

THE ENTREPRENEUR'S WAY

Your business is one thread in the tapestry of your life. Before establishing goals for your business, it is essential to reflect on what is important to you as an individual — your personal vision. This chapter explores the power of planning, when owners integrate their personal goals into their business.

"BUSINESS, MORE THAN ANY OTHER OCCUPATION, IS A CONTINUAL DEALING WITH THE FUTURE; IT IS A CONTINUAL CALCULATION, AN INSTINCTIVE EXERCISE IN FORESIGHT."
- Henry R. Luce

by LUKE R. REINHARD,
CFP®, CHFC, REBC, RHU, MS
FINANCIAL ADVISOR

Typically, entrepreneurs consider their businesses to be part of their investment portfolios — it is their "ticket home." However, in truth, many small business owners only have the job to show for all those endless hours of work and frustration.

Scores of entrepreneurs never achieve their personal goals; they find themselves tied down to the business. By not integrating their personal goals into the business planning process, many small business owners take excessive risks because they risked everything on one endeavor. If the business fails, so does their goal of accomplishing financial independence.

Many small businesses never produce enough profits to allow the owner to save outside the business, and in many situations, the business cannot find a buyer, because no one is willing to buy a job. However, by not tying personal goals to the business, the entrepreneur has done just that: he/she has simply given him/her self a job.

When entrepreneurs integrate personal financial decisions into the business, the business takes on a new meaning. The business becomes more of an instrument to accomplish personal goals; it is viewed as an investment in the overall plan.

How do you begin integrating your small business with your long-term personal financial planning? Start with your personal goals.

HOW DAVID BECAME A FINANCIAL GOLIATH

Consider the following example of an entrepreneur named David. I will tell his story throughout this chapter, and use him to exemplify my advice, and, hopefully, by seeing how my advice helped his family, you will gain insights into your own situation. The measures I recommend in these pages are not theories but actionable steps that can help you reap tangible rewards.

Let us start at the beginning. The dry cleaning business was 60 years old that year, and in trouble. David, the manager of the family business, was facing a problem that many small business owners face come tax time. How was he going to pay his tax liability and fund the businesses' retirement plan? The business could not afford both. If he funded the retirement plan, he would owe the IRS less, but not have the funds to pay the income taxes which was not an option. If he paid only the IRS and did not fund the retirement plan, he would owe additional taxes and let his family down. David's extended family had come to anticipate the retirement contribution.

David was looking for a quick fix to a deeper problem. He had trouble focusing on anything except the immediate issue at hand and he resisted any attempts to discuss his personal goals.

Randolph, David's father, the sole owner of the dry cleaning business, could not see the changes taking place. Randolph, turning 82 that year, was enjoying life. For the last 15 years, he and his wife took nice trips to Europe with family and friends. The Maine business paid for all his insurance, provided extra cash, and allowed him to help his other children who were always in trouble and needed money. He took pleasure coming to the rescue.

Randolph's family moved to the United States from Europe in 1941 to escape the coming war. David's grandfather, Joseph, started the dry cleaning business in 1942 and he built the business through hard work and by providing good customer service at a fair price. Randolph had worked for his father, Joseph, for most of his adult life, taking over the family business at Joseph's death. Since graduating from college, David has worked for Randolph for almost 25 years and had taken over the management 15 years ago. David was the oldest of five children.

For David, the business had lost its charm. He dreaded going to work and viewed the business as a ball and chain. David had worked nights and weekends, six days a week, for more than 25 years to grow and develop the family business. He wanted out but felt trapped by his immediate and extended family, who depended on the business for their livelihood.

Insider Notes: Why Goal Setting is Important! In 1984, a follow up study was done on the Harvard Business School graduating class of 1964. In the fabled Harvard University study only three percent of Harvard students set and wrote goals on a regular basis. The stunning revelation of this study is that 30 years later, 50% of the total net worth of the group was held by just three percent of the group. You guessed it! They were the three percent that had a habit of setting and writing goals as students, and then continued to write goals and review them regularly. Do not be afraid of wanting too much — Write it Down; Make it Happen and Plan to Succeed!

THE BUSINESS TAKES ON A NEW MEANING, WHEN YOU INTEGRATE PERSONAL FINANCIAL DECISIONS INTO YOUR BUSINESS. IT BECOMES OKAY TO CEASE SINKING EVERY DOLLAR BACK INTO THE BUSINESS, SINCE THE BUSINESS IS VIEWED AS AN INVESTMENT IN AN OVERALL PLAN — YOUR PLAN.

David was tired of the headaches from unruly employees with an attitude and no work ethic; of making the never-ending weekly payroll; of paying state, federal, social security, Medicare, and unemployment taxes; of responding constantly to ever-changing governmental regulations; of his customers not paying their bills; of his employees stealing from him; and of the stress of making a profit to support the family. The business was crushing him.

Randolph's exit plans from the business consisted of David working until Randolph's death, as he did for his father, Joseph. Randolph took over the business, at his father's death at age 62, almost 20 years ago. In those years, the business was a moneymaker; employees valued their job and put in an honest day's work.

At Randolph's death, David would get the business, but then what? David's kids took no interest in running the family business. They would work during the summer months to earn some extra spending money for school but they saw the commitment needed and wanted nothing to do with it. David envied, and yet encouraged their insight. How clear it became to David over the last few years that running or even owning the business was a dead-end! So much time had been lost; David was approaching 50. He did not see a way out except for the path laid before him, like his father, and David wondered if he could make it.

Randolph could not understand why David wanted out and felt betrayed. After all, where else was David going to make the money he makes? The business provided for David and his family, it provided the fine home, the children's private high schools and the nice vacations. If David ever truly needed money, Randolph knew he would come to the rescue.

Typically, entrepreneurs consider their businesses to be their "ticket home" like Randolph. However, in truth, many small business owners have only the business to show for all those endless hours of work, and in most cases, not even the business. This perceived ticket home becomes a problem when stacked up against the facts: over one million businesses are started each year in the United States and by the end of the first year, only 60% are still operating. Within five years, only 20% will be in business and by the 10-year mark, only 4%. So only 4 out of 100 make the 10-year cut. Grim odds, indeed (Department of Commerce, 2002 Report).

This chapter explores the power of planning when owners integrate their personal goals into their business and the potential consequences when owners do not. From my experience, dealing with either side in isolation creates a disservice to your business and your family. Setting goals and implementing a plan that integrates your personal and your business planning issues is the basis of a business owner's success. David wanted financial independence i.e., (the financial security, control, money and power to do the things he wanted, at the level he wanted, when he wanted). David could not see the path....

The business takes on a new meaning, when you integrate personal financial decisions into your business. It becomes okay to cease sinking every dollar back into the business, since the business is viewed as an investment in an overall plan — your plan.

Insider Notes: Looking to recruit, retain and — when the time comes — generously reward key employees, deferred compensation fills this niche by rewarding select executives by helping them set money aside for retirement, death and disability. A deferred compensation arrangement can provide you with the kind of flexibility that is quite simply unavailable in a qualified plan. And it can provide generous benefits to select executive employees, including a different level of benefits for different employees. Consult with legal counsel.

Your business will become less individual and more a tool to accomplish your goals. David found this to be true. By viewing the business as a tool to accomplish his personal goals, David was able to make tough decisions and move the business to profitability.

THE PLANNING PROCESS

Creating a vision of where you see yourself in the future is the first step in developing an overall plan. A vision is a coherent statement of what you would like to become. David's vision was to achieve financial independence at age 55 and completely exit the business in eight years, without relying on his family or the business at that time.

The chart below outlines the process on which I placed David. No short cuts here, nothing new, just a time-tested process of helping clients achieve an ever-increasing degree of financial independence. David wanted financial independence but could not see the path, because the business took precedence over his personal goals.

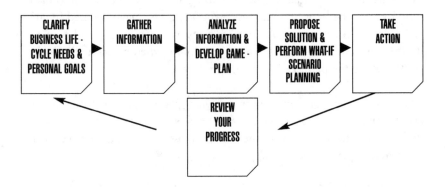

If you separate your personal goals from your business goals, as most owners do, typically, the business demands will overshadow your personal goals. However, if you ask a business owner to look into the mirror and say what they see, it is usually a father, a husband, a mother, a grandfather, not a business owner. Yet, running a business demands so much of the owner's time, energy and thought, it virtually absorbs the owner's identity. Business growth can bring exponential headaches due to the hassles of payroll, cash flow, management, etc. Many owners describe day-to-day activities as running an adult daycare center. The realities of running a small business can change your vision, particularly if the business was not grounded to your personal goals. Your vision provides the anchor that prevents you from drifting when responding to employees, competitors and market conditions. By starting at the personal level, and identifying those one or two goals that will make your life complete, you can use the success of the business to accomplish what is truly important to you.

Integrating personal goals into the business involves the process of separating your goals from your desires. A desire involves other stakeholders (investors, partners, employees, etc.) who will determine the outcome. For example, David desired for Randolph to give him the business, while Randolph wanted David to continue supporting him and his extended family.

At this stage in the process, you need to overcome the natural desire to protect your personal goals from the ferocity of the business climate. Many owners are often fearful of integrating their personal goals into their business planning, since if the business fails, so do their most precious goals. Overcoming this fear is a factor in any major decision and can mean the difference between failure and success.

For David, bringing Susan, his spouse, into the process was instrumental in helping him overcome his fear. Moreover, once Susan got caught-up into the process, she became supportive in helping David overcome some difficult roadblocks, such as dealing with Randolph and the extended family. She brought a different perspective to the progress that supported David's actions.

As with David, a starting point in the process is to discuss your vision with your advisors and stakeholders and involve them early, like a spouse or a significant other. Your stakeholders need to buy into the process, otherwise it will be difficult to maintain momentum and focus while building the support network needed to overcome roadblocks. When you develop your vision, think long-term. Most people are multigenerational investors; we are not only planning for our well-being but for our kids, grandkids, and our greater community.

DEVELOP A S.M.A.R.T. VISION

A vision is where you see yourself in the future. It is created from within, from personal hopes, values and interests. After you have developed your vision, you are able to identify your financial goals. Goals shape your plan by helping you determine your time horizon, how much risk you should be taking, and what strategy is most appropriate.

A well-stated, attainable goal should be S.M.A.R.T.

- **Specific** — Ensure that your goals express what you want to say and achieve.
- **Measurable** — Include a target such as a dollar figure or timetable to measure your progress.
- **Actionable** — There should be clear steps you can take to help you attain each goal.
- **Realistic** — Make the goal achievable so you will not get discouraged at the outset; make sure it is consistent with your lifestyle and expectations.
- **Time-bound** — Set a deadline for realization to add urgency and motivation for action.

First, focus on the top one or two goals and separate them from wishes. Unlike wishes, goals are obtainable outcomes that you can control. Do you have an emotional tie to this goal? If not, the likelihood of success is extremely small. If the goal did not take place and you did not feel deeply disappointed, then the goal was only a wish.

A goal is truly worth pursing once it passes a series of acid tests:

- **First Test:** How important is it? This is an emotional test. Your goal passes this test if you feel that achieving it will give you emotional satisfaction.
- **Second Test:** Will I do what it takes? This is a practical test. Can you afford the goal in terms of time, money and effort?
- **Third Test:** This is a logical test. Ask yourself, "If I do not achieve this goal, will I stop wanting it?" In addition, you should ask yourself and your loved ones how your goals and their goals would change in event of a death or a disability.

Many small business owners set financial goals dependent on their current business cycle. For example, David measured his success based on sales for the week: "If I keep outpacing last year's sales, I will be OK." Many owners and advisors believe that success comes from growth. What they are saying is that we will be all right if we do better than last year. In reality, this is not tied back to their personal goals. If your life raft only gets you halfway to shore, you still drown.

Typically, when you integrate your personal goals into the business, you will find it is easier to focus and stay true to those profitable activities that lead to personal success. Most growth targets are actually desires or outcomes, not the activity required to accomplish the goals. Very seldom do businesses tie their personal goals back to the business, let alone provide specifics. For example, this year, I want to invest $10,000 into my kid's college fund or invest $25,000 towards financial independence.

By sharing your goals with your loved ones, and seeking their input, it helps to build accountability, support and motivation, similar to what David did with Susan. In large part, the overall success of your vision depends on you building accountability to your loved ones.

Once your vision and goals have been pinned down, it is prudent to identify "roadblocks" that could prevent you from accomplishing your vision. Usually, roadblocks can be prevented or anticipated with a well-thought-out gameplan. Consider David's current goal of funding his retirement plan while also addressing IRS liabilities. This dilemma is nothing new for him; he struggles with this situation every year. For many owners, April can be a stressful time. Your retirement plan contributions are due, last year's taxes are outstanding, and your first quarterly tax payments are also unpaid, and of course, year-end receivables are up, creating a cash flow

Insider Notes: Keep your real estate holdings separate from your corporation for liability and flexibility reasons. Have your corporation lease back the buildings at fair market prices. When you sell the business, you can lease or sell the property separately. Consult with legal counsel, tax and financial advisor on the most appropriate entity for ownership.

crunch which often leads to borrowing from future cash flow to fund last year's obligation, allowing the crisis to repeat itself, like David.

Many start-up businesses do not have valid gameplans due to lack of experience and a track record. Creating an undeniable gameplan requires a commitment to the vision, building critical data for projection and planning and, of course, time, knowledge and energy. Otherwise, the plan turns into an exercise in creative writing.

Many owners do not think they have the time to act globally or execute a long-range plan. But without a gameplan, a business is unprepared for adversity, such as a slow year or a couple of slow years, a new competitor with better service and products, conflicts with employees and clients and, of course, the macro environment. In these situations, planning takes on the immediate crisis, leaving you open to repeat problems. The response typically addresses the symptom not the underlying problem.

In many cases, owners have achieved a degree of comfort; the business provides a good living and, after all the hard work and many years of sacrifice, they feel they deserve a break. The goals have adjusted to the realities of the business; the focus and the fun are long gone. Complacency sets in. The owner is biding his or her time and would sell if they could; however, the business has no value to anyone but the owner. The business produces a livelihood for the owner and his family, but not the extra profit that holds true value for a potential buyer.

GETTING YOUR HOUSE IN ORDER

What steps can you take to help you avoid these adverse outcomes? Get your own house in order. Start with your vision and goals; this is where it all begins. Where do you want to end up? What legacy do you want to leave?

Financial planning is the development and implementation of a total, coordinated plan to achieve your overall vision and goals. Documenting your baseline provides you the means to track and monitor your progress towards your goals. The baseline also allows you to perform what-if scenarios and see potential outcomes, like the death or disability of the owner or a key employee or changing your business structure and/or your retirement plan.

Many individuals falter and fall at this stage since it requires some heavy lifting. Documenting your assets, liabilities, insurance, income and expenses requires time and effort. As simple as it sounds, taking inventory can seem like an overwhelming task, especially when many of us do not know what we have, where it is, and why. Few individuals have an idea of their current net worth, let alone a personal budget.

Most owners view their business as their primary investment, and typically, it is their sole asset outside their home. Many believe that investing into the business will yield the greatest return compared to other potential investments. In a sense, you are saying that, "no other company can do better than I can given the risks." It is like advising a client to invest all their money into one small, unknown stock.

Many owners are so close to the business that they severely underestimate their risk, which can lead them into a false sense of security. Randolph and David provide a good example; neither accumulated funds outside the business, always reinvesting and growing the business.

Even if the business does provide a good rate-of-return, it is not usually prudent to invest all your funds in one business. Generally, business owners have unrealistic ideas about the value of their business or the potential of "cashing-in" by going public or selling the business to employees that yet exist. Google's lucrative IPO notwithstanding, most owners do not realize what little value their businesses have in the open market — until it's time to sell. Many focus on building and growing the business without any concrete plans to harness the wealth through an exit plan.

Insider Notes: Having trouble saving money? Does money slip through your checking account? Divide your income and expenses by setting-up a system that separates all your income from your expenses into different accounts. Live on a fixed monthly allotment and save or invest the balance.

Many business advisors assume that what is good for the business is good for the owner. If you keep the business healthy, then by default, the owner's healthy.

For example: in David's case, it may be in the best interest of the business (an S-Corp) not to put the kids on the payroll because of the additional payroll cost, potential FICA taxes, and the downside of bringing family members into the business. Moreover, owners are unwilling to commit cash flow that does not directly benefit the businesses growth, since the growth of the business is the driving force, not the personal goals of the owner.

However, if you look a little deeper, David's overall tax burden would decrease since the kids are in a lower tax bracket than David and Susan. If you ask David or most owners what is more important, funding your kids' college or growing the business, the overwhelming majority will answer funding their kid's education. However, few, business advisors, including corporate attorneys and CPAs, could articulate your personal goals, if pressed.

CHOOSING THE RIGHT BUSINESS STRUCTURE

Assessing your business structure is one part of this stage. Without the right business structure, you may find it difficult to take advantage of planning opportunities.

As a general rule, if your business is a start-up or is planning to lose money out of the gate, you may want to consider a Sole Proprietorship for simplicity. A sole proprietorship is an unincorporated business which is owned and usually managed by one person. The business has no separate existence apart from the owner. The owner and the business are one and the same. Business property is owned by the proprietor and not by the business. The business may only sue and be sued in the name of the owner, and all business assets and debts are personal assets and/or debts of the proprietor. Of the types of business organizations, sole proprietorships are by far the most common.

There are three principal reasons why the sole proprietorship enjoys such widespread popularity: ease of formation, unified management and freedom from much government regulation.

Obviously, the sole proprietorship is not free from disadvantages. If it were, there would be no need for partnerships or corporations. Here are the disadvantages: only one manager, limits on capital, and unlimited personal liability.

The sole proprietorship is not recognized as a separate tax entity. It is neither a tax-paying entity like the corporation nor a tax-reporting entity like the partnership. No tax return is filed by a sole proprietorship. Instead, the profit or loss from the business is reported on Schedule C (Schedule F in the case of a farm) and filed with the owner's Form 1040. The business income or loss is treated as the owner's personal income or loss and, of course, is taxed at the rates that apply to individual taxpayers.

When a proprietor dies, business assets become part of the deceased owner's estate, and business debts become debts of the estate. So, the personal representative of the estate may be forced to sell the business assets in short order to pay estate debts. Thus, the business inventory and equipment may have to be sold piecemeal and/or at sacrifice prices.

A corporation is a legal entity having an existence that is separate and distinct from its owners. The corporation, unlike a sole proprietorship or a partnership, is considered by law to be a separate legal "person." As a result of this separate existence, the corporation, not the shareholders, owns the corporate assets.

Insider Notes: Wanting to reward key employees for growing the business with equity without giving-up ownership, control or cash flow, A Phantom Stock Option plan provides selected employees a form of deferred compensation by awarding "units of participation." Each unit is equivalent to a share of stock, so if the stock appreciates in value so does the units. Upon maturity, the key employee receives appreciation which occurred during their tenure. Employees have no rights in the units and can be used with S-Corporation without creating a second class of stock. Consult with your legal counsel.

The corporation can sue and be sued in its name. The business debts are those of the corporation and not those of the shareholders (unless, as often happens in closely held corporations, the corporate debts are personally guaranteed by the shareholders). The corporation pays taxes on business income, and the corporation's existence is not automatically terminated by the withdrawal of a shareholder from the business.

Corporations may be generally divided into two types: publicly held and closely held. A publicly-held corporation, also called a public or open corporation, is generally characterized by a large number of shareholders, most of whom do not take an active part in the management of the corporation. Further, the corporation's stock is generally traded either on a stock exchange or an over-the-counter market.

In contrast, a closely-held corporation is one in which the shares are usually owned by only a few individuals who usually take an active role in managing the business as directors and/or officers of the company. Stock in a close corporation is rarely traded on the open market.

While it is relatively uncomplicated to launch a sole proprietorship or partnership, a corporation is a creature of law and can be created solely by the authority of government. A corporation cannot legally exist without receiving permission from the state government.

In a sole proprietorship or general partnership, an ownership interest in the business usually automatically entitles a person to share in the management functions. In a corporation, however, the owners and managers are, in theory, separate persons. So an owner of a corporation, unlike the general partner in a general partnership, is not automatically entitled to a direct voice in management.

For a person who wants to make a limited investment in a business, one of the most disturbing characteristics of either a sole proprietorship or a partnership is likely to be the possibility of unlimited liability for business debts. So the partners could lose not only their business investment, but also all or part of their personal property.

The situation is entirely different with a corporation. The corporation is a separate entity. And one of the most important economic characteristics that stems from this separate existence is that debts and liabilities incurred by the corporation are the debts of the corporation, not those of the shareholders.

The shares of the deceased shareholder simply pass to the shareholder's heirs who, in turn, become shareholders. Unless some limit has been set in the Articles of Incorporation, a corporation's life is perpetual until dissolved by law. This continuity is in sharp contrast to the uncertainty about the future of businesses formed as sole proprietorships and partnerships.

Regular or "C" corporations pay tax on their corporate income as a separate taxpaying entity. But the owners of a corporation can elect to be taxed under Subchapter S of the Internal Revenue Code. An S-Corporation is one whose owners have elected not to pay any corporate tax on its income. Instead, the shareholders elect to pay taxes on their respective shares of corporate income at their individual income tax rates, even when income is not distributed to them.

An S-Corporation is similar to a partnership in that both are tax conduits. The character of items of income, deductions, losses and credits passes through to the shareholders. Although an S-Corporation does not usually pay a tax, it must file an annual return on Form 1120S.

Fringe Benefits for Shareholder/Employees: S shareholder/employees who own 2% or less of the corporate stock are generally treated the same as other employees for fringe-benefit purposes. When an S shareholder owns more than 2% however, restrictions do apply.

Insider Notes: "The Kiddie Tax" is the nickname of the tax on the unearned income of children under the age of 14. Generally, such income is taxed at the parent's marginal tax bracket, not the child's, once a small exempted amount has been exceeded. If your children are 14 or older, consider paying them through the business for their work. Consult with your tax advisor and beware of the side effects on your kid's financial aid.

GOOGLE'S LUCRATIVE IPO NOTWITHSTANDING, MOST OWNERS DO NOT REALIZE WHAT LITTLE VALUE THEIR BUSINESSES HAVE IN THE OPEN MARKET UNTIL IT'S TIME TO SELL. MANY FOCUS ON BUILDING AND GROWING THE BUSINESS WITHOUT ANY CONCRETE PLANS TO HARNESS THE WEALTH THROUGH AN EXIT PLAN.

Professional Corporations: Beginning in the 1960s, a number of states passed laws enabling statutes that permitted professionals — physicians, lawyers, dentists, accountants, etc. — to incorporate their practices. The shareholders in these "professional corporations" must be licensed in the field in which the corporation will practice. Historically, licensed professionals had operated as either sole proprietorships or as partnerships. For a time, the primary incentive to incorporate were the more generous benefits available under corporate retirement plans. But in 1982, Keogh retirement plans for the self-employed were brought to "parity" with corporate plans (with a few lingering exceptions), so the original, primary incentive for incorporation has largely disappeared.

Nevertheless, incorporation offers a number of residual advantages. First, there are the familiar non-tax benefits of doing business as a corporation: centralized management, continuity of life (i.e., the death of an owner does not dissolve the business, as in a partnership), and ease of transferring interests. Moreover, the incorporated professional may gain a measure of limited liability. While the professional remains liable for his or her own negligent acts (e.g., malpractice), in most states he or she is not liable for the negligent acts of a co-shareholder. This contrasts favorably with a partnership, in which each partner is jointly and severally liable for the negligent acts of the others.

In some years, you may find a pass-through corporation as the S-Corporation provides the best planning platform while, in later years, a different entity form may prove to be more advantageous. Your business structure is fluid. Do not feel that you cannot change. Many businesses have outsized their existing business structure, which no longer meets their current needs. Since the choice of a business structure is an important decision, you should seek legal, financial and tax counsel.

Again, let us turn to David's situation for insights. David's spouse, Susan, runs and owns a one-person consulting firm providing turnkey software services to occupational therapists. Last year, she netted $85,000 as a sole proprietor. After she complained to her accountant about her taxes, he advised her to purchase her next car through the business since a portion of the car used for the business may be written off for tax purposes. Of course, in her mind, a more expensive car generates more deductions, so she bought a Lexis.

This decision was not necessarily in line with her and David's goals to achieve financial independence when David turns 55.

If David and her personal goals drove the decision, she could have incor-porated into an S-Corp, saving approximately $5,300 in FICA taxes by paying herself a fair and reasonable salary of $40,000 and drawing $45,000 from distributions. She could also setup a solo 401(k) Profit Sharing Plan, and invest $13,000 through salary deferral and $10,000 into the profit sharing plan, deferring (saving) $7,705 in state (8.5% bracket) and federal taxes (25% bracket) that year. Overall, she stood to save close

Insider Notes: Do you or your spouse have a defined pension plan? Purchase a sufficient amount of life insurance on yourself prior to retirement, naming your spouse as beneficiary. The death benefit is earmarked to help replace the lost pension if you die first. To get the best insurance rates, the younger and healthier you are when you make this decision, the better. But it may still work, in some cases, even if the policy is purchased shortly before retirement. The idea is to use a portion of your full benefit to help pay the insurance premium. At retirement, you and your spouse opt to take the single-life benefit option, receiving your maximum pension benefit for as long as you live.

to $13,000 in taxes per year with these two changes. If she continues funding the solo 401(k) for eight-years or until retirement, assuming a 7% rate of return, David and her could have accumulated more than an additional quarter million dollars, before taxes, toward their financial independence, which more than pays for that second home they wanted in Florida, but did not believe they could afford.

Taking it one-step further, if Susan plowed the tax savings of $13,000 and the financing savings for three-years into her savings account, she could purchase that Lexis with cash for $40,000 and save more than $6,000 in financing costs for a 5-year note at 6%. You see? Once we identified that financial independence was the number one goal, the course of action was straightforward!

BUSINESS LIFE CYCLES

I explained to David that businesses have life cycles and each stage holds unique challenges, concerns and strategies. The issues, needs and your decisions are largely dependent on your current business cycle. Is the business a start-up and in the survival mode or has it moved on to the emerging growth and expansion phase? The following diagrams list some of the issues each phase can bring to a business and action steps that can be taken.

Your current business life cycles will likely dictate your course of action. For example, Randolph's youngest brother, Scott and his wife Brianna, met after a second marriage. Brianna started a graphic design firm in 1988, specializing in working for large paper manufactures in Maine. During 2000 and 2001, her business was off and many of her clients were going out-of-business, merging together and struggling to stay afloat. In response, she started taking on other clients in other industries. With no industry experience in these new areas, her profit margins continued to drop. She was underbidding the jobs due to a lack of industry expertise and out of fear of not making payroll.

Insider Notes: Selling your Corporation? Consider selling your business assets and keeping your corporation open for the fiscal year without employees and set-up a qualified retirement benefit plan. Consult with an actuary and a pension consultant.

BUSINESS LIFE CYCLES

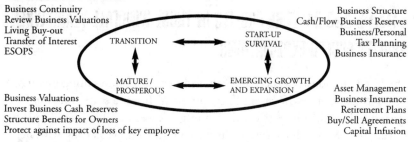

Business Continuity
Review Business Valuations
Living Buy-out
Transfer of Interest
ESOPS

Business Structure
Cash/Flow Business Reserves
Business/Personal
Tax Planning
Business Insurance

TRANSITION ⟷ START-UP SURVIVAL

MATURE / PROSPEROUS ⟷ EMERGING GROWTH AND EXPANSION

Business Valuations
Invest Business Cash Reserves
Structure Benefits for Owners
Protect against impact of loss of key employee

Asset Management
Business Insurance
Retirement Plans
Buy/Sell Agreements
Capital Infusion

STAGES AND BUSINESS CONCERNS

START-UP AND SURVIVAL

- WRITE A GAME PLAN
- DETERMINE BUSINESS LEGAL & TAX STRUCTURE
- MANAGE & TRACK CASH FLOW
- DEVELOP CASH RESERVES STRATEGIES
- DEVELOP A TAX MANAGE-MENT STRATEGY

MATURE AND PROSPEROUS

- ENHANCE & MANAGE EMPLOYEE BENEFITS
- SET-UP NONQUALIFIED PLANS FOR KEY EMPLOYEES
- DEVELOP A BUSINESS PRO-TECTION STRATEGY
- UPDATE BUSINESS VALUATION
- REVIEW LEGAL & TAX STRUCTURE

EMERGING GROWTH AND EXPANSION

- BUILD THROUGH CAPITAL REINVESTMENT OR OUT-SIDE FINANCING
- ATTRACT & RETAIN GOOD EMPLOYEES — THE 5RS
- PROVIDE MANDATORY INSURANCE & BENEFITS
- REVIEW ELECTIVE BENEFITS & SET UP RETIREMENT PLANS

TRANSITIONAL

- ENSURE SUCCESSION OR CON-TINUITY WITH BUY/SELL OR STOCK REDEMPTION
- CONSIDER BUSINESS SALE, MERGER OR AN ACQUISITION
- IMPLEMENT STOCK INCENTIVE PROGRAMS FOR OWNER & EMPLOYEES
- IMPLEMENT AN ESTATE PLAN

TAX PLANNING ALLOWS YOU TO BETTER CONTROL COSTS AND CAPTURE PROFITS IN THOSE WINDFALL YEARS WHEN PROFITS EXCEED EXPECTATIONS.

She hired an industry expert and retooled her business, resulting in a new business name, a new focus and new products. It was a scary time for Brianna, since the business continued to go deeper into her line-of-credit during the 18-month transition. In the end, though, by starting with her personal goals to have more fun with her family, Brianna's company went through a complete transition, from being a mature business to a start-up with a more profitable client base, more energy and a happier owner.

Once you have developed your vision and goals and have identified your business structure and its lifecycle, you should begin to develop your team and a strategic approach. Often, we have good intentions to plan but falter due to other demands. While others seek help too late, the business is in a decline, the owners' energy and ambition are waning, the business is in a crisis, and planning takes on a sense of urgency — a predicament similar to David's when he first walked in my door.

A team approach can dramatically increase the likelihood of success by allowing you to anticipate problems. Going it alone is often a reckless endeavor, since most business owners need advice concerning insurance, investments, taxes and legal issues. It is easy to miss opportunities by not having all the facts available to make educated decisions at the right time, as we saw with Susan and her shiny new Lexus.

THE TEAM LEADER

Entrepreneurs are a proud bunch and many resist advice from outsiders. Surprisingly, many entrepreneurs lack basic knowledge about investments, accounting, legal issues, operations management, human resources, trust management, estate planning, etc.

The difficult part is determining which strategies to deploy. Taxes, insurance, estate, and legal issues have become complicated and most business owners do not have the time to research them. This is where assembling a good team comes in. Either the owner needs to act as the quarterback, or hire a financial advisor to take on that role. I recommend the owner hire a team leader. Owners can easily lose focus and put these responsibilities on the back burner. In addition, many owners do not have the objectivity or temperament for this detailed type of work.

Once the team leader has been secured, other members of the team need to be identified and brought in. A typical team involves the accountant, personal/business financial planner, owner, owner's spouse, business lawyer, estate lawyer, and banker. Other team members could include the auditor, controller, key management, and trust officers.

The team leader draws advice and guidance from other members, based on the owner's personal goals. In regards to any advice, always ask yourself: Am I closer to my goals if I do this today? I suggest that you would rather be a wealthy investor than a perfect investor. By not using a team approach, many owners get sidelined in the technical analysis, which leads to "analysis paralysis" or inaction. Moreover, if you are about to embark on anything expensive or painful, get a second opinion!

Your team should initially focus on developing systems to track your personal goals. Establishing a timetable, a written action plan and a system to hold each team member accountable increases the ability for the owner to execute action steps. Many owners wait too long before seeking help when roadblocks are encountered, which forfeits many planning opportunities. Often, the result is that drastic actions are needed, instead of small, corrective steps.

The systems need teeth to hold each team member accountable. If a team member is not performing to expectations, the team leader needs to have the authority and your support to replace that member. Many owners have stumbled by using family members or friends for advice. It is very difficult to fire your brother-in-law or a longtime, family friend. Your team should be impartial, competent, professional, knowledgeable, and hopefully wise. Act cautiously when considering friends and family members for your team of advisors.

WHERE THERE'S A WILL...THERE'S AN ESTATE

Small businesses present special estate planning dilemmas for entrepreneurs. Many small business owners are shocked by the elements that Uncle Sam counts when determining their taxable estate. When tallying up the value of your estate, don't forget the following:

- full value of the property of which you are the sole owner;
- half the value of the property you own jointly with your spouse with right of survivorship;
- your share of property owned with others;
- half the value of community property if you live in a community property state;
- the value of proceeds of any insurance policy on your life, you own or have an interest in the policy;
- money owed to you, such as mortgages and rents;
- your interest in vested pension and profit-sharing plans;
- the value of revocable trust property;
- the value of gifts made within three-years of your death if you retained power to alter, amend, revoke or terminate the gift; and
- the value of gift tax paid on transfer within three-years of your death.

Many successful owners have addressed the need for a feedback system by developing the team approach. Each member of the team holds other members accountable and the team holds the owner to their vision. Members of the team are the best of the best: your partner, best accountant, or best lawyer. Armed with your vision statement, your advisors and loved ones can be a guiding light through dark times and help you stay focused.

HOW TO BE A GOLDEN GOOSE, NOT A COOKED ONE

Comprehensive planning involves at least six key areas: net worth, protection planning, accumulation planning, tax planning, retirement planning, and estate planning. Many plans are actually issue plans. Issue plans limit their scope of analysis to a particular question with little or no regards for other planning aspects.

In many cases, issue planning leaves gaping holes in your planning and can actually be counterproductive. The power that comes from planning is getting all aspects of your life working together for a single purpose. There are no short cuts. Issue planning can actually create competing strategies for your resources, limiting your progress towards your goals.

Let us get back to our saga of David and his family. Joyce, David's youngest sister, met Eric in college. After falling madly in love, they married and had four kids by age 30. Eric was an entrepreneur by nature and had a bit of a green thumb. He started a home plant business in New Hampshire, and over time, Eric built a very profitable business through personal connections and had hired three assistants to help him care for the plants. Eric was branching out into the flower delivery service and had just leased three more vans when he was severely hurt riding his bike with his youngest daughter.

In a matter of six months, Eric and Joyce had depleted their savings, were delinquent on their home mortgage payment, $20,000 in credit card debt, and were quickly draining their retirement and college funds. The business was virtually dead, since not enough income was coming in to support the lease payments, let alone Eric and Joyce's lifestyle and the business' payroll.

Eric had handled everything, from securing new accounts, to the payables and the billing. Joyce tried to keep the business afloat, but with four kids in school and taking care of Eric full-time, it was a doomed enterprise. In the end, they were forced into closing the business and filing for personal bankruptcy. Joyce is now working evenings as a nurses' aid at a local hospital and relies on Randolph's help to stay afloat.

Eric and Joyce had homeowner's insurance, car insurance, liability insurance, health insurance, dental insurance, and business insurance but did not protect their most valuable asset, Eric's ability to work. If Eric and Joyce had completed a comprehensive plan, instead of just setting-up retirement and education funds, they would have addressed this financial void. Nobody really believes they will end-up disabled and many only fully insure the golden eggs (i.e., the cars and homes) but not the golden goose, which is you. With a little planning and foresight, Eric could have entered into a cross purchase agreement with a key employee, Paul the florist. A cross-purchase agreement is a type of buy/sell agreement designed to allow the business to go on without you in the event of your death or disability, while safeguarding your family's financial future. Paul would take over the management of the flower delivery business at Eric's disability or death. Simple, yet effective.

The cross-purchase agreement would take effect upon the death or the disability of Eric. To cover any potential outstanding short-term financial obligation, he could purchase a business overhead disability policy, as for long-term disability concerns, Eric could purchase a disability buyout policy.

REACTIVE AND PROACTIVE TAX PLANNING

In determining a course of action, taxes should always be considered. However, tax planning is a means to an end. There are two types of tax planning, reactive and proactive. Either way, tax preparers generally have little, if any, incentive to provide tax advice, especially when you consider the current enforcement structure of fees and penalties.

Tax preparers are keenly aware that their reputations are at stake and do not want to draw attention to themselves from local IRS agents. The tax preparer typically has to defend their work during an audit, which is expensive and time consuming. So why take the risks? They sometimes avoid the trap, by not providing the advice to begin with. Tax law is neither black nor white; some provisions require interpretation. A good tax advisor should give you the facts and render an opinion, but you should make the decision. The tax advisors role is to interpret the IRS rules and help you make tax decisions.

Unfortunately, the way our tax system is structured, most accountants are trying to survive the tax season and do not have the time to discuss non-pressing issues, (i.e., like next year's planning opportunities) let alone do projections and what-if scenarios. Taxes are one aspect of a much larger plan. Yet, many business owners rely solely on the advice of their accountant or CPA for advice on hosts of issues that would typically be better served with a team approach. Any significant recommendation needs to be balanced against other planning objectives and the side effects of the advice.

Tax planning involves analyzing several competing strategies in unison. Owners can get in a rut, and view transactions in a one or two-dimensional frame of mind, locking them into a zero-sum situation. By integrating your personal taxes into the business, tax planning can reduce your overall tax burden, allowing you to potentially fund personal goals. A lower tax burden also creates a business with a greater value. Tax planning allows you to better control costs and capture profits in those windfall years when profits exceed expectations and adjusts to the businesses' profitability, since many businesses go through cycles with great years and potentially large tax bills, and down years with potential losses.

Many owners do not use a team approach and rely heavily on the experience of one advisor to provide advice on investments, business structure, employee benefit programs, health insurance, and tax planning. Business and personal planning are complex areas and require expertise from tax professionals, the legal community, and the insurance and investment community. Taxes are an important factor in many decision-making processes but should not be the sole driving factor.

Too often, fortunes are lost because taxes were the deciding factor. For example, Gray, Randolph's youngest brother, established a Subaru automotive parts store in Maine. At his retirement, he found a large publicly traded company to purchase his business. He had an option of taking cash, a taxable transition that year, or merging his company into the public company, which would be taxed when he sold the public stock, the difference being Gray could defer the taxes with the stock transaction.

He spent countless hours working with his accountant projecting out the different tax options, but no time researching the stock. He took the stock deal without protecting his downside risk. On the day of the transaction, the stock dropped by one-third because of an accounting scandal and declined further over the next year. He went from achieving financial independence to needing income to supplement his retirement. It's not unlike many retirees who chose not to sell highly appreciated stock in the late 90s, to avoid paying capital gains taxes, only to find that their potential gain turned into a potential loss.

CREATE AN EXIT PLAN

Many successful owners do not exit the business in a timely manner because they fear not having the ability to maintain their financial independence. They stay on well beyond what is healthy for the business, themselves and the next generation.

Randolph is a perfect example; by not having a valid exit strategy, Randolph has placed his livelihood and the business at risk. Many advisors focus on accumulation without planning for the exit. In achieving and maintaining financial independence, an exit strategy is often more important than accumulation, since you only have one shot. Whatever the desired outcome, planning is essential to help ensure an orderly change of ownership when you retire, become disabled or die.

Start with an exit plan first and work backward into the gameplan. Sometimes it's better to grow small than big. If your industry or business does not provide a platform to build equity within the business, focus on developing strategies that allow you to build value outside the business, like a 401(k) or a profit sharing plan.

Your personal plan should determine the exit strategy and your timeframe. Let your goals drive the decision of when, and how, to exit the business. Developing a toggle switch that identifies when you have reached financial independence will help prevent you from staying too long. For example, in David's case, it was determined that they would need an additional $1.4 million, in today's dollars, to achieve financial independence.

Here are important questions to consider when setting-up a transition plan for your business:

- What are the potential tax obligations connected to the death of the owner?
- Has a successor/buyer been identified? Are they trained and ready to step-in?
- Will cash be available to purchase all the outstanding shares from all the heirs?
- Is management a sole individual or has responsibility been transferred?

■ Is there a plan to provide for the heir when the business is liquidated?

Planning for the business transition can help you select and evaluate the most appropriate strategies for the transition. You can run what-if scenarios to see the full extent the transition has on you, your heirs and key employees. Your current and future business cycle will likely dictate your approach and the type of transition available.

YOU DO NOT NEED TO BE CHARITABLE TO BE CHARITABLE

For example, David friend's Derek sold his highly depreciated "mature business" for $3.1 million in an asset sale, netting $2.2 million after federal and state taxes, at an effective tax rate of 29%. Derek was tired of running the business and over a dinner party got introduced to a buyer, and looked at the deal as a godsend. The price he got for the business was more than fair. However, Derek never articulated that his goal for selling was for him and wife was to maintain their luxury lifestyle.

The accountant did an excellent job of projecting the taxes due from the sale and the attorney did a superior job on the purchase and sales agreement, anticipating the needs of both the buyer and seller. Unfortunately, neither advisor ever asked Derek what he needed to maintain his lifestyle and achieve financial independence.

In the end, the net dollars leftover, after taxes, did not allow Derek to achieve financial independence. For example, Derek could have set-up a Charitable Remainder Unitrust Trust (CRUT) that would pay an annual income for rest of his life, and at his death, the remaining balance would go to the charity of choice. He could gift his shares of business to the CRUT, receiving a charitable deduction of approximately $450,000, (subject to charitable gift limitations) and then the CRUT would sell the shares to the new owner with no taxes due at the time of sale.

(In compliance with the American Job Creation Act of 2004, Derek would need to obtain a qualified appraisal of the business and attach the details of the appraisal to his tax return for the year the deduction is taken.)

Derek and his family could be receiving income from $3.1 million in assets compared to the $2.2 million. The difference in income is $81,000 per year. It is also the difference between achieving financial independence and seeking a second career to augment his retirement income.

Furthermore, if done correctly, Derek could set-up an irrevocable life insurance trust and the trust could purchase a $3 million dollar life insurance policy, so at his death, his family would receive the $3 million, tax-free and not subject to estate or income taxes. Derek could fund the policy from the CRUT.

Many successful business owners fail to achieve financial independence and their retirement dreams, due to lack of preparation. Your business relationships, established over many years, go well beyond just business and provide a social network. Your standing as a business owner provides links to friends, associates and the greater community, and for many, these relationships are intertwined with social activities like community involvement, hobbies and volunteerism.

Replacing these relationships with new activities and interests takes time and effort. By developing these interests early on in the process, you will begin to look forward to letting go instead of dreading it.

For example, if you desire to sail around the world at retirement, take a few sailing classes now and develop relationships with individuals who share your interests. Alternatively, if you plan to write that great American novel, take a few writing classes now and start to foster relationships within your writing community. By looking forward, it is easier to not look back.

Once you have identified your goals, you need to determine your strengths and weaknesses compared to your goals. This step will help to clarify a course of action. Typically, you will need to develop a net worth statement, income and expense statements and a budget. With these figures, you can start the process of analyzing your goals against your means.

As stated earlier, a typical baseline analysis addresses education, retirement and accumulation goals, along with estate, and tax planning. It is also important to integrate your protection goals into the other goals. Ask your significant other(s) what they would like to see happen at your death or disability; the answers may surprise you. For example, if you are hurt and cannot work, how does that affect your children's education and/or your retirement goals?

WHAT-IF SCENARIOS

Once you have completed the baseline analysis that identifies your strengths and weaknesses, you can start the process of running what-if scenarios.

For example, a local shoe store was losing money. At first, the owner believed it was just cyclical, but his team identified a long-term, developing trend. The owner was taking too much cash out for personal uses, sales were down, and their inventory was up. It all added up to the business losing money, but the losses were not showing up in the checking account yet. Based on a thorough analysis by his team of advisors, they identified the losses to the store's lack of upscale appeal, a new competitor in the neighborhood and the owner's increased personal needs.

For the business to remain healthy, the owner needed to invest into the business by strengthening financial controls, establishing compensation guidelines and expanding floor space. With a plan in place, instead of taking cash out to fund personal goals, the owner tightened his belt and invested heavily into doubling the sales floor, purchasing two new European designs, increased training for the sales staff, and hiring a sales manager. The million-dollar expansion was done solely through debt.

The problem was identified quickly, which allowed the owners to make structural changes and track the changes before a crisis developed. The advising team had timely information in diagnosing the problem early, providing the owner time to meet this new challenge with a confident,

Insider Notes: Update your game plan at least annually since tax law, your business, and investment opportunities change with time. Small changes now can make a big difference later in moving you to financial independence. Pick a time in the business cycle that is historically slow so you have the time and energy to focus.

head-on plan. Because the banker was involved in the analysis, securing the debt was less troublesome.

All too often, owners fail or lose opportunities because adverse or positive scenarios were not fully analyzed and the underlying assumptions were not tested. If roadblocks are encountered, it is easier to overcome them if guidelines are developed in anticipation and corresponding strategies have already been identified. It is not practical or feasible to plan for every potential scenario. Nonetheless, some occur with predictability, like a key player leaving for a competitor, the death or disability of the owner or a key employee, and of course, a cash flow crunch.

On that day when David walked into my office, he resisted discussing his personal goals and bringing Susan into the process. David believed that Susan did not grasp the business and would confuse the issues with personal concerns. To keep David's interest in the planning process, we discussed strategies that he could use to improve the business' cash flow. After the first meeting, it became evident to David that these strategies were relevant to his personal situation, so we brought Susan into the progress, and eventually Randolph, and his accountant and his attorney. That was three years ago. Now, after seeing the benefits of starting with personal goals first, our meetings usually start with, "How are we doing in achieving financial independence?"

During those first meetings with Randolph and his accountant, it was obvious that Randolph felt trapped too. He wanted to give the business to David, as his father did for him, but was afraid to give up control and the income. By all accounts, at age 82, Randolph had achieved financial independence, but how much was enough? Randolph, however, viewed financial independence as the business. He offered to sell the business to David, but the purchase price turned out to be inflated for a business that was losing money. If David purchased the businesses at that price, he would end up tied to a bank note for the next 20 years.

Over the three-year period that I have worked with David and Susan, we have accomplished the following:
- ■ Changed the way Susan now pays herself through her business, by putting her on a salary;

- Worked with her tax and legal advisor to change her business structure from a Sole Proprietor to an S-Corp;
- Set up a Solo 401(k) through her business;
- Set-up a retirement plan that benefited David's business and that also rewarded employees for staying and removing promised benefits to those employees that left;
- Put David and Susan's kids on the payroll through David's business

Moreover, David and Susan refinanced their home at a lower interest rate and a shorter duration. With each change, we set-up a system to capture the savings. Their current savings exceed 30% of gross income, compared to 3% when we first met, and yet, their lifestyle has improved.

The exciting news is that at age 53, David and Susan have achieved financial independence, two years earlier than planned. When you step back from the business, you can begin to view it as a tool to help you accomplish what is truly important: your personal goals. Just ask David.

■ ■ ■

Luke R. Reinhard, a Senior Financial Advisor and a Business Financial Advisor is the registered principal of Reinhard & Associates Inc., a financial advisory practice of American Express Financial Advisor Inc. and has provided financial advise to business owners for more than 10 years. He was previously an Investment Manager for a privately-held, international investment firm in New York, New York. He holds the following designations: a Chartered Financial Consultant, Certified Financial Planner™, a Registered Employee Benefits Consultant and Registered Health Underwriter, a B.S.C.E in Engineering from Purdue University and a Masters in Finance from the University of Chicago. He can be reached at (207-771-5300; luke.r.reinhard@aexp.com).

American Express Financial Advisors Inc.and IDS Life Insurance Company. Members NASD. Insurance and annuity products are issued by IDS Life Insurance Company, an American Express company, Minneapolis, MN. American Express Company is separate from American Express Financial Advisors and is not a broker-dealer.

[10]
MACRO STRATEGIC
PLANNING®: YOUR ROADMAP
TO PERSONAL FULFILLMENT

You need more than an investment plan — you need a philosophy and proven formula for a happy, successful and fulfilling life. Learn how to use your time, talents and resources to become self-reliant, with a "Big Picture" perspective. By the end of this chapter, you'll be better equipped to create a personalized roadmap to fulfillment.

"KNOW THYSELF."

- Socrates

by PAUL CAPUZZIELLO

In the next few pages, I will introduce you to Macro Strategic Planning®, an overarching set of principles that can help you develop and follow your "compass" to achieve the best life that you can imagine. This concept is built on universal truths that will lead you down the path of self discovery, and help you see new possibilities and achieve what matters most to you.

It will help you transcend the micro issues, such as self-serving advisors, temporary market movements, and distracting personal hassles, so you can reach your qualitatively highest goals.

Put simply, Macro Strategic Planning® is a tool for self-empowerment. It helps you actually live your Ideal Life and Perfect Calendar™.

> **The Perfect Calendar™:** "Spending your time, talent and resources doing what matters most to you (your most fulfilling life)."
> — **Bruce Wright**

In his book, *The Seven Habits of Highly Effective People,* Dr. Stephen Covey writes that we often spend our lives and careers climbing the ladder of success, then, near the top, look around only to discover that our ladder was against the wrong wall or not the best wall. My goal for this chapter is to introduce you to a revolutionary new way to make sure that your ladder is always on the best wall or the right wall for you. This process, called Macro Strategic Planning®, was created by my good friend and mentor, Bruce Wright. He defines Macro Strategic Planning® as follows:

"Macro Strategic Planning® is a revolutionary process for defining and writing down your greatest vision for your life and the necessary action steps, personnel, timeline and capitalization plan to turn that greatest vision into reality. The focus of that vision can be something as simple as losing weight and increasing physical fitness to something as complex as starting a new company, deploying a new division of your company or developing and marketing new product lines for your customers.

Macro Strategic Planning®, in its most comprehensive form, can show you how to achieve your greatest vision for your personal life and how to utilize all of your time, talent and resources on purpose, by design. It helps you live a more passionate life. It helps you articulate then achieve the quality of life you want for yourself and your family members for generations to come." — Bruce Wright

The model for Macro Strategic Planning® focuses on the above-the-line issues — your vision, commitment and goals — as well as providing the catalyst for the below-the-line issues — the strategies, tactics and tools.

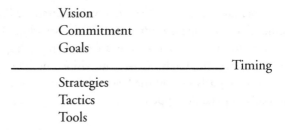

Vision
Commitment
Goals

_____ Timing

Strategies
Tactics
Tools

Macro Strategic Planning® is unique in that it is truly client centered rather than being built around some type of sales process. It has nothing to do with selling, selling tactics, closing techniques or psychological manipulation. Its simple premise is very different from all other planning processes in the marketplace. When you discover your ultimate vision and see it in writing, you understand what will bring you the greatest joy in your life as you look forward, as well as the things that would cause you the most pain.

The premise of traditional financial services is flawed from the beginning. The prominent existing models require that advisors discover just barely enough about what you think and what your goals are, so they know what to sell you. However, the good news is that the consumer is becoming more discerning and better able to recognize when they are being sold to, rather than truly being helped.

Unfortunately, most people cannot articulate their greatest vision for their life, their business or their relationships with their spouse, children or

Insider Notes: Unfortunately, most people cannot articulate their greatest vision for their life, their business or their relationships with their spouse, children or grandchildren. Macro Strategic Planning® is about thinking and behaving with tangible physical deliverables in ways that are completely beyond the scope of financial and estate planning.

grandchildren. Macro Strategic Planning® is about thinking and behaving with tangible physical deliverables in ways that are completely beyond the scope of financial and estate planning.

The fundamental challenge or flaw that Macro Strategic Planning® fixes is that, rather than focusing on some superficial discussion of goals, it is about getting to the very root or core issues. There is a gap that exists between the above-the-line issues — your vision and your commitment to it and its specific goals — and the below-the-line issues-the strategies, tactics and tools to make it happen.

In fact, this is no small gap; it is a great chasm, and it exists because the culture of the financial industry is about money and selling, and not about helping the client connect the above-the-line dots with the below-the-line dots. Macro Strategic Planning® helps you build a bridge over that chasm to lead you to the outcomes that you desire most. Here's a common example:

> A couple sits down with an attorney to discuss one of their greatest concerns: They do not want their wealth to destroy their grandchildren or great-grandchildren (make them lazy or rob them of a sense of self-determination). What they get from the lawyer is a series of documents that shows them how to hold title to their assets-the focus is on below-the-line strategy.

> There is nothing in the documents that reinforces or advocates the teaching of principle-centered living. The attorney appears to hear the couple's concern, but the outcome does not address their problem at its core. This is partly the attorney's fault and partly the client's. Why? Because the couple did not know how to articulate their greatest vision, and the advisor didn't know the correct questions to ask and/or accepted inadequate answers to the questions he did ask.

As the consumer, you must have a clear vision of what you want to achieve and take an active roll in making sure that you achieve your vision, your 100-year plan and your Perfect Calendar™.

The 100-Year Plan: "Because almost everything is in a constant state of change, a 100-year or layer perspective is essential to our ongoing effectiveness and balanced state of mind. Those who choose not to develop a long-term vision and action plan are destined to suffer less peace of mind, less effectiveness and less fulfillment. Acknowledging that some things must change, while some will not, is a critical point of discernment and necessary to increasing your wisdom. Those who can articulate the constant from the transient possess a decided advantage in life, family and business matters." — **Bruce Wright**

Bruce Wright, creator of Macro Strategic Planning®, helps people understand the concept with the following story, an ancient tale from India.

THE PRINCE AND THE BLIND GURUS
Once upon a time, a wise Rajah (Indian Prince) conducted an experiment in human nature. He put on a contest to see who was the wisest guru in all the land. Many gurus came to the palace to participate. To be recognized by the prince as the wisest guru would mean great success. The wisest guru would be considered superior to all the lesser gurus and could charge much more money for giving advice.

Quite unexpectedly, after many tests of wisdom, all of the six finalists turned out to be blind. For the last test, the prince decided to introduce each of the remaining gurus to a newly discovered creature. The gurus were asked to describe the true essence of the creature.

One at a time, the gurus were allowed to experience the creature. Then the prince brought them all together to discuss their findings and decide the outcome of the contest. The first guru described the creature as being like a wall. The second guru defined the creature as being like a spear. The

Insider Notes: There are people for whom money is the end goal, who measure success by the size of their net worth. I suggest that it is not how much money you have, but what you achieve with your life that counts. After all, money is a tool, no more and no less.

third guru boldly stated that they were both incorrect because he was certain that this creature was a large, powerful snake.

The fourth guru adamantly argued that they were all wrong, as she knew what she knew: the creature was like a fan. "You're all crazy!" stated the fifth guru. "Anyone can tell that the creature isn't even a creature at all. In fact the 'creature' is actually a tree with a unique type of bark."

Finally, the sixth guru made his claim to being the wisest of all. Dismissing the rest as fools, he stated: "After all, anyone should be able to tell that the creature is like a strong and lively rope!"

A very bitter argument broke out, because each was certain they were correct. They were all quite confident in their conclusions. Each of them knew what they knew. After much name-calling and bitter debate, the Rajah stepped in and ended the contest. This is what he said:

> All of you are correct, yet all of you are profoundly mistaken. Your egos have gotten the best of you. Had you opened your minds, put your egos aside and worked together, you would have been able to understand the true essence of the creature. Each of you described only the one piece of the creature you personally experienced. Had you applied the principle of interdependence, you would have learned that the creature is an elephant, and like all creatures, the elephant is greater than the sum of its parts.

The story demonstrates how people — and who they really are — happen to be greater than the sum of their parts. In this chapter, I use the word "elephant" to mean a person who sees the big picture and approaches life and wealth management in a holistic manner. The fact is, we have the ability to be majestic beings, like the elephant, but most of us don't see ourselves that way. We surround ourselves with lawyers, accountants, financial planners, consultants, and business gurus — all of whom deal with one small piece of the elephant. They do not communicate with one another or with us in writing as to what we really are in totality.

Real power and beauty derive from thinking of your perfect vision in macro terms, and writing it down. The tangible nature of the written document eliminates the ability to hide behind lack of clarity. Without a written plan, it's all too tempting for you and your advisors to avoid accountability for the achievement of your vision.

Whether you delegate the achievement of your vision to division managers, vice presidents, lawyers, accounts advisors or consultants, if they don't all have a physical document — an action plan and timeline — in writing, they are likely to come up with a series of excuses. When every member of your advisory team has the written plan, including action items and timeline, you are less likely to hear excuses such as, "I didn't know exactly what to do," "I didn't realize that was my responsibility," or "I thought someone else was supposed to do that."

There are people for whom money is the end goal, who measure success by the size of their net worth. I suggest that it is not how much money you have, but what you achieve with your life that counts. After all, money is a tool, no more and no less than that. Lack of clarity about how you want to live your life and apply the use of your money to reach your objectives can be dangerous. Many people who have a lot of money are not happy. People can spend a lifetime pursuing the glittering prizes, only to discover too late that these prizes come with a built-in tarnish. Materialism for its own sake is a blueprint for unhappiness.

Focus on quality of life, not money. What good is having a lot of money, if it doesn't give you the freedom to do the things you want to do? If you're spending all of your time making money without building in time to live your Ideal Life, then aren't your efforts in vain?

Bruce tells another story that illustrates how important it is for you to know what is really important:

Insider Notes: People often fail to implement good ideas because they lack clarity above the line and/or commitment to see their goals through. Once you have gained this clarity and commitment by creating your Macro Strategic Plan, you will not need anyone to sell you anything.

A father and son asked their accountant and financial advisor to help them devise a plan, so that they could buy out the dad's two sisters from the family farm in the most tax effective way. The accountant and advisor came up with a brilliant plan, making sure to cross all of the t's and dot all of the i's.

Then, at the last minute, Bruce was brought in for a second opinion. In reviewing the plan, Bruce saw that they were planning to pledge their entire combined net worth of about $10 million and borrow an additional $20 million, to buy out the two sisters at $10 million each. He asked them targeted questions designed to get them to thinking about quality of life issues, such as how would they spend their time if they could wave a magic wand and live as they please. Bruce helped them discover that their Ideal Life and Perfect Calendar™ would not involve working seven days per week running a farm.

In fact, each of them already had enough personal net worth to exit their careers as farmers and support their desired lifestyle without having to work for money. Amazingly, they were about to borrow $20 million dollars and go into debt for the next 20-30 years, just so the two sisters could effectively exit from any attachment to the farm, move to Hawaii and live their ideal lives. You'd have to be insane to exchange financial freedom and your Ideal Life and Perfect Calendar™ for a business that requires a 24/7 schedule! This was a classic example of A) a client not knowing what questions to ask, and B) advisors being absolutely ignorant about what questions to ask, and C) a profound lack of big picture vision.

A Macro Strategic Plan is not just a roadmap of where you want to go or who you want to be down the road. It does those things, but it also tells you what kind of personnel you need on your advisory team, and it defines the core competencies you want from them. Don't do business with an advisor just because she's convenient or he was a fraternity brother. Choose your advisors on their ability to dynamically execute and deliver what you need from them.

THE FIVE OBSTACLES TO SUCCESS

Most of the country's most famous tax, financial and estate planning professionals do not address the above-the-line issues in a tangible, measurable way. According to Bruce Wright, there are five key reasons why:

1 They have not learned how to begin with the client's best interest in mind. They do not think in terms of resolving the above-the-line issues before proceeding with below-the-line issues.

2 They have not learned the skill sets to deliver anything truly meaningful, tangible and measurable-above the line.

3 Virtually all but a tiny bit of the training and skill sets learned by most professionals revolves around below-the-line solutions or products.

4 Most professionals are compensated only for below-the-line products or solutions. Most have no business model that compensates them for above-the-line services or deliverables.

5 Many advisors are embarrassed to ask the right questions-even if they know what they are. The very questions that would clarify the client's greatest needs and best interests can be considered intrusive by some people.

When you can answer the question, "What is the highest and best use of my time, talent and resources?" — when you see the answer on paper and say, "Yes! That is exactly what I want!" — you then have to ask yourself, "Am I committed enough to this vision to get all of my advisors to make it a reality?"

As part of your Macro Strategic Plan, your commitment needs to be measured mathematically. Rate your commitment from -5 to 5, with 5 being completely and unwaveringly committed, -5 being completely opposed to any sort of commitment, and 0 being indifferent.

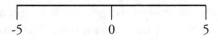

-5   0   5

Once you have a numeric commitment level, then you and your advisors can be held accountable to the achievement of your vision.

People often fail to implement good ideas because they lack clarity above the line and/or commitment to see their goals through. Once you have gained

STARTING OR EXITING A BUSINESS

Starting or exiting your own business is a life event in which a Macro Strategic Plan can greatly influence results. Most start up businesses, especially if they are looking for funding, begin with a business plan that discusses the management team, background, competition, market, marketing strategy, income, expense projections, etc. — all critical information to determine whether or not your business venture will be a viable concern. Common business plans usually fail to address some important issues, such as:

- Why do you want to start the business? What is your or the owner's motivation?
- How big do you want to get or how small do you want to stay? What are the measures?
- At what point do you want to exit the business?
- How will you exit?
- What role will your children play in the business, if any, upon your exit?
- How will the business be owned and by whom?
- Do you desire to take it public?

For most business owners, their business is like a child. The owners are intimately involved from conception to birth, and there are emotional decisions along the way that have to be made. However, the owners may be too close to the business to see and do what's best for it to thrive. Not only does their business plan not address the issues, they haven't seen that document since they gave it to the bank.

So whom do you ask for advice? Your financial advisor? Your CPA? Your corporate attorney? If each of these people is operating independently — not **interdependently**, the answers you get may leave you more confused than if you made the decision on your own. Your advisors will make recommendations based on their individual areas of expertise. When bombarded by conflicting information, some business owners get "paralysis by analysis" and don't make a decision at all, or make one based on flawed logic.

That's why, from the beginning, you should supplement your business plan with a Macro Strategic Plan that includes the following:

- The principles on which the company is being established.
- How, when and why you want to start it.
- Your goals for the company's size.
- Your short-, mid-, and long-term personal financial goals.
- How the business would integrate with your personal Macro Strategic Plan® and Perfect Calendar™.
- The role of family members.
- How you will exit the company and what the terms will be.
- Your goal for company value or selling price that would trigger your exit.
- How you will hold title in the beginning, before the business becomes valuable, so you can manage taxes proactively rather than reactively.

By establishing all of the parameters up front, in writing, and integrating them with your personal and family goals, you have a centering point to help you make these difficult decisions. If you have given your dream team of advisors a copy of your Macro Strategic Plan, and they agree to work interdependently with each other to make your desires happen, then very little is left to chance.

With tough decisions made at the outset, you can, as Michael E. Gerber points out in his book *The E-Myth Revisited,* set out to work on your business and not in it. In other words, your vision and priorities, not the exigencies of your business, should drive the critical decision-making.

About a year ago I met two gentlemen who had a business that was doing quite well. I was asked to help them decide what their next steps should be. I started by asking them when they wanted to get out of the business. Both of them stated that they loved what they did and wanted to keep working as long as possible. One was in his late fifties, and the other was in his mid sixties.

My next question was, "If a buyer came in with a cashier's check for $10 million, what would you do?" They both immediately said, "Here are the keys." It wasn't just that they loved their business or working; they didn't think they had enough value in the business to live their Perfect Calendar™. But for each of them, it seemed that $5 million was enough. How much is enough for you?

this clarity and commitment by creating your Macro Strategic Plan, you will not need anyone to sell you anything. You will be self-motivated to seek out professionals to help you dynamically execute your Macro Strategic Plan and turn your vision into reality. You will have a written document asking and answering the right questions and defining the needed personnel, greatly increasing your chances for optimal results with regard to achieving financial success and living your Ideal Life and Perfect Calendar™.

FORMING YOUR ADVISORY TEAM

The Internet, CNBC, MSNBC, and a host of media outlets spew forth a bewildering amount of financial information. During the last 10 years, this information has encouraged many to make their own decisions, and question the wisdom of the advice they get from their advisors. Corporate scandals, misinformation from investment advisors and a slow economy have created many "do-it-yourselfers."

Who can blame investors for wanting to go it alone? There are a lot of snake oil salesmen out there. I'm reminded of a great one-liner from Woody Allen: "I help people with their investments, until there's nothing left."

To be sure, it's crucial to be skeptical of advisors and to think for yourself. However, you also must find a balance between interdependence and independence. To quote a great poet: No man is an island. A crucial step to achieving your Ideal Life and a Perfect Calendar™ is to recognize your own core competencies and expertise, acknowledge those of your advisors, and then leave your ego at the door and let someone help you.

When choosing advisors, know the limits of your knowledge. No one person can be an expert in all areas in which you need assistance, and there may be options that you don't even know exist. As the client, you are the creator of the team, picking professionals in each position to create your own "Dream Team."

You need to create the vision and the environment in which your team will play. This will help you achieve greater effectiveness. Choose people who possess the appropriate core competencies, understand you, and know where you want to go. They must be people who can work collaboratively and proactively. When you choose the right team, the probability of achieving your vision and optimum effectiveness increases exponentially.

Knowing whom to choose as an advisor can be difficult. Everyone claims to be an expert, or to have a specialty. But even someone who graduates at the bottom of his or her medical school class is called "doctor." If you or a loved one had a very dangerous brain tumor, would you want a minimally-qualified physician operating? Likewise, what is the minimum level of core competency you want your advisors in each area of your life to possess?

You'll also find advisors who say, "I'll give you a discount, or won't charge you, for the above-the-line services in exchange for the below-the-line business." If they are willing to do this, they probably do not highly value their above-the-line skill sets, so why should you? Above-the-line advice can be priceless, while the below-the-line advice and especially products and services are available from just about everywhere, often at discount prices. Short-term prices often come with long-term costs.

RATE YOUR KNOWLEDGE

To help you choose the right advisors, Bruce created an evaluation system called the Rate Your Knowledge Exercise. Take a few moments to rate your knowledge of the following subjects, using the scale below:
0 = You've never heard of the subject.
1 = You have at least heard of the subject.
2 = You have a vague understanding of the subject.

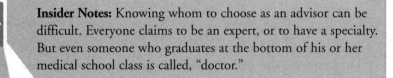

Insider Notes: Knowing whom to choose as an advisor can be difficult. Everyone claims to be an expert, or to have a specialty. But even someone who graduates at the bottom of his or her medical school class is called, "doctor."

3 = You have been involved in some meaningful exploration of the subject.

4 = You can provide a reasonably accurate verbal or written summary of the subject.

5 = You can provide a very accurate verbal or written summary of the subject.

6 = You have firsthand personal and/or professional experience with the subject.

7 = You are considered by many of your peers to be the best local authority on the subject.

8 = You are highly compensated for your work in the area. Peers, friends and even competitors recognize you as being an expert in the top five percent in your field.

9 = You are highly compensated for your work in the area. Peers, friends and even competitors recognize you as occupying the top five percent in your field. Not only do you have technical ability, but your total breadth of knowledge and creative ability empower you to apply your skills in a macro sense.

10 = You are considered to be an international authority, and/or you are in the top one percent in your field or niche.

11 = With apologies to *Spinal Tap,* there are no 11s.

Rating
(0 — 10) Subject Area
Insert in the blank spaces the appropriate numbers from above.

____ The rollover, effective, and appropriate reinvestment of qualified plan assets

____ Avoiding the triple or quadruple tax on qualified plans

____ Irrevocable life insurance trust design and funding

____ Specific advanced strategies that provide 'living benefits' vs. 'inheritance benefits'

____ 1035 exchanges

____ Rule 144 stock transactions

____ 1036 Exchanges

____ Mergers and acquisitions

____ 664 exchanges

____ The formation and administration of asset protection trusts and vari-

ous offshore financial and/or business strategies
___ Current income, capital gains and estate tax rates, deductions, and exclusions
___ Proposed or recent changes to the tax rates, deductions or exclusions
___ Multi-generational quality of life and behavioral planning
___ Generation skipping trust parameters and planning techniques
___ The limitations, disadvantages and advantages of living trusts
___ Social security rules, regulations, and procedures
___ Medicare rules, regulations, and procedures
___ The use of tax-exempt trusts to sell highly appreciated assets without capital gains taxes
___ Business macro strategic planning™
___ Limited Liability Companies (LLCs)
___ Family Limited Partnerships (FLPs)
___ Grantor Retained Income Trusts (GRITs)
___ Grantor Retained Annuity Trusts (GRATs)
___ Grantor Retained Unitrusts (GRUTs)
___ Qualified Personal Residence Trusts (QPRTs)
___ Self Canceling Installment Notes (SCINs)
___ Family Macro Strategic Planning™
___ Private family foundations, supporting foundations/organizations
___ Gifting & freezing strategies
___ Trustee, custodial, and administrative services
___ Tax filing, tax projections, and related accounting services
___ Income, capital gains, estate tax reduction and elimination tactics
___ Risk reduction through diversification
___ Financing arrangements for business and personal needs
___ Real estate sales and exchanges (IRC Section 1031)
___ Fulfilling philanthropic desires through charitable planning
___ Goal identification and problem recognition techniques
___ Growth investment selection and ongoing portfolio timing and management

Insider Notes: The stock market of recent years has crippled the financial dreams of many. However, as mentioned earlier, money is just a tool and should not affect your overall vision of who or what you want to be.

____ Income investment selection and ongoing portfolio timing and management

____ Personal Macro Strategic Planning™

____ Paradigm recognition and shifting techniques

____ Interdependent facilitation of business or personal goals

Use the *Rate Your Knowledge Exercise* with any prospective advisor. Decide the minimum level of competency you will accept — generally the higher the level of competency, the greater the level of execution. You probably don't want to work with those that rate themselves one through five. Six through seven is better, and eight through 10 is where dynamic execution occurs. When you must achieve brilliant results, you must rely on brilliant people.

In addition to having the right expertise, your advisors must all work like a team toward your greatest vision and your "tangible, measurable" goals. Just one advisor who wants to remain independent could ruin your entire plan. Everyone must contribute and take from the relationship in an equitable but not always equal manner. Some advisors and professionals have a transaction-oriented mentality; they will do what they need to do with you and quickly move on to the next client. This type of advisor is rarely client centered enough, and usually not good prospective members of your team.

One caveat to this is that the nines and 10s may be so busy speaking and teaching their subject that they are not in the trenches, so to speak, working one-on-one with people. Have you ever sat in the class of a fully tenured college professor who had not practiced in his field in years? Typically, the best professors aren't just master theoreticians; they're still active in their fields. You may sometimes get better results with an eight who is still active on a day-to-day basis. Generally, the higher the level of competency the higher the price, but the lower the cost. But please keep in mind, paying less up front may cost more in the long run, because of lost opportunity, bad advice or less effective execution.

Look for advisors who are client centered, honest, dedicated, and creative. You do not want a group of "Blind Gurus" working on your team — they will never see you as an elephant and, therefore, you will be less likely to obtain optimum results in your life, business and finances.

PRINCIPLES VS. VALUES

People often ask: "How much money do I need to be an Elephant; do I need to be wealthy?" The answers to both is NO. History tells us of many people who spent their time, talent and resources doing what mattered most to them, with money being a secondary concern. Think of Mother Theresa. Here was a small, elderly woman with no money, and yet, she impacted the lives of millions of people. She was an Elephant.

The concept of Macro Strategic Planning® is becoming more important because the world is finally ready for it. While there are still plenty of dual income households, a new trend is emerging: more and more families are sacrificing the material benefits of two incomes so that one parent can stay at home with the children.

Most people will tell you that their values are superior to all others, but this often puts them in conflict with universal laws or principles. For example, the followers of Islam value peace, however, al Quaeda believes that those who do not believe in Islam should be punished or killed. This value goes directly against the principle of self-selection. As we can see, values are defined and interpreted by groups or individuals, and Principles are universal truths—gravity, for example. Has there ever been a time when the law of gravity did not apply or could be interpreted any differently than, "What goes up must come down?"

Some of the universal Laws or Principles essential to optimum effectiveness and becoming an Elephant are as follows:

Insider Notes: By establishing for your family a 100-year plan, or better yet a 500-year plan, that is communicated to all generations of the family, your vision and the teaching of those principles that will lead to an effective and fulfilling life, will last long after you are gone.

Self-Selection: The ability to make personal choices and act of your own free will, to make your own decisions without being forced by others.

Self-Discovery: Learning of or awakening to an idea, concept or belief in a way that fosters an individual's ownership of the discovered concept.

Win/Win: All parties must benefit from any agreement, or there is no deal. Benefits cannot be solely for one party to the agreement or relationship.

Other Messengers: Allow other messengers to help an individual accept a different or challenging idea. You can use media, friends, or family members to communicate a point more effectively than you could do yourself.

Interdependence: Work collaboratively with others to accomplish far superior results than could be attained by working independently

These universal truths, as with gravity, are at work in our daily lives whether we choose to acknowledge them or not. What sets Macro Strategic Planning® apart is that it will take you on a journey of self discovery with a trained individual to discover and achieve that which matters most to you. You are a key component to achieving success. The most skilled Macro Strategic Planning® advisor will not be able to help you if you do not articulate what is important to you.

The stock market of recent years has crippled the financial dreams of many. However, as mentioned earlier, money is just a tool and should not affect your overall vision of who or what you want to be. In creating your Macro Strategic Plan, you write down your perceived fears, obstacles and limitations. You can then use your plan to more easily, effectively and systematically overcome them.

Can you think of any fears, thoughts, people, or behaviors at play in your life that prevent you from becoming an Elephant? Becoming an Elephant is up to you — it isn't going to happen unless you believe that you can achieve it and apply the mind set and action steps to become the powerful and majestic being within you.

HOW MACRO STRATEGIC PLANNING® CAN HELP YOU DEAL WITH VOLATILE MARKETS.

The stock market of 2000 though 2002 greatly impacted the lives of many people, not necessarily for the better. Most people made decisions to buy or sell based purely on fear and emotion because they were considering only the short-term results. They had no long-term plan or vision to help them transcend economic and market conditions.

No one wants to lose money or throw good money after bad, but what if your short-term investment results did not matter? What if you knew that your vision and goals would still be accomplished regardless of current or future market conditions? What if your financial success or failure was not based on an assumed rate of return, but rather on your commitment to your vision and goals and a well thought out, written document that's been communicated to all of the professionals you work with?

What if you determine that short-term results are often not as important as the long-term outcome? With the right mindset, action plan, accountability, and adequate diversification, you can still accomplish your vision and goals. Wouldn't this help you transcend the volatility of the stock market? Your financial advisor, attorney, CPA, broker and insurance agent can be very important in helping you implement the necessary strategies, tactics and tools you need to succeed.

You will find many of those professionals to be knowledgeable, caring and honest people. You will also find that some have a specific area of focus or objective. In a perfect world, you would have shared your vision, commitment, and goals with them so that you, as the elephant, can hold them and yourself accountable for remaining on track with the bigger picture, as well as relevant below-the-line details.

Insider Notes: For most business owners, their business is like a child. The owners are intimately involved from conception to birth, and there are emotional decisions along the way that have to be made. However, the owners may be too close to the business to see and do what's best for it to thrive.

If you had done this over the last four years, you would have been in a position to transcend the current market and economy and continued to work on and live your Perfect Calendar™ and vision. Do you think Bill Gates made drastic changes to his life because his net worth went down billions of dollars? I am not saying that it is okay to accept mediocre or poor performance; but if you have a direction and a measuring stick for your progress, returns become secondary to the ultimate goal and the emotional stress is reduced.

HOW MACRO STRATEGIC PLANNING® CAN HELP PARENTS AND GRANDPARENTS

I recently tried to obtain information about assets that a mother was holding for my client. I explained to the mother why I needed the information. She told me that she did not feel ready to release the assets to her daughter and son-in-law because she did not want a sudden financial windfall to exert a disruptive effect on their lives.

I had known and worked with the son-in-law for more than 11 years and the daughter for two years. I have never met a young couple that was better mannered, more responsible, and more goal-driven. I found it curious that the mother could not see these sterling qualities in her own children. She was afraid her gift of money would "ruin" them, yet she and her son-in-law's parents had already instilled the right principles to keep that from happening. Frankly, I had no worry at all because her daughter, son-in-law and I had spent a great deal of time discussing their Macro Strategic Plan and life vision — something the mother had not done.

I often have similar conversations with parents and grandparents, whether they are giving $500,000 or $500 million. It seems that most parents and grandparents can't get past their parental relationships with their progeny to see them as responsible adults. How do you think my conversation would have gone if the mother had created a Macro Strategic Plan and saw her daughter as an elephant, or if she actually knew that her daughter was applying correct principles in her life? If the mother had done her own Macro Strategic Plan, she would have a better understanding of who her daughter really is and to what degree she could be entrusted with wealth. Nonetheless, even the best of intentions, the best parenting and the best planning still can result in a wayward child. A family may have to make the tough decision to do no more for a profligate child. They might choose, rather, to focus on those family members who want to participate in the family vision. When grappling with these difficult decisions, it's important to have on hand a document reflecting your vision, commitment and goals, to guide your family.

By establishing for your family a 100-year plan, or better yet a 500-year plan, that is communicated to all generations of the family, your vision and the teaching of those principles that will lead to an effective and fulfilling life, will last long after you are gone. An added bonus will be the likelihood that the wealth you create, regardless of how vast, will not corrupt future generations.

If you hired an average estate planning attorney, he or she would create a series of trusts, allowing you to control the money from the grave and distribute it to your children or grandchildren at certain ages or over their lifetimes. In the absence of principles, this would solve the problem of "ruining" them, because they'll know exactly how much they'll be getting and when. But will this foster self-discovery? Creating a clear Macro Strategic Plan that is communicated to your advisors and family greatly eliminates many of the stresses of leaving money and passes along your full legacy — it bequeaths not just your money, but the principles essential to living and an effective, joyful, fulfilling life.

TODAY'S VERSION OF RETIREMENT

As with everything else, the definition and perception of retirement has changed dramatically over the years. It used to be that people would work for a company for their entire lives and, at 65, walk away with a nice pension and a gold watch. Today, with an ever-changing global economy, a mobile workforce and retirement funding responsibility falling on the employee, retirement has changed dramatically.

The average person sets a date or age for retirement and does not think much more about the details-such things as why they want to retire, what they will do, where they will live, their desired lifestyle, and how they will spend their newfound "free time."

Bruce tells a story of a man who, when asked what his Perfect Calendar™ would look like at retirement said, "Just play golf." When asked what else he was going to do, he said, "Just play golf."

Consequently, the Macro Strategic Planning® advisor filled his Perfect Calendar™ to read: Monday 8:00 a.m., wake up and have breakfast; 9:00 a.m., hit a bucket of balls; 9:30 a.m., play 18 holes; 1:30 p.m., have lunch; 2:00 p.m., play 18 holes; 6:00 p.m., hit a bucket of balls; 6:30 p.m., dinner; 7:30 p.m. hit another bucket of balls; 9:00 p.m., bed.

This was entered every day for 365 days. When the man was presented with his "Perfect Calendar™", he realized how absurd it was and decided to do more than play golf. He now travels and, among other things, teaches golf to children in underprivileged neighborhoods and countries.

This story illustrates the need to put a great amount of thought into your ultimate vision of retirement. Maybe you retire from your stressful demanding job and begin a second career or business, predicated on something you love. Maybe you choose part-time work, or volunteer for a cause for which you never had enough time in the past.

Financial planning will ask you your desired age of retirement and the amount of money you want, and it will tell you how much you need to invest and earn on your investments to have that nest egg. However, what happens when the market doesn't cooperate, as in years 2000-2002? People panic, they get depressed, and they make rash decisions they often regret later. They watch the CNBC ticker all day, or their computer screen at work, and pray things improve. It's not a recipe for contentment; it's a recipe for misery and Maalox.

A Macro Strategic Plan helps us remember that, although money does play an important part in our retirement, it is a means to an end, not the end itself. Equally important is a well-considered plan communicated to each of your interdependent advisors — a plan that's flexible, continually monitored and updated on a regular basis. With that in place, wouldn't you rest easier when the market is down?

What if, by creating your Macro Strategic Plan, you learn that you've already been living much of your Perfect Calendar™ and desired lifestyle? Then instead of quitting work altogether, maybe you cut back to 20 hours a week for a couple of years to continue doing what you love and to have added time for the other things you enjoy.

No matter what you do, there are no guarantees or absolutes. You always have the right to change your mind. By following a Macro Strategic Plan in addition to your financial plan, you will be in a position to see the forest from the trees. You will hold your advisors accountable, and decisions will be based on long-term life goals instead of short-term emotions and piecemeal product solutions. The ability to make proactive decisions versus reactive ones will allow you to put choices in a win-win format that, in turn, will allow you to be the elephant you desire to be. Most important of all, you can focus on your well-earned retirement, rather than worrying about your portfolio.

MACRO STRATEGIC PLANNING®: YOUR STEADY RUDDER

The issues that are mentioned here are but a few of those that need to be addressed and each person's issues will be different. Putting your vision and goals in writing will greatly affect the success of your business, as well as allows you to focus on what is important to you. Things will change, and that is okay. Use your Macro Strategic Plan as your rudder to keep you heading in the right direction.

The remainder of this book focuses on the strategies, tactics and tools used by attorneys, CPAs, insurance agents, brokers and financial advisors — all of them important pieces of the puzzle. However, having a tool, like a Macro Strategic Plan that encompasses sound principles, and your ultimate vision, commitment and goals is priceless to help guide you through the good and bad times.

It is up to you to seek out the right professionals to deal with each aspect, including Macro Strategic Planning®. Then provide copies and communicate it to all of your other advisors so that everyone is acting in your best interest. Do not be led by blind gurus who do not see you as an Elephant.

For them to view you in that light, you must truly believe that you are a powerful, majestic being that needs to have your greatest human need ful-filled — the need to be understood — for if they do not understand you, they cannot help you achieve optimum results!

■ ■ ■

For the last 14 years Paul Capuzziello has helped discerning affluent people and their advisors see new possibilities and improve results in their lives, busi-nesses and finances. After years in the financial services industry, Paul became tired of product-centered solutions. He wanted to focus on his clients' greatest needs and wants, not solely on their finances, and subsequently was introduced to Bruce Wright the creator of Macro Strategic Planning®.

Paul was among the first Licensed and Certified Macro Strategic Planning® Advisors in the United States and founded the LifeBridge Company. LifeBridge helps its clients articulate their Ideal Life and then helps them build a bridge that spans the chasm that exists between their current life and their desired results. Paul's passion is helping people discover their options and opportunities and then facilitating the execution of a well thought out written plan through dynamic execution of the details.

The LifeBridge Company has been working with clients in the New England area and is now expanding to accept clients nationally. If you would like infor-mation about the LifeBridge Company, you can visit the website at www.thelifebridgeco.us. Paul can be reached at 401-475-2675, or paul.t.capuzziello@thelifebridgeco.us.

Macro Strategic Planning® is a registered trademark of the Wright Company.

[11]
MANIFESTING WEALTH: CREATING FINANCIAL ABUNDANCE THROUGH APPLIED THOUGHT

Learn the formula to creating endless wealth in your life. Getting rich isn't merely a matter of dollar and cents — it's a function of the right attitude coupled with sufficient desire. You don't necessarily need to be "smart" to be wealthy, but you do need to be wise. What follows are the immutable Laws of Wealth creation.

"NOTHING IS REAL UNTIL IT IS EXPERIENCED."

- John Keats

by AVERY KANFER

Life may not seem very fair. Right now people all around you with less smarts, initiative, integrity, people skills, investment knowledge and ingenuity are striking it rich — while you look at them and wonder, why not me?

JUST AS THERE ARE PHYSICAL LAWS, SUCH AS GRAVITY OR MAGNETISM, THERE ARE ALSO MENTAL LAWS OF ABUNDANCE THAT GOVERN WEALTH AND ACCUMULATION.

The answer is simpler than you may think. Those that create riches in their lives do things differently than those who haven't yet achieved financial abundance. And I'm not talking *Millionaire Next Door* kinds of things, like buying used cars and clipping coupons.

Specifically, they think about money and wealth differently.

I want to prepare you — the information in this chapter will be quite different from the others in this book. Previous chapters detailed the secrets and advanced strategies towards investing, managing and safeguarding your money. That information is undoubtedly important and will be an invaluable complement to what you learn with me here. My mission involves sharing some information that you will probably find a little (or a lot) strange in the beginning. However, I hope you'll agree that learning how to create wealth endlessly in your life is worth the diversion.

So, to make good on my promise of teaching you how to create endless wealth, I need to establish a few ground rules for the road ahead:

❶ **Put your inner critic on pause.** There will be plenty of time to be skeptical later on. For now, just relax and be open minded;

❷ **Acknowledge that wind is real.** Even though you can't see wind, it can ruffle your hair or knock you down. Acknowledge that like wind, there are plenty of other things that are real that we can't see with our eyes, such as: electricity, feelings and microbes.

❸ **Be willing to do something silly for a million dollars.** I've worked with enough clients one-on-one to know that you will think some (if not all) of the items that follow are silly or trivial. You'll have to take a leap of faith and trust me on this one, but nothing could be further from the truth. You will only know the reality of what I'm sharing once you experience the truth of it for yourself. You might as well try it; what do you have to lose?

This information has been around since the beginning of time and has been utilized by everyone who has managed to create financial abundance in their life (consciously or unconsciously), including myself. Though the subject matter involves complex physics, I've tried to package this in a way that will make complete sense to you regardless of your background.

THE LAWS OF WEALTH CREATION

Just as there are physical laws, such as gravity or magnetism, there are also laws of abundance that govern wealth and accumulation. These are all universal laws and they work regardless if a person is consciously aware of them or not.

These laws have been in existence long before being "discovered" and named by man. Laws, unlike religion, don't require that you believe in them. Just as you don't need to "believe" in gravity to come back to Earth after you jump in the air, you don't need to believe in the Laws of Wealth Creation for them to exert their forces on you as well. However, as with aeronautics engineers who have conquered gravity through knowledge, you can create financial abundance in your life through mastery of the Laws of Wealth.

Knowing the laws begins with knowing what they are not.

A catastrophic, yet unrecognized, trap people fall into that sabotages their desire for wealth accumulation is their belief in "Faux Laws." These Faux Laws or myths are insidiously detrimental because they are usually passed down to us from well-intentioned authorities in our lives (parents, bosses, mentors, etc.) and adopted by us as truisms or realities in our lives. They not only have the "ring" of absolute truth to them, but are also accompanied by huge amounts of statistics and other corroborating evidence

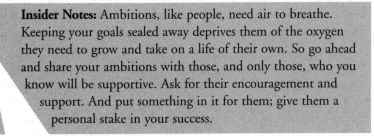

Insider Notes: Ambitions, like people, need air to breathe. Keeping your goals sealed away deprives them of the oxygen they need to grow and take on a life of their own. So go ahead and share your ambitions with those, and only those, who you know will be supportive. Ask for their encouragement and support. And put something in it for them; give them a personal stake in your success.

demonstrating their validity. Unfortunately the more true they appear, the more true they'll become in your life if you are not aware.

A law that doesn't work all the time is not a law.

Pursuing wealth utilizing Faux Laws as your guide is like going on a journey with an inaccurate map. For us to identify the true laws (the ones that *always* work) behind creating wealth we must begin by separating out the Faux Laws or myths that are commonly misperceived as the prerequisites to wealth.

THE TOP 10 MYTHS OF WEALTH CREATION

Myth #1: You Must Be Smart (or Have a Great Education) to Create Wealth.

Hundreds of millions of people believe brainpower (IQ) is a valid prerequisite to wealth. That is a mistake.

Yes, many wealthy people are smart. Yes, many have IQs that are above average. Yes, Bill Gates, the richest man in the world, has a genius level IQ. With evidence like this, it's easy to see why so many people fall into this trap.

Did you know Bill Gates never finished college? And, for every Bill Gates there are thousands of other "geniuses" (with even higher IQs) who can't even function in the real world. Not only are they not wealthy, many are destitute relying on the charity of others to provide food, clothing and shelter.

If smarts were a governing factor to wealth, then wouldn't the smartest among us also be the wealthiest? A quick glance at he tax returns of every brilliant university professor, brain surgeon and NASA rocket scientist will show that Forbes magazine did not mistakenly leave any of these people out of their annual ranking of the world's wealthiest individuals.

Just as a high level of intelligence won't guarantee you wealth, lack of intelligence or college degree will not disqualify you from the accumulation of riches. More millionaires have been created in the United States from the dry cleaning business than any other industry. That's a labor intensive, not brain intensive business. Certainly not an industry requiring a college degree to break into. What is the second ranked industry in millionaire creation you ask? Vending machines. No one's screening your résumé for an Ivy League pedigree in that industry either!

What's the biggest source of wealth creation in the U.S.? No, it's not the lottery (further proof that smarts are not required to create wealth in your life). It's inheritance. More people acquire their wealth through inheritance than any other way. So much for smarts.

Myth #2: You Must Have Great Parents to Create Wealth.
Like all Faux Wealth Creation Laws, this one has some degree of truth in it. Great parents can be a phenomenal help in acquiring wealth. For one, they can bequeath it to you. As I've said many times to my clients, it's certainly not the worst thing in the world to have wealthy parents.

Moreover, parents don't have to be wealthy to be great parents, either. Mothers and fathers can, through their encouragement, belief and support, spur their children to great achievement and wealth. Children raised in these kinds of nurturing home environments will almost certainly have wealth creation advantages over children raised in an environment filled with fear, guilt and deprivation. These kinds of negative formative experiences can cause great mental blockages in creating wealth.

But, if great parents were absolutely necessary for creating great wealth, then how can one explain an orphan who accumulates great wealth? Or the child of two abusive, alcoholic parents who becomes a multi-millionaire? Or Oprah Winfrey? Her unmarried parents separated soon after she was born. Raised by her maternal grandmother she's overcome sexual

> **Insider Notes:** The process of creating begins with knowing exactly what it is you want and then having the unshakeable desire to manifest it in your life. The clearer and more compelling you can visualize and actually feel what you intend to create, the higher you will be able to raise your level of desire. The stronger your intent, the greater your ability to manifest. Weak desire, weak results.

THERE IS NOT A RACE OR RELIGION ON THIS PLANET WHOSE PEOPLE HAVE NOT AT SOME TIME CREATED ENORMOUS AMOUNTS OF WEALTH.

abuse by male relatives to become one the most powerful and financially successful people of our time, amassing a fortune worth in excess of one billion dollars.

Or what about people like Patty Hearst, heiress to the Hearst publishing fortune, a woman born with all the advantages of wealth and education but who nonetheless became a notorious bank robber and radical?

Myth #3: You Must Be a Good Person to Create Wealth.
In my practice I hear this one all the time. People say things like "I'm a good person, why can't I pay my bills" or "buy a car" or "pay for my kids college?"

The answer is simple: Creating Wealth has nothing to do with being a good person, or what humanity calls a good person.

If it did, Hitler, Saddam Hussein, Osama Bin Laden, Manuel Noriega, Yassir Arafat and Fidel Castro wouldn't have become phenomenally wealthy.

Myth #4: You Need a Good Economy to Create Wealth.
Sure it helps when the stock market is going through the roof and there is such low unemployment that recent college graduates can command six-figure salaries and companies can afford to pay huge signing bonuses to attract new employees.

However a good economy is not a Law of Wealth Creation.

In amazing economic times there are millions who lose their shirts, and in times of great recession there are many who became phenomenally rich. Short sellers profited handsomely during the dot-com crash just as construction company executives in Florida reaped a windfall during the economic devastation in late 2004 caused by the four hurricanes hitting the state.

The most insidious consequence of this Faux Law is the self-fulfilling desperation created during periods of economic downturns. We can all learn from a wealth creation master like Donald Trump who is brilliant in his understanding that every economic situation offers its own, albeit unique, path to wealth.

Myth #5: You Need the "Right" Job to Create Wealth.
"Study hard so you can get into medical (or law) school" is a common refrain from parents. The underlying message imparted is that becoming a doctor or lawyer will guarantee the child's financial well-being.

Sure, many doctors, lawyers and other professionals create substantial wealth for themselves. It's this kernel of truth that makes this Faux Law a trap for so many.

Entering a specific field does not guarantee anyone wealth. You may enter the field of professional acting. You may get rich, or you may not. No guarantees. Did you realize that today doctors are leaving the field of medicine in record numbers because malpractice insurance and fee limitations imposed by HMOs make it difficult for them to eke out a living? Or, that the glut of attorneys graduating law schools has increased unemployment among attorneys, forced down salaries and made getting on the "partner track" much more difficult than in years past?

On the flip side, any field can generate fantastic wealth for any individual. In virtually any industry you can think of, there are people who have become extremely wealthy. From botany to pig farming, or garbage collection to education, you can find example after example of those who've cre-

Insider Notes: The American Dream is rooted in millions of real life examples of people with absolutely nothing, except an unquenchable desire to succeed, who pulled themselves up by their bootstraps to escape their circumstances. Conversely, there are many children born into a life of "privilege" who do nothing but squander their opportunities and inherited wealth.

ated financial abundance for themselves. The truth is, you can become wealthy beyond your wildest dreams regardless of where you work.

Myth #6: You are Too Old (or Too Young) to Create Wealth.
This is nothing but a sad excuse. Choose to believe in it and it will unfortunately become true for you in your life.

Age is not a determinant of wealth. Wealth has absolutely nothing to do with age or time. Colonel Sanders made his fortune in his senior years. He was 65 years old and penniless when he started Kentucky Fried Chicken. His cooking skills became widely known, prompting him to open a restaurant. He persuaded others to invest in his recipe and a franchise was born. He retired wealthy at 80 years of age.

Alexander the Great controlled half the planet in his 20s. Michael Dell became a millionaire in his 20s and a billionaire in his 30s. Jeff Bezos (Founder of Amazon.com) became a billionaire in his 30s, while Athina Roussel (granddaughter and heir to shipping magnate Aristotle Onassis's fortune) became one of the worlds wealthiest people while still a teenager. Frank Lloyd Wright became famous and wealthy in his late 60s.

There is no age that either stops people from or enables people to create wealth in their lives.

Myth #7: You Come From the Wrong Upbringing to Create Wealth.
This is a twist on Myth #2, whereby people feel that only those born in the "right" place or from a "proper" station in life are the ones who can create wealth in their lives.

For those living in areas of urban blight, surrounded by poverty and despair, this is a common trap to fall into. When you can't see any way out of your current circumstances, it's easy to reach the conclusion that "it's not meant to be for me."

This of course would be wrong.

The American Dream is rooted in millions of real life examples of people with absolutely nothing, except an unquenchable desire to succeed, who through their desire pulled themselves up by their bootstraps to escape their circumstances. Conversely, there are many children born into a life of "privilege" who do nothing but squander their opportunities and inherited wealth.

Can your upbringing put you at a disadvantage or put you on a longer path to wealth creation? Sure it can. But, if Frederick Douglass can conquer the shackles of slavery and poverty, then anyone living today can accomplish their desires too.

Myth #8: Your Race and/or Religion Stops You from Being Able to Create Wealth.
You don't have to look too far to see where a myth like this could get legs. Jews in Nazi Germany...Kurds in Saddam Hussein's Iraq...Blacks in Colonial America or Apartheid South Africa.

However, wealth is not aware of one's skin color. Wealth has no knowledge of one's religion. Race and religion do not guarantee wealth nor does it automatically preclude it.

So even though millions of Jews were murdered in Nazi Germany, that didn't stop Jews in other countries from achieving great wealth and success at the same exact time. While blacks in Colonial America we're turned into slaves, blacks in Africa (and Northern Colonial America) we're free to work, invest and own property.

There is not a race or religion on this planet whose people have not created enormous amounts of wealth or at some time suffered from lack of it.

Insider Notes: Age is not a determinant for wealth. Colonel Sanders made his fortune in his senior years. He was 65 years old and penniless when he started Kentucky Fried Chicken. His cooking skills became widely known in his 60s, prompting him to open a restaurant. He persuaded others to invest in his recipe and a franchise was born. He retired wealthy when he was 80 years old.

IN AMAZING ECONOMIC TIMES THERE ARE MILLIONS WHO LOSE THEIR SHIRTS, AND IN TIMES OF GREAT RECESSION THERE ARE MANY WHO BECAME PHENOMENALLY RICH.

Myth #9: Your Nationality Stops You From Creating Wealth.
If this were true then it would also be true that coming from a specific nationality would guarantee your wealth.

There is no nationality in America or around the world whose people are either all wealthy or all poor. Every nationality has millionaires and every nationality has those living below the poverty level.

Myth #10: You Need Wealth to Create Wealth.
The old adage "it takes money to make money" seems to be ingrained in our collective psyche. And, when it comes to investing, there is an element of truth to it. The more you can afford to invest, the greater your potential return.

But is this a Law of Wealth Creation? Are only those people currently possessing wealth the only ones who can create more wealth? Or, does that mean that if you currently have no money are you forever destined to always have no money? Of course not.

To get the answer you could look to millions of immigrants. People who came to this country with nothing but desire and the shirts on their backs. Many didn't even speak the language! Another common example are the vast majority of teenagers who leave their homes each year (without a trust fund) to make their way in the world. They start with next to nothing and most succeed at creating increasing amounts of wealth for themselves each and every year of their lives.

THE FORMULA FOR CREATING WEALTH

So far, we've only succeeded in identifying ways that won't guarantee wealth and abundance in your life. That and $3.50 will get you a soy latté at Starbucks.

The key question really is:
Are those that create abundant wealth in their lives doing something different than those who haven't created wealth?

Do billionaire investor Warren Buffet, steel magnate Andrew Carnegie, serial entrepreneur Richard Branson, retail legend Sam Walton and your wealthy uncle all have something in common? And, if there is commonality, can it be repeated with the same effect by the rest of us?

OUTCOOKING WOLFGANG PUCK

I love to cook, but I'm no Wolfgang Puck.

Despite my inferior talent in the kitchen, I know that I could tie (if not, with a little luck, beat) famous Chef Wolfgang Puck in a blind cook-off. I'd even be willing to bet that I could pull this off if our contest was baking pizza, his most famous dish, where he's worked for years perfecting the crust and tomato sauce from scratch.

I'd only need one thing — his recipe.

While Chef Puck may have labored for years through trial and error in the kitchen to perfect the exact ingredients, measurements and cooking temperature, I could replicate it if I had the explicit recipe and I followed it exactly.

The same is true of creating wealth. All you need is the recipe and to follow it exactly.

THE SECRET RECIPE OF WEALTH CREATION

There are four ingredients to creating wealth. Each ingredient can be

Insider Notes: Entering a specific field does not guarantee anyone wealth. You may enter the field of professional acting. You may get rich, or you may not. No guarantees. Did you realize that today doctors are leaving the field of medicine in record numbers because malpractice insurance and fee limitations imposed by HMOs make it difficult for them to eke out a living?

found in active use by *every* person who has ever created wealth in their life. Those who haven't created sufficient wealth in their lives can trace it back to a missing or insufficient quantity of one or more of the following ingredients, they are:

Wealth Creation Ingredient #1: Desire

The process of creating begins with knowing exactly what it is you want and then having the unshakeable desire to manifest it in your life. The clearer and more compelling you can visualize and actually feel what you intend to create, the higher you will be able to raise your level of desire. The stronger your desire, the greater your ability to manifest. Weak desire, weak results.

Keep in mind that your desires are neither good nor bad, they just are. Many people limit the amount of desire they can muster by judging themselves or making themselves feel guilty for their desires. Don't do this.

Wealth Creation Ingredient #2: Certainty (Absence of Doubt)

Doubt decreases desire. Those that successfully create are assured, resolute and certain that they can achieve their desires. They have no fear and they don't concern themselves with unnecessary details, like where the money will come from. They just know, not just believe, but KNOW that they will create the specific wealth they intend for themselves.

Wealth Creation Ingredient #3: Know That Your Desire is Possible in This World

To create whatever it is you desire, you must first believe that your desire is possible on this planet. If you want to be a millionaire, you need to know that it's possible to amass a million dollars. It's a great help when you have role models that already have what you want. But that's not necessary. Wilbur and Orville Wright believed they could fly, even though they had no rational reason to feel this way. They just knew they could. Eventually they turned their knowing into reality and were rewarded handsomely as a result.

If I wanted to create a new color I'd have great difficulty because deep down I don't think a new color is possible in this world. This doubt would insure my failure. Sorry Crayola.

Wealth Creation Ingredient #4: Know That Your Desire is Possible For YOU

Just because you know that something is possible, believing it is possible for you is a whole other kettle of fish. To successfully create, you've got to believe that it's within your abilities to attain your desires, not just that it's possible or possible for someone else.

THE PHYSICAL POWER OF BELIEF

When Roger Bannister broke the four-minute barrier in the mile (previously thought by scientists to be a mark humans did not have the physical capacity to break), he not only had to believe that it was possible in this world, but that it was possible for him. Within one year of Bannister breaking four minutes in the mile, scores of other runners also eclipsed the mark. They had the ability all the time; the only thing standing in the way were their limiting beliefs.

At some point, J.K. Rowling (British author of *Harry Potter*) had to believe it was possible not just for a novelist, but for her specifically, to become wealthier than the queen. Jerry Seinfeld had to believe he could earn one million per episode (higher than any one person had ever earned on a TV show before). And, Rudy Giuliani had to believe it was possible for him to earn $100,000 (plus travel expenses) for a speech (despite earning absolutely nothing for longer speeches as Mayor of New York). Belief is the father of reality.

If you don't know your desire is possible for you, it isn't.

Insider Notes: Think you need college to get rich? More millionaires have been created in the United States from the dry cleaning business than any other industry. That's a labor intensive, not brain intensive business. What is the second ranked industry in millionaire creation you ask? Vending machines. No one's screening your résumé for an Ivy League pedigree in that industry either!

THE TRANSFORMATIONAL EFFECT OF DESIRE ON WEALTH CREATION

Desire is the key element affecting manifestation in the universe and definitely the key ingredient in the creation of wealth.

In fact, wealth creation ingredients two through four are important mainly because of their substantial effect in reducing or neutralizing desire.

Desire's effect on creating wealth (or anything else for that matter) is like boiling water. The point where water boils is a transformation point, where one element (water) is transformed into an entirely different element (steam). There is no middle ground. Fail to heat the water high enough and no transformation will occur.

The same is true with desire and creating wealth. If you don't get your desire to a high enough intensity you won't reach the transformation point — the point where your desires are transformed from thought to reality.

Unfulfilled desires are the cause of frustration to so many, and it's completely unnecessary. In most cases all that was needed was to either increase their level of desire to the necessary transformation point, or just sustain the appropriate level of intent a little longer. (You can't even make spaghetti by dropping hard pasta into boiling water for only a few seconds!)

Those who are successful at creating the things they want in their lives have been able to raise and keep their desire at the necessary boiling point. Serial creators, like Steve Jobs (Apple Computer, iPod, iTunes and Pixar Films) are able to get their pot boiling time and time again. Some do it consciously, others unconsciously. It doesn't matter, as long as you do it.

TOP 10 WAYS TO INCREASE YOUR LEVEL OF DESIRE TO ITS "BOILING POINT" — WHERE TRANSFORMATION OCCURS

❶ **Watch the "Movie"** — Create a mental IMAX version of what it is you're trying to create. When you close your eyes, watch your movie on the Technicolor three-story screen with Dolby surround sound blasting from the speakers. You're the director, writer and star...so you can make changes whenever you want, to make your movie more compelling. It doesn't need to be long, just motivating. Watch it often, the more the better.

❷ **Play the Part in Real Life** — Act like the person who already has what it is you're trying to create. With your desires clear in your mind, go through your daily activities acting "as if" you ARE the person who has already manifested the wealth you desire. What do you wear? How do you treat people? How do you feel? How do you walk? How do you present yourself?

❸ **Remove Fear, Uncertainty and Doubt** — These are the three killers of desire. The good thing is, like in the 1400s when most people were certain Columbus was going to sail off the "flat" Earth, most fears have no truth to them. A good technique to eliminating these saboteurs is to sit back and remember past times in your life where you had great fear, uncertainty or doubt and feel what actually happened. Did the event you feared actually take place? If it did, was it anywhere near as bad as you imagined it would be?

❹ **"I Am" Statements** — Psychologists have long known about the power of self-suggestion. However the key element to engaging the power of self-suggestion is not the actual words themselves, but the emotion and feelings behind the words. Begin by thinking up a series of "I am" statements that describe that which you are intent on creating. Here are a few examples:
  ■ I am a multi-millionaire
  ■ I am a wealthy entrepreneur
  ■ I am of complete abundance

> **Insider Notes:** Yes, many wealthy people are smart. Yes, many have IQs that are above average. Yes, Bill Gates, the richest man in the world, has a genius level IQ. With evidence like this, it's easy to see why so many people think "smarts" is a prerequisite for wealth. But, did you know Bill Gates never finished college?

Then repeat these over and over again with as much emotion as you can work up. Do this whenever you have a few seconds free throughout the day. I know it may sound silly but "I am" sends a signal to your subconscious that you are accepting the command and, when said with emotion, the power is profound.

❺ **Prove To Yourself That It's Possible** — You'll never generate enough desire to get you to the transformation point if you don't know, in your heart of hearts, what you want to create is possible. One way of proving this is through real life examples of people who've created in their lives what it is you want to create in yours. Put together a little scrapbook that has their pictures and stories so you can look through it and educate your skeptical conscious mind that not only are your desires possible, but there are many others who have accomplished exactly what you're intent on creating in your life.

❻ **Prove To Yourself That It's Possible For YOU** — You can see example after example of people who've already achieved your goals, but if you don't sincerely believe that it can happen to YOU, then you're going to keep your desire from reaching the necessary transformational boiling point. In these cases the easiest solution is to temporarily modify your intentions to be something you feel is definitely possible for you. For example, if you have a net worth of $5,000 and you have a goal to create a billion dollars in wealth, that goal may be too big of a stretch for your conscious mind at this point. Instead, start with a goal to be a millionaire or even a hundredthousandaire. Once you've accomplished a smaller benchmark, you will probably find much less internal resistance to your larger ambitions.

❼ **Tell Supportive People** — Ambitions, like people, need air to breathe. Keeping your goals sealed away deprives them of the oxygen they need to grow and take on a life of their own. So go ahead and share your ambitions with those, and only those, who you know will be supportive. Ask for their encouragement and support. And put something in it for them; give them a personal stake in your success.

❽**The Contract** — Put what you intend to create, in very specific terms, in a formal contract. Include a section on the benefits you (and those close to you) will receive when you are successful...and the consequences if you don't succeed. Then, when you're 100% committed to making this happen, sign it and keep it somewhere where you can look at it regularly.

❾**Desire Enhancing Reminders** — It's easy to lose focus on what you're trying to create and get wrapped up in daily trials and tribulations. To fight this tendency, which effectively reduces desire, put pictures or quotes that remind you of your intentions in places that you'll see throughout the day. When you see these images, take a quick moment to focus on what you're looking at and FEEL "as if" you already have created that which you seek. The feeling part of this is critical, because it creates the necessary neuro-association and energy field.

❿**Meditate** — This last suggestion, when used, is the most profound of all. Go to a quiet, peaceful place and communicate to your inner-self that which you are intent on creating. The cosmic force in which we all operate is your partner in this process; you don't have to do all the work yourself. Pick a certain time of the day to regularly communicate with your partner, the universe, and it will respond by delivering to you that which you strongly desire. You didn't think those billions of people meditating for hundreds of years in the Far East were *all* crazy, did you?

WHY THIS PROCESS WORKS

Knowing what to do to create wealth in your life is worthless, unless you're willing to actually do what you know. The saddest thing is that the neediest of you, those who desperately want more money won't even *attempt the process I've laid out for you.*

It says a lot about you and your desire, if you're not even willing to try? For heaven's sake, there is absolutely no downside to just giving this process a try. Some people would be willing to stand on their heads and spit nickels for the chance to have the financial abundance of their dreams. If you're not willing to try, then why not stop being miserable and at least choose to be happy with what you've got?

TO CREATE WHATEVER IT IS YOU DESIRE, YOU MUST FIRST BELIEVE THAT YOUR DESIRE IS POSSIBLE ON THIS PLANET. IF YOU WANT TO BE A MILLIONAIRE, YOU NEED TO KNOW THAT IT'S POSSIBLE TO AMASS A MILLION DOLLARS.

The good news is that you don't have to stand on your head, and you can be as skeptical as you want. As long as you're able to put a firewall around your skepticism and follow the process. Suspend disbelief for a little while and let the results speak for themselves.

While your conscious mind may throw out all sorts of excuses for not wanting to follow the process, they all boil down to one real reason — your mind doesn't believe the process will work. This uninformed opinion isn't based on a modicum of fact, but unless you have great wisdom of how the process works you probably still won't *take action*.

To overcome this, I've found it helpful to share the scientific underpinnings to the entire Create-by-Thought process.

THE SCIENCE BEHIND THE LAWS OF WEALTH CREATION

Everything in the universe — plants, animals, minerals, water, cars, paperclips, cat food, air...everything — is constructed out of atoms named protons, electrons and neutrons. These electronically charged particles are not only all about us everywhere we go, they are us. The entire universe, and all of creation, is essentially a massive electromagnetic "swimming pool" of protons, electrons and neutrons.

Because the core building blocks of mass are particles with varying levels of electromagnetic energy, every substance known to man has it's own, measurable electromagnetic energy field.

Over the years, scientists have invented a dizzying array of devices and calculators to measure energy. Common examples include: thermometers (heat energy); Geiger counters (radiation energy); therms (natural gas energy); and calories (energy content of food).

Scientists can not only measure the energy field associated with every object, but when it comes to humans, they can even measure energy levels of various organs. For example, when our hearts stop working, doctors may apply electrical energy (in the form of defibrillator paddles) to get them working again.

Our brains work because each individual brain cell communicates with tiny electrical impulses. Doctors can measure this electrical communication through an EEG (electroencephalogram) test. Treatments of many brain-related disorders involve electrical stimulation of various parts of the brain.

Our thoughts each have differing electromagnetic energies that can be measured by an EEG no different than a test for epilepsy, encephalitis (inflammation of the brain) or dementia. Thoughts with stronger intensity have different electrical measurements than those with weak intensity. The electrical energy of thoughts is no different than the electrical energy of any other matter.

Each of us is part of a mass electromagnetic "pool" that pervades all physical existence. When we make a call on our cell phones, the electronic cell phone signal doesn't stay inside the phone. Rather it is transmitted through invisible waves from you into the universe and then back in similar electronic waves from the universe to you.

The same is true for our thoughts.

Every thought goes out from you in electromagnetic waves and then returns to you in a similar fashion. This is simply another example of Newton's Third Law: for every action, there is an equal and opposite reaction. This explains why those who send out thoughts of unworthiness get back less than stunning financial remuneration and those that send out

Insider Notes: Knowing what to do to create wealth in your life is worthless, unless you're willing to actually do what you know.

feelings of intense desire and expectation for financial abundance become the wealthiest amongst us.

That's the science. Here's where it gets weird or, maybe more appropriately, where science hasn't yet come up with instruments sophisticated enough to explain.

Thoughts sent out that are at a high enough intensity level return to the individual in the form of physical manifestation. In other words, you actually get the stuff you were thinking of. It's strange, but it's true. And it will work for you, regardless of whether you believe it or not.

■ ■ ■

Born in Brooklyn, NY, Avery Kanfer is a a nationally known Intuitive Counselor & Holistic Healer whose over 3,500 individual clients include world famous athletes and entertainers. Headquartered in Rockville, MD, Avery lectures at psychological institutions and colleges across the country. His teachings have been the feature of numerous radio and television broadcasts. You can reach Avery at 301-315-2230, avery@helpfromavery.com, www.helpfromavery.com.

LARSTAN's
THE BLACK
BOOK™ ON
PERSONAL
FINANCE

NOTES

BLACK BOOKS ON PERSONAL FINANCE — 2006 ADDITION:

Larstan Publishing is looking for qualified subject matter experts to work with us to author new sections for the second edition of The Black Book™ on Personal Finance.

Larstan is now accepting author applications. To be considered, please complete your author application which can be found at www.blackbookfinance.com.

UPCOMING BLACK BOOKS:

Larstan's influential **The Black Book Series™**, is looking for experienced "thought leaders" to contribute to a number of new books we are publishing in 2005-2006. Larstan is now accepting author applications for these and other upcoming titles, including:

- **The Black Book on Marketing**
- **The Black Book on Safety**
- **The Black Book on Supply Chain**
- **The Black Book on Business Continuity & Disaster Recovery**
- **The Black Book on Government Security**
- **The Black Book on Corporate Security 2006**
- **The Black Book on Government Technology**
- **The Black Book on Healthcare Technology**
- **The Black Book on Financial Services Technology**
- **The Black Book on Retail Technology**
- **The Black Book on Transportation & Logistics**
- **The Black Book on Manufacturing Technology**

For more information on these or other titles, Larstan Publishing or The Black Book Series, please contact Group Publisher Mike Wiebner at 301-637-4591 x903 or mwiebner@larstan.net.

The Finance Institute @

www.BlackBookFinance.com

Head to our website at www.BlackBookFinance.com and find an array of free informational resources at your disposal. Items include:

» Daily Personal Finance News Feed
» Newsletters by World Class Financial Experts
» "Ask the Experts" — Get Your Questions Answered
» Research
» Articles
» Case Studies
» Vendor Resource Guide
» Educational Seminars & Webcasts

...and much, much more!

We'd love to hear about your successes, challenges and comments on the book. Email us at comments@blackbookfinance.com. If you send it, we will read it!

www.BlackBookFinance.com

GET THE SECRETS

LEARN FROM THE NATION'S LEADING FINANCIAL ADVISERS HOW TO CREATE WEALTH AND MANAGE MONEY LIKE A MILLIONAIRE

LARSTAN'S THE BLACK BOOK ON PERSONAL FINANCE

- TODD BAUERLE
- CHERYL BURBANO
- PAUL CAPUZZIELLO
- BRIAN EVANS
- AVERY KANFER
- LUKE R. REINHARD
- SCOTT B. ROSE
- STAN SKLENAR
- STUART J. SPIVAK
- LORI WATT
- GREG WERLINICH

"FINALLY, A HANDY REFERENCE ON HANDLING YOUR MONEY THAT DOESN'T TALK DOWN, BUT RAISES YOU UP."
— NEIL CAVUTO,
HOST OF FOX NEWS' YOUR WORLD WITH CAVUTO AND AUTHOR OF THE NY TIMES BESTSELLER, MORE THAN MONEY.

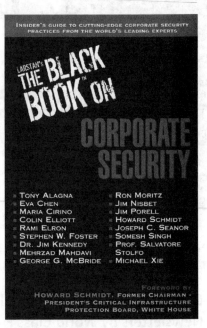

INSIDER'S GUIDE TO CUTTING-EDGE CORPORATE SECURITY PRACTICES FROM THE WORLD'S LEADING EXPERTS

LARSTAN'S THE BLACK BOOK ON CORPORATE SECURITY

- TONY ALAGNA
- EVA CHEN
- MARIA CIRINO
- COLIN ELLIOTT
- RAMI ELRON
- STEPHEN W. FOSTER
- DR. JIM KENNEDY
- MEHRZAD MAHDAVI
- GEORGE G. MCBRIDE
- RON MORITZ
- JIM NISBET
- JIM PORELL
- HOWARD SCHMIDT
- JOSEPH C. SEANOR
- SOMESH SINGH
- PROF. SALVATORE STOLFO
- MICHAEL XIE

FOREWORD BY
HOWARD SCHMIDT, FORMER CHAIRMAN - PRESIDENT'S CRITICAL INFRASTRUCTURE PROTECTION BOARD, WHITE HOUSE

COMING SOON TO A BOOKSTORE NEAR YOU

 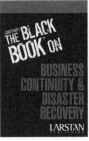   

For a free first chapter sample email freechapter@theblackbooks.com. Specify which book you're interested in.

LARSTAN
PUBLISHING
WWW.LARSTAN.COM